I0660131

Reckless HEART

THE HEARTS OF SAWYERS BEND
BOOK EIGHT

IVY LAYNE

GINGER QUILL PRESS, LLC

Reckless Heart

Editing by:
Samamntha Skal, samanthaskal.com
Olivia Zugay, storyflowsolutions.com

Find out more about the author and upcoming books online at www.ivylayne.com

Contents

Also by Ivy Layne

Don't Miss Out on New Releases, Exclusive Giveaways, and More!!

Join Ivy's Readers Group @ ivylayne.com/readers

THE HEARTS OF SAWYERS BEND

Stolen Heart

Sweet Heart

Scheming Heart

Rebel Heart

Wicked Heart

Wild Heart

Broken Heart

Reckless Heart

Forbidden Heart

THE UNTANGLED SERIES

Unraveled

Undone

Uncovered

Chapter One

My small, cluttered office didn't feel like the place to have a serious meeting, but I couldn't think of another option. I sure as hell wasn't going to do it around any of my other employees. Definitely not in the taproom where anyone could walk in. This time of the morning, we were unlikely to have a crowd, but in a tourist town, you never knew. There were a lot of reasons people visited Sawyers Bend, and the active foodie and brewery culture in the area was at the top of the list. I'd had more than one group stop in for a breakfast beer.

I was stressing about the location of the meeting, because I didn't want to think about the reason we were having it in the first place. I mentally reviewed my arguments, hating that my mouth was bone dry and my heart thudded in my chest. Why should I be nervous? I'd fired more than a few employees since I'd started my brewery. Why was this one any different?

Because it was. Hiring Matthew Holt was arguably

the worst mistake I'd ever made, both as a woman and a business owner. Matthew had to go. It had taken me far too long to reach that conclusion, and my gut told me he wasn't going to go quietly, hence the dry mouth and pounding heartbeat.

The pen I fiddled with slipped out from between my fingers, rolling across the desk to fall on the floor, and I added sweaty palms to the mix.

"Fuck, Avery, get your shit together," I told myself. "Everybody messes up. Time to clean up and move on."

Firing Matthew was the right thing to do. My gut knew it. My head knew it. So why was I dreading saying the words? I couldn't answer that question, and as knuckles rapped on the doorframe, I knew I was out of time.

I looked up to see Matthew's familiar, charming smile spread from ear to ear, a shock of his golden blond hair falling in his eyes.

"What's up, boss?" he said, folding his lanky frame into the chair beside my desk. "I was just about to head out to the Orchard to go over plans for the Halloween party. The new fall brew is going to make a splash. It's fantastic. We make magic together."

He winked, and my stomach squeezed, reminding me exactly why I was firing Matthew. We hadn't developed the recipe *together*, unless you counted his standing behind me, second-guessing every choice I made as collaboration, which Matthew did. As far as I could see, his presence had only served to get in my way until he could take credit once the job was done. And I was pretty damn sure that if the new recipe wasn't as amazing as we thought it would be, he would quietly slide into the shadows, leaving me to take the blame. Because that was how Matthew worked.

I'd finally reached the point where I could recognize the formula: step one, compliment me enough to get me excited, so I'd work my ass off; step two, swoop in and take the credit. But this was my brewery. My work. And I was done letting him manipulate me.

"Matthew," I said, threading my fingers together and resting my hands in my lap. "I appreciate everything you've done here at Sawyers Bend Brewing, but I think it's time we part ways."

I expected shock and anger. Even rage. I was prepared for it. I didn't expect Matthew to fold his arms over his chest and lean back in the chair, giving me a gentle, condescending smile.

"Ave, baby, I think you were right to break things off between us. At least for now. I haven't given up completely." He winked again. How had I ever found this man charming? "But you can't deny that I'm a hell of a brewmaster, and I've made all the difference around here."

A spurt of rage burned through my chest, firing hotter as I had to concede and recognize he wasn't wrong. Not entirely. He was a great brewmaster. I'd learned from him, and Sawyers Bend Brewing was better for his tenure here. But that wasn't the whole story. Being good at his job wasn't enough.

I tried for a professional smile. I could guess from his expression that what I managed was more of a stretch of my lips over gritted teeth.

"Matthew, you're an excellent brewmaster. But at the end of the day, I don't think our visions match. I think you'd be happier somewhere bigger."

Matthew shook his head and tried again. "Ave, sweetheart—"

His use of my nickname grated.

"My name is Avery, and I'm not your sweetheart. Do I need to point out that this is part of the problem?"

He gave a confused shake of his head, and I didn't know if he was being obstinate or if he just didn't get it. I had a feeling it was door number two, which didn't say a lot about my taste in men. I was pretty sure he had no idea what a dick he was. How could he when he had so much to offer? Brewing expertise and orgasms—what more could a woman want? How about mutual respect, or letting me run my own goddamn business rather than coming in once I'd gotten some traction and trying to take over the whole place?

I'd had such high hopes when I hired Matthew. He had the kind of experience I needed to take the next step in the world of craft brewing. Sawyers Bend Brewing had been barely more than a hobby back then. I'd been able to cover expenses only because my brother Ford had strong-armed our father into cutting me a break on the rent. I'd hired my first employee a few months before I took the leap and brought in Matthew as brewmaster.

Even now, we still worked in small batches and served a local market. I created the recipes, worked with artists on the labels, and ran the bottling machine. I had a hand in every aspect of the business. I didn't care how much expertise Matthew had. He wasn't taking any of it from me.

He'd been great at first. A team player eager to help me expand my reach. The change had started slowly. A lingering hand on my shoulder, or one of those flirty winks. Late nights talking beer and strategy. My hormones had gotten the better of my business sense. I'd been going through an endless dry spell.

Running my own place on a shoestring budget didn't leave me much time for socializing, and I had a strict policy about hooking up inside the industry. The brewers in the area had created a strong community, including places smaller than mine, all the way up to national corporations. In this world, being a Sawyer wasn't an asset, not when I was also a woman in a traditionally male-dominated field. The last thing I needed was a messy romantic relationship to get in my way. But the first time Matthew kissed me, standing right here in this office, I'd given in to the flash of lust. For a while, things had been great. We'd run the brewery together. It had felt like a partnership. Things had been good in bed and great at work.

And then, little by little, Matthew started taking over. I hadn't noticed at first. He'd encouraged me to focus on recipe development and let him handle little details and small tasks until eventually it was Matthew representing the brewery while I was in the background, working my ass off and getting none of the credit. Slowly, the suspicion had grown that Matthew didn't want me. He wanted my brewery.

On top of that humiliating realization, it had

occurred to me that while we worked well together, I didn't really like being with him that much. To be fair, the sex was pretty good—a hell of a lot better than no sex at all—but it wasn't life-changing. And neither was Matthew. He was an asset to the brewery, but as a person, he was boring. All he could talk about was himself. What Matthew wanted, what Matthew thought. He wasn't interested in being a partner. What he really wanted was an audience.

Two months ago, I ended our personal relationship. He'd taken that so well that it had confirmed that his real interest lay in Sawyers Bend Brewing. Once orgasms were off the table, my vision cleared, and I realized that Matthew's skills as a brewmaster weren't enough to put up with the rest.

"You know we make a great team," Matthew said, bringing me back to the conversation. "I can't leave you on your own, Avery. This place will fall apart."

The soothing tone in his voice had my hand itching to fly up and smack the smug expression from his face.

"I was hanging in there before you showed up, Matt. I'll make it work without you," I said, managing to keep the fury out of my voice.

"You won't be able to hire another brewmaster with my experience," he said, shaking his head. "Not with what you're willing to pay."

"Probably not," I agreed with a hint of a smile. "One of the things I've realized over the last year is that I miss being the brewmaster."

Matthew scoffed.

"Avery, you were barely making it before I showed

up." He leaned forward, bracing his elbows on his knees, his expression so sincere, I knew he believed what he was saying, which only made it that much more infuriating. "You could be so much more than a small-time brewer. You have so much talent. You have an instinct for the process, for flavor and timing that's unique and can't be taught, but you just need guidance. With my help, you can be so much more."

"I don't want to be more." My chest burned as I spoke the lie. I did want to be more. I just didn't want the *more* Matthew envisioned.

I'd known this was over the day he let it slip that his long-term plan was to build up Sawyers Bend Brewing to sell to a multi-national. Hell no. Not happening. Did I want to reach more beer lovers with my craft brews? Abso-fucking-lutely. Could I create great beers? I had no doubt. But this was my place. I hadn't built it up from nothing, so I could sell out and let a conglomerate slap my logo on their beer in exchange for a fat check.

"Like I said, Matt, I think we have different visions for Sawyers Bend Brewing. I'm sure you won't have any trouble finding a place somewhere else." Matthew had a good reputation in the industry, and he wasn't short on employment options in this area of the country. Between Western North Carolina, Georgia, and Tennessee, there were plenty of breweries who'd love to get their hands on him. They were welcome to him. I was done.

He studied my face, his features gradually hardening as he read my resolve, and he understood he wasn't going to be able to get his way. The friendly expression in his eyes flicked off as his gaze chilled.

"You're going to regret this," he said, his voice low and hard.

I raised an eyebrow as my shoulders relaxed.

"Really? That's what you're going with? I'm going to regret this?" I let out a sigh. "Maybe I will. But I won't know until I do it." I stood, ready for Matthew to exit my brewery and my life.

He rose from the chair, stepping closer, looming over me. "Don't expect me to come back and save your ass when this place goes under," he said.

I gestured to the door. "Thanks for your concern," I said dryly. "I'll be okay. I appreciate everything I learned from you, but it's time for you to move on. If I regret it, that'll be mine to live with."

"I've invested too much in this place to walk away," he protested, refusing to back up when I stepped forward, trying to urge him to the door. A frisson of alarm skittered down my spine. I had two part-time employees in today, and neither was close enough to hear if I called out.

"You've invested your time for which you were compensated," I said, keeping my eyes locked on his. "I'm not going to change my mind."

Cold fury flashed across his face before a vaguely genial expression took its place. He shoved his hands in his pockets and shook his head.

"I made you what you are, Avery. Without me, you're nothing. One way or another, you're going to pay for this." He turned and strode through the door.

As much as I wanted to let him make a dramatic exit and then never see him again, practicality had me trailing him as he left, crossing from my office to the other side of the warehouse style building that housed the brewery, stopping only to grab his wallet, keys and jacket as he went. The heavy metal door slammed behind him.

Letting out a long, slow breath, I tried to shake off my unease. The hard part was over. Matthew was gone, and I was free to start a new chapter as a brewer. I was ready for this. I didn't need Matthew.

I looked around the brewery, drawing in the smell of hops and malt. This was my home. The invader had been tossed out. All was right in my world. Wasn't it?

Sure, it was, I told myself. It had to be.

Shaking off my unsettled mood, I ran down a list of things I had planned for the day. I needed to check in with the Orchard we were co-hosting the annual Halloween party with. Verify the delivery estimates for the new labels. Sweet talk Hank from the hardware store into installing new locks now that Matt was gone. Call my local hops supplier and see if he could increase my usual order. And when that was all done, I'd man the taps until Cammie showed up.

I expected phone calls or texts as word got around about me firing Matt, but my phone stayed silent. Customers came in, drank beer, and left with a six-pack or some merch. I met a sweet, retired couple from Michigan and a nice group of guys making the rounds of local breweries as their bachelor party.

None of it helped change my mood.

When the taproom was quiet, I stepped into the small kitchen space connected to the bar. It had been there when I'd moved in. So far, I'd used it only for tinkering with smaller recipes I wasn't ready to brew at scale. It wasn't much bigger than the inside of a food truck, but my brother Finn, a classically trained chef, was looking for an occasional workspace. His primary job at the moment was head chef at Heartstone Manor, our family home. He claimed he was happy feeding his family, glad to enjoy life with his new wife and son, away from the rat race of cooking in a high-pressure kitchen. But he'd been toying with the idea of doing some pop-ups here and there. He said he missed feeding people, but he wasn't ready to start his own place.

I wasn't looking to turn Sawyers Bend Brewing into a restaurant, but I thought my little kitchen off the taproom might be the answer to Finn's itch to cook for the public and mine to level up the Brewery. If word got out Finn was cooking, the place would be packed. I wasn't adverse to the increase in sales that would lead to. I had bills to pay, and this felt like a win-win. Matthew had hated the idea. I think he'd worried Finn would take over his territory.

Making a note that the small kitchen needed a thorough cleaning before Finn could use it, I got back to my to-do list. Work had always been my cure for everything that ailed. But by the time Cammie showed up, I was a ball of nerves, jumping every time the door opened. I thought once the confrontation with Matthew was over, my anxiety would dissipate. I'd done the hard thing. What was there to be nervous about?

Instead, it only got worse. I drove back to Heartstone Manor, wishing that my father hadn't left behind a complicated will that forced me to move home if I wanted to keep my business. I loved my family—a surprise after so many years of keeping them at a distance—but I missed the days when I'd occupied the tiny living quarters above the brewery. The rooms had been tacked on as an afterthought. Drafty in the winter and hot in the summer, they were spare and small, but they'd been mine.

"I just need a good night's sleep," I said aloud as I drove through the iron gates to the Manor, waving at the security camera tracking my arrival. "I'll shake off the day and start fresh tomorrow."

I woke early, skipping breakfast to head back to the brewery, eager to take back the reins of my business. Sleep had helped, but I was still feeling off.

Pulling my car into my usual parking space at the side of the building, I sat for a second, something tugging at me. Something wasn't right about the brewery, but I couldn't pin down what it was. Getting out of the car, I locked the door and instead of heading to the big metal door into the brewery, I walked to the front, scanning the building for whatever had tweaked me as I'd driven in. The small parking lot was empty, as it should have been at this hour, and the pumpkin display I'd arranged was bright and festive beside the door to the taproom. The open door to the taproom.

I reached out to push it all the way open and stopped cold, my hand dropping to my side.

Cammie wouldn't have forgotten to close and lock

the door. She never did. And she and I were the only two with the keys to the new locks I'd had installed yesterday.

Which meant that no matter how much I needed to see what was waiting inside, I wasn't going in by myself. I was headstrong, not stupid.

I pulled my phone from my pocket, scrolled through the contacts, and hit the one I was looking for.

Chapter Two

WEST

My cell phone rang as I reshuffled the stack of paperwork on my desk. I dropped the file in my hand and reached for it. Anything for an excuse to push the paperwork off a little longer.

It was a toss-up whether the incoming call was personal or business. In a small town like Sawyers Bend, it seemed like everyone had the police chief's cell number. I glanced at the screen and paused, not expecting to see Avery Sawyer's name on the screen.

I'd known Avery practically since her birth. She wasn't just a citizen in my town; she was my closest friend's younger sister, and Griffen and I had been best friends since kindergarten. Although he'd left Sawyers Bend at twenty-one and had disappeared for a while, since he'd been back, we'd been as tight as ever. He hadn't held it against me when I'd put his brother in jail for killing their father. He hadn't said "I told you so" when Ford came home, exonerated by an alibi that had shown up, in my opinion, a little too conveniently.

I knew Ford hadn't killed his father. I just hadn't been able to prove it. It wasn't for lack of trying. Whoever had killed Prentice Sawyer had been very smart or very lucky. Probably a combination of both. I was going to find him. I wouldn't stop looking until I did.

The phone rang a second time. I stared down at Avery's name on the screen, not liking the twinge of concern at the sight of her name on my phone. I wouldn't say Avery and I were friends, but we were more than friendly, and I could count on one hand the number of times she'd called me in her thirty-one years on earth.

Growing up, the eight years between us might as well have been a lifetime. On top of that, Avery Sawyer did not ask for help. Avery kept to herself and solved her own problems. She worked her ass off to get what she wanted, refusing to ride on her father's coattails or make anything of her family name. I suspected she saw being a Sawyer as more of a burden than a blessing. If she was calling me this early on a Friday morning, something was wrong.

I tapped the green circle on the screen. "Avery, what's up?"

"West." She sounded breathless. "I just got to the brewery, and the taproom door is open."

"Who worked last night?" I asked, standing and grabbing my keys. "Cammie?"

"Yeah, she's never forgotten to lock the door."

"Have you talked to her since?" I asked, closing my office door behind me. If it were anyone else, my mind would have stuck on a simple B&E, but Avery was a Sawyer. Their lives had been complicated since Prentice

14

was killed. Murder. Sabotage. I wouldn't make assumptions until I saw what was going on.

"No. Do you think...?" She cut off, and I could feel her tension in the quick intake of breath in my ear.

"We don't know anything yet, Avery," I said, hoping she wasn't going to lose her cool. "I'm just gathering information. Did you go in? Did you touch the door?"

"No," she said, the word coming out sharp and quick. She stopped and drew in a slow breath. When she spoke again, she was calmer. "I didn't touch the door or go in. I saw it was open. I thought I should call you first."

"Smart," I said. "Where are you right now?"

"At the back door of the brewery by my car."

"Go to the front, to the street where you're in plain view. I'll be there in a few minutes. Don't go inside."

"I won't," she said. "Thanks, West."

"That's what I'm here for," I said. "I'll meet you out front." I was already striding out of my office. At the dispatch desk, Amanda waved at me.

"Headed to the brewery," I called out. "Call me on my cell if you need me."

"Avery okay?" she asked.

"Yep," I answered, not wanting to share details I didn't have.

I could have walked down Main Street to get to her. The distance between the police station and Sawyers Bend Brewing wasn't that far, but I hadn't liked the fear I'd heard in her voice. I didn't want to leave her standing there alone longer than I had to.

I hopped into the Sawyers Bend Police SUV that served as my regular transportation and rubbed the heel of my palm against my chest. Concern was usually the last thing I felt for Avery. After growing up with Griffen, it was a habit to keep an eye on his sisters. I worried about Quinn who led strangers on hikes in the mountains, about Sterling who had been arrested for public intoxication more than once before she cleaned up her act, about Parker when she'd married that dickhead Tyler and moved to New York.

Avery always had her feet on the ground and her head on her shoulders. She kept to herself and didn't start drama. While she had a temper—I'd seen it fly at Griffen more than once—it never led her into trouble that brought her into my path. She was smart and self-sufficient.

She stood in front of her brewery wearing a red Sawyers Bend Brewing polo shirt, her sleek dark hair pulled back in a braid, her dark eyes worried. Tall, with milky skin set off by dark brows and dark hair, and a wide, expressive mouth that I tried not to think about, she was more than beautiful. Avery Sawyer packed a punch I don't think she was aware of. That was fine with me. She was eight years my junior and my best friend's sister. Plenty of reason to remember she was one of my citizens, and I was here on business.

"Hey," I said as I got out of my vehicle. "Let's go see what's going on." No light shone from inside the taproom. "Wait here."

Not wanting to alarm Avery further, I decided against pulling my sidearm just yet. I nudged open the door with my shoulder while glancing back at Avery, following just behind me.

"Stay out here," I ordered, shaking my head firmly at the protest on her face. "Don't make me lock you in the back of the SUV."

"Fine," she huffed and shoved her hands into her pockets before taking a step back.

With that settled, I turned my attention back to what awaited in the taproom. Flicking on the lights, I stood in the doorway and studied the familiar space.

Avery's place was small, but her beer was some of the best I'd ever had, which was saying something considering it was hard to turn around in this part of the country without tripping over a great brewery. Before she took it over, her place had been a bar and pool hall. She'd stripped the building back to bare bones and added details to bring out the simple post and beam construction. It reminded me of a cabin in the fall, all warm wood and stone, accented with bright colors.

I walked through the taproom, taking in the clean tables, chairs stacked upside down, and the floor freshly washed before Cammie had closed up the night before. No surprises here, and no clue who had left the front door ajar. I crossed to the door beside the bar. Pushing it open, I entered another world.

This was where the magic happened. In a square metal frame building with a concrete floor sat two shiny stainless-steel vats that were Avery's pride and joy. The air was scented with hops and malt, every inch so clean I bet the health inspector loved her. Nothing looked out of place until I got to Avery's office. There, it looked like a bomb had gone off. My first instinct said the place had been ransacked, but just as I was about to call out for

Avery, I gave the space a slower once-over and saw a discordant sense of order among the stacks of papers and piles of boxes. It could have been ransacked, or this could have been the way Avery had left it.

Leaving her office, I checked the restrooms to verify that the building was empty, and I went out the front door. Avery paced in the parking lot, her teeth gnawing at her lower lip, her dark brow pulled together in worry.

"What did you find? Is everything okay?" she asked.

"It's fine," I said. "I can't see any damage done. It doesn't look like anything's missing, and there wasn't anyone in there. I want to go through it with you to see if you spot anything out of place."

We retraced my steps more slowly than I had before; her anxious eyes double-checking every detail. "Everything looks fine in here," she muttered. "I called Cammie, and she's absolutely sure she locked the door last night. She said she remembered because she left her phone inside and had to get the keys back out to lock up after she got it. She said she always checks to make sure it's locked after she turns the bolt."

"Who else has the keys? Did you give one to Dave?" I asked, thinking of her other part-time employee as I followed her through the brewery to her office.

"Only me and Cammie. Dave wasn't working yesterday," she answered absently, her voice fading away as we entered her office, her eyes narrowing on the stacks of papers and files. She didn't react to the mess, telling me that the organized chaos was business as usual. "Everything looks fine. I—" She cut off as she looked at the center drawer of her desk. It wasn't open, but it was ajar just enough that I could see it hadn't been locked.

Avery shook her head, staring down at it. "I locked that drawer, West. I always lock it."

She yanked the drawer open, sending a pen and two pencils rolling wildly. I saw a few markers and a notepad. That was it.

"Avery, what was in there?" I asked.

"Fuck," she said, crouching to look in the back of the drawer. Reaching in, her hand slid across the wood, fingers seeking and coming up with nothing.

"Ave, what's missing?" I pressed, but she didn't answer.

"Oh, goddammit," she turned around, her eyes wildly skating over the piles of papers and boxes, clearly looking for something.

"Avery, stop. Tell me what's going on so I can help you." I closed a hand over her shoulder and forced her to look at me.

"I only had two things in that drawer, West. The new recipe I've been working on for our Halloween beer, and —" Avery bit her lip, her dark gaze skating away from mine.

"And what? What else was in there?" I demanded, knowing I didn't want to hear the answer.

"My research file," she gritted out, still not meeting my eyes.

"Research file on what?" I asked slowly, though my gut already knew the answer.

"On the necklace Quinn found in Dad's cabin," she forced out, jerking her shoulder free of my grip.

"Are you kidding me?" I exploded. I tried to keep things professional with people I was supposed to protect, but Avery was Griffen's sister—as good as family —and she was playing with fire. "What are you thinking? Whoever murdered your father is still out there. And that necklace is a dead end."

"You don't know that! It's the only clue we have," she fired back, her dark eyes blazing with fury.

I wanted to argue with her. She didn't belong anywhere near that necklace or her father's case. Ford had been poking around in their father's business, and he'd ended up framed for murder.

She crossed her arms over her chest and raised her chin. "I'm going to find out who left the necklace in the cabin."

"The fuck you are!" I shot back. "Have you talked to Griffen about this? Or Ford?"

"I talked to Sterling," she said, tossing her braid over her shoulder. "And Quinn."

"Oh great. Two people with even less experience in investigations than you. This isn't a game. Or did you forget that someone tried to kill Ford in prison, and before that, they came after Griffen, and they did kill Vanessa when she threatened to spill what she knew?"

Her face paled, but she didn't lower that stubborn chin. I stared down into the open drawer, trying to think like a cop and not a surrogate older brother. "Avery, we'll talk about you pursuing your father's killer on your own later—and we're definitely going to talk about it. But for now, let's focus on your break-in. I'm going to check the door and your desk for fingerprints. But I need you to think—whoever got in here took the recipe and your file on the necklace. Any chance the same person could want both?"

She bit her lip again and looked at the ceiling. "I don't... I can't think of anyone who would..." She cut off and let out a sigh. "You should know, I fired Matthew yesterday."

"Your brewmaster? Why?" I'd never liked the guy. He was conceited, convinced he was God's gift to beer, Sawyers Bend, and women, not necessarily in that order.

She shrugged. "It was time for him to move on," she answered cryptically.

"Did he go quietly?" I asked, surprised when she nodded.

"Quietly enough. You know, the typical, 'You'll never make it without me, I'll make you pay.'" Avery rolled her eyes.

"He said that? He'd make you pay?"

"Yeah," she admitted. "But I had the locks changed yesterday. Only Cammie and I have keys right now. And no one has the key to my desk." Her eyes flicked down to the open drawer. "It doesn't look like it was forced."

"No," I agreed. "It doesn't. Where else do you keep your recipes? Were they all in the drawer?"

"Only that one. The rest are all on my laptop. This one was new. I'm still tinkering with it."

She let out a long breath, seeming to deflate. "It was my only copy. Matt kept his own notes. He wouldn't have had to steal the notebook for the recipe."

"The recipe was in a notebook?" I asked. Avery nodded.

"Was that the only thing in the notebook? If someone had opened it, would they have known what it was?"

She shook her head. "It was my *everything* notebook. I jotted down everything in there. To-do lists, random stuff, and sometimes, recipes I was working on or ideas I was still playing with. Whoever was after the file probably grabbed it thinking they were connected." She rubbed her palms over her face. "Fuck!" Tipping her head back, she squeezed her eyes shut. "What are the chances Matt would let me see his notes on the recipe?" Shaking her head, she answered her own question. "Zero. Considering he hates me. Fuck."

"Can you recreate it?" I asked.

She lifted and dropped her shoulder. "Exactly? I don't know. I had different drafts of the recipe. My memory isn't bad, but it's not photographic. I have an idea of what I did, but— Fuck! It was going to be so good. And now, even if it's as good as I hoped, I won't be able to make it again."

"Forget the recipe for a second," I said. "If whoever broke in was after your research, we have a problem. I don't want you on this guy's radar." I stared down into Avery's eyes, her long, dark lashes doing nothing to hide her frustration.

"Then I guess you'd better help me catch him," she said.

"Do you think I haven't tried?" I asked. I'd been looking for the son of a bitch since the day Prentice was shot, and everywhere I turned, I came up empty. My eyes dropped to the open desk drawer, my gut icing over as the implications of what this break-in could mean sank in.

"It's likely that whoever killed your father also killed Ford's ex-wife and was behind the assassination attempt on Ford last spring. Now he's looking at you."

If I was hoping to scare Avery off, I was out of luck. She glared up at me, that stubborn chin raised, her eyes hot with emotion. "Then I guess you'd better help me track down the necklace before he gets to me, too."

Chapter Three

WEST

I was halfway through the stack of paperwork on my desk when a quick triple knock sounded on my open door. I wasn't expecting to see Avery Sawyer standing there. Avery didn't show her face in the police station often, a good thing, since it meant she mostly stayed out of trouble. It wasn't her presence that had me concerned. It was the big, bright smile on her face. With that wide mouth and her full lips, her smile was a show-stopper. Always had been, even when she'd been tiny.

As her brother's best friend, I never got that smile. That was her tourist smile. Her—*Don't you love my beer? Spend some money in my taproom!*—smile. I was more likely to get a scowl for bossing her around. If I was getting her tourist smile, she had to want something. And I had a good idea what it was.

If I was right, I was going to make her work for it.

"Avery. Everything okay at the brewery?"

"So far, so good," she said, inclining her head at the

empty seat on the other side of my desk. "Do you have a minute?"

"Sure. It's been a few days. You here for an update on the break-in?" I straightened the stack of paperwork, setting it out of sight, and picked up the pen on my desk, flipping it through my fingers.

Avery nodded, though I didn't think details on my investigation were her reason for stopping by. She knew I would have called her if I had anything, and getting news about the break-in wouldn't call for that smile. It was easy enough to fill her in on what little info I had. She'd get to the real reason she was here eventually. And maybe I'd get another of those smiles along the way. I wasn't susceptible to her charm, but that didn't mean I couldn't enjoy it.

"I don't have much," I admitted. "The prints all belonged to people who were cleared to be in the brewery. You didn't keep your office locked, so any of your employees could have tried that drawer looking for a pencil or rubber band and left their prints behind."

"Shit," Avery said under her breath. "And the cameras?" She spoke the word *cameras* as if it had four letters and they all tasted bad. I thought I understood.

The cameras were part of being a Sawyer. Avery liked to think of herself solely as the proprietress of her brewery. I got it because I'd been in the same situation. Being the son of the mayor in a small town wasn't always simple. Especially when your father expects you to live your life following precisely in each of his footsteps. Valedictorian in high school, off to Chapel Hill, then to law school, and then finally into his seat in the mayor's office so I could kiss Prentice Sawyer's ass the way my father had spent his life doing.

No thanks. It had come as a great shock to both my father and Prentice that I didn't intend to join his crowd of enthusiastic lackeys. I knew all about wanting to be your own person, but Avery couldn't escape being a Sawyer, and these days that came with security.

Ever since Prentice had been murdered, his killer had been coming after the remaining Sawyers. While he was away, Griffen had worked for Sinclair Security, one of the top private security agencies in the country. He knew what he was doing. When he moved in, he had his former employers set up Heartstone Manor's alarms and cameras and brought in Hawk Bristol to oversee everything. Hawk didn't take any chances. He hadn't just wired Heartstone Manor—he'd tightened security everywhere: Quinn's guide business, the Inn at Sawyers Bend, and Sawyers Bend Brewing.

I'd learned from talking to Hawk that the door the perp had used at the brewery was the one door they didn't have coverage on—a pushback from Avery. Whoever had broken in had used Avery's alarm code, and either had a key or had expertly picked the lock. Since Avery had changed the locks that day, and only she and Cammie had the keys, I was going with option two. That left the suspect pool wide open, including Avery's asshole ex-brewmaster. Unless Cammie was in on it. As much as my gut had a firm line through her name, I had to keep Cammie on the list of potential suspects. At this point, I couldn't discount anyone. Except maybe Avery. And that was only because Hawk had confirmed she'd come home in time for dinner and hadn't left the Manor until the following morning.

I wished I had something concrete to tell her. "Whoever it was got in and out without being caught on the cameras. Which meant they either got lucky, or they knew there was a blind spot because they worked there, or scoped it out ahead of time. I'm not giving up, but I don't have much at this point."

Avery nodded, accepting my lack of news more easily than I expected. That couldn't be good. Proving me right, she leaned forward, her dark eyes intent on mine. "I want to see the necklace. I asked Quinn, and she said you had it, that you took it for safekeeping after the break-in at Harvey's offices."

I was shaking my head before she could finish, trying not to smile as she ground her teeth at my negative response. There'd always been something about Avery Sawyer. In a house full of children who lived on guard against their father, against each other, she'd always burned bright. She kept to herself, but she wasn't timid or afraid to go after what she wanted. Sitting there with her cheeks flushed pink and her jaw set, she was almost irresistible. Almost. I wasn't going there. Aside from the fact that she was eight years younger than me, and she was Griffen's little sister, she'd drive me insane in a week. She was too headstrong, too reckless. I liked order in my life, and Avery was the opposite.

"I don't have the necklace," I said. "I gave it back to Harvey."

"Why?" Avery protested. "It was evidence." She

slumped back in her chair and crossed her arms over her chest, momentarily stymied.

"Not officially," I told her. "Harvey asked me to hold on to it, and then he asked for it back. And as much as you might think that necklace is proof of anything, right now, it's just a necklace. We don't know who it belonged to or how it got to the cabin. I had no good reason to keep it."

Avery's eyes narrowed, but she didn't say anything. I guessed she was formulating an argument. She and her sisters believed the necklace was the key to finding Prentice's mystery bride, the woman he'd hinted he was bringing back to the Manor to install as the new Mrs. Sawyer. Their theory was that he'd been murdered over their relationship, and if they could discover who she was, they'd know who killed Prentice. Maybe. But Prentice Sawyer never had any shortage of mistresses or enemies. People all over the country hated him for a wide range of reasons. Any one of them could have shot him. We had no proof that the murder had anything to do with the new Mrs. Sawyer.

Whoever she'd been, she hadn't married Prentice or moved into Heartstone Manor. No one had claimed the boxes of baby things Savannah and Hope had found in the attics. Prentice had abruptly fired half the staff, stopped taking care of the Manor, and became close to a hermit in his final years. His death was a tangle of mysteries. I didn't blame Quinn, Sterling, and Avery for pulling at whatever threads they could find. We all wanted answers.

Avery shoved herself to her feet and glared down at

me, her hands on her hips, her long dark hair sliding over her shoulder. "That's fine," she said, her cheeks still flushed pink, her dark eyes flashing in annoyance. I had to wonder what the fuck the ex-brewmaster had been thinking to let Avery get away.

"I'm going to see Harvey," she announced. And then I remembered the downside of a headstrong, capable woman.

"Wait," I said, standing. "I'll come with you."

Her eyes narrowed on mine, and I wished I knew what she was thinking. I thought it likely she was about to tell me no, but if that were the case, she was shit out of luck. I was going to Harvey's with her, in part because I wanted to talk Harvey into letting me put the necklace back in the property room. But mostly because I didn't trust Avery to go haring off after her father's killer on her own.

Talking to Harvey was safe enough. He was the family lawyer, loyal to the Sawyers, every one of them. He wouldn't hurt Avery, but where she'd go after she talked to Harvey was anyone's guess. I was going as much for damage control as to satisfy my curiosity.

"I don't need a babysitter," Avery muttered, striding down the hall beside me.

"That's debatable," I said, placing a hand on her lower back as we passed through the front door, giving in to the urge to touch her, to lay a finger on all that sparking energy, as much as I was being polite.

"I'll drive," I said, nudging her towards my SUV. She climbed into the passenger seat without argument.

"What did Harvey say when he asked you to give the

necklace back?" she asked as we turned onto Main Street, heading out of town in the direction of the Victorian where Harvey had his offices.

"That he was still looking into the source of the necklace, and he wanted to have it on hand in case he needed to send pictures or show it to someone."

"And you didn't think that was suspicious?" Avery asked.

"Do you?" I countered. She had a point if I thought Harvey was up to something. Which I didn't.

"I wouldn't have," she said. "Except someone stole the file. I don't know. Everything is suspicious. Especially when nothing makes sense."

"Yeah," I agreed. "Welcome to your father's case. Too many suspects, too many motives, no answers."

"I like my job a lot better than yours," Avery said, sending me a sidelong glance.

"Yeah, I like your job, too. Especially since you're so good at it. You ever find your notes on that recipe that's missing?"

She shook her head. "Only what's up here," she said, tapping her temple. "What I wouldn't give for a photographic memory right now. I know the ingredients, I think. It's the proportions and some of the timing I can't remember."

We pulled into the gravel lot, only seeing Harvey's and his secretary's vehicles. Louise was seated at her desk when we pushed open the door, her eyes brightening when she saw us. "Chief Garfield. Avery. Everything okay?"

"Everything's fine," I said. "Harvey available? We won't take much of his time."

"Sure, I'll just—" She was lifting the handset on her phone when Avery crossed the room and dropped a quick knock on Harvey's door, then swung it open. Avery wasn't waiting for permission. She was a client, not a public servant, and she wasn't going to let anyone tell her no.

I took advantage, following her in just in time to see the concern in Harvey's eyes smoothly concealed by a friendly welcome.

"Avery. West. What a surprise," Harvey said, levering himself out of his desk chair. A rotund man with apple cheeks, he could have played Santa with the addition of a red suit and white beard. "What can I do for you two? Is everything all right?" His bushy eyebrows pulled together as his bright eyes flicked from me to Avery and back to me.

"Everything is fine," Avery said. "We just wanted to see the necklace. You know the one that Quinn found in the cabin? West said that you took it back from his property room and that you had it here. I've been looking into it, and I just wanted to—"

She stopped at the morose shake of Harvey's head.

My cop's gut pinged. Hard.

Chapter Four

WEST

"Avery," Harvey said, "I'm so sorry." The glance he shot me was heavy with guilt and a little chagrin. "It was stolen."

Not what I expected Harvey to say. And somehow, not entirely a surprise. Fuck. Why couldn't anything ever be simple? But this was—

"Weird," Avery said. "What do you mean it was stolen?" she asked, and for once, I didn't mind sitting back and letting someone else lead the charge on the questioning. I was curious what she'd be able to get out of Harvey that I might not.

His glance flicked to me again, and when he saw I wasn't going to interrupt, reluctantly, he looked back to Avery and let out a sigh. "I had it in my desk. Someone broke in. And when I came in, it was gone."

"When?" Avery challenged.

"A few weeks ago, I didn't write the date down."

At that, I was done letting Avery take the lead. "Harvey, you had another break-in, and you didn't call me?"

Harvey looked down at his desk, then up at me. "I'm sorry. I just... I know Hawk and Griffen wanted that fancy security system here, but I keep forgetting to set it. This is Sawyers Bend. What do I need a security system for? All these years, I've never had one."

"All these years, you've never had multiple break-ins," I reminded him.

"I know, I know, I know." He sounded like a broken record. Harvey shoved his hands in his pockets. "I'm sorry to disappoint you. I should have known better. It's just... Well, when I forgot to set the alarm, there had only been the one break-in, and that was related to whatever was going on with Quinn and Hawk. Didn't seem like it had anything to do with me, and I just..." He looked down at his feet and shrugged a shoulder before looking back at me, all sheepish remorse. "I've gone a lot of years not locking my door, son. The idea of doing that, plus setting an alarm, just slips my mind."

I could practically hear Avery's teeth grinding together, but she didn't say anything. Not yet.

"Fine," I conceded. I knew enough people in Sawyers Bend, especially the old-timers, who couldn't get their heads around locking their doors, much less setting security alarms. "But that doesn't explain why you didn't call to report a theft."

Harvey looked around the office for a moment, making me wonder if he was looking for escape or hoping someone would appear to rescue him from my questioning.

"Do either of you want coffee? Tea?" he asked, brightly.

"No," Avery said sharply. "I want to know how you let the necklace get stolen and why you didn't tell any of us. You knew it was important." Her voice cut off, and she swallowed hard.

I didn't believe the necklace had anything to do with Prentice's murder, but it was all they had to go on. I set a hand on Avery's shoulder, half expecting her to shrug it off, but she leaned into me just a fraction, her gaze hard on Harvey's face.

"I should have called," he said, talking mostly to me. "I should have reported the theft. I understand that. It's just..." He let out another huff of breath. "Honey." He looked at Avery. "It's just a necklace. Your father was murdered in his office, not in the cabin, probably because of a business deal. And it's been making me nervous, you girls are so obsessed with finding the woman who owned that necklace. You're only going to stir up trouble that could get you hurt. When I came into my office and found the necklace had been stolen, I thought maybe it was for the best."

A sound rumbled from Avery's throat that was suspiciously like a growl. "Are you kidding me, Harvey?" she said. "Seriously? You got robbed, and you didn't do anything about it because you hoped we'd be quiet and let it go?"

"That's about it," he admitted. "Though now I'm seeing that wasn't such a great plan."

Avery shook her head and stormed past me. I caught her by the elbow, handing her the keys to the SUV.

"Wait for me," I said. "I'll be right there." I hoped giving her the keys was the right idea. I was pretty sure she wasn't going to steal my police issued SUV, but I couldn't entirely rule it out as an option.

We watched her leave, and Harvey sighed. "That girl's always been too headstrong for her own good. She does brew a good beer, though."

"That she does," I agreed. "And she's not wrong. You knew that necklace was important to them."

"Do you really think it's evidence?" Harvey asked.

Once, I might have told him exactly what I thought, but I had learned a lot in the last few years on the job. Since Prentice Sawyer had died, I didn't trust anyone. It didn't matter that we were a small town filled with mostly good people. Everyone had their breaking point, had the one thing that would get them to do something they never would otherwise. No one was innocent. Not completely. Even Harvey, the trusted Sawyer family lawyer.

"Harvey, you have to understand how this looks. You knew someone had broken in once. You didn't secure your office. And now you're telling me the one piece of evidence we had that might point to the identity of the mystery woman the Sawyers have been looking for is now gone. Gone because you removed it from my property room and left it in an unlocked drawer in your unlocked office."

"Well, when you put it like that, it doesn't sound so great." Harvey looked to the door Avery had closed behind her, maybe wishing again for rescue.

"No, it doesn't," I agreed. "I need a better timeline on when the theft occurred. Don't give me this bullshit that you don't know the date. I understand that you're trying to divert Avery, and good luck with that. You've known her as long as I have. She's not easily distracted when she sinks her teeth in. If she were, she wouldn't have her brewery."

"Let me pull up my calendar," Harvey said in defeat. He was too much the attorney not to have noted the date. I followed his fingers as he flipped through the appointment book on his desk. Nearly five weeks before.

Fuck. Whatever trail we might have would be stone cold. There were cameras on Harvey's building. I'd talk to Hawk and see what he could pull, but I wasn't feeling hopeful. Even Hawk didn't hold on to footage forever.

"What are you going to do?" Harvey asked.

"About what?"

"About the necklace and the girls looking into all this."

"What do you suggest I do?" I asked, already knowing what he'd say.

"Tell them to let it go," Harvey said, his voice sharp. "I should have reported the theft, I know that, but I hoped that if the necklace went away, they would drop it. This is a ticking bomb. You and I both know Ford is innocent. Whoever manufactured the evidence that forced you to put him in prison also supplied the alibi that got him back out."

I nodded. I didn't need Harvey to tell me that.

"And you and I both know," Harvey went on, "that the reason they got Ford out of prison was because they couldn't take him out inside."

I gave a sharp nod. That was my guess as well. Not long before video evidence of his alibi appeared in a pawnshop, someone had tried to assassinate Ford Sawyer in prison. The guards had stopped the attempt. And now Ford was out—a far easier target than he had been in prison. For now, he was sticking close to home, letting Hawk and Griffen's tight security keep him safe, but he wouldn't let himself be caged forever. As soon as he got restless, it would be open season on Ford Sawyer.

I hadn't figured out the why of it all. My best guess was that Ford knew something—maybe something he didn't know he knew. A part of me wondered if it was possible Ford had been the target all along. If not the primary target, a secondary one? Had whoever showed up at the house and assassinated Prentice Sawyer planned to go after Ford next? The not knowing would drive me mad if I thought about it too much.

I had a town to protect—a town filled with people who weren't Sawyers.

"You know this is dangerous," Harvey said, leaning in, his eyes on the door Avery had exited through only a few minutes before. "We don't know who's behind this. We don't know what they want or who they'll go after next. The girls shouldn't be poking around. Quinn was kidnapped and Sterling—"

"None of that had anything to do with Prentice," I said. The details weren't Harvey's business, but I knew that with one hundred percent certainty. "No one's come directly at the family in a while. What makes you so sure the girls are in danger?"

Harvey leaned back, looked down at his desk. "It just seemed safer if it all went away."

"Safer for who?" I pressed. "For the girls or for you?"

Harvey just shook his head, refusing to meet my eyes.

My gut didn't like any of this. I wouldn't have said I trusted Harvey with my life, but I'd never thought of him as one of the bad guys. Now I wasn't so sure.

"I'm going to talk to Hawk and see what the security team can pull from the date of the break-in here." I watched his face carefully, but there was no reaction, no request that I just let it go and not investigate. "I'll keep you posted," I said and turned for the door.

Harvey let me go without a farewell.

I nodded at Louise on my way out, glad to see my SUV was still where I'd left it, Avery in the passenger seat, her arms crossed over her chest, fuming quietly until I got in.

"I never thought I'd say this," she said, "but I don't trust Harvey. Am I off base here, or was that really odd?"

I started the car, meeting her eyes for a second as I looked over my shoulder to back out. She was riled up and beneath that, uncertain. Harvey had been one of Prentice's buddies. More than just a lawyer, Harvey was almost family, and he'd always looked out for Prentice's children, doing his best to take care of them in his own way. I wanted to say he was trustworthy, but I shook my head.

"I'm there with you," I said. "His judgment was questionable."

"Is there any way—?" She shook her head. "I'm trying to imagine Harvey sneaking into the brewery and breaking into my desk drawer." She let out a sigh, leaning her head against the car window and staring at the tourists crowding Main Street. "I can't see him out of bed after 9 p.m., much less sneaking around town in the dark.

And why? What could he possibly gain from stealing my file?"

I raised an eyebrow, unable to get the picture to gel in my head either. "One thing I've learned in this job," I said, "Is that most people are capable of a lot, depending on the motivation. I wouldn't have put Harvey on the list for the break-in at the brewery, but I also wouldn't have thought he'd let his office get robbed and keep it a secret. Everything about that situation is sketchy."

"What do we do now?" Avery asked.

I stared up at the headliner of my SUV for a second, calling on every ounce of patience I possessed. "*We* aren't doing anything," I said. "You're going back to the brewery to figure out that recipe and do whatever else you need to do now that you fired your brewmaster and are taking over his job yourself." I raised an eyebrow. "I'm assuming that's your plan."

"Yeah, that's my plan." She let out a huff of air and tucked her hair behind her ear. "I have a crazy list of stuff to do. But I can't just let this go, West. That was our only lead, and now it's gone."

"The necklace is gone," I found myself saying, kicking myself mentally even as the words left my mouth. "But you still have the pictures. You can look for the designer. You were doing that anyway, all three of you, right? And you didn't actually have the necklace? It's not the necklace that's important. It's where it leads you." What the hell was I doing encouraging her?

"Good point," she said, settling back into the seat. "I just have to figure out—" Her voice trailed off.

"Avery." She snapped back to attention, her eyes

catching on mine. "I want you to think hard about letting this go." She sucked in a breath and leaned forward, her mouth opening to speak. I held up a hand, and she stopped. "It's dangerous," I reminded her. "Your brother's out of prison. His record has been cleared. You can let it go."

"And he'll never be safe unless we find who put him there in the first place," she said.

The bitch of it was, she was right. Ford would never be able to relax as long as Prentice's murderer was out there.

"I haven't stopped looking for the killer," I said.

"I know, West, and I know you're good at your job," she acknowledged. "That doesn't mean fresh eyes can't help."

"I don't need a partner, and I don't need to worry about keeping you out of trouble."

"I can't stand seeing him the way he is, West," she said, the sadness in her voice getting under my skin.

I didn't have to ask what she meant. I hadn't been tight with Ford Sawyer since he'd stabbed Griffen in the back and gotten my best friend exiled from town, but we'd been close when we were kids—not as close as Griffen and I, but close enough. In the years since Griffen left, Ford had matured into a man who was dynamic and authoritative, a man who wielded power comfortably. Since he'd come back from prison, he was diminished. He'd lost everything, and he didn't seem to be making any moves to take any of it back, seemingly content to hide himself away in the library at Heartstone Manor, reading and doing who knows what else.

He'd made no effort to find his father's killer or clear his own name beyond what the alibi had given him. He wasn't the same Ford I'd known most of my life, and while he'd been a jackass to a lot of people, he'd always looked out for Avery. He was a large part of why she had her brewery, and Avery didn't forget who she owed her loyalty to.

"I know you want to save him, Ave," I said gently, "but maybe this time you can let Ford solve his own problems."

"You blame him for what he did to Griffen," she said. "But he doesn't deserve this."

I let out a sigh, flicking on my blinker to turn into the station's parking lot. "I don't have the luxury of that opinion," I said, honestly. "As your brother's friend, I have a lot of feelings about Ford, but I'm the police chief of this town, and he's one of my people. That means something to me. I've never stopped looking for your father's killer, and I won't until we find them."

"Well, neither will I," she shot back, mutinously, reaching down to unsnap her seatbelt.

I opened up my mouth to threaten her with something—I don't know what—but the words didn't come out.

Avery was headstrong and reckless, and this was a terrible idea from start to finish. I didn't bother to tell her to stand down. I already knew she wouldn't listen. Bossing her around wasn't the way to keep her safe. If I wanted to keep her out of trouble, I'd have to figure something else out.

Chapter Five

AVERY

I wandered the brewery, fiddling and fussing, double-checking my stock of ingredients, even grabbing a cloth and polishing a scuff on one of my shiny, stainless-steel tanks. I was procrastinating. I checked on my attempt at recreating the fall brew, currently fermenting in one of the tanks, and right on track to start bottle conditioning next week. My gut told me it was going to be good, better than good, that it could be something extraordinary. Yet again, I cursed my faulty memory. I always kept notes. I had a database of recipes on my laptop, and my notebook was filled with ideas and musings about flavors that might be good together.

But with this recipe, I just couldn't nail down the details. I'd gone back and forth over so many things, changing my mind on technique and proportions, finally writing down my final decisions in the notebook that had been in my desk with the file on the necklace. It had never occurred to me that anyone would empty out my desk.

I knew the basic ingredients. It was beer, after all. Water, hops, malt, and yeast. But this one, a fall brew, had a hint of apple and the tiniest aftertaste of spice. I wasn't one for over-flavoring my beer. I liked beer to taste like beer.

But within that definition, there's so much variation. Lagers, ales, stouts, porters, sours, and my favorite, IPAs because I was a sucker for hops. I stopped in front of the hops bin, drawn there by instinct. I needed the comfort of pulling apart the bright green buds between my fingers, the deliciously acrid, piney, citrusy scent of the hops sneaking up my nose and filling my brain, spreading happiness with every deep inhalation. The sticky shreds clung to my fingers, staining them lightly with green and soothing my soul.

I'd been accused of making more than a few too-hoppy IPAs, and I refused to apologize. In the new recipe, I hadn't gone overboard, the bitterness of hops running counter to the hint of apple and spice I'd wanted for the fall brew.

I paced the open space, my boots thudding on the concrete floor, my brain sifting through what I could remember of the recipe and what my gut told me would give me the result I was looking for. For the millionth time, I stopped, pulled the note card out of my back jeans pocket, and jotted down an idea, the whole time my stomach was tight. I hated this feeling of uncertainty.

Usually, when I came up with recipes, I was led by my senses, my instincts, to the ingredients I'd use. Once I had that down, I fiddled with the proportions, with the process, the science of it at the front of my mind. But smell and taste, the heart of the beer, always came first. I rarely did anything this way with bits and pieces of incomplete memory. Normally, I was trying to create something new, and wherever my vision led, so be it. Not everything came out great, but some things did, and that was enough. But with this, I wasn't looking for something new. I wanted exactly what was in that vat. Nothing else would do.

It was possible I could reverse engineer it. I shoved the note card and pen back in my pocket and crossed the room to look at a stack of labels that had come in. The artwork was brightly colored, in deep reds, oranges, and yellows, a reflection of the gorgeous fall leaves that drew so many tourists this time of year. Designed by a local artist, they were vibrant and unique, perfect for the new recipe. I needed a special label since this might be the only bottling I'd have.

I wished Matt were the one who'd broken in and stolen the file and the recipe. If he had, I wouldn't think twice about storming over to his place and demanding my recipe back. It could have been him, but the more I'd thought it through, I didn't think so. For one thing, he didn't need to steal the recipe—he'd worked on it with me; he'd been the fucking brewmaster—and he probably had his own copy. I could ask.

I could. But every time I tried to envision doing it—picking up the phone or going over there after I'd fired him, I couldn't do it. Matt would know exactly how much I needed that recipe and what it meant to me. I wasn't going to ask Matt for the recipe; if the cost of my pride was losing it, so be it.

I'd told him I didn't need him. If I went over there now and asked him to bail me out, it would just be proving him right. I could do this without him. Right? I would have given anything to feel a resounding answer in my chest—in my gut—*Yes, you're in control, you can run this business just as well as you can brew beer*.

But there was a part of me that didn't entirely believe it. I wanted to—God, did I want to—but the hollowness in my chest, the clench of my stomach—argued back. *You've never done this without a brewmaster—not at this scale.*

In the beginning, I'd barely had a taproom or business, selling just enough beer to break even, Ford's well-timed infusions of cash keeping my head above water until I'd gained just enough of a foothold to afford hiring a real brewmaster who could teach me what I didn't know. That had been Matt.

And now that I'd booted him out, I was going to have to sink or swim on my own. *This is what you wanted*, I reminded myself. And it was. I dropped the rag in my hand in surprise as a fist pounded on the metal door to the brewery, my mind going immediately to the intruder the cameras hadn't caught. My phone was in hand, West's number on screen, when I heard a familiar voice call out.

"Ave, open up." My brother Finn. The tension drained out of me, and I pulled the door open to see his often surly face brighten with a smile.

"Hey," I said, smiling back.

"Did I interrupt?" he asked, walking past me to the taproom.

"No, I'm just..." I looked around. How to explain? "Procrastinating, I guess."

"I've been there," Finn said with an understanding nod. "I was heading into town for supplies, and I started thinking about that little kitchen you've got here. Maybe doing an apple pumpkin fall pop-up thing. After Halloween, maybe?"

"That would be awesome," I said. Now that Matthew was gone, nothing was stopping us from bringing Finn's culinary excellence to Sawyers Bend Brewing. "The kitchen isn't much."

"Yeah, I know, I've seen it. I've worked in worse. Anyway, we're not talking about a full menu at this point."

I tilted my head to the side and studied Finn's face. Since he'd come home, we'd seen many evolutions of Finn: surly and angry, not unlike the teenager he'd been years ago. Then, after he took over the kitchen at Heartstone Manor, a settled, focused, creative Finn had emerged. He still had a temper and an attitude when he was annoyed, but I felt like, for the first time in our lives, I was seeing the real him. And I liked him.

I'd always loved my siblings, but liking is different. This new Finn made me regret all the years he'd been away from home, but I suspected he'd needed that time to become the man he was now. Since he'd fallen in love with our housekeeper, Savannah, and married her, he'd become a father to her young son, another role I'd never thought I'd see my rebellious brother fill, but he filled it happily, loving both of them so much it radiated whenever they were together.

The side of Finn's mouth quirked up, and he shrugged his shoulders.

"Yeah, just pop-ups for now, but, and I'm not horning in on your brewery, Ave, I swear. I know how you are about this place. But, you know, we own the land next door, right?"

"I didn't," I said, surprised. There was a parking lot on one side of the brewery, and on the other side, a small lot with a ramshackle building that until recently had sold generic tourist crap. Sawyers Bend had a lot to offer in that area, and generic didn't cut it. The tenant, a transplant from Florida who thought selling cheap junk would be easy, had packed up and left a year before. The place was growing more decrepit by the day.

"I was thinking," he said, gesturing to the far side of the bar, "on this side of the building, the taproom is almost on the property line. If you wanted—" He raised two hands fending off the protest he thought was coming. "Only if you wanted, we could talk to Griffen about tearing down that building and extending your taproom and the kitchen."

I closed my eyes, letting the image Finn had described sink in. The small kitchen off the taproom was on the side of the building that abutted the property in question. Finn's proposal would work. I could see it, the way the stone and beam architecture of the taproom could extend into a dining room.

"We could have indoor and outdoor seating," I said. "The views from over there aren't anything spectacular, but it's pretty. The woods and the trees are cool in the summer, protected in the winter. We could have space heaters or a cast iron wood stove." I looked back at Finn to see that a slow grin had spread across his face.

"Now you're thinking," he said. "I don't want to jump in headfirst or anything. We're talking about a lot of work —planning, designing, building."

"And you're not in a rush to leave Heartstone's kitchens, are you?" I asked. I wasn't in a rush for him to leave the kitchens either. I'd never eaten this well in my life. Six months before, Finn had pissed off the chef enough that she'd quit. And as Griffen had threatened he would, he'd given Finn her job. It was either that or get kicked out and lose his inheritance. Finn had given in so easily, I suspected that's what he'd been after all along.

It was typical of Finn to go after what he wanted with the most amount of chaos possible. But now that he was in charge of the kitchens, we were treated to crispy, fluffy Belgian waffles in the morning. Divine omelets and light, buttery biscuits. His simple lunches were anything but boring. And the dinners... He could do home cooking, soul food, and gourmet, and all of it was amazing.

"If we do this," I said, raising an eyebrow, "who's going to feed us at home?"

Finn laughed. "We'll figure it out. I was thinking I could find an apprentice. There's a lot of talent in the area. It shouldn't be hard to track down somebody eager to learn and doesn't annoy the shit out of me. If I can do that, we should be able to put together a decent kitchen schedule to cover feeding you guys and running a restaurant. I've got a family now. I'm not looking for high stress—"

"—but cooking just for the family isn't enough," I finished for him.

"Exactly. You know how it is. You could have stuck to home brewing. You didn't need to start a beer empire."

"It's hardly a beer empire," I laughed. "But yeah, home brewing wasn't enough. This is what I wanted."

"And this plus a restaurant?" Finn asked.

If I told him no, he'd take it gracefully, because he was my brother, and as ornery as he could be, he also loved me. I'd just booted one partner. Did I want to take on another?

"Yes," was the answer, immediate and true. Because this wasn't a partner in my brewery. This was something else. This was sharing space. Finn wasn't looking to tell me what to do with my beer any more than I'd be micro-managing what he did in the kitchen.

Together, we could bring in more tourists. We could feed them. Give them beer. Sell them some t-shirts or a few six-packs to go. The only side benefit of my father's insane will was that he'd brought my family back to me. And working with my brother?

"I'd love it," I said. "Let's talk to Griffen. And let's figure out this pop-up for November."

"Awesome," Finn said. He started toward the little kitchen off the bar and stopped, turning back to me. "I heard you fired—What's his name? Mike?"

"Matt. And yes, I did."

"Are you looking for a new brewmaster?" he asked, raising one dark eyebrow.

"Not yet," I said.

He reached out and squeezed my shoulder.

"You've got this, Ave. Look what you've done so far. You didn't need him."

"Thanks, Finn," I said, wishing I had his confidence. Even without it, I'd put myself in this situation. I'd have to figure it out, one way or another.

I thought about what to do next. Go back to fiddling with the recipe, inventory the taproom, or check supply orders and the schedule for the week? The phone in my pocket rang. My sister Sterling.

"Hey," I said, answering. "I didn't expect to hear from you today." Her fiancé's mother and stepfather were in town for the fall craft fairs. Emily, Forrest's mother, seemed to have her finger in a bit of everything, crafts-wise. And Jerry, his stepfather, was a potter.

Sterling had shown me his website and a mug she brought home from Oregon that he'd made. From what I could see, he was talented. He'd love the craft fair, as would Emily.

"I was thinking," Sterling said, "there's supposed to be a lot of jewelers at this one. Do you want to tag along and bring pictures of the necklace? See if we can find anybody to talk to? Emily and Jerry are probably going to wander off. They're on a mission to find some potters Jerry knows."

Yes. This was exactly what I needed. Maybe it would clear my head to actually get something done instead of being frustrated here. "My to-do list is annoying me," I said. "I'm in."

"Cool," Sterling said. "We're headed out in an hour or two. We'll swing by and pick you up."

"Works for me," I said. I might have lost my file on

the necklace, but I had pictures. The sight of it—the shape, the colors—was ingrained in my memory. "See you soon," I said and hung up.

Now that I knew I didn't have all day, I found some motivation. I filled the time dealing with the dreaded to-do list—approving the beer labels, checking supplies, and making notes of glassware. In the background, I heard clangs and bangs from the tiny kitchen. Finn emerged looking a little dusty, shaking his longish hair out of his eyes, with a grin on his face.

"It's a mess in there," he said, but he didn't sound upset about it.

"Is it too small?" I asked.

"Nah. It's bigger than a food truck, and you'd be surprised what I could do with a food truck. It just needs a little reorganizing. I can definitely make it work."

"What about seating?" he asked, his eyes scanning the taproom. It wasn't a huge space. There was standing room at the long, wide bar, some high-top tables with two or four chairs, and some lower tables, but not as many as you'd have in a restaurant.

"I have small square folding tables in the back," I said, "and chairs to go with them. I bought them for an event a couple of years ago, and they come in handy. We've done a few collabs with food trucks before, and we use them every year for the Halloween party at the Orchard. They're not fancy, but they get the job done."

"For now," Finn agreed, "that's all we need."

"How many can you seat?" We walked the space, pacing out where the tables could go; discussed and vetoed the prospect of outdoor seating. By the time Finn headed off to do his grocery shopping, we had a pretty good idea how we'd handle the pop-up in November and a few thoughts on what we might do after that.

I looked at the taproom again, trying to imagine the changes Finn had proposed: the space opening up into a dining room in the same style, outdoor seating that brought the woods inside.

And unlike the hollow feeling I got when I thought about my recipe problem, this felt solid and right. This was going to be great. If only I had a new flagship beer to celebrate with.

Ugh, get it together, Avery. I'd come up with the missing recipe on my own. Mostly. Matt had helped me with the business side and the techniques of scaling up from small batches to commercial levels, but we'd both known my recipes were better than his. When I'd contemplated firing Matt, I'd worried about the mechanics of running the place, but not the beer itself. I wasn't loving the irony of the intruder taking the one thing I'd assumed I had under control. Whatever. I'd figure it out. I had to.

Chapter Six

AVERY

By the time Sterling pulled up with Emily and Jerry, I was more than ready to get out of my place for a while and focus on something else. I let Dave know I'd be back later and headed out to the parking lot.

Jerry started to unfold himself from the front seat, saying he'd sit in back with Emily, but I took one look at the length of his legs and shook my head. "I'm good. You sit up front. Your knees will be in your chin otherwise," I said as I slid into the back seat.

Forrest, Sterling's fiancé, was the CFO of the Inn at Sawyers Bend. More often than not, he was in a button-down and tie, pretty formal for our neck of the woods. I don't know what I'd expected of his mother, but the pixie sitting beside me with hot pink streaks in her gray hair had not been it.

She gave me a bright smile. "Avery, I had some of your beer last night and it is fantastic. A friend of mine's daughter is a brewer in Portland." We fell into a conversation about the brewery the daughter worked for, a place I recognized, and the ride to the craft fair flashed by. Sterling slowed when we got there as a man in an orange vest waved us to the gravel parking lot beside the Convention Center.

Beside me, Emily rubbed her hands together, her eyes wide with glee. "This is going to be fun." I looked around with fresh eyes and realized it really would be, especially for Emily. We were spoiled by all the artists and craftspeople in this area of the country. After a while, we came to expect it—the beautiful wares and art available all around us; the regular craft fairs bringing in more artists, more opportunity to surround ourselves with lovely things. I forgot sometimes not everybody lived with amazing potters and weavers and jewelers, and painters right next door.

As soon as we were inside the vast building, as Sterling had predicted, Emily and Jerry peeled off and disappeared into the crowd. We didn't bother to follow. They were on a mission. And so were we.

"Everyone's scattered all over the place," Sterling said. "I guess the better to browse. We're going to have to cover a lot of ground."

"I'm not in a rush," I said. "Just keep me from shopping."

Sterling laughed. "I'll try, but you know—same. My room's already full."

"You have Forrest's house," I suggested.

She bit her lip and then shook her head; "No, we left it furnished for the renter."

"But eventually you two are going to move in, right?"

I asked as we walked down the first aisle, scanning for a jeweler whose work matched the necklace.

"Eventually, yeah, I mean, after the will terms are up and we're allowed to move out of Heartstone Manor. I love his house. It's so cool. With so much wood, it blends into the trees. But it's bright and open too. He has good taste," she said with a smug smile.

"Obviously, because he picked you," I said, nudging her with my shoulder.

Sterling flashed me a radiant smile. I loved my littlest sister, always had, even when she'd been a hot mess of self-destruction. But I adored seeing her like this, happy and in love, sober, and working her ass off on a coding career of all things. To be honest, I didn't really understand what it was she was learning. She'd tried to explain it, especially her new cybersecurity interests, but it all went right over my head. She was working with some of the tech guys at Sinclair Security, the company our brother Griffen and Quinn's husband Hawk used to work for. They were serious. Uber high-end security to the stars kind of thing, and they'd offered her a kind of internship. I knew it was a big deal.

Her confidence had taken a boost as she settled into pursuing her career goals, but it was Forrest who'd put that blissful look in her eyes. Sterling was happily in love, and I had to admit I had the tiniest twinge of envy. For a moment with Matt, I'd hoped—but I'd never loved him. Been attracted to him, yeah. Appreciated his expertise and everything I could learn from him, but we hadn't had that connection, that spark beyond the hormones of it. Not like—

I cut that thought off before I could finish it. The only man I'd sparked with lately was one I wasn't touching with a ten-foot pole. West was hot, sure. He'd always been hot. I'd picked up on that when I hit puberty and noticed that boys were good for something other than hunting frogs and playing in the woods. But West was eight years older than me. Back then, I'd looked, maybe imagined a time or two, but absolutely nothing more than that.

My older brothers and their friends had felt like surrogate parents more than regular people when I was a teenager. I'd appreciated West's thick, dark hair and the broad shoulders he'd had even back then. He was tough and didn't take any bullshit, but he'd also been kind, which a lot of my brother's friends hadn't been. Why would they be? The rest of us were kids and, by their definition, annoying. Even with years of familiarity, I'd never grown used to West's good looks. Maybe because he was so much older, and our paths didn't cross often.

I stayed out of trouble, and Griffen had been gone from Sawyers Bend for years. There'd been no reason to see West. It was weird to know someone my whole life and not really know them well, but that's how it was with Weston Garfield. That didn't mean I'd lost my appreciation for his charms. Those shoulders were even broader. Whatever workout he did had left him with some pretty spectacular muscles.

But he was still my oldest brother's best friend, and the police chief of Sawyers Bend. He was also bossy as hell and overly responsible. Definitely not my type. I mean, I like responsible, but...

"Are you brooding over the break-in?" Sterling asked as we turned down another aisle.

I stiffened, afraid my little sister could read my mind. I debated lying. I wasn't sure I wanted to talk about any of this. But lying and deception were my father's way, and he was gone. If I couldn't be honest with my little sister... I shrugged. "Not about the break-in exactly, though it freaks me out that somebody knew I had that file and went to all the trouble to get in and take it."

"Ave, you're there alone a lot." She slid me a sidelong glance, concern darkening her eyes.

"Yeah, and I know Hawk has the place wired, but apparently not enough to keep someone from breaking in," I said. I should have listened to him when he said I needed more cameras. But it had bugged me to think about being watched. I suppose I needed to get over that.

"Yeah. You should have heard him this morning. I know he didn't call you because he said he wasn't going to." She gave an adorable imitation of Hawk's growl. "'I *don't give a shit what Avery thinks. I'm going out there and locking that place down. Nobody's getting in again.'* He was pissed," Sterling said in a regular voice. "The idea that you could have been there, working late—" She shivered.

"I have a feeling whoever broke in knew I wasn't there," I said, "but yeah."

I'd had the same thought earlier. What if I had been there? I knew some self-defense, but it was a terrifying thought, and it made me feel vulnerable. I hated feeling vulnerable. Hawk would take care of making sure it didn't happen again, but maybe the violation was bugging me more than I was ready to admit.

"You don't have to worry," Sterling said. "Hawk is going to fix it."

"I know," I agreed. "'I was just...'" I wrinkled my nose, trying to think of how to say what had been on my mind without starting something I wasn't prepared to finish.

"West is mad, too," Sterling said quietly with a sparkle in her eye. "I overheard him talking to Hawk. He's really bossy. Like, hot bossy."

Before Sterling could say anything else about West's bossiness, I distracted her. "He's pissed at me for having that file. He's pissed at all three of us."

"Yeah, Hawk yelled at me. And Quinn." Sterling shook her head. "If I didn't know he loved her to pieces, I might have worried. Because he was furious. *'None of you should be doing enough investigating to have a file, for fuck's sake,'*" she said in Hawk's voice.

"Has he heard you imitate him?" I asked, smiling at her. "I'm not sure if he'd be pissed or die laughing."

"Quinn has," Sterling said with a giggle. "She thought it was funny."

"I bet. I think I'm glad West yelled at me instead of Hawk, but honestly, I'm not sure which of them is scarier when they're angry."

Sterling nodded in agreement. "Anyway, West is pretty bossy, but he's also West." She wiggled her eyebrows at me, and I knew she wasn't going to drop it.

"He's too old for me," I said. It was a weak excuse, and Sterling knew it.

Sterling's eyebrows pulled together as she thought about that, her eyes scanning the aisle ahead of us. We passed one booth that had a gorgeous array of lampwork beads, and I thought of Scarlett, my twin brother Tenn's wife. She was a glass artist who did lampwork, making jewelry and small sculptures. She'd displayed at a craft fair already this season, but she'd given this one a pass, saying she didn't have enough time to keep up with inventory for the shops in the area that carried her work and stock another booth. A good problem to have. She was hoping to have enough for a booth here next year. Based on what I was seeing, she'd do a lot of business if she did.

"He's not too old for you, but I know what you mean. I love him, but he's—" Sterling looked up to the ceiling as she searched for the right word. "Rigid."

I smirked, and she laughed.

"Not like that, you perv. I mean, maybe." Another eyebrow wiggle. "But you know what I mean. Letter of the law and all that. He's always been kind," she said, echoing my earlier thoughts. "But he's black and white. Not a lot of room for grey."

She would know. When Sterling had been drinking, West had thrown her in jail more than once. It hadn't taken him long to cure her of trying to drink and drive. She'd been young and stupid, but a night in jail had impressed upon her the importance of not getting behind the wheel when she'd been drinking. After the first time he'd thrown her behind bars, she hadn't tried to drive drunk again. I knew there'd been a night or two when she'd slept in the chair in his office or an empty cell because she couldn't drive home and didn't want to ask our brothers for a room at the Inn.

"I don't have a problem staying on the right side of the law," I said, frowning to myself as I thought it through. "It's not that. I deal with enough regulations running a brewery. I know how black and white things can be and when it's important to do things the right way," I said. "It's the bossiness."

"You never liked anyone telling you what to do."

"Hello, pot calling the kettle black," I said with a laugh.

"Yeah, yeah, I know we all have that problem. Except Parker. She doesn't seem to mind being bossed around as much, but she picked a better one to do it this time."

"Definitely," I said, thinking of Nash, Parker's fiancé. "I'd let Nash boss me around any day," I joked. "Not that he has eyes for anyone but Parker."

"I think when it comes to West," Sterling began, and then stopped. "Hey, look." A few feet ahead was a booth draped in rust-colored fabric, trays and cases laid out, filled with bracelets, necklaces, earrings, and rings, all in a nature theme. My heart kicked in my chest. I pulled out my phone, scrolling through to find the picture of the gold oak leaf necklace Quinn had found in what used to be our father's hunting cabin.

As we neared the booth, I looked from the picture on my phone to the stock the jeweler had displayed. It wasn't an exact match, but it was pretty fucking close. I scanned the booth and found a woman about my age hovering by a display of earrings, dressed all in black, her copper-colored hair pulled back in a sleek ponytail. She smiled as I approached. I stopped at a tray of necklaces similar to the picture on my phone.

No oak leaves. I spotted a beautifully crafted tree branch and a goldfinch. Then I saw it—a maple leaf. Not an oak leaf, but it was a gold charm hanging from a chain —almost exactly like the one in the photograph.

"Can I help you find something?" the jeweler asked.

I glanced at Sterling, whose eyes were on the maple leaf necklace. She didn't say anything, so I took the lead. "Actually, yes." I tapped my finger on the maple leaf and showed the artist the picture of the oak leaf necklace on my phone. "Is this your work?"

"I, uh," she took a step back, shaking her head. "I recognize it, but—I mean—I don't know. Where did you find it?"

"It belonged to a friend," Sterling lied easily. "We've been admiring it, and she couldn't remember where she got it except that she knew it was around here some- where. She got it a few years ago. Could it have been yours?"

Sterling blinked her big blue eyes up at the jeweler. Sterling was dazzlingly beautiful. Long golden curls and those Sawyer blue eyes. Her smile had been known to turn people to mush—male or female, it didn't seem to matter. The jeweler didn't fall under her spell, but she eased slightly. I kept my mouth shut. Between the two of us, Sterling was more likely to get information. I was too upfront, too demanding. Not assets in a conversation where someone had something to hide.

The jeweler shook her head again. Sterling fluttered her lashes and gave a smile so sweet it made my teeth hurt. "Are you sure? It looks so much like this maple leaf here, but we really wanted an oak." She looked at me and back at the jeweler. "For all the oak trees by our house, you know? And this one—" She tapped on the screen of my phone. "It's just so pretty. Are you sure you didn't make it?"

"I'm sure," the jeweler said shortly. "I've made a couple of leaves like that one there," she pointed to the maple in the case. "But no oak leaves—not a couple of years ago."

"Okay, well, if you're sure." Sterling let her shoulders sag in disappointment.

"I'm sure," the jeweler said again shortly and turned to another customer hovering at the edge of the booth.

We walked away. As soon as we were out of earshot, Sterling said, "That was weird, right? Because that maple leaf—the style of it—the way she pressed the pattern of veins into that leaf…"

"I know," I said. "It looks exactly like the oak except it's a maple. But, yeah, the style, the execution, everything. Why wouldn't she just tell us?"

"I don't know." Sterling glanced back over her shoulder. "I don't think she's going anywhere. We can keep looking and see what we find."

We did. I ended up buying a pair of fingerless gloves with a matching hat because the knitter had embroidered hops at the wrists and on the hat brim, and I couldn't resist. Sterling walked away with a small stone sculpture she said was for Forrest. We saw more jewelers. Beautiful work. More nature-inspired pieces, but nothing like the maple leaf necklace or the oak leaf on my phone.

When we were done, Sterling turned back towards the first jeweler's booth. "I want to talk to her again," she said. The jeweler spotted us as we approached, her spine going stiff, her hands fidgeting as she straightened a tray. The maple leaf charm was gone.

"Hey," Sterling said in a friendly, ditzy-sounding voice. "You still have that maple leaf?"

"Sold. Sorry," was the terse reply.

Something told me she was lying. I didn't know if it was her quick response or the way she couldn't meet Sterling's eyes, but I would have bet that maple leaf pendant was still somewhere in this booth.

"Oh, that's such a shame. It's not the oak leaf we wanted, but we thought— Are you absolutely sure you didn't make the necklace we showed you earlier? Maybe you just forgot. It looks so much like your work."

"I didn't— I—" Her eyes skipped from one side of the booth to the other, and seeing no other customers, she leaned in, glancing down at the phone in my hand. "Could you put that away?"

Curious, I slid it into my pocket and waited.

"Here's the thing," she said. "I didn't make that oak leaf necklace. The reason the maple leaf looks so much like it is, well, I know the artist who made the oak leaf. I admired her work, and I was going through a creative dry spell, and I kind of—"

"Stole her designs?" I asked.

She flinched at the words and gave a shamed nod, her eyes glued to the tray of bracelets in front of her. "Look, I'm not proud of it, okay? But times were tough, and you know how it is."

I shook my head. I did and I didn't. Times were always tough. And while I'd been inspired by other brewers' creations, I'd never ripped one off. I was an artist, not a thief.

Sterling edged me back with her shoulder and flashed another of her saccharine sweet smiles. "I get it. It's not always easy to come up with new ideas. And you did a beautiful job with that maple leaf. But we are really looking for the oak leaf. Do you remember the name of the designer? I swear we won't say anything."

The copper-haired jeweler's eyes flashed from side to side again, as if making sure no one was close enough to hear. She hesitated.

"Please," Sterling cajoled. "It would mean so much to us."

"Buy the maple leaf and I'll give it to you," the designer said quickly. "But I don't have her contact info, just a name."

"How much is the maple leaf?" I asked, my voice considerably less sweet than my sister's. Sterling could be a little con artist when she wanted to. For better or worse, I didn't have that in me. The jeweler inched closer to Sterling and said, "Two hundred fifty."

"Done," Sterling answered, shooting me a quelling glare.

I started to say something, and she whacked me with her elbow. "Done," she said again, and I shut my mouth.

"I'll pay you back half," I muttered as the jeweler turned and dug in a bin beneath the table, coming up with the gold maple leaf.

Pulling out a business card, she wrote a name on the

back. "This is her. I don't know if she's still in the area. Honestly, I haven't seen her around in a while. But, you know, that doesn't necessarily mean anything. I'd appreciate it if you kept me out of it when you find her."

"Oh, don't worry," Sterling said. "All we want is the necklace. And thanks for this," she held up the box with the maple leaf. "It's really pretty. You do nice work."

We strode away, Sterling gripping the box with the necklace so hard her knuckles were white. "It's a little scary," I said, "how full of shit you can be."

"I know," she said brightly, "but I only use it for good these days."

"What are you going to do with that name?" I asked, sensing that with her programming skills and close relationship with Hawk, she was the best person to hunt down the name the jeweler had given us. "I don't recognize it, but that doesn't mean much."

"You're a beer hermit. You don't know anybody unless they're in brewing."

"True," I said. "But at least now we know where to start."

Chapter Seven

WEST

> Your mother wants you to come for dinner tonight. 6:30 p.m.

> Don't be late. We haven't seen you in weeks.

I tried to ignore the twinge of annoyance at my father's text. It was so typical of him. First, the command performance. Of course, he'd assume I'd be there just because he said so. Also, on brand for my father: using my mother as the excuse, because God forbid, he takes full accountability for anything. And no communication would be complete without the sprinkle of guilt at the end, the seasoning on the meat of his demand.

We haven't seen you in weeks.

Bullshit. I'd seen my mother just a few days ago when she'd stopped in to drop off cookies at the station. Everyone loved my mother, the sweet, slightly dotty mayor's wife. At least that's what she wanted everyone to think.

She showed up with baked goods, smiled, batted her eyelashes, patted my head, and left, vacuuming up every bit of gossip she could along the way. She'd always been the perfect partner for my father—genuinely beloved by the town, and sharp enough to use her information network to her—and his—advantage.

She and I would never see eye to eye when it came to my father's role as mayor, but I could live with that. I loved my mom, and in her own way, she'd always been in my corner. To her, I wasn't a tool to be used.

My father and I would have had a better relationship if I'd let him steer me through life the way he'd wanted to, but unlike my mother, my father had his own plans, and no one, especially not his wayward son, was going to get in his way.

I thought about turning down his summons. Tempting, but I had a feeling this dinner was less about filial duty and more about my father going after something he wanted. If I were right, I'd be better off if I knew what that was.

Now that Prentice Sawyer was dead, I had a chance to clean up Sawyers Bend once and for all. At the moment, the main force standing in my way was my father. As the mayor of Sawyers Bend, he was the most visible of the good ol' boys' club that ran the town. His more powerful and wealthy compatriots came to him when they needed the rules bent, or town policy 'adjusted.' My father gave them what they needed, and in return, they cut him in on 'investments' profitable enough to ease any ethical dilemmas he might have had.

The police chief before me had been in on the game. I could only assume that my father and Prentice thought I'd happily take his place. They should have known when I'd refused to go to law school and follow my grandfather's footsteps into a judgeship that I wasn't going to play along. I didn't want to be a lawyer, a judge, or the mayor—the only three professions acceptable for Garfield men. I wanted to be a cop—a respected profession to the rest of the world—but in my father's eyes, I was a fuck-up.

My father's perks from kissing Prentice's ass had included tuition for Laurel Country Day, the same private school the Sawyer kids went to, but it hadn't created the distance from my fellow citizens my father had hoped. I'd grown up in the big brick house just off Main Street that they still lived in, and when I wasn't in school, I was on my bike, riding around town to the playground or the baseball fields, to get an ice cream or a piece of pie at Maisie's place. By the time I was a teenager, I knew everyone in Sawyers Bend. Not as the son of the mayor, but as me. And unlike my father, pretty much everyone liked me. Not a huge surprise. I'm a likable guy, as long as you aren't breaking the law.

I'd always wanted to be a cop. It was the first Halloween costume I'd chosen for myself, complete with a shiny badge and a plastic gun on my hip. It wasn't until later that I understood that what I wanted was justice.

Just because Prentice Sawyer owned most of the town didn't mean it was okay for him to talk the police chief into enforcing parking and loitering laws to target those they felt were undesirable, or to look the other way when one of their cronies broke the law. Sawyers Bend was filled with mostly good people who were just trying to make a living and enjoy life with their families. It was my job to make sure they could do that without bending to the wills of the men who wanted to run my town like their own personal fiefdom.

I still didn't know why they didn't get rid of me the first time we'd butted heads. Prentice had demanded that I serve an eviction notice to a woman who was behind on her rent. She had two young kids and had recently lost her husband, but that wasn't of concern to Prentice. He had plans for the house she was renting, and he wanted her out. Immediately.

I'll never forget the look on his face when I'd informed him it was the County Sheriff, not Sawyers Bend Chief of Police, who executed evictions, and if he wanted his tenant out, he'd have to initiate the legal process of eviction, which would take time. His face had turned scarlet with rage, and he'd thrown me out of his office at Heartstone Manor, swearing he'd have my badge. I didn't care. I wanted to stay in Sawyers Bend, but not at that price, and I could be a cop anywhere.

I'd never asked, but I suspected Ford had played a role in keeping me on the job. Here and there, problems were sometimes quietly solved, actions taken to subvert Prentice's goals that only someone on the inside could have pulled off. Like the newly widowed mother behind on her rent. The pastor at her church had helped her with childcare and a deposit on a new apartment, thanks to an anonymous grant. I couldn't prove it was Ford, but my gut was sure.

Trying to level the playing field in Sawyers Bend had been an uphill battle—if the hill was the size of Mt. Everest. With Prentice gone, I had the chance to make real progress. In the time since Prentice's murder, my father had made it clear he didn't see an opportunity for change, but a power vacuum he badly wanted to fill. That he'd never have a fraction of Prentice's resources wasn't going to stop him. As long as he could get more than what he had. For men like my father, there was never enough *more*. If I wanted to stay ahead of him, I had to know what he was up to.

> I'll see you at 6:30.

I hit send on my text and tried to push the upcoming dinner out of my mind. At the least, I'd get a good meal out of it. My mom was a great cook. I stayed at my desk and handled paperwork until 6 p.m., then swung by the florist for a bouquet of flowers for my mom.

My father met me at the door, a cut crystal glass in his hand, bourbon on his breath.

"Your mother's back in the kitchen," he said. "Dinner's almost ready." He turned to follow me to the dining room, the table set with fine china and linen napkins, same as it would have been even if dinner had been only the two of them. Once, when I'd asked why go to all the trouble, I'd been informed that standards were what set the Garfields apart. As if eating on fine china somehow made us better than everyone else. If my mother knew how many dinners I ate on the couch, she'd have an old-fashioned attack of the vapors.

"Quiet day around town," he said, pausing in front of the crackling stone fireplace and raising his glass for a sip of bourbon.

"As quiet as it ever is," I agreed.

"Any word on who broke into the brewery?" He looked casual, sipping his bourbon in front of the fire, his hair a little mussed and his tie loosened, but his eyes were sharp and his question had the hairs standing up at the nape of my neck.

I couldn't think of a single reason my father should know about the break-in or be interested enough to ask. "It's an open investigation, Dad. You know I can't talk about it."

My father shook his head. "Always a stickler, son. Things have changed. It's time for you to loosen up for the good of the family."

I rolled my eyes. I'd heard a version of this lecture for years. I'd been ignoring it just as long. "Dad, let it go," I said, "Prentice is gone. Your whole southern gothic 'we own this town' bullshit has had its day. I'm sure as hell not going to support it."

My father clenched his jaw, his eyes hard and cold. "You never did have any goddamn respect."

"You haven't done a hell of a lot to earn it," I said with a shrug, keeping my tone easy and relaxed. I didn't want my mother to hear us arguing.

He ignored me, turning to the bar in the corner of the dining room. "Bourbon?" he asked, already pouring. Clearly, whatever he was after was going to wait.

I shook my head. "I'm still on call." I wouldn't have a drink until 8 p.m., when my second deputy went on shift, and when I could have one, I didn't want bourbon. At that thought, I could almost taste Avery's flagship crisp, hoppy IPA. That was what I wanted. Maybe when I escaped our family dinner, I'd stop by Avery's place and have that beer—a flare of anticipation followed that thought. Sitting at her bar, listening to the hum of conversation as I sipped an IPA was exactly what I needed after a few hours dealing with my father. It didn't have anything to do with Avery herself.

I turned at the sound of footsteps, handing my mother the bouquet of flowers when she entered. Her eyes lit as she took them, her mouth curving into a genuine smile.

"West, they're so lovely." She leaned in to kiss my cheek, enveloping me in the light floral scent of her perfume. "You're such a good boy, even if you haven't come to dinner in weeks."

This time, my eye roll was affectionate, and I hugged her. "Been busy, but it's always nice to get a hot meal." *It'd be nicer*, I added silently, *if my dad hadn't been here, but I couldn't have everything.*

Leaving my father sitting at the head of the table in the dining room, I followed my mother back to the kitchen and started dishing out pot roast, my favorite, while she arranged her flowers in a vase. "West, I can do that," she chided, glancing at the door to the dining room. "You should go visit with your father."

"I've got it," I said, ignoring the suggestion to spend more time with my father. The familial harmony my mother wanted was never going to happen. We both knew it, but she'd never stop trying. I grabbed my plate and the basket of freshly baked rolls and followed her to the table.

As soon as we were seated, I asked, "How's the garden club coming along with decorating the town for Halloween?"

With that one prompt, my mother would dominate the conversation for a solid twenty minutes. It was a bonus that I was actually interested. My father straightened in his seat, scowling down into his bourbon. He wasn't happy that I'd derailed his agenda for dinner, but for all his other faults, he loved his wife, so he didn't interrupt as she told me all about the papier-mâché skeletons they'd made in the grade school to decorate windows around town and the deal they'd gotten on pumpkins for the carving party they'd sponsored to raise money for the food pantry.

She was the perfect mayor's wife. She liked her position, both the power and the wealth it afforded her, but no one could deny that she spent a lot of time and effort making Sawyers Bend a better place to live for everyone, not just for herself. By the time she was done filling me in, I'd finished most of my dinner, and my father looked ready to explode.

"And how about you, dear?" she asked. "Anything interesting going on in town?" She waggled her eyebrows at me with a smile, already knowing I wouldn't tell her anything. And we both knew, with her resources, she got the best gossip, usually before a whisper reached my ears.

"I heard," she said, leaning in with a smug smile on

her face, her voice dropping as if there were anyone to overhear, "that Avery fired her brewmaster."

"I think that's common knowledge by now," I said.

"Well, the firing is, but did you know he may already have a new position?" She mentioned a brewery that was, sadly, fairly local. I didn't know Matt that well, but my gut said the farther he was from Avery and Sawyers Bend Brewing, the better.

"And," she went on, "The brewmaster has been sharing some stories about his time at Sawyers Bend Brewing." My mother shook her head, her expression genuinely troubled. "It sounds like Avery's in over her head. I always wondered what Prentice was thinking, letting a young lady like her run a brewery. It's not proper."

"Mom, you sound like a dinosaur," I said, wishing I were surprised by her line of thought. I loved my mom, but she was perpetually stuck in the fifties. "Avery brews an excellent beer, and she knows how to run a business."

"Then she should have turned her recipes over to the brewmaster and let him run the place," my father grumbled. "Your mother's right. It's not appropriate. She's a Sawyer. It never sat right with Prentice. He only let her have the place to keep Ford happy."

"I don't know what that has to do with anything," I said stiffly, annoyed on Avery's behalf. As much as I wasn't Ford's biggest fan, I knew without him in her corner, Sawyers Bend Brewing wouldn't have gone anywhere. "I don't know what stories Matthew is spreading," I said. "But I'm not sure you should take the word of a guy who just got fired."

"She did have a break-in, though, didn't she?" my mother asked, gently probing for more details. My eyes went to my father.

"Why is everyone so interested in the break-in at Sawyers Bend Brewing?" I asked, uneasy. "Dad asked about that, too. Where did you hear about it?"

My mother remained silent. After a long silence, my father said, "Harvey mentioned something."

"Harvey," I repeated. That was plausible. My parents were good friends with him, as were most of Prentice's generation. And a crime against a Sawyer business was unusual enough to make it a hot topic for gossip. I still didn't like it. Considering he'd kept his mouth shut about his own break-in, why was he talking about Avery's? She'd hate being the subject of town gossip. Harvey should know better than to talk about her personal business.

"So, how's the mayor business, Dad?" I asked, changing the subject away from Avery. There was no way I was getting out of here without hearing whatever it was my father wanted to say. We might as well get it over with.

"Frustrating," he said, letting out a gusty sigh.

"Frustrating how?" I prompted.

He set his empty bourbon glass on the table with a thump and drew in a breath. I braced for the bullshit to come. I was not disappointed.

"Things have been done a certain way here for a very long time," my father said, his deep voice reverberating as if he were giving a sermon. "The fabric of our town is woven with the threads of history. Without respect for the past, we have nothing."

He paused, as if waiting for a response from me. Since he hadn't said anything worth responding to, I stayed silent, waiting for him to get to the point. He forged ahead.

"Change is rarely good, and too much change can be disastrous. We need to hold tight to our ways. That's where we find security and positive growth."

Another expectant pause. And still, he hadn't actually said anything. He'd thrown out some vague concepts dressed up in pretty words, but he hadn't said anything concrete at all. I knew this game just as I knew what he was getting at.

I wasn't in the business of vague promises. The law doesn't work on vague. If he wanted my help, he was going to have to articulate exactly what he needed, which I knew was the last thing he wanted to do. But I had a life to live and a cold IPA in my future. I'd had enough of my father's machinations.

"I don't see the problem," I said. "Change is a constant. Adapt or die." I could throw out cliches, too.

Another gusty sigh, accompanied by a heavy shake of my father's head. "The problem is that your friend Griffen doesn't want to play ball."

"Are you surprised?" I asked, trying not to laugh in my father's face, if only for my mother's sake.

"I'd hoped the boy would have matured in his time away, at least enough to see sense. But he's as hard-headed as you are. Everything has to be above board. No backroom deals. No gentlemen's agreements." He changed his tone, losing his trace of a Southern accent, and said, "*Just because it's the way it's always been done doesn't mean it's the way we're going to do things from now on.*'"

It was a poor imitation of Griffen, but I got the point. I wondered how many times Griffen had repeated those words since he took the reins of Sawyer Enterprises.

"I don't know what you expect me to do about it, Dad. I'm the police chief," I reminded him. "I'm the last person to convince anyone to bend the rules."

"I'm not talking about anything illegal," my father said. "I know better than that. It's about doing things the way they've always been done. He doesn't respect history, or precedents, or contracts that his father negotiated. Or the way we do things."

"You mean he doesn't want you and the rest of your buddies making backroom decisions that affect the entire region, but only benefit you?" I tried to keep the acid out of my voice, but caught my mother's wince and knew I hadn't been successful.

"It's more than that." My father waved his hand in a circle in the air. "It's everything. The businesses he's trying to attract, the salaries he's paying. He's making everything more complicated."

"And you want me to do what about this?" I asked, trying to imagine a world in which I'd ever ask Griffen to stop bringing better jobs to our town. Just as hard to imagine was a world in which Griffen would listen.

"You two have been friends since you were children," my father said in a coaxing tone. "I want you to talk to him. I want you to explain to him how important history is."

"Sure, I'll talk to him," I said easily. I'd tell Griffen every detail of this conversation, not that it would help my father.

My father's eyes narrowed. "Both of you were always ungrateful little shits."

"Howard," my mother cut in. "That's uncalled for. West is his own man, and so is Griffen." She shook her head at me and reached out a hand to cover mine, squeezing. "Your father always did hate change. He could use your understanding."

I nodded, and she turned back to my father, who glared at her. "Bets, you just don't understand how serious this is. You've never had a head for business and—"

"I don't need a head for business to know that you're a smart man, Howard," she said, her voice sharp but her eyes warm as they met his. "You'll figure out a way to work with Griffen because you have to. And it won't be by trying to strong-arm the boy into seeing things your way. I'm ashamed of you trying to rope West into your shenanigans. You should know better."

I tried not to grin. My father dropped his head like a recalcitrant school boy, muttering, "You don't understand."

"I understand enough," she said, standing. "Dessert? I made coconut cake."

I wasn't going to turn down my mother's homemade coconut cake, even if it meant more time with my father. "She's right, you know," I said. "Griffen isn't unreasonable, just ethical. If you put more energy into working with him instead of trying to change him, you'd get a lot further. He's not interested in joining your good ol' boys' gang. Edgar already tried that when Griffen married Hope."

"Edgar still thinks the boy will come around," my father said, lifting his chin. Edgar was Hope's uncle and had been Prentice's business partner. I didn't trust him any more than I'd trusted Prentice.

I absorbed that, turning it over in my mind before shaking my head. "No, he doesn't. He knows Hope is working side by side with Griffen, and she's even more ethical than Griffen. Edgar knows they won't blur any lines. If he's telling you they will, he's playing you."

My father's brows drew together in a scowl, but he didn't argue my point. Instead, he admitted, "If I'd known Prentice was going to get himself shot, I would have done a few things differently."

"You're one of the few people truly mourning him," I said.

"Prentice was a friend for most of my life," my father admonished me, and I felt a twinge of real guilt. I had so many reasons to dislike Prentice Sawyer, sometimes I forgot there were a few people out there who'd liked him. My father's next words wiped away my guilt.

"Prentice's murder has cost me a lot of money," my father said. "Being mayor doesn't exactly pay the bills." He raised an eyebrow, his gaze sweeping around their elegant dining room furnished with antiques.

I thought of the two luxury cars parked in the garage, the vacations he took my mother on, and the fur coat hanging in her closet. Being mayor of a small town in North Carolina didn't pay enough for all of that. My father had always been good at turning connections and opportunities into cash in the bank. But with Griffen in the way...

My cop's brain couldn't help following that thought to its most obvious conclusion. Someone had sent a killer after Griffen, not once, but multiple times. It was nearly impossible to believe that my own father could be responsible. On top of that, we'd assumed that the person after Griffen and the other Sawyers was the same as the person who'd killed Prentice. That made the most sense.

I was damn sure my father hadn't killed Prentice Sawyer, if for no other reason than sheer greed. Everything was better for my father with Prentice alive to lend him the power and the connections to make profitable investments. And getting rid of Griffen didn't necessarily solve his problem. With Griffen gone, he'd still have to deal with Hope and Royal, neither of whom would be interested in bending their ethical standards.

As I worked my way through the logic of it, I felt a weight lift from my chest. Yes, Griffen was in my father's way, but my father was still better off with him alive. The risk/reward matrix wasn't enough for my father to consider murder a solution to his problems.

My mother returned with generous slices of cake and launched into a story about a woman at church who'd been badgering her for the recipe for her award-winning coconut cake. My mother was an amazing cook, and she did not share her recipes. Ever. Everyone knew that, but the woman at church had apparently decided she was special. My father and I laughed at the right moments in the story, and as soon as she was done, I escaped with a hug, a kiss, and a full stomach. My father's pensive glare followed me out the door.

I rolled my shoulders as I walked, trying to leave behind the weight of his disapproval. I knew I was a disappointment. In my younger years, that had burned some, but most of the time, I thought I'd grown past needing anything from him. I loved my job. I loved this town.

I took a minute to notice the papier-mâché skeletons decorating the window of the town drugstore. My father was wrong. The changes caused by Prentice's death were good. He'd adjust. Eventually.

My feet took me past the police station, and I felt a vague wash of surprise that I hadn't turned into the parking lot to get my vehicle. I didn't want to go home. Not yet. I wanted to move, to walk.

And—I realized as my feet took me through town and out the other side—what I really wanted was a cold beer.

Chapter Eight

I pushed open the door of Sawyers Bend Brewing and let the warm air and golden light surround me. Conversation was lively but not boisterous. Small groups clustered around high-top tables; a few people sitting at the bar. Avery stood behind the long expanse of wood, pulling a beer from the tap and smiling at a customer as she listened to whatever he was saying.

I was hit by an odd wave of pleasure at seeing the smile on her face, at seeing her at all. Before I could wonder where that had come from or why, it occurred to me that Avery was rarely here in the evenings. Usually, if she was behind the bar at all, she handled days. Cammie or Dave usually handled evenings.

I shouldn't have expected to see Avery here, and I wasn't sure why I was so glad that she was. She slid the beer to her customer, and her eyes lifted, meeting mine. Her smile spread wider, her gaze pulling me to the bar like a tractor beam, and I decided I didn't really care why I was so glad to see her. I was just glad I was here.

"What can I get you?" she asked.

"White Water IPA."

"Good choice," she said, grabbing a pint glass. "Late night at work?" she asked.

"Dinner with my parents," I answered.

Avery slid me my beer and let out a short sigh, her eyes leaving mine only to scan the bar and make sure no one needed anything. "That sounds like fun." Her dry tone told me she knew dinner had been anything but fun. "How's your mom?" she asked with genuine warmth in her voice.

"Mom's good. I see she talked you into some papier-mâché skeletons in the window."

Avery tossed her dark ponytail over her shoulder and laughed. "Those elementary school kids are pretty industrious. At least I got one of the skeletons that looks like a skeleton instead of a worm with weird legs. It's pretty cool. I like how they decorate the whole town. Everybody gets in on it. It's cute for the tourists, but it's also..." She shrugged, a little smile curving the side of her mouth. "It makes the town even more homey, you know what I mean? Like we're all here together, celebrating the season. I can't wait to see what they do for Christmas."

"I know what you mean," I said. My father's proprietary attitude about the town got under my skin, but I did love the way my mother and whoever else she could rope into community service helped to keep us a community, not just a tourist destination. "I heard Finn's been around," I said.

Avery glanced to the side, to a closed door that led, I

thought, to a small kitchen. "Yeah, we're working on some ideas."

"Good ideas?" I asked, raising an eyebrow and taking a sip of my beer, letting the bitter, bright hops wash over my tongue. Avery knew her stuff when it came to beer. My eyes skimmed the taproom—not crowded, but doing steady business. She knew what she was doing there as well, despite the rumors her former brewmaster was spreading. It didn't look to me like she was in over her head.

"You two going to team up?" I asked, my mouth watering at the idea of Finn's cooking being as accessible as Avery's taproom. I could always bum a meal at Heartstone Manor. Griffen would never turn me away, but then I'd have to deal with the entire Sawyer clan, which, while they were like family, could also be a lot.

"We're working up to it," she said slowly. Her eyes caught on something across the room, and she said, "One sec," headed down to the other end of the bar, took an order, filled it, and came back I was pleased to note that while she smiled at her customer, it didn't have the same warmth as the smile she'd given me.

Why did I care? I hadn't quite figured that out. She was Griffen's little sister. She'd been in the background of my life for as long as I could remember. Until the morning after the break-in, I hadn't thought of Avery as more than that. Now I couldn't stop thinking about her.

I wasn't exactly sure what I planned to do about that.

Ignore it until it went away?

That was the simplest answer. Watching the curve of

her lip as she smiled, walking my way, I wasn't sure it was the most satisfying answer, or the answer I wanted.

"The town could use another restaurant," I said when she was close enough.

"That's what we were thinking. Nothing fancy. Small menu. Not every day, to start. I don't know. We're tossing stuff around, but I like it," she nodded. "I'd mentioned it before, but Matthew—" Avery cut off abruptly and shook her head at herself, clearly not wanting to talk about him further. It gave me the opening I wasn't sure I wanted but knew I had to take.

"You know he got a new job? At Bear Run Brewing?"

Avery shrugged one shoulder. "I guess that's not a surprise. I was done working with him, but he's a good brewmaster. He just—" her eyes scanned the bar again, came back to mine. "He wanted to take over, you know."

"He's been running his mouth," I said, slowly.

Avery's jaw set, and she drew in a breath slowly before letting it out, fighting, I thought, to control her temper. "What's he saying?" she asked slowly, grudgingly, as if she didn't want to know.

I lifted one shoulder, wishing I had news that wasn't going to piss her off. "I only know what my mom heard. Mostly that he was the brains behind the business, and you're in over your head."

Avery nodded and didn't look as upset as I'd expected. "That's the story he gave me when I fired him. He's not wrong," she said. "And he's also completely wrong. I hired him as brewmaster because I needed to learn from him, and I paid attention over these last two years. If I can't do it on my own by now—"

She cut off as a group of five came through the door and headed to a high-top table. One of them broke away and came to the bar. Avery moved to take her order.

I watched her talk and smile, charming and friendly, as welcoming as her taproom. She'd created the kind of place you wanted to hang out for a while. In one corner, she had a bookshelf with games and decks of cards. One group had grabbed a board game and a big round table. It looked like they'd been working their way through pints of beer as they played, laughing the whole time.

Avery carried a tray of beers to the new group and made her way back, picking up the conversation where we'd left off. "So that was it? Non-specific bragging about how great he is and how I'm incompetent without his guidance?"

"Pretty much," I said. "At least, as far as I've heard."

She let out a huff of breath and shook her head. "For now, I'm going to ignore it, no matter how much I want to shut him up. Protesting isn't going to make me look more competent, you know? And complaining about gossip just makes me sound like a whiner."

I didn't like the passivity of it. I wanted her to fight back, but I knew how this would go. I might be a man, but I wasn't blind. Matthew was getting a pass on his gossip. If Avery spoke up, she risked being labeled emotional or catty. It wasn't fair, but she was right. For now, she was better off ignoring him.

"Did you make any progress on the missing recipe?" I asked.

She shrugged a shoulder as she dried and polished pint glasses she removed from an under-counter dishwasher. "Maybe. It's too soon to say. We have the Halloween party at the Orchard next week. The first and maybe last time we serve the original version of the fall brew. I don't know if I'm hoping it's amazing or hoping it sucks so I don't feel bad about losing the recipe." She sighed and glanced at me. "I don't suppose there's been any clues about who broke in?"

I hated having to shake my head. "Not yet. I'm not giving up."

Avery reached out and laid her palm over my hand, her fingers curling around mine to squeeze once before she slid her hand away.

"I know you won't give up."

"You have any luck tracking down that jewelry designer?" I asked quietly, though there was no one close enough to overhear. I wasn't taking any chances.

She shook her head. "Not yet. Sterling's trying to get the address." She raised an eyebrow, and the corner of her mouth curled up. "I'm not going to say anything else about that."

"Probably better that you don't," I said, my tone dry. "When it comes to Sterling and her new connections, I figure the fewer questions I ask, the better."

Avery grinned. "I think you're right. Who knew she had all those numbers and formulas running through her head?"

"I'm not surprised," I said. "I always had a feeling there was something more..." I searched for a better word. "She was always so angry—angry at your father, angry, I think, at the rest of you for going on with your lives and leaving her."

Avery winced, and I shook my head, "Not saying you should have done anything different. You had a life to live, too. And it wasn't easy for any of you in that house."

"Still, we should have done better by Sterling. Maybe by Brax too," she said, her eyes shading dark as she thought of her younger brother, dead these last few months. The Sawyers' grief had been a painful tangle. Their brother was dead, shot before he could carry through with his plan to murder Sterling and Forrest. No one had wanted Brax dead, but in the moment, there hadn't been a choice.

I didn't have anything comforting to offer on the subject of Brax. He'd lost any compassion I had when he tried to kill his sister. They'd all grown up with the same nightmare of a father. Only Brax had chosen murder. Instead, I said, "We all have our own road to go down. This was Sterling's. She had a messy start, but it feels like she's hit her stride."

"Yeah, she has," Avery said with a genuine smile. "I'm so proud of her. And a little afraid of what she'll do with all of this—you know, working with Sinclair Security. What if she moves to Atlanta?"

"Atlanta isn't that far. She'll figure it out," I said, taking another sip of beer.

A customer at the end of the bar caught Avery's eye. "One sec," she said before moving to take his order. Once that was taken care of, she grabbed an empty tray and circled the room, clearing empties and taking new orders, ringing them up on various tabs, running cards, and making change.

I could tell she loved seeing people enjoy her taproom.

I was surprised when my phone beeped with an alert, and I realized it was after 10 p.m. With an early morning in my future, I didn't need another beer. I should pay my tab and walk home. As I pushed my stool back, I realized I didn't want to. I felt good sitting in Avery's taproom, talking about nothing and everything in the short chunks of time she had free. She was closing soon. I could stay and walk her to her car.

"You ready to cash out?" she asked. "I'd say it's on the house, but..." I shook my head, and Avery grinned back. "Yeah, I know, Chief West Garfield does everything by the books."

"What time do you close?"

Her eyes flicked to her wrist. "In about half an hour, though I might stay later if these guys haven't finished their game," she said, lifting her chin at the group with the board game.

"They driving?"

She shook her head. "I don't think so. They're staying at the Inn. It's only a few blocks away. I figure they'll walk home and sleep it off. They're my favorite kind of drinkers. Happy, never get wasted enough to be a problem, but keep buying beer."

"The board games are a good idea," I said, tapping my phone on the small card processor she slid my way. "You don't usually work this late. Somebody call out?"

"Cammie," she said. "I think the break-in spooked her. Or maybe she's just got stuff going on, because she's called out more than usual in the past few weeks. Tonight being one of them. If it keeps up, I may have to figure something else out. I'd hate to do it. She's been with me practically since the beginning, but..." She rolled her shoulders back and tilted her head to the side, stretching her neck. "It's a long day, on top of running the brewery."

"What time did you get here this morning?" I asked, shoving my phone back in my pocket.

"Early," she said. "Too early. I'm sleeping in tomorrow just to make up for it."

"Are the cameras working on the front of the building? Is somebody at Heartstone keeping an eye on you when you go out to your car?"

Avery's mouth curled up, her eyes warm on mine. "Yes, Chief, I promise. Hawk makes me text before I leave so whoever's on cameras can make sure they're watching to be sure I get to my car safely."

Good. That was good. I didn't have to make an excuse to linger and walk her to her car. I could go home, get a good night's sleep, to start my own early day tomorrow.

So why did I feel a pang of disappointment where there should have been relief?

"See you around," I said. "Keep an eye out when you leave."

"Will do. Bye, West."

The door shut behind me, cutting off the golden light, the warmth, and the cheerful voices, leaving me alone in the cold fall air. I shoved my hands in my pockets, turning back toward town and the short walk home. My evening had ended a hell of a lot better than it started. I hadn't expected that.

As I walked, I found myself making a plan to keep an eye out for Avery's car at the brewery in the evenings. It wouldn't hurt to stop in when she was working late. It would send a message to whoever had broken in that the police had their eye on the place. Just part of the job, right?

Sure.

I didn't bother bullshitting myself any further. It wasn't about sending a message. It was about seeing Avery. I couldn't forget the warm clasp of her fingers around mine when she told me she knew I wouldn't give up.

In so many ways, Avery and I were strangers. And in the ways that mattered, Avery knew me to the bone. I doubted she knew what kind of pizza I liked, but she knew what my job meant to me. How much I loved this town, and the tangle of irritation and love that was my relationship with my parents. And on top of all of that, I thought I could still feel the heat of her fingers on my skin. She had strong, capable hands. I couldn't stop wondering how it would feel to have them all over me. I'd have to figure out what I was going to do about that.

Chapter Nine

AVERY

My feet were killing me, my lower back was on fire, and my cheeks hurt from smiling, but I couldn't have been happier about any of it. Our second annual Halloween collab with Rivers Bend Orchard was well into its fourth hour, and so far, it had been a smashing success.

There were people everywhere. Tourists, locals, families with kids, all roasting marshmallows around the huge bonfire, bobbing for apples, and buying tickets to shoot the potato guns at scarecrows. At this point in the evening, it was too dark to see where the potatoes landed if they missed the spotlit targets, but that didn't seem to be stopping anyone. A local band played bluegrass and folk rock by the barn. People were gorging themselves on fried apple pies, cider donuts, and barbecue from a food truck.

And everyone was head over heels in love with the fall brew. It was a triumph.

Except that I didn't have the recipe anymore.

One thing at a time, I reminded myself. Right now, I was going to enjoy that I'd made something so many people agreed was amazing. I'd planned to serve whatever we didn't sell tonight in the taproom, but it looked like the crowd here might drink every drop.

A crew of kids in costume ran by, a mummy's white streamers trailing behind them as they zigzagged from one candy station to another. The Orchard staff had set up a scavenger hunt of candy, challenging enough for the older kids and easy enough that the little kids still got their share. All of us working the event were in costume, like a lot of the kids, adding to the festive air. I'd kept it simple with a black dress and fangs that were still attached to my teeth because I hadn't tried eating yet.

My stomach growled, reminding me how long it had been since breakfast. I thought I'd gotten used to the tantalizing scent of barbecue drifting in the air, but I saw someone walk by with a huge pulled pork sandwich, and my stomach made itself known. Glancing around, I thought I might have time for a quick break.

I turned for the food truck and almost bumped into August, my brother, Tenn, and his wife Scarlett's youngest son. Looking up, I saw him accompanied by Nicky, Finn and Savannah's son, and August's older brother, Thatcher. Griffen and Hope's nanny, Paige, stood a few feet away, wearing baby Stella in a carrier.

"Hey Paige, hey guys," I said. "How long have you been here?"

"A while," Nicky said, bouncing on his toes. "We went and shot the potatoes, and I think I decapitated one of the scarecrows—" I glanced up to see Thatcher shaking his head.

"Didn't even get close," he said under his breath, but Nicky didn't pay attention.

"—and then Paige said we could get some donuts after we bob for apples," Nicky finished.

Paige smiled at me over Stella's head. She was sweet and quiet, and great with the kids. I hadn't been sure about having someone in the house who wasn't family. Savannah didn't count. Even before she married Finn, she'd grown up with us as the daughter of the house-keeper, Miss Martha, who'd run Heartstone my entire childhood.

But Paige had fit in seamlessly, first living in town and only coming in during the day to help Griffen and Hope with Stella, filling in when anyone needed help with the older kids. A month ago, she'd moved into Heart-stone Manor, and by all I could see, she was making everyone's lives easier. I liked her.

"Who else is here?" I asked.

Paige looked back over her shoulder at the food truck. "Griffen and Hope. That's why I have this one here," she said, smiling down at the top of Stella's fuzzy pumpkin hat. "Finn and Savannah, too. Sterling said she was going to come by, but she isn't with us yet. And Ford."

"Ford? Really?" I asked, surprised. Ford didn't come out in public much, especially among crowds. I don't think he'd been to a single town event since he'd been sprung from prison months before.

Paige pressed her lips together, nodding. I wondered if he'd been dragged or come willingly, but it wasn't the kind of question I'd ask Paige. I'd ask Ford myself when I saw him.

"Have fun," I said to the kids. "Don't make yourselves sick on those donuts." They laughed and rolled their eyes, August and Nicky bolting for the big metal tubs set up for apple bobbing.

"Good luck," I said to Paige, squeezing her shoulder as I walked past her, my eyes on the long line at the food truck, the smell of barbecue making my mouth water.

A man walked by, holding a red and white paper container mounded high with mac and cheese. I started making a list in my head: a barbecue sandwich with plenty of coleslaw, some of that mac and cheese, maybe they'd have collards with bacon. I hadn't eaten since breakfast—a million years ago—and I'd been on the move since I woke up. I could devour a whole platter of barbecue and all the sides.

I scanned the crowd for any of my siblings or their spouses and came up empty. The turnout had been wonderfully big. Rivers Bend Orchard was popular, which sure didn't hurt, but neither did having the name Sawyers Bend Brewing on the banner at the front. I was almost at the food truck when I had a thought and diverted back to where my staff was pouring beer.

Dave looked up. "I thought you were on break."

"I'm working on it," I said. "I'm getting some food. You guys want me to get you anything?"

"I'm good," Cammie said. "I'll eat when you take my spot here." I'd been thrilled when she hadn't bailed on me for this. We needed every hand on deck for today.

"I'm good too, boss," Dave said. "I ate earlier. Definitely get some of that mac and cheese. It was—" He rolled his eyes in bliss. "Life changing."

"It's on my list," I said, my mouth watering again. "All right, if you guys are cool—"

"Better than cool," Dave said. "Everyone loves the fall brew."

"Congratulations," I heard from behind me.

I turned to lock eyes with Matthew, my appetite dying a quick death as I took in the smirk on his face. I was not talking to him in front of my employees. Turning, I paced back toward the food truck, letting him hurry to keep up.

"Avery," he started, and I slowed down, realizing my determined stride was attracting attention.

"What's up, Matthew?" I asked, my voice as neutral as I could keep it.

His hand closed over my elbow, stopping me in my tracks, his grip too tight for me to break without drawing the eyes of everyone around us. That was the last thing I wanted. Second only to Matthew being here at all.

"I bet you think you pulled this off, don't you?" Matthew said in a low voice. "But you're on borrowed time. I heard you lost the recipe for the fall brew. Everyone loves it, but that won't do you any good, will it?"

"Where'd you hear that?" I asked, ignoring his smug expression.

"Word gets around," he said easily. "It's possible I have the original on my laptop. I might be willing to part with it. For a price."

My chest burned with sudden fury. I yanked my

elbow free of his grip, too angry to care who saw. I had to shove my hands in my pockets to stop myself from throwing a punch right to that perfect nose.

The businesswoman in me said I should find out what his price was and get my recipe back. The rest of me rejected that idea. Fuck that and fuck him. It was my recipe. I'd made it in the first place. I'd make it again. I'd make it better.

What I would not do is give Matthew Holt another dime of my money.

"No thanks, I'm good," I said, fighting to keep my voice even and friendly, aware of the way some of the people around us had stopped talking, their heads tilted in our direction, ears tuned for gossip, for trouble. I didn't want to give them either.

This was my night. My triumph.

"Why are you here, Matthew?"

"What? Can't I hang out in my town? Have some barbecue and drink a beer? I brewed it after all."

"I thought you had a new job. You're not a part of Sawyers Bend Brewing anymore," I reminded him.

"You think you can get rid of me that easily?" Matthew asked, leaning in and lowering his voice. "Enjoy your night, Avery. It feels like a triumph, but it'll be the last you ever know. You can't reproduce this beer without me. Everyone will realize what a failure you are when you never make another decent beer."

He straightened, raising his voice just enough to be overheard by the crowd around us. "If you change your mind, you know how to find me. I've saved your ass before. I might be willing to do it again for a price. Then at least you could have some talent behind your beer."

I didn't realize how close I was to punching the arrogant expression off his face until an arm came around my shoulders, pulling me back. I looked up to see my brother Ford, his usually impassive face set in hard lines, his eyes furious.

"You're not welcome here," he said to Matthew. "Leave now or I'll make you leave."

"You can't fucking tell me what to do," Matthew spit out, taking a step forward.

"No," West said from behind Matthew, "but I can. One of the hosts of this event has asked you to leave." West looked at me with raised eyebrows. I nodded with a jerk of my head, forcing my fingers to open from clenched fists.

"Yes," I said, in case it was unclear to anyone. "I want him to leave." I wasn't sure how much I cared if he left quietly as long as he was gone.

West looked to Ford. They shared a look that I was pretty sure meant, *You got her while I take care of this?*

I didn't love the whole "men saving the little lady" vibe, but at the moment, as long as it resulted in Matthew being gone, I'd take it.

Ford nodded back, his arm tightening around my shoulders as he turned me and led me toward the side of the barn, pulling me toward the shadows, away from the crowd. "I thought you were going to break his nose," Ford said in a low voice.

"I wasn't planning on it, but—" I shook my head,

pulling my hand out of my pocket, clenching my fist and releasing it, trying to force the rage out of my body.

"He doesn't know you're a scrapper. I almost wish I'd let you hit him, but I figured you'd regret it later."

"Maybe," I said, not sure if I would have regretted it. He certainly deserved it.

"He probably would have had you charged with assault. And with that many witnesses, West would have had to arrest you," Ford said, making me laugh.

"West wouldn't need the crowd of witnesses," I said, shoulders shaking with amusement at the idea of West having to arrest me. "You and I both know he never lets anything slide."

"True," Ford agreed, with a dry laugh. It had been a while since I'd heard my older brother laugh. When he finally did, I wouldn't have thought it would be over a bad joke about West throwing me in jail. All of us, including West, had known Ford was innocent of our father's murder, but the evidence had pointed to Ford, and West had done his job. By the books, as always.

"Thanks for keeping me out of jail," I said, shoving my hands back in my pockets. I stopped at the far corner of the barn, the dark, cold air a buffer from the crowd gathered by the front of the barn.

"I don't know what Holt was saying, but you looked like you were about to explode."

"I was," I agreed. "I don't know why I let him get under my skin like that."

"He's an asshole," Ford said. "You were smart to fire him, and your beer is fucking awesome."

I let out a gust of a sigh, feeling the same twist of joy

and despair I did every time I'd heard that tonight. "I just wish…"

Ford shook his head, the movement barely perceptible in the dark. "Don't, Ave. You made it once. You'll either make it again, or you'll make something better. I know you. You won't give up until you kick ass. You never do."

A group came around the corner of the barn, talking and laughing. Ford and I inched back toward the far corner, deeper into the dark.

"I just need a minute to get my shit back together," I said. "Thanks for saving me from embarrassing myself."

"That's what he wanted you to do," Ford said. "While he was baiting you, I could see him looking around. He knew people were watching. He wanted you to react. Now he's thrown out on his ass, and you can enjoy the rest of the night."

I should have caught that, but I was glad I'd managed to keep my shit together.

"So," I prodded, "who forced you to come tonight?"

Something moved in the dark on my left, and I turned, my feet going out from under me abruptly, something heavy hitting my back, shoving me forward into the rough barn wall. Fire slashed along my collarbone and down my arm.

Someone screamed. Me? I tried to get my feet under me. They tangled, and I pitched forward, smacking my head into the side of the barn before I twisted and landed on a body. A groan told me it was Ford. Why was Ford on the ground?

I couldn't get my bearings. There was a scuffle of

footsteps. The shadows had seemed safe before, a cocoon away from the crowd, but now they were impenetrable. And they held danger. I could barely see Ford's face, his grey shirt and jeans all but invisible against the dark ground.

I felt movement on my left, cold air stirring against my cheek, the whites of someone's eyes, and the grind of a shoe on gravel. Metal flashed, a blade catching the light from the bonfire so far away. It came down, aiming for Ford or me, I couldn't tell. I never found out. Pinned half beneath me, Ford wrapped his arms around my torso and rolled, shielding me as the dark figure lunged in, the blade scraping the dirt where we'd been a second before.

We knocked into our assailant's legs, sending the murky figure sprawling in the shadows, the blade in his hand flashing in the firelight.

There was a laugh and a shout, the noise terribly incongruous. A group of kids raced by in the dark, screaming, throwing something at each other as they ran. When they'd passed, he was gone, melting into the dark beyond the barn.

"Are you okay?" I asked. "Say something." I slid to the side, getting off Ford, shoving his arms away.

"I'm okay," he said, his voice low and tight.

I didn't believe he was okay. I wasn't sure I was either. My collarbone and arm burned. My fingertips came away sticky and wet. Blood. I could tell it wasn't very deep, a scrape more than a stab. Fuck. It had happened so fast. It didn't hurt yet, but I knew it would.

"Can you stand?" Ford asked.

"Yeah," I said, not sure if I could. I managed to get to my knees and immediately knew they wouldn't hold me up. Not yet. I was a wobbly mess. I rocked back on my butt and leaned against the side of the barn, the rough wood cold. "I just... I just need a second. I'm okay."

"Stay there," Ford said.

"Where are you going?" I asked, my voice thin and high-pitched, brittle with panic.

"Nowhere. Just sit still." I heard a rustle and saw the light of his phone as he tapped the screen. The screen flashed, and he said, "Someone just jumped Avery and me. I think they had a knife. She's hurt. We're on the north side of the barn. We were trying to get away from the crowd for a minute."

"I see you," West said in response. The call went dead. West was there a moment later, crouching in front of me.

"He had a knife?" he asked, scanning the light from his phone over my body.

"Yeah," Ford said. "Where'd he get her?"

"Collarbone and arm," West answered, both of them talking as if I weren't there.

Normally that would irritate the shit out of me, but in that moment, I didn't want to talk. I couldn't get my brain to catch up. Five minutes ago, I'd been furious with Matthew, trying not to make a scene. And five minutes before that, I'd been reveling in the success of this year's Halloween party.

Now I was sitting in the dirt, bleeding. Someone attacked us with a knife? Why? It didn't make any sense.

"He got you, too," West said, his light on Ford's grey shirt, stained dark with blood across his chest. "I'm taking you both to the ER."

"I don't need—" Ford began. West cut him off.

"Shut it. You're going. Don't piss me off." He looped his arm around my back, pulling me to my feet. My joints felt slippery, like the bones in my legs wouldn't line up right. I leaned into West, my cheek resting against his chest, the beat of his heart reassuringly solid under my ear.

"Can you walk out of here?" West asked, his breath warm on my cheek. "I can carry you."

That vision sprang to life in my head—West's strong arms taking over for my wobbly legs. West, making all of this go away, bringing me somewhere safe. I liked that. Then there was the image of him carrying me through the crowd. After my altercation with Matthew, that was the last thing I needed. Fucking hell. I squeezed my eyes shut.

"I can walk," I forced out, not sure if I was lying.

West took a step. I tried to keep up, but my feet weren't cooperating, my head still spinning. Pulling out his phone, he made a call. "Hey," he said to whoever answered. "We have a situation. I need a pick-up. Come around the back of the barn using the side access road. You know where it is?" He paused for confirmation. "See you in a minute."

He looked up, scanning the dark around us. "Jim is on his way." Sliding his arm down my back, he bent and lifted me in his arms, cradling me against his chest. "We'll get you out of here the back way. No one will see. Just close your eyes for a minute."

I thought about arguing or asking questions, but I settled for closing my eyes and letting the dark take me under. I'd worry about everything later. For now, I just wanted the quiet.

Chapter Ten

WEST

A very went limp in my arms, and for a second, my heart stopped. Her breath against my neck brought me a degree of relief, but not enough. Ford was on his feet. There was a gash at the side of his head, bleeding freely, but he was steady enough. His eyes darkened with concern as he saw Avery out cold.

"She hit her head when she fell," he said in explanation. "Is she still bleeding?"

"Not much. Whoever jumped you, got her with the knife, but she looks better than you," I said, not liking the blood soaking into his shirt. "I'm not sure she'll need stitches, but we need to get you to the ER. Can you walk to the back of the barn?" I looked past Ford to gauge the distance. It was dark back here, but I guessed the light on the far corner of the barn was maybe fifty feet away.

Ford lifted a hand to press his shirt into the bloody slash across his chest. "Yeah, but I'm fine. I don't need to go to the—"

"I don't want to hear it," I said, cutting him off. Ford

opened his mouth to object again. I said the only thing I knew would shut him up. "Look, Avery needs to get her head checked at a bare minimum. And if you bail on the ER, I'm going to have a fight to get her there. So could you just do me a favor and let me take both of you in?"

Ford knew my game, but he also got the logic of it. Avery was sweetly compliant when she was unconscious, but I knew well that when she woke up, compliant wasn't a word I would use to describe Avery Sawyer. The surprise was how much I liked the way she pushed back at me.

My head had been spinning since I first caught sight of her moving through the crowd in her Halloween costume. Avery had always been striking. With her dark hair and bold eyebrows, that wide, full mouth, and bitter chocolate eyes. Even as a child, she'd been compelling. Then she grew from a little girl into a woman, and she'd become more than just striking. Avery was beautiful on a bad day.

Tonight, though. Tonight, she was stunning.

She didn't put a lot of thought into her looks. Most of the time, she didn't bother with makeup or coordinate her clothes. I was used to seeing her in jeans and a Sawyers Bend Brewing polo shirt, her long hair pulled back into a braid or twisted up and held in place with a chopstick or pencil. I was not used to seeing her like this.

Her hair flowed like a shining curtain over shoulders bared by her black dress, the sleeves hanging past her fingers in ragged points, the skirts swirling around her legs. Her lips were blood red to go with the fangs in her mouth, her lashes so long I was pretty sure they weren't real. The dress dipped to show the slightest curve of cleavage, the skirt revealing only a bare hint of long legs ending in worn black combat boots I remembered from her teenage years. Her costume was completely appropriate for a family night at the Orchard, and so fucking sexy I'd had trouble thinking clearly every time I'd spotted her in the crowd.

I was off duty, but whenever a lot of people were combined with free-flowing alcohol, anything could happen. I'd skipped a beer, as good as I knew it was, and went for a soda, watched the kids bobbing for apples, took a few shots with the potato gun, won a prize, so at least I didn't embarrass myself and tried not to keep an eye on Avery. I failed miserably at the last part. When Matthew had intercepted her in the crowd, I was headed their way a second later.

Ford must have been watching her, too. We came in from opposite sides, making a beeline for Avery to stop whatever the fuck Matthew was up to. We'd both watched as Matthew had grabbed her arm, and my gut burned at seeing the way she started to yank her arm free, then stopped, not wanting to cause a scene. A smirk had twisted Matthew's mouth as he'd realized he had her trapped. For the first time in memory, I'd wished I wasn't the police chief so I could tear him away from her and beat the shit out of him for daring to touch her.

That wince on her face when he squeezed her elbow —he deserved a broken nose just for that. But not only was I the police chief, beating the shit out of him for touching her was exactly the kind of scene Avery wanted to avoid. Instead, I'd gotten him out of there, and the next thing I knew, Ford was calling to say he and Avery had been jumped.

The sight of Avery covered in blood was fucking with me. I didn't like seeing anyone hurt. But Avery...

I had to focus. My deputy pulled around in his department SUV. We traded keys.

"My vehicle's parked in the lot in front," I told him, and turned to Ford. "You get in and slide over. I'll pass her to you."

Avery's eyes fluttered open as I placed her gently on the seat, nudging her to lean against her brother. "West? What happened?"

"It's okay. Ford's got you. I'm going to take Ford to the ER. We'll get you checked out while we're there."

"I don't—" she started to protest. Ford wrapped his arm around his sister, pulling her close. "Just close your eyes, Ave. It won't be a long ride. Everything's fine now."

"My head hurts," she grumbled, her eyes meeting mine just before her lids slowly drifted shut again.

The ER was quiet when we got there, or as quiet as a rural ER ever gets. I took Avery from Ford, leaving my vehicle out front, and carried her in. Ford followed behind, still moving under his own steam, but slowly. He needed some stitches, probably some antibiotics, maybe even a pint of blood or two. I had to respect the guy, though. The slice across his chest had to hurt, but he didn't complain, more worried about Avery than himself.

I let the doctor nudge me out of the way after depositing Avery on a hospital bed in a room next to Ford's. The second my hands were free, I called Hawk, filling him in on what had happened.

"I'm sticking with Avery. At this point, we don't know which one of them the attacker was after, and I'm not leaving her. I need you to send someone over here to cover Ford. I don't have the staff to spare," I said.

I hung up in time to see a nurse cutting open the sleeve of Avery's vampire costume to reveal a long, thin slice that started at her collarbone and extended down her arm. Most of it had stopped bleeding. I didn't like the way Avery lay there, passive and pale. Shock? Disorientation from hitting her head? I wasn't a doctor. I only knew that this wasn't Avery.

"It's better than it looks," the nurse said. "A few deeper spots here and there, but it should heal up just fine." She looked up at me. "She passed out?"

"Yes," I confirmed. "Not long after I found them. Her brother said she hit her head on the barn pretty hard when she fell."

"How does your head feel, honey?" the nurse asked.

Avery lifted her hand towards her forehead and slid it back to graze a spot above her ear. "It hurts the worst right here. When he jumped us, I slammed into the wall."

The nurse took a closer look and turned worried eyes to me, then made a note on her chart. "We'll take a look at that," she said. "You might have a concussion."

"I don't want a concussion," Avery said, startling a laugh out of the nurse.

"Well, you don't always get what you want, honey. But at least we can find out what you're dealing with. I'm going to get this cut cleaned up, then see about taking a closer look at your head." She stood. "I'll be right back." The nurse stepped out of the room, I guessed to make arrangements to get Avery an MRI or a CAT scan or whatever they'd use to check out that hard skull of hers.

"You still with us?" I asked. Avery wasn't back to herself, but her eyes looked clearer than they had a few minutes before.

"Yeah, I'm okay." She let out a long sigh. "Everything hurts. My arm. My head. It's annoying. Is Ford okay?"

"He's probably going to need a few stitches, but otherwise, I think he's in better shape than you are. Do you know who attacked you?"

Avery started to shake her head and stopped as a wave of pain hit her. Squeezing her eyes shut, she kept her head very still as she said, "No. It was dark, and it happened so fast. I saw his eyes, but that was it. It wasn't anybody I knew, not that I could tell. And then some kids ran by and he disappeared."

She sat back into the bed, settling her head into the pillow. Her eyes drifted closed, but there was nothing restful about her. After a minute, she said, "He was trying to stab Ford. He knocked us down, and I fell into the barn, then onto Ford, but he was there with the knife, pushing me out of the way, I think, trying to get a better angle on Ford." She opened her eyes, her dark gaze locking onto mine.

"Are you sure?" I asked. "You said it happened fast. How do you know he was after Ford and not you? He could have been trying to get you into a better position, not Ford."

Avery opened her mouth, then closed it. Finally, she asked, "Why would they be after me?"

I shook my head as the nurse came back in, a

plastic bin filled with supplies in her hands. "I've got your scan ordered," she said cheerily. "While we're waiting, let's get you cleaned up." She looked at me. "You staying?"

I sat on Avery's good side, taking her hand. "I'm staying," I said, unable to explain why I wasn't going anywhere.

I couldn't get it out of my head. The hint of cleavage I'd admired was stained red to match her lips. She'd been so vibrantly gorgeous, so alive, and a knife had split her skin while I'd been only feet away. It was too close. Until I saw all that blood, I'd never considered what I might lose if something happened to her.

I wasn't leaving until I was sure she was all right. I'd work out the why of it later.

The nurse wiped at the dried blood on her skin, and Avery winced, her face going a little pale. I wasn't sure if it was at the sight of her own blood or the pain from the nurse cleaning her up. Either way, I said, "Hey, don't watch. Look at me." Obedient, for possibly the first time in her life, she rolled her head to the side and met my eyes.

"This was not how the rest of my night was supposed to go," she said.

"I know," I said. "You were kicking ass. I think you doubled the crowd size from last year."

She smiled. "People looked like they were having fun. The music was good, I heard the food was great, everyone loved the beer."

Her pride was evident, and I grinned back.

"You did good," I said.

"Yeah," Avery agreed with a sigh. "Yeah, we did good. For tonight."

"I know this part's not great," the nurse murmured, but I don't think you'll need stitches." She fastened what looked like a butterfly bandage over the deepest part of the cut, pulling the sides of the torn skin together until the cut almost disappeared. "We'll start antibiotics since we don't know where that blade was, but it's not too bad. It should heal up without much of a scar. We just need to take a look at that head." She finished bandaging Avery's arm. "Hang tight for a few minutes. I'll be back to bring you up for the scan, okay?"

"Okay," Avery said.

The nurse laughed, and her eyes flicked to me. I nodded, understanding. "I'll make sure she stays put."

"West," Avery said, "I'm okay."

I didn't know what to say. Technically, she was okay. I wanted her under guard until we figured out what the fuck was going on, but did she need me sitting next to her bed holding her hand? Probably not. I could have stood up, untangled my fingers from hers, and stood guard in the hallway. I could have, but I didn't.

I leaned in close until my forehead rested against hers and murmured, "You scared the shit out of me."

And then I did the thing I'd wanted to do most. The thing I'd told myself I definitely wasn't going to do. All my logic, all my defenses fell apart at the thought of how close she'd come, how much damage that knife could have done. I tilted my head and pressed my lips to hers, wondering what she would do.

Pull back?

Slap me?

Ask me what the hell I thought I was doing?

She didn't do any of that. Instead, she lifted her mouth to mine, her lips warm, giving. I cupped her face in my hands, feeling the throb of her pulse under my fingertips as I parted my lips and kissed her again, longer, deeper, my tongue sliding against hers, tasting Avery.

And I was lost. The soft rush of her breath, her lips curious and eager against mine. I didn't want to stop kissing her. I couldn't remember why I should. Shifting, I slid my hand to cup the back of her head, lifting her mouth to mine, my other arm wrapping around her waist, easing her closer. Her good hand came up, her fingers wrapping around the back of my neck, pulling me in, a low moan vibrating in her throat.

Fuck, I was in trouble. So much trouble, I didn't hear the beeping. Not until the footsteps squeaked behind me and Avery went still against me.

Then the shrill, urgent alarm cut through the haze in my brain, right along with the glare of Avery's nurse. "Behave yourselves and stop messing with my sensors," she ordered. I thought there was a glint of amusement in her eyes, but that might have been wishful thinking.

"Yes, ma'am," I said, settling Avery back against the pillow, my hand finding hers and giving it a squeeze. Her eyes, when they met mine, were wide with panic. Over getting caught or from kissing me? If it was from the kiss, she wasn't the only one.

Part of my brain was going off with clanging alarms that matched those coming from her heart rate sensor. I'd kissed her because I wanted to. Needed to. Even though it was the last thing I should do. She was lying in a hospital bed, possibly with a head injury, for fuck's sake. I was the police chief and her brother's best friend. So many fucking reasons I shouldn't have kissed her.

Reality was, I didn't give a shit about any of the reasons I shouldn't have kissed her. Something had happened inside me when I'd seen her on the ground by the barn. Maybe I could have put aside the vision of her in her vampire costume. Maybe. That hint of cleavage would have tortured me. But everything had changed at the prospect of losing her.

I wasn't going to turn away from Avery Sawyer. I wasn't going to forget our kiss. And neither was she.

Chapter Eleven

WEST

By the time Griffen walked in the room, followed by Hawk, I was sitting a respectable distance from Avery, nothing to hint at what had happened except for my fingers still tangled in hers. Griffen didn't miss a thing, his eyes lighting on our clasped hands for a split second that was just long enough.

I'd deal with that later. My stomach was twisting at the thought of telling my oldest friend I'd kissed his sister. It would be awkward, probably uncomfortable, but that wasn't enough to scare me away. Not from Avery. Not now. I don't know what I had intended with that kiss. Maybe a brush of the lips to test the waters. That was assuming I was thinking at all. I hadn't expected her response. If I'd known she could kiss like that—

Avery shot me a guilty, embarrassed look, shocking me back to reality. Damn, that kiss was hard to shove to the back of my mind, but somehow, I needed to. There would be time to deal with that later. For now, we had business to discuss.

"Ford's getting stitched up," Hawk said, taking a position in the open doorway, where he could keep an eye on us and the traffic in the hall at the same time.

"He's okay?" Avery asked.

"He's fine," Griffen answered, standing at the foot of her bed, his arms crossed over his chest. "Ford said you hit your head pretty hard."

"It hurts," Avery said, "but not as bad as it did before. I was woozy. I think I passed out for a minute, but I don't know if that was from hitting my head or just shock. It happened so fast, and there was so much blood."

"And you had no idea who it was?" Griffen asked, his eyes glued to his sister, soaking in every detail—her pale cheeks, the bandage covering the cut on her collarbone and arm.

"No," she whispered. "I wish I did."

"Give me a description," Hawk said. Before Avery could start, he looked at me.

I pulled out my phone. "I'll take your statement now," I said to Avery. "We might as well do it this way and save you coming in later."

"Sure," she said, eyeing my phone as I hit record. I added the identifying info—who I was interviewing, time, date, all that. Then I said, "Tell us what happened. Start with the altercation with Matthew."

Her dark brows pulled together, and I knew she wanted to argue. She didn't want to talk about Matthew, especially not in front of Griffen and Hawk. She was embarrassed and angry. I knew all of that, and still, I needed her statement. All of it. She eyed the screen of my phone, watching the stopwatch tracking the length of the recording. I squeezed her fingers. "Forget about the recording. Just tell us what happened."

Avery nodded. "Matthew approached me while I was on the way to get dinner," she began, telling us step by step everything that had happened from when we'd parted ways to when I found her on the ground covered in blood.

"All I saw were his eyes. Really just the whites of his eyes. I want to say they were dark brown, but they could have been hazel. It was so dark. His clothes were dark and—"

"You sure it was a man?" I asked.

She closed her eyes for a second, I thought to replay the attack in her head. Her eyes still closed, she said, "I'm pretty sure. He was tall, taller than me, almost as tall as Ford. Not bulky though. He was rangy. Lean, but strong. He had something over his head—a costume or a mask. I wish..." She let out a short laugh. "I was going to say I wish it had lasted longer so I could have gotten a good look, but if it had lasted longer, one of us would probably be dead."

"Before," I said, "you thought he wanted to stab Ford. What made you think that?"

"Because he had a knife, and he came at us," she answered, her eyes wide. "It seems kind of obvious he wasn't there to play chess or ask for my beer recipe."

"How do you know?" I asked. I could practically hear Griffen's teeth grinding together at the question. None of us liked the idea that the stranger with the knife had been after Avery. Ford seemed like a logical target. Someone had already tried to kill him in prison. Now that he was out, he'd stuck close to home, reluctantly putting up with the security that Griffen and Hawk assigned. Whoever wanted him dead hadn't had a lot of opportunity to go after him. Until tonight.

"I just, I guess I just assumed they were after Ford," Avery said, letting out a breath. "I mean, who would come after me?"

"The same person who broke into the brewery?" Hawk asked with a raised eyebrow.

"But they just stole my file and my recipe, they didn't try to hurt me. And I don't even know what that was really about. Maybe..."

"Did he say anything?" I asked. "Anything that indicated that Ford was the target?"

"He barely made a sound," she said, her voice rough with frustration.

Griffen, Hawk, and I exchanged a long look.

"At this point," Hawk said, "we need to assume either one of you could have been the target."

"No," Avery protested, trying to push herself into a higher sitting position. "No, it couldn't have been me. I don't want—"

I squeezed her hand. "Hey, I know you don't want to think about it. I know it's fucking scary. And I know you don't want the added security that your brother and Hawk are definitely going to put on you after this."

"I really don't," she said, sending a frightened glare at her brother and Hawk.

"But until we know what's going on," I went on, "the

priority is keeping you safe. It's better to waste manpower watching your back than to assume we know what's going on and put you at risk. Do you understand?"

She didn't answer, just huffed out a breath. Hawk took a step into the room to make space for the nurse pushing a wheelchair. "Anybody want to go for a ride?" she asked, and I clicked off the recorder on my phone.

"I do," Avery said, sounding grateful for the excuse to escape the conversation. I helped Avery into the wheelchair, ready to follow them, when Hawk smoothly stepped in my way.

"I'll escort the patient," he said, his gaze flicking from Griffen to me. Hawk hadn't missed anything either. "You can question Ford while we're gone."

I didn't need Hawk's permission to question my witness, but I knew it wasn't about permission. In his own tight-lipped way, he was giving me a minute with Griffen. I took it. We watched Hawk wheel Avery out of the room, following the nurse down the hall.

"This is a fucking mess," Griffen said, his arms dropping to his sides.

"I can't get it out of my head," I admitted. "It was a great night. Huge crowd, everyone loved her beer, and then Matthew was there, getting in her face."

"That fucking guy," Griffen said. "You kicked him out? I was at the craft tables with Hope and missed what happened."

"I escorted him off the property," I said. "I wanted to do a hell of a lot more than that, but—"

"It would have been awkward if your deputy had to

arrest you for assault," Griffen finished for me, raising an eyebrow.

"Yeah, something like that. I went to find Avery to make sure she was okay." I shook my head, the image of her covered in blood flashing behind my eyes again. It would be a long time before the memory didn't make my heart freeze.

"I kissed Avery," I admitted, annoyed that Griffen didn't look surprised. His only response was a small curl to his lips and a slight shake of his head.

"What?" I demanded. "Do you have cameras in here or something? How did you know?"

"I didn't know," Griffen said with a shrug, "but I had a feeling."

"Well, I didn't," I said, shoving my hands in my pockets. "Until I did. And now..." Griffen just raised an eyebrow. "If you have a problem with it, you might as well say something."

"Would you back off if I did?" Griffen asked, his voice tight, but run through with a thread of amusement. Since he was my oldest friend, and this was his sister we were talking about, I figured I was better off being honest.

"No, I'm not backing off unless she wants me to."

"I didn't think so," Griffen said. "Did you think I'd have a problem with it?"

I rolled my shoulders back, annoyed that he wasn't giving me a straight answer.

"I don't know, man. She's your little sister. I don't have a sister. I'd think you'd want to beat up anyone who kissed her, even your best friend. Maybe if we were still teenagers—but if we were still teenagers, she'd be in grade school and that would be fucked up." For a second, I felt like *I* was in grade school again. "You know, I never thought about her like that. Not back then."

Griffen snorted a laugh. "Yeah, I know. I would have killed you. And you're not a creepy weirdo, so obviously. But now she's an adult. She can handle herself. If she doesn't want you kissing her, I'm pretty sure she'll let you know."

My cheeks felt hot for a second. I was not going to talk about Avery's response to my kiss with her brother, best friend or not.

"West, you're my best friend for a lot of reasons, one of them being that you're not an asshole. You're a good man. You're not going to be a dick to my sister, yeah?"

"Of course not."

"Then, I'm not going to get in your way. She could do a fuck ton worse than you, and not much better."

"Thanks, man." A knot in my chest I hadn't fully realized was there loosened. I didn't know where this thing with Avery was going. I'd barely gotten past the fact that I'd kissed her, and she'd kissed me back. But at least I didn't have to worry about hiding it from Griffen. Or him being pissed I'd dared to touch his sister.

"I want her to stop investigating the necklace," I said, changing the subject to take advantage of our temporary privacy.

Griffen sighed. "Do you think she was the target?"

I shook my head. "We don't have enough evidence either way. It's clear that one of them was. That wasn't random. They waited until those two were away from the crowd. I think it's even odds it could have been her." I paused, gathering the thoughts I'd been keeping at bay. "She's not exactly keeping a low profile in this whole fucking mess. If she is the target, it means her lead on the necklace isn't a dead end."

"And if she's not the target, the lead could still go somewhere," Griffen said. "Somebody needs to find that jeweler."

He was right, and this attack could mean that the jeweler was exactly the person we needed to find to solve the biggest fucking question of all: who had killed Prentice?

It burned that while Ford's name had been cleared, until we knew who'd killed Prentice, people would think he was the killer—only free on a technicality. As much as I wasn't Ford Sawyer's biggest fan, I didn't want him to live with that for the rest of his life.

"So, what are you saying?" I asked, knowing Griffen was getting at something.

"I'm saying," he said, "that I don't think she should stop. She's getting somewhere, she and Sterling. And Sterling has access to sources you can't use."

I shifted, pulling my hands from my pockets to cross my arms over my chest. For one, this could be dangerous for both Avery and Sterling if the attacker had anything to do with the jeweler. Second, there were things I wouldn't do, even for my closest friend. And that included using information obtained illegally. "I'm not going to break the law to solve this, Griffen."

"I'm not asking you to, but you can keep an eye on one of your citizens, can't you?"

I stared him down. "Let me get this straight. Not only

are you not mad, you want me to spend more time with Avery, helping her investigate your father's murder—an act which may have almost gotten her killed?"

Griffen shrugged, his eyes glinting with what I knew from long experience meant trouble. "Do you think you can stop her or Sterling at this point?"

"No," I answered immediately. "They'll just lie and go around us. They're too invested."

"Exactly. So, rather than waste our time trying to stop them, take advantage of what they can do that you can't. Stay close. Maybe we'll finally figure this thing out."

"Fine," I agreed. "Let's go talk to Ford."

"Works for me," Griffen agreed, following me out of Avery's room and into Ford's, where Ford corroborated everything that Avery had said, adding little of any use.

Avery returned, wheeled in by the same nurse who confirmed her diagnosis of a mild concussion. She'd have to stay until the next day while Ford was going home with Griffen and Hawk. Griffen looked at me, eyebrow raised. I nodded.

"I'm staying," I confirmed. "I'll bring her home later, when they spring her. Probably mid-morning."

"West, you can't sit in the chair beside my bed all night," Avery protested.

"I'm not leaving until you do," I said, too exhausted to argue.

Griffen nodded again and left, taking Hawk and Ford with him. I sat in the quiet room, holding Avery's hand until I thought she was asleep. Just when I was sure she'd drifted off, I heard her voice in the dark.

"Did you kiss me, or did I make that up?"

I pressed my lips to the back of her hand. "I kissed you," I said. "And I'm going to do it again."

"Right now?" she asked, her voice caught between interest and alarm.

I thought about the beeping of the heart rate monitor and shook my head. "Not now. I don't want the whole nursing staff running in." A quiet giggle took the weight off my heart. "But soon."

"Okay." Avery's fingers squeezed mine. She whispered, "Soon," as her eyes slid shut, and I started to calculate exactly how soon "soon" would be.

Chapter Twelve

AVERY

I wiped a damp rag across the bar, my eyes on the door. Whoever was escorting me home would be here any minute, and Cammie hadn't shown up yet. She'd always been a little flaky, but mostly reliable. Since the break-in, she'd been all over the place, canceling at the last minute more often than not. I didn't want to fire her. Despite her recent flakiness, I liked her. I didn't like coming into work early and staying to clean up after closing. It was a long day, and more than once lately, I'd felt the exhaustion to my bones.

A wave of relief washed over me as the back door to the brewery slammed open, and Cammie exploded through, all apologies and waving arms. "I'm so sorry. The dog got out, and I couldn't get him back. I'm so sorry, Ave."

"It's all right," I said, as I always did, slinging an arm around her shoulders and giving her a quick hug. She wore a low-cut Sawyers Bend Brewing t-shirt and red lipstick, and her frizzy hair smelled of perfume and ciga-rettes. Her dark eyes were heavy with remorse.

"Seriously," I said with another squeeze of her shoul-ders, "It's okay. My ride isn't here yet anyway."

Cammie slung an apron around her waist and tossed her hair back off her shoulders. "They're still keeping you under guard?"

"Looks like it," I said. "After what happened at the Orchard, I'm not as annoyed by it as I used to be."

The cut had been shallow and was mostly healed, but overall, two thumbs down on knife wounds from me. I wasn't too keen on my brother almost getting stabbed either.

Cammie took her place behind the bar, grabbing a pint glass and pulling a beer for a customer. I patted her on the shoulder and headed back to my office to grab my bag and my jacket. I needed to stop at the drugstore on the way home. Hopefully, whoever Hawk sent after me wouldn't mind a quick stop. I liked his team well enough, but I was hoping none of them showed.

In the week since the Orchard and the hospital, I'd only seen West a few times. He'd come to the taproom to bring me home, and both times, police chief stuff had gotten in the way. We both acted like his chauffeur service was run-of-the-mill, like he was just up on rota-tion, but I thought we both knew it was more than that.

Or maybe that was just wishful thinking. I couldn't forget that kiss. I'd been woozy and in pain, but that kiss had blown it all away. His lips had been so soft, his hands strong as they held my face, reigniting every lustful thought I'd ever had about West Garfield.

He was my brother's best friend. Too old for me, too serious for me, too bossy for me. All of that was true.

But hey, West was hot. I had eyes, so I'd noticed. I'd filed him away under "never going to happen."

He'd also never given me the slightest indication he saw me as anything other than Griffen's annoying little sister. Until lately. Lately, he'd looked at me differently, and I'd realized I liked it.

I still hadn't seen that kiss coming. And damn, I wanted another one.

I didn't care if I should, or if it would be good for me, or if it would cause a mess when, inevitably, we stopped kissing. We'd deal with that when it came. In light of all the other crap going on, getting tangled up with West didn't seem like the worst idea I'd ever had. I slung my purse strap over my shoulder, zipped up my jacket.

Who was I kidding? I was making excuses because I wanted to kiss the police chief again. The first time he'd come to bring me home, he had to bail when his phone rang. Fender bender in town. I'd been disappointed, but I knew it came with the job. Two days before, we'd been about to head out the door, and it happened again. This time, a domestic disturbance. I didn't know more than that. West knew how to keep his mouth shut. I could respect that, even when it was annoying.

It was leaf season in Western North Carolina, and the height of tourist season. The Inn was booked to the max, every short-term rental in a 50-mile radius was taken, and there were more out-of-state plates in town than locals. Sawyers Bend was a madhouse, but those of us who catered to the tourist trade weren't complaining.

Even my quiet little brewery on the far end of Main Street was packed daily.

I glanced out at the taproom. Cammie and Dave could handle it. They'd have their hands full, but their pockets would be stuffed with tips by the end of the night. My feet ached as I pushed through the door to the taproom and took a spot at the end of the bar, watching Cammie and Dave pull beers, make change, and run credit cards. I just wanted to get home. Maybe the drugstore could wait. But if I didn't do it now, it'd just be there for me later. I let out a sigh, pushing my hair back from my face. I might as well just get it over with.

The door shoved open, letting in a blast of crisp fall air, and there was West, his dark hair falling in his eyes and his Sawyers Bend police coat hanging open. Here was a man with a gun on his hip who I didn't mind following me around. My heart lurched as his eyes locked on mine. He crossed the room in that long-legged stride I'd always found so appealing.

For a second, disappointment threaded through me as I wondered if he was here for a beer and not for me. It faded as he headed to my end of the bar.

"I'm your ride tonight. You ready to go?" he asked, reaching to close his hand around my upper arm.

"I'm ready," I said, letting him tug me close enough to slide his arm around my shoulders, leading me to the door, West angling himself into the crowd, using his shoulder to clear a path. That was the thing about West; sometimes he could be bossy and overbearing, but I liked the way he protected me. I hadn't had a lot of that for most of my life. Everyone assumed I could take care of myself. I could. I did. But sometimes it was nice to know someone else was taking care of me, too.

I followed West out to his Sawyers Bend Police SUV. He held open the passenger door. "You hungry?" he asked, not waiting for an answer. He closed the door, and I watched him round the front of the vehicle, my stomach grumbling.

"I'm starving," I said as he got in. I'd missed dinner at the Manor, but I'd see if Finn would take pity on me and give me some leftovers.

West glanced my way, putting the SUV in reverse. "Do you have plans tonight?"

"Not really," I said, deciding to run my errands another time. "I was going to eat, put my feet up, and go to bed early. The usual, if I can get out of the brewery before close."

"Good," was all he said.

I wanted to ask what that meant, but a wave of fatigue hit me, and I settled into the passenger seat, leaning my head back, giving myself up to the flow. It sounded like he was going to feed me. I wanted food, and I wanted to see West, so whatever happened next was fine with me. In the back of my head, I must have expected him to turn toward town and one of the many restaurants we'd find there. Maybe we could get a table at the Inn.

Instead, he went the other way, toward the Manor. Why would he ask about dinner if he was just taking me home? Before we got to the Manor, he flicked on his blinker and turned left onto a narrow road.

"Where are we going?" I asked.

Without looking at me, he said, "My place."

Anticipation rippled through me as my heart picked up speed in my chest. Maybe I was going to get my wish about that kiss. My stomach rumbled again. "Do you have food at your place?" I asked. I wanted to see where West lived. For all that we'd known each other most of my life, I'd never been to the house he'd bought as an adult.

"I do," he answered.

"Works for me," I said, straightening a little in my seat, the fatigue gone. My heart hadn't slowed. I waited to feel cautious, for the doubts to creep in. I wanted a kiss, but going to his house at night—that seemed to imply a lot more than just a kiss.

Was I ready for that? Was it what I wanted?

I watched the trees flash by under the headlights as we wound further off the main road, turning at a bank of old mailboxes.

"Hang on," West said. "Driveway's a little bumpy. We need to get it regraded, but all the neighbors can't agree, so at the moment it's a mess."

He wasn't wrong. I gripped onto the oh-shit handle above the door, gritting my teeth as the SUV bounced beneath us. After a very long, bumpy minute, we turned onto a neatly graveled drive.

Chapter Thirteen

AVERY

The headlights penetrated the growing dark, illuminating a neatly adorable craftsman cottage painted a light green, trimmed in darker green, with two pumpkins on the front stoop. West parked in front of the matching single-car garage.

"This is your place?" I asked.

"Yeah. Why? You look surprised."

"It's so pretty," I said.

He laughed. "Did you think I'd live in a log cabin or something?"

"Yeah, I guess I did," I said, trying to figure out what I'd pictured for West. "I don't know. Something manly, with a stuffed bear on the porch."

He laughed again. West wasn't overly serious, but he wasn't a big laugher either. The sound of it, rich and full and true, did something to my insides. I loved making this man laugh.

"Nah, log cabins are drafty, and when they really start settling, they're a pain in the ass to keep up. This beauty was built eighty years ago, and it's rock solid. It needed some new appliances, a few coats of paint, floors refinished, and a little work in the bathrooms. Now it's good as new."

"How long have you lived here?" I asked, opening my door before he could round the SUV to do it for me. I ignored his slight scowl and followed him to the front porch.

"I bought it six years ago, not long after I got the job as chief." West unlocked the door and swung it open. "I was renting, had been saving up, and I decided it was time to find my own place. I wanted a little space from town. It was a little too easy for people to ring my door-bell when I was in the apartment above the pizza place, you know?"

"I can imagine," I said. The lights were already on inside, and the smells—fresh baked bread, lemon, basil—had my mouth watering. "Did you cook?"

"Yeah, Finn gave me the recipe," he said with a shrug, a hint of pink hitting his cheeks. "You can leave your jacket and your purse over there." He lifted his chin in the direction of an antique bench with a tall back that had coat hooks running along the top. I hung my jacket, my purse, and sat to take off the boots I was wearing. "This is perfect." It looked like an antique.

"My mom did some of the decorating. I didn't have the heart to stop her."

I looked around. "Your mom has great taste, and she didn't make it fussy." I didn't know Mrs. Garfield well, but I'd seen her ruffled blouses and pearls. None of that was evident here. It wasn't overly masculine. No antlers or buffalo plaid. I couldn't see West searching through antique stores in his free time to pick out the bench where I'd taken off my boots or the hickory coffee table, the black iron lamps in the living room, or the rustic kitchen table, which looked both well-loved and fit the space perfectly. It was clear she both knew her son and had excellent taste.

The kitchen was bigger than I expected, the cabinets creamy white with black iron handles, the countertops granite, the center island topped with butcher block, the cutting board there spread with freshly washed basil and sliced lemons. On the gas stove, a stainless-steel pot held water, and a package of pasta on the counter beside it.

"Did Finn give you the recipe for my favorite dinner?" I asked, the familiar ingredients making my mouth water.

"Kind of," West said, going to the refrigerator to get out a container of ricotta cheese. "He said your very favorite dinner was steak with asparagus and hollandaise, but I got to the butcher too late. They didn't have anything that looked good. Finn said this lemon ricotta pasta was your second favorite."

My heart squeezed at the sweetness of it—that he hadn't just picked up pizza or wings, which I would have been perfectly happy with, but had taken the time to ask my brother what I'd want for dinner. "Finn give you a hard time?" Knowing Finn, I had to ask.

West shook his head, leaning into the fridge. He pulled out a beer and held it up. One of mine, my favorite IPA.

I took it. "Good taste."

"My favorite," he said. "And, you know, it's Finn, so of course he gave me shit."

"I think he's constitutionally incapable of not giving shit if he has the opportunity," I said after a long pull on my beer. "At least since Savannah and Nicky, he's graduated from surly to just occasionally obnoxious."

"Yeah, talk about a good influence," West said, turning up the heat on the pot of water. "You know, Savannah wouldn't put up with surly for long. She'd smack him upside the head."

I laughed. I had no doubt that was true. Savannah didn't take shit from anybody. When she'd hooked up with Finn, who was brimming with attitude on a good day, I'd figured one of them would end up dead. How wrong I'd been. They'd fallen head over heels in love, and all of Finn's surliness had melted away, leaving him with a sharp tongue and a wicked sense of humor, but more often smiling than snarling.

I took another long pull of the crisp, hoppy IPA and smiled. "Goddamn, that's a good beer," I said.

"You should know," West said, slicing a shallot almost as well as Finn did. He wasn't messing around. He actually knew how to cook. Sexy. And helpful since I could brew a hell of a beer, but I wasn't much good in the kitchen otherwise.

"That's what I love about being a brewer," I said. "I love beer. I love stouts and porters. I love a pilsner, but my favorite is a crisp, citrusy IPA. And I get to make all of them exactly the way I like them."

"Lucky for you, a lot of people share your taste."

"True," I agreed, "lucky for me."

"How's the new recipe coming along?" he asked, drizzling olive oil in a pan.

I let out a breath and shook my head. "I don't know. I think it's close." I paused, watching as he added garlic and a handful of spinach. My stomach rumbled again, and my mouth watered, though I wasn't sure if it was from the delicious smells in the kitchen or from watching West.

There was something about his strong, capable hands slicing the basil into thin strips, the bright scent of it filling the room that was so fucking sexy. I couldn't remember the last time I'd watched a man cook. Finn didn't count. This was a whole different bag than watching my brother in the kitchen. I shifted on my tired feet and took another long sip from my beer, telling my hormones to chill the fuck out. Food first. I was going to be civilized about this, right?

"It was hard," I said. "Watching everyone fall in love with the fall brew that night at the Orchard. They loved it."

"They were crazy for it," he agreed. "Did you have any left at the end of the night?"

I shook my head. "Nah, Dave told me they sold out of all of it. People were asking if they could come by the brewery and pick up a six-pack or a growler, but they drank it all. I held back a few bottles to sample as I work on the recipe, but that's it."

"I can see where that would burn a little," he said. "I mean, great to know you made something everyone loves that much, but—"

"Yeah," I agreed. "It was amazing how much

everyone loved it, but I not only didn't have any more, I also don't know how to make it."

"Sure you do," he said. "You made it in the first place, right?"

I took another sip of beer, the familiar flavor bursting over my tongue. "Yeah," I said, sounding less than confident. "Yeah," I said again, this time meaning it. "I did. Fuck, I hate how I let him get in my head. You know, they were my recipes."

"Why'd you hire him anyway?" West asked, looking back at me.

I sighed. "There's a big gap between brewing beer on a small scale and being able to brew it on a commercial scale. I knew how to brew beer, knew what I liked, knew it tasted good, made enough friends in the business to talk recipes, and experiment with ingredients, but I didn't know the ins and outs of running a commercial brewery. I needed someone to teach me. He was qualified. He just..." I shook my head.

West finished my thought. "He wanted to be more than just the brewmaster."

"Yep. He saw me as a way to get his own place. But I don't want to give up Sawyers Bend Brewing. I don't want to sell out, and I don't want to put somebody else in charge. I love what I do, even when it's long days and my feet hurt. Even when things go wrong."

"Yeah," West said. "I know what you mean. This time of year, I wonder, what the hell am I thinking? Police chief of a small town in Western North Carolina seems like an easy gig, except this time of year, when it's anything but." He shrugged, rolling his shoulders back, and lifted his chin. "It's not like I'm dealing with heavy drug trade or a ton of violent crime, but we've got a lot of people coming into town. They think it's like a fairyland. The mountains and rivers are pretty. They're used to things being safe and packaged, you know? Half the time, the trouble is just tourists drinking a little too much, getting into a fight like the other night, or car accidents, petty larceny, stuff like that. But then we get people who go hiking or tubing, don't know what they're getting into. Those aren't my favorite."

"Yeah, I bet," I agreed.

"And the waterfalls," he said, shaking his head. He didn't need to go into detail. I knew exactly what he meant. Western North Carolina is chock-full of gorgeous waterfalls—big ones and little ones, all beautiful, most accessible by easily marked hiking trails, and every single one deadly. These days, tourists want to get a selfie at the top of the falls and think, *I'll just climb over this rail that says, "Do not pass. Slippery terrain."* They climb over, take a step too far, lift their phone to get a great pic, and boom—right over the edge.

Sometimes they could be rescued, but at the bottom of waterfalls, you've got churning water and sharp rocks, neither of which gently receives a falling body. We tried to educate visitors, but people having fun don't always like to listen. I knew West had accompanied a body bag out of the rivers more than once every tourist season. Every time, it was heartbreaking.

"Your job is definitely rougher than mine," I said.

"When it gets bad, yeah," he said. "Fortunately, most days it's not. You want to slice the bread?"

"Sure, where is it?" I asked, looking around the kitchen. I could smell it, but I didn't see it.

"In the oven."

I grabbed potholders and pulled out the crispy loaf. "Did you stop by Sweetheart Bakery?" I asked.

"I did," he said.

"Really?" I wondered if there was anything in the fridge for dessert. My brother Royal's girlfriend Daisy ran the bakery with her grandmother, and those two were geniuses when it came to anything bread or pastry related. My stomach rumbled again, a loud, angry growl. I looked over my shoulder at West. "Sorry, I missed lunch."

"Don't apologize," he said. "It's just making me want to feed you more."

I set the bread on the cutting board. Before I could reach for the knife, his arm snaked around my waist and pulled me back. "Just an appetizer," he murmured, his lips against my ear. Then I was turning, my face lifting, my arms sliding around his shoulders as if we'd done this a million times. His lips didn't touch mine. They skimmed the side of my jaw, dipping down to my neck, sending shivers down my spine.

I strained towards him, the kiss in the hospital flooding my brain. West. I wanted West. I turned my head, catching his mouth as he straightened. He tasted just like I remembered, his lips soft but firm. My empty stomach was forgotten. I arched into him, sinking my fingers into his hair, my body flooding with heat. This is what I'd wanted ever since he'd kissed me the first time. My mouth followed his as he stepped back.

Chapter Fourteen

AVERY

"**D**inner first," he said, his voice rough. "I don't want to rush this."

"Fine," I agreed. "Dinner first."

I finished slicing the bread, putting it on a plate to bring to the table, where he'd already set out softened butter. I turned to see West, a pasta dish in each hand, piled high, decorated with ribbons of basil, creamy lemon scents filling my nose.

"Oh, that looks good."

"Yeah," he agreed. "Smells amazing. Finn said the recipe wouldn't be too hard, but I didn't believe him."

"But it's not?" I asked. Finn had made it for me plenty of times, but I'd never done it myself. He didn't like people in the kitchens at Heartstone. He got cranky if you touched his stuff. Considering Finn was a way better cook than I'd ever be, I didn't argue that much.

"No, it really wasn't. Want another beer?"

"Sure," I agreed, realizing the one I'd been holding was empty.

We sat at the table and I dug in, twining pasta around my fork. It was perfect, the creamy lemon flavors exploding on my tongue. We didn't talk much, too focused on filling our bellies.

"I missed lunch too," West said in between bites. "I brought a sandwich, but somebody broke into the gear closet at the Inn, and I had to head over there."

"Oh shit, really?" I asked after swallowing. "Are they still having trouble over there? Royal and Tenn haven't said anything." Not long after my father had died, Royal and Tenn had a problem with sabotage at the Inn, but I didn't think they'd had any issues recently.

West shook his head. "Teenagers staying at the Inn with their parents. They wanted to go out on the river in the kayaks."

"Do they not know how cold that water is?" I asked.

"Apparently not," West said dryly.

I shook my head. "I'm always surprised by how many people forget we may be in the South, but we're still in the mountains. It gets cold up here."

"Exactly. Fortunately, we caught them before they got in the water. No life vests, no helmets." He shook his head. "Dumbasses."

"Well, that's teenagers for you."

"You weren't a dumbass when you were a teenager," West said. "I would have heard about it."

"Nah, not me. It wasn't worth getting on my father's radar. Neither were you. Son of the mayor, future police chief. You stayed out of trouble."

West smirked and shook his head. He swallowed a bite of pasta, took a sip of beer, before he said, "It's not so much that I stayed out of trouble as I knew how to not get caught. Someday, maybe you can get your brother to tell you all the shit we got up to."

"Why don't you tell me, and then I can torture Griffen with it."

He laughed. "Can't do it. Best-friend code."

"Huh. I'll get it out of you. I have my ways," I said, leaning forward and looking up at him through my eyelashes.

His eyes darkened. "I bet you do."

Heat spiked through me. *Dinner first*, I reminded myself. This pasta was too fucking good to leave behind. I watched West's fingers twirl his fork in the pasta, his hands strong and a little banged up from whatever he'd been doing all day. He lifted the fork to his mouth, pasta neatly twirled around it, his jaw flexing as he chewed. How was it that everything this man did was hot?

There were a lot of things I didn't know. If I could really run the brewery by myself. If I were going to figure out the recipe I'd lost. If I were able to find out who killed my father. But I knew one thing: I wanted to strip West Garfield naked and have my way with him. And when I did, it was going to be amazing.

I looked down at my mostly empty plate, and shot a glance at his before taking another bite, and another, steadily finishing my dinner. Finally, I dropped my fork back onto my plate with a clatter. I took a long sip of beer, watching West wipe his mouth with his napkin and do the same. I was already standing when he pushed his chair back.

He never made it to his feet. I stepped in front of him,

my hands on his shoulders, and swung a leg to straddle his lap. Leaning forward as I made myself comfortable on his lap, I cupped his bristly cheeks in my hands and pressed a kiss to his lips. Before it could go anywhere, I leaned back, heat spiraling through me as his hands settled on my hips, his fingers curling in a tight grip.

"We're going to do this, right?" I asked, raising an eyebrow.

"Hell, yes," he answered.

"Is it going to get weird?"

"Weird how? Like kinky-weird?" He raised an eyebrow, the side of his mouth curling up.

"Well," I considered, "it could get kinky-weird, but that's not what I meant. I mean like you and me and you're Griffen's best friend and, you know, that kind of weird." I shifted on his lap, the heat of his body between my legs doing things to my head.

"No," he said. "Not unless we make it weird. I talked to Griffen already."

That was a bucket of ice water, though a small one. "What do you mean you talked to Griffen already? When? What did you say?"

"In the hospital. I told him I kissed you."

"What did he say?" I asked, curious. "He didn't punch you or anything, did he?" I studied West's face, looking for signs of a black eye I'd missed.

"No." West grinned.

"Did you think he was going to punch you?" I asked.

"A little bit, maybe," West said. "He said you could do worse and told me to not be an asshole, which I try not to do anyway."

"And that was it?" I raised an eyebrow, not sure how I felt about this.

"That was it," he said, running his hands up my back, sliding under my t-shirt, his callused fingertips delicious on my skin. I tried to focus on the conversation, just a little longer.

"No big brother posturing," I pressed. "No 'break her heart and I'll break your face'?"

West shook his head, hands dropping to squeeze my hips. "I think that was all implied. I'm pretty sure if you told him I was being a jackass, he'd beat the shit out of me. Or he'd try. And if I really was being a jackass, I'd probably let him."

"So... So we're good to, you know, whatever?" I asked, butterflies taking off in my stomach.

"Assuming you're up for—" he raised an eyebrow. "Whatever."

"All these years," I said, tracing a finger along the curve of his lower lip. "You were Griffen's best friend. I always thought you were hot, but, you know, brother's best friend, too old, too grown up, all that stuff."

"I'm not that much older than you," he said.

"Yeah, but when you're fifteen..."

"You thought I was hot when you were fifteen?" His lips curled in a satisfied grin.

I rolled my eyes. "You knew you were hot when I was fifteen."

"Yeah, but you were just a kid."

"Not that much of a kid. Not at fifteen. Anyway. I always thought you were hot, but somehow I never thought we'd end up here." I squirmed on his lap, feeling the ridge of his growing erection exactly where I wanted it, minus the layers of clothes between us. "But now that we're here..." My hands dropped to the button at the top of his shirt.

"Now that we're here," he repeated.

"Now that we're here, I can't figure out why we didn't do this sooner." I dove in, pressing my lips to his, done with talking. I didn't get very far with the buttons before West surged to his feet, his hands sliding down to cup my ass, tightening, lifting, and settling me against him. He carried me down the hall, I was hoping towards his bedroom, but at this point, I'd take any flat surface if it meant West would be there with me, preferably naked.

I had a split-second view of his neatly made bed in muted greens before he set me on my feet, and I went after the rest of the buttons on his shirt. I hadn't seen him without a shirt on in years, and I needed to, desperately. I needed to get my hands on his warm skin, needed to touch and taste.

I stripped the shirt over his shoulders, letting him handle getting it off his arms as I went for the hem of the white t-shirt beneath, yanking it up. He pulled it over his head, dropping both to the floor, and my mouth went dry. The sprinkle of dark hairs on his chest only highlighted the lean muscle, his broad shoulders. He wasn't weightlifter-built, but there was power there. I ran my hands over his shoulders and down his arms, feeling the hard curves, the heat of his skin.

His fingers closed over the bottom of my sweater, pulling it over my head. "Fuck, Avery," he let out a breath. My bra wasn't the sexiest in my collection, but that didn't seem to matter. He traced a fingertip over the curve of my breast before sliding the straps off my shoulders and unsnapping it in the back. "Goddamn, you're gorgeous," he said, cupping my now bared breasts in his palms. "Fucking amazing."

He slid his hands down my sides, closing them around my waist, turning me, easing me back onto the bed, the comforter cool under my bare back, his fingers working at my zipper, then sliding my jeans over my hips, taking my underwear with them. I was spread out in front of him, naked, legs parted, looking up into West's dark, hot eyes.

He moved forward, and I shook my head. "Don't even think about getting in this bed until you lose the rest of your clothes."

West's eyes narrowed further, drinking in every inch of me, lingering on my breasts, my legs, the shadows between. He flicked the button open on his jeans and shoved them down. His cock sprang free, thick and hard. My fingers stretched, itching to touch. I needed to know what he felt like in my hands, in my mouth, inside me. He kicked off his jeans and socks and landed on the mattress beside me, pulling me further onto the bed, wrapping me in his arms, his legs twining with mine.

This kiss was so different from the one in the hospital. That one had been tender, slow, and filled with promise. This one was so much more—hot, wet, devouring. I held on to his shoulders, kissing him back, my tongue brushing his, before I shifted to suck at his lower lip. I wanted more. More of everything, more of West, and the feel of him against me.

He pulled back, his mouth grazing my neck, my collarbone. His hand cupped my breast, lifting it to his mouth. He nipped at the tip, shards of pleasure spiking through me and straight between my legs. I moaned, arching up into his mouth. I twined my legs around him, my brain coming online just long enough to say, "Please tell me you have a condom."

In answer, West shifted to the side, reaching for the bedside table. I heard the crinkle of plastic, and he came back with a bright green square in his hands. "Hang on to this for me," he said, pressing it into one hand as he dipped lower, his mouth sliding between my breasts, tongue tasting my belly button. I had a moment of panic, a flush of unexpected shyness. I'd kissed him, had been eager, no, desperate to get naked with him. But now, his face between my legs, my brain started to spin from desire to nerves, right up until his tongue flicked out, hot and wet on my clit. My brain shut off abruptly. Anything that felt that perfect had to be a good idea.

"Oh God, West." A finger slid inside me, then another, stretching me, getting me ready as he licked and sucked, every pull on my clit sending sharp waves of pleasure up my spine and into my brain. It was too much. Too much and so good. The orgasm hit me out of nowhere. I should have seen it coming, but the heat and weight of him, his mouth on me, it was too much. And then it was everything. I screamed out his name, my fingers clawing at the bedsheets, hips rocking into the hot suck of his lips, his thrusting fingers, and then it was all gone, his fingers nipping the condom out of my hand, and he was moving, the hard nudge of him filling me all the way until I let out a low groan.

"Oh, fucking God, West, you feel so good."

"Avery," was all he said. My knees came up tight to his sides, my hips rocking up, taking him deeper.

"So good," I murmured, my eyes shut tight. I wasn't usually a multiple orgasm kind of woman, but this, this was like nothing else. He filled me right to the point of too much, the steady, hard thrusts hitting every nerve.

"Oh God." In the end, all I could do was hold on, my fingers grasping his shoulders, my hips rocking up, my eyes opening to see his face so close, his dark eyes half-lidded, hot with pleasure. "Avery," he breathed. "Avery." My body convulsed around him, pleasure spiking through me. West followed, gasping my name over and over, rolling at the last second so I settled on top of him. His mouth touched my neck in a soft kiss.

"Fucking amazing," he breathed. "You're fucking amazing."

"Ditto," I said, still trying to get my breath as he shifted me to the other side.

He disappeared across the room into what I guess was the bathroom. A minute later, he was back, slid into the bed beside me, pulling up the covers, drawing me into his arms. I collapsed against him, his shoulder under my ear, his bristled cheeks so close. I reached up to trace that full lower lip again.

"You've got a hell of a mouth there," I said. Nudging his softening cock with my thigh, I added, "The rest of you isn't bad either."

"Right back at you," he said, a laugh in his voice.

"Once is definitely not going to be enough," I said, half to myself and half to West.

His chest rumbled with a laugh, sending a warm sensation spilling through me. "Once was never going to be enough, Avery. But now that I've had you, fuck no. Once is definitely not going to be enough."

I was so warm, so comfortable. I snuggled in, stretching against him. "How much would be enough?" I mused aloud.

"I don't know. We'll just have to find out."

Chapter Fifteen

AVERY

I had marketing materials to go over, but I gave in to the urge to lean over the vat of mash and take a deep, long breath. Sour, tangy, yeasty. God, I fucking loved it. My first attempt to recreate the fall brew was getting there. So far, so good.

I didn't want to review new label designs and social media posts. I wanted to do something physical. Move those bags of hops from the pallet to the bin, maybe, or play with a new recipe. I needed to get my hands dirty. But work was work, and dealing with the office shit was part of running the brewery. At some point in the hopefully not-too-distant future, instead of hiring a new brewmaster, maybe I'd hire an office manager or whatever you call the life-saving person who wrangled the endless piles of paper and logistical phone calls that came with running a business—the stuff I didn't like.

Someday. For now, except for Dave and Cammie and the rest of my skeleton staff, it was all me. *This is why you fired Matthew*, I reminded myself. Because that was what I wanted—for it to be all mine, the good and the bad, including the paperwork. I turned and headed back to my office, sliding the piles of stuff on my desk out of the way and pulling my keyboard closer. I could answer some emails before I got to the rest. Blessedly, my phone rang. I knew that tone. Sterling.

"Hey, what's up?"

"You busy?" Sterling asked.

I eyed the screen of my computer and my full inbox. "No," I lied. "Why? What are you up to?" I glanced at the clock. Too late for lunch, too early for dinner. She wasn't calling to see if I wanted to grab a meal.

"I'm at Quinn's, waiting for a guide group to come back, so I can't leave the desk," she said. "Can you come over?"

I caught the thrum of energy in her voice. She was excited about something. My mind immediately flipped to the night before. Fuck, how did she know about West already? Normally, I might have spilled to one of my sisters by now, even if it was just a silly text. I didn't hook up a lot. I hadn't dated anyone since Matthew, and not a whole lot before. But even so, I might have shared the news the morning after.

It was different when it came to West. I was trying to avoid dwelling on how complicated this could get. I hadn't wanted to before, blinded by the idea of getting my hands on him. The lust had hit me out of nowhere. Maybe not completely out of nowhere, but after a lifetime of knowing him, everything had shifted in a heartbeat.

I told myself I'd figure it out later, half convinced that maybe it'd be a one-time thing. Curiosity satisfied, no need for repeats. Except *hell no* to that. Curiosity had only been whetted, and repeats were absolutely in order.

"Avery, are you there?" Sterling demanded, interrupting my thoughts. "Are you coming over?"

The anticipation in her voice had me squirming in my seat. I wasn't ready to talk about this.

"What is it?" I asked. "I kind of am a little busy here," I hedged, "but I could come over. Is everything okay?"

"Yeah, yeah, it's fine, it's fine. I just... I don't want to talk on the phone. If you're not busy, come on. I'm not far away. It's important," she said, putting the nail in my coffin.

I wasn't 100% sure what was important to Sterling these days, though I could make a list: Forrest, school, and whatever sketchy hacker stuff she was doing with Griffen's friends from Atlanta; her family; finding that jewelry designer; and yes, most likely, needling gossip out of her older sister—especially if it concerned the police chief, who was as good as family. But if Sterling said it was important...

I let out a sigh. We'd ignored what was important to Sterling for too long. No more. If she needed her big sister, I'd haul my ass over there, even if it meant her giving me crap about West. We hadn't exactly been discreet. There'd been a ton of tourists in the draft room the night before, but plenty of locals had seen me leave with West. Fuck.

"Be there in five," I said. I put my computer to sleep, grabbed my bag, and poked my head through the door to the taproom, catching Dave's eye where he worked behind the bar.

"I'm headed out for a bit. Call if you need anything, okay?"

"Got it, boss," he grinned back.

I waved and headed out the back door. It wasn't a long walk to Sawyer Outdoor Adventures. Hawk and Griffen, and probably West, too, though we hadn't talked about it directly, didn't want me wandering around by myself. I wasn't calling for a pickup to go three blocks on Main Street. Even if this side of town wasn't as well-trafficked, it was still tourist season. Everything was crowded. There were eyes all over the place. The only people who bothered me on my walk were locals, shooting me a smile and a raised hand. I waved back.

It wasn't long before I found myself in front of Quinn's guide business. The parking lot was full, and the Sawyer Outdoor Adventures van was gone. Quinn could be anywhere, but my guess was leading a leaf season hike. We'd gotten lucky this year with the right temperatures, the perfect amount of rain, and the mountains were a riot of color. Yellows, oranges, reds. Everywhere I turned, it looked like a postcard. Days like these, I remembered how lucky I was to live here.

My phone beeped with a text, and I looked down, stopping in the middle of the parking lot. West.

Staying out of trouble? What are you doing tonight?

Hmm, how to answer that question? What did I want

to be doing tonight? Every cell in my body answered that question with one simple answer: West. West was what I wanted to be doing tonight. Was it too soon? Was that going to make this like a thing? Definitely not casual if it was two nights in a row. We hadn't talked about anything. We'd eaten dessert in bed, then licked chocolate sauce off each other, and then had mind-blowing sex again. I'd woken up at 6 a.m. to West sliding from the bed, saying, "No rush to get out of here, but I have to be at the station in an hour."

"I have to get to the brewery," I'd answered.

I'd made coffee while he showered. We swapped places, and I emerged in a soft flannel robe I found in his bathroom to a breakfast sandwich waiting next to a steaming cup of coffee. We ate together as if we'd been sharing breakfast our whole lives. West had dropped me at the brewery on his way to work; that was the last we'd seen of each other.

My finger hovered over the keyboard. Yes, or no?

Fuck it. Maybe this was going to burn itself out. Things had been too easy, too good. The more time we spent together, the more we'd find the cracks. The glow would fade, the sex would get mediocre, we'd tire of each other, and all my anxieties would be solved. But right now, I didn't want to go back to Heartstone, eat with my family, and go to bed alone. I wanted more of West.

> No plans tonight. What did you have in mind?

I'll pick you up at 5 and we'll figure it out.

I gave his text a thumbs up and squeezed my eyes shut, annoyed with myself. I could *feel* the dopey expression on my face. The last thing I needed was for Sterling to lock onto that. She'd tease me for the rest of my life.

Was I getting a little gooey over our hot police chief?

Yes, maybe I was.

Did I need anyone to know about that?

I absolutely did not.

I was a grown woman. It was my prerogative to get all dopey over a hot guy who was amazing in bed, even if he was my brother's best friend. I didn't owe anyone an explanation. Fine. Good.

Before I could shove my phone in my pocket, it rang. I glanced down, not recognizing the number. I stopped on the first step of the porch, bringing the phone to my ear.

"Avery Sawyer," I said.

"Avery, hey, it's Bob James."

"Oh, hey, Bob. I've been meaning to call you."

Bob James ran Wild Haven Brewing, a small place on the outskirts of town. Small, but bigger than Sawyers Bend Brewing. They didn't have a taproom, but you could find their six-packs in most local grocery stores. I'd heard through the grapevine they'd gotten distribution to grocery stores in Charlotte and Atlanta. Bob and I had been planning a joint event with a local restaurant. Barbecue, pies from Sweetheart Bakery, Bob's beer, and my beer. We were wrapping it up into a charity drive—

Christmas presents for kids—but we needed to nail down some details.

"I've got some time on Thursday. What does your schedule look like?" I asked.

"Yeah, um, that's the thing..."

I didn't like the hesitation in his voice. A sense of doom settled in my gut.

"What's the thing?" I asked, my feet clunking hollowly up the rest of the steps to the front porch of Sawyer Outdoor Adventures.

"We're, uh, well, we talked, me and Jamie—Jamie runs the restaurant—and, uh, we're going to do it with Bear Run Brewing. It's not personal, Avery," he blurted out. "It's just, we've been hearing things."

"I bet you have," I said and immediately wished I'd kept my mouth shut. Bear Run Brewing was Matthew's new employer, and I wasn't surprised. I should have seen this coming. "What have you heard?" I asked, trying to keep my voice calm and friendly, hiding the rage that threatened to explode out of me. I wasn't going to yell. I wasn't going to throw my phone. I wasn't going to murder Matthew. Yet.

"Just that you're in over your head over there. There's a lot going on, and now that you don't have a brewmaster, you're juggling. We really need this event to go off well, you know, for the kids. It's important, and Jamie and I feel like coordinating with Bear Run Brewing is just a more solid bet. You understand, right?"

"Have you talked to Daisy?" I asked. Daisy and I weren't super tight, but she was my sister-in-law, Hope's best friend, and head over heels in love with my brother,

Royal. One of these days, he'd drag her down the aisle, and she'd be my sister too. No way would she pick Matthew over me.

"Uh, yeah," Bob said slowly.

"And what was Daisy's opinion?"

"Daisy's no longer participating," he admitted. "Without Sawyers Bend Brewing, Sweetheart Bakery is out."

That was something, at least. My family had my back.

"When did you talk to her?" I asked.

"Just a few minutes ago. Look, Avery, I'm not trying to start anything. I know you and Matthew have had tensions, and, you know, relationship stuff doesn't have any place in business."

"I'm not sure what this has to do with relationship stuff," I said, gritting my teeth and pushing open the door of Sawyer Outdoor Adventures.

Sterling sat behind the desk in front of me at her laptop. Her eyes brightened as she saw me, then narrowed when she caught the expression on my face.

"I can't say I understand, Bob, but this was supposed to be a collaboration. If two of you don't want to collaborate with me, there's not much I can do about it. I would like to know, though, more specifically, what the fuck Matthew said." I bit my lip as the profanity escaped. *Inappropriate for business*, Avery, I told myself. The fact that I hadn't set the phone on fire with the force of the fury pouring out of me was a miracle. A paltry *fuck* sneaking in was nothing.

"Avery, you make a good beer. Everybody knows that.

But running a brewery, it's a business. It's not just the brewing, you know? And without Matthew there, we need someone reliable."

"Fine," I said. "I wish you all the best. It's about the kids, right?"

"I'm so glad you understand."

I tapped the red icon on my phone, hanging up.

Chapter Sixteen

AVERY

"Fuck him," I said, slamming my phone down on the counter in front of Sterling. "Fuck him and fuck every single person who thinks I can't do this. Goddammit."

"What happened? Avery, who was that?" Sterling asked.

I crossed my arms over my chest and started to pace, stomping across the hardwood floor, my boots echoing in angry thumps. "That was fucking Bob James."

"Do I know who Bob James is?" Sterling asked cautiously.

"Bob James runs Wild Haven Brewing."

"Oh, you guys were going to do that thing with the toys for kids for Christmas or whatever with Daisy and that barbecue place out on Route 191?"

"*Were* being the operative term," I said, squeezing my eyes shut to fight back my anger.

"What happened?" she asked, shoving back her chair and rounding the counter.

"Fucking Matthew is what happened. Fucking Matthew telling everybody I'm in over my head and can't handle running the brewery. That I'm unreliable. And under all of it was the 'stay in the kitchen' bullshit line I've been hearing since I started this. No fucking wonder there's not a lot of women brewing beer. It's not that we don't like it. It's that we have to deal with fuckheads like this. I make a goddamn good beer, and I can run a business. Motherfucker."

I bent over, bracing my hands on my knees, letting my head hang down. "Why did I ever get involved with him?"

"Hey," Sterling said, crossing the room. She pulled me back to standing and hugged me tightly. "Hey, don't do this. First of all, you hired him because he was qualified, and you wanted to learn what he knew. And you learned, right?"

"Yeah," I said grudgingly.

"So, he also turned out to be a manipulative asshole. That happens. Not your fault."

"I should have known."

"Jesus, Avery. I mean, we all tell ourselves that after we fuck up, but the truth is none of us are perfect. We use the best judgment we have in the moment, and Matthew puts on a really good front. I'm pretty good at reading people, and even after I sobered up, I didn't see what a shit he was. He was cute, and you never have time to date. Yeah, okay, hooking up with your employee, not great judgment."

"Yeah, I figured that out." I hated remembering what an idiot I'd been.

"Hey, I'm not giving you shit. Lesson learned, but it doesn't mean you deserve this."

"Goddamn right." I spun around and paced in front of the counter, my feet hitting the floor in angry thuds. Sterling was right. I didn't deserve this blowback. But it had happened. So, what came next? That's what I had to focus on. "It's not like this event was make or break for Sawyers Bend Brewing. I mean, I'm probably better off spending my time really getting a handle on running the brewery by myself. But it was going to be fun."

"What about Daisy?" Sterling asked.

"Daisy's a rock star, and she bailed. She told Bob that if I'm out, she's out."

"I love Daisy," Sterling said, "and not just for her brownies."

"I know. I owe her a thank you. It could have been good for them."

Sterling shrugged. "Daisy and Grams have more business than they can handle. Those pop-ups that they do? Best lunch ever. Now that J.T. is so busy with school, they've had to hire extra hands to keep up. My guess is Daisy signed on half because it would have been fun to work with you, and half to get presents to needy kids for Christmas. She and Grams will probably do something. Maybe you and Daisy can figure it out together. You could get her to try your new version of the fall brew and make an apple pie that goes with it."

"That would be awesome. Sweet and spicy. I can give her the flavor profile—" The idea exploded into my brain, chasing off my anger. "Sterling, you're brilliant."

"I know. It's a curse." She slung an arm around my shoulder, giving me a tight hug. "You okay?"

I shrugged. "Yeah, I guess. I'm just frustrated and annoyed that the default is always doubt that I can run my brewery. Because I'm young. Because I'm a woman. Because I'm a Sawyer. There's always a question mark. I don't want to have to prove myself all the time. I just want to make really good beer and sell it at a decent price so I can keep my doors open and pay my staff. All of the rest of this sucks."

"Yeah, it really does. You want some good news?"

"Yeah." I suddenly remembered why I'd been nervous about coming in. But Sterling didn't look like she was digging for sisterly gossip. This was something else. "What's up?" I asked.

"I know it's been a while, but I gave Emmett the name of that jewelry designer."

I allowed myself a wave of relief that she didn't know about West, at least not yet. There was no way she'd be talking about the jewelry designer if she knew I'd spent last night with him.

"Emmett?" I asked.

"You know, Hawk's friend." She bit her lower lip, pausing.

I decided to take pity on her. "I know, the one we're not supposed to talk about, who kidnapped Quinn. He's helping you learn cybersecurity stuff." I knew *cybersecurity stuff* didn't really cover what Sterling was doing, but the accounting software on my laptop was as techy as I got, so it was the best I could do.

"Yeah," Sterling confirmed. "He works for Sinclair Security now. And if those guys can't find somebody, they don't exist. He said this one took a little bit because they had an all-hands-on-deck situation over there. So, he had to put it on the back burner for a few days, and then the name the jewelry designer works under is actually a pseudonym, a DBA, *doing business as* kind of thing. So, it took a little bit longer to find out who she is, but—" Sterling lifted a Post-it. "I have an address."

"No shit. Really?" The call from Bob James and Matthew's bullshit slid into the background. "That's very interesting." I reached for the Post-it, but Sterling tucked it in her back pocket.

"Nuh-uh, not without me."

The front door opened. "Not without you, what?" I heard West say from behind me.

"Hey," I said, spinning around to see him filling the doorway, his cheeks pink from the chill in the air, his dark eyes curious.

A stab of pure lust hit me so hard I almost gasped. Fuck. I had it bad.

"What are you doing here?" Sterling asked, one eyebrow raised in suspicion.

"I heard Avery was here." West looked between us and grinned. "Since the two of you together means trouble, I thought I'd stop in. Where are you going?" he asked Sterling.

"Nowhere," she lied.

"Uh-huh." West crossed his arms over his chest. "Sterling?"

She crossed her arms over her chest and lifted her chin. "Nowhere," she said again.

"Look," West shook his head. "I talked to Griffen. I know you two aren't going to let this go. Fair enough. I want to find out who killed your father and put Ford in prison just as much as you do. I'm not having a lot of luck doing it my way," he admitted. "And I know you can do things I can't."

Sterling's defiant expression cracked, the side of her mouth curving in a grin. "True," she agreed.

"I'm not going to break the law, but if you have information—something we can follow up on—I can help you with that. If we find who did this to your dad, to your brother, we need to do it right," he said. "So they can end up in prison. The last thing we want is to find out who it is and fuck it up, so they get off on a technicality."

Sterling dropped her arms to her sides. "Yeah, good point." She looked at me, raising an eyebrow.

I let out a breath. I was at my limit with men telling me what to do for the day. But this was West. He wasn't like that, even when he was being bossy and annoying. And on top of that, working together wasn't the worst idea in the world. It didn't mean he had to be in charge. I looked at him, absorbing the patience and intelligence in his eyes. I could trust West. I wanted to trust West. He wasn't Matthew. He wouldn't diminish or disregard me. He could have tried to manipulate, but instead, he'd laid it out.

I turned to Sterling. "I think we should let him help." Sterling rolled her eyes. "He has a gun," I added. "Who knows, maybe the jewelry designer is dangerous."

"Whatever," she said. She reached into her back pocket and pulled out the Post-it. "This is the address of the jewelry designer we're looking for."

West reached for it. Sterling yanked it out of reach. "You have to take one of us with you, if not both of us."

"I'm not going to investigate while trailing a team of civilians behind me," he said.

"Not a team of civilians," I added. "Just me."

"Hey," Sterling said.

"You want to go instead?" I asked.

She handed the address to West and shrugged. "Actually, I get more of a kick out of finding the information, though Emmett did most of the work this time. And that address is up by the Highlands. It's going to take more time than I have to spare to go out there and talk to her. So, fine. But you have to take Avery. No going off on your own with our info."

"Agreed," West said. He looked at the address. "We don't have time today. I'll pick you up after work. We can look at our schedules and figure it out."

"Sounds good to me," I said, trying to keep the flush of pink out of my cheeks and failing as I felt them get hot. He wasn't even doing anything—hands to himself, not staring at my boobs, no smirk. He didn't need any of that. Just those dark eyes on mine, the promise in them, the way his strong hands folded the Post-it so precisely before tucking it in his shirt pocket. I knew what those hands could do. And then there was that mouth.

I let out a breath and looked back at Sterling. She was observing the two of us, her eyes bright. Fucking fuck.

She didn't know where I'd spent last night, I was sure. But now...

"You're picking Avery up from work?" she asked innocently.

West shoved his hands in his pockets. "Griffen, Hawk, and I agreed that since the incident at the Orchard, we don't want her on her own too much. Not until we figure out what's going on."

"Good plan," Sterling said.

"Hey, you're supposed to be on my side," I said.

"Not in this." Sterling shook her head. "I like you in one piece without, you know, knife wounds and stitches. So, yeah, I'm with them."

"Do as I say, not as I do?" I asked, making sure my voice dripped with sarcasm, remembering the way she'd gone running off with Forrest on their scavenger hunt with the mob following them. She hadn't exactly been playing it safe then.

"Something like that," she said, and sent me a prime little sister smirk. "Anyway, you should know," she said to West, "Matthew's spreading gossip about Avery, like she's in over her head, can't handle the brewery, bullshit like that. Avery just lost the thing she was going to do with Wild Haven Brewing and Sweetheart, and that barbecue place. I just thought you'd want to know."

"Sterling!" I shouted. I did not need my baby sister telling my—whatever West was—about Matthew's big mouth.

"Hey, am I wrong?" She looked back at West. "You want to know that, right?"

"Yes," he said, his eyes on me. "Yes, I want to know."

I knew he wasn't talking as the police chief now. He was talking as my lover. Ugh, weird. "Fuck, Sterling," was all I could come up with.

She was completely unrepentant. "He should know."

"Fine," I spit out.

"We don't have to talk about it if you don't want to," West said.

"You're not going to go beat him up?" Sterling demanded.

"I can't assault a citizen of my town for spreading gossip, even if he is a raging asshole," West said.

As ticked as I was at the two of them talking about me like I wasn't there, I found myself smiling at his reaction.

"You're not going to do anything?" she pressed. "I told you, so you'd do something."

"I didn't say I wasn't going to do anything," West said.

Sterling grinned. "Ooh, sneaky West. All right, I'll be patient."

"I need to talk to Avery, get more information," he said to Sterling before turning to me. "Are you two done here?"

I knew if I stayed, Sterling would just give me the third degree about whatever was going on with West. I didn't have an answer, which meant I wasn't sticking around. "I guess."

"Then let's swing by Sweetheart and grab something, and then I'll walk you back to the brewery."

"If you've got time," I said. "I wouldn't mind a cookie and a chai."

Sterling watched the two of us, her arms crossed over her chest, one eyebrow raised. I knew she was recording every detail for later, but later was later. And now I was headed for a cookie and a tea with my new boyfriend, lover—I didn't know what he was. I didn't like any of those words. I just knew as we walked out the door that there wasn't anyone I wanted to be strolling through town with more than Weston Garfield. And that was enough for now.

Chapter Seventeen

WEST

"What happened to you?" I asked after I'd tracked Avery down in her office after work, trying to mop herself off with a fistful of rags. From the shoulders down, she was soaked, and from the smell, I was guessing it was beer. Not a surprise, considering, but the quantity was unexpected. "Did you stand under an open keg or something?"

"No," Avery said with a laugh and a rueful shake of her head, her dark ponytail swinging. "I wasn't looking where I was going. I came around the corner of the bar, Dave called my name, and I turned but kept walking right into Cammie, who was holding a full tray of beer."

"I was going to see if you wanted to go get some barbecue, but maybe we'll swing by Heartstone first."

"Definitely," Avery agreed. "Yes, on the barbecue after a pit stop for a change of clothes. I love my beer, but I don't want to wear it."

A knot in my chest unraveled at her easy agreement to dinner. I hadn't realized how much it had mattered that she wanted to go get barbecue with me. I'd had her over the night before, all night, waking with her curled in my arms, her head on my chest.

'I didn't date a ton. It could get complicated for a small-town police chief who left too many relationships behind. I couldn't remember the last time I'd woken up with a woman, and never like this—comfortable, satisfied, resenting the alarm that would pull us apart.

I was trying not to overthink this thing. I wasn't going to treat Avery like an afterthought or a hook-up, but I wasn't ring shopping either. We were just feeling things out, seeing how it went, enjoying each other while it worked. All of that made it seem easy and casual, and maybe, on the surface, it was. But underneath, there was my reluctance to let her slide from my arms, that knot in my chest that she might not want to eat dinner with me or come back to my bed. It surprised me how much I wanted her with me.

At least for the moment, I didn't have to worry about it.

Avery grabbed her bag from the back of her chair, started to pull on her coat, then threw it over her arm and headed out, waving at her two bartenders. As far as I could tell, Cammie and Dave tended the bar at night when it was busy, helped in the brewery in the afternoons, and basically did whatever needed to be done. Avery managed them like she did everything else, with ease and empathy. I thought again, as I had many times since seeing her earlier, about how much of a dick Matthew Holt was. Avery was a far better manager than he'd ever be, but it only took a few stray comments to completely fuck up her business. It was bullshit.

Matt had always been on my radar as someone to keep an eye on, but now he was on my shit list.

I hooked her arm through mine, and we left out the side door.

"So, Heartstone and then barbecue?" Avery asked as she fastened her seatbelt. "It won't take me long to change."

I hesitated about bringing up the thing on my mind— but this was Avery. I didn't need to waste time beating around the bush. Not with her. So, I jumped in. I reached across the center console and slid my hand over hers, taking my eyes off the road for a second to shoot her a quick look. She was smiling, her fingers twining with mine.

"I want to ask you to come home with me after dinner," I said. "But I know there's a limit on how many nights you can spend away from Heartstone."

Avery let out a breath. "Yeah, it's a pain in the ass. My fucking father and his stupid will." She was quiet for a second, looking out the window, then sucked in a breath and said, "It's not as if staying at your place is more discreet, considering everybody knows I didn't come home and can guess who I'm with."

"Kind of what I was thinking," I said, relieved we were on the same page.

"How do you feel about staying at Heartstone with me?" She asked, the hint of hesitance in her voice telling me I wasn't the only one trying to feel this out.

"I'm up for that," I said, slowly. "It might be a little

weird at first. But we have to get over the weird eventually if we're going to do this. Assuming we're doing this." I didn't think I had to define what *this* was.

The side of Avery's mouth curled up. "After last night," she said, "I vote that we are absolutely doing this."

"Agreed," I said, more relieved than I was prepared to be. "For more of you, I'll happily put up with weird."

I turned onto the long drive to Heartstone Manor. Thanks to Hawk, it had changed in the last few years. Prentice, for reasons unknown, had neglected Heartstone Manor in the two years before he died, including the long drive in from the main road. When Griffen came home after Prentice's death, it had been choked with weeds, crumbling potholes dotting the asphalt, not the driveway you'd expect to lead to a grand estate.

Hawk had been busy keeping the Sawyers alive, but he'd found time to clean the place up. It had seemed odd at first, Griffen's security expert doubling as the groundskeeper. But I'd learned Hawk loved few things more than getting his hands in the dirt. One of those things was Quinn, Griffen and Avery's sister. I had a feeling that if we ever found Prentice's killer and things calmed down, Heartstone would have gardens that would be the envy of everyone in Western North Carolina. Someday. But Heartstone's grounds were no longer choked by weeds, and that was progress.

We emerged from the tree-lined drive to the courtyard in front of the big house. I wasn't expecting to see two cars parked in front, especially not cars I recognized.

"Who's here?" Avery asked, leaning forward. "Are those Edgar and Harvey's cars?"

Edgar was Griffen's wife's uncle and one of Prentice's former business partners. "Do they come to dinner often?" I asked, knowing the answer but wanting confirmation anyway.

"Sometimes on Sundays, you know, for family dinner," Avery said, squinting at the two cars as I pulled up behind them and put the SUV in park. "But it's not Sunday." A thought occurred to her, and she straightened, eyes widening. "It's not Sunday, is it?"

"No, it's Tuesday," I confirmed with a smile.

"That's what I thought, but sometimes the calendar gets away from me," she said. "If it's not Sunday, why are they here?"

"I don't know," I said. "But how would you feel about taking a rain check on that barbecue?"

"Done," Avery agreed. "I want to know what's going on. But first, change of clothes."

I followed her up the front steps and opened the door. "I'll go see if I can find Griffen."

She nodded, jogging up the stairs with a wave. My eyes followed her, lingering on the flex of her legs and her round ass. Looked like I was going to get to see inside Avery's bedroom. Not that I'd be paying much attention to the decor. Not if I had her all to myself.

The front hall was empty. I could hear movement in the dining room to my left, but not voices—probably Savannah or one of the day maids, Kitty or April, getting the table ready for dinner. In years past, and probably still on Sundays, there would have been a cocktail hour before the meal. But the current crop of Sawyers weren't big drinkers in general, and most of them had busy days—no time to hang around socializing before dinner.

I found Griffen in his office behind his desk, baby Stella strapped to his chest in a carrier.

"Hey," he said with a smile as I walked in after dropping a quick knock on the open door. "What are you doing here?" His eyebrows drew together. "Everything okay?"

"Yeah, everything's great." I dropped into the chair in front of his desk. "Avery walked into a tray full of beer. We were going to head out for dinner after she changed, but..." I raised an eyebrow. "Edgar and Harvey are here."

Griffen let out a grunt and nodded. "They're with Hope right now. Edgar was interested in those diaries from the housekeeper around the turn of the century that she and Savannah found. Harvey tagged along. They'll be back."

"Turn of the century diaries?" I asked. Not that it was my business, but I'm the police chief. It's my job to be a nosy fucker. And while I didn't have anything concrete on either of them, I didn't fully trust Edgar or Harvey. Edgar, because he'd been up to his nose with Prentice and, to a degree, my father on business dealings that, while they might be legal, weren't what I'd consider above board. And Harvey... Harvey, for a lot of reasons, was primarily at the top of the list for letting the necklace get stolen and not calling me about it.

"I think the diaries were a bonus," Griffen said, stroking Stella's back through the carrier. "They both just showed up. Apparently, they called Finn to make sure there was enough and said they'd see us at 6 p.m."

"Weird."

"Yep." Griffen closed his laptop, leaning back in his desk chair. "Any movement in Sterling and Avery's investigation?"

"Actually, yes. Hawk's friend dug up the designer's address."

"Have you checked it out yet?"

"Tomorrow," I said. "Avery couldn't get away today, and neither could I. But I've got double coverage tomorrow, so I should be good to play hooky for a few hours."

"Is she local? The designer?"

"Local enough. Out by Wolf Mountain. I can't find a phone number—not one that gets answered—so we'll go out there, see what we see. If it gets us any information we can use, I'll owe your sisters one."

A deep, resonant bong echoed through the house. When we'd been kids, Miss Martha, Savannah's mother and the housekeeper of Heartstone Manor for most of my life, had used the gong to call the family to dinner—a tradition that went all the way back to William Sawyer. These days, I can't remember the last time I'd heard it. Everyone showed up to dinner on time, or Finn would refuse to feed you. Nobody wanted to risk missing one of Finn's meals.

"You guys back to using that thing?" I asked as we walked down the hall to the dining room.

"Only when Edgar or Harvey are here," Griffen answered in a low voice. "Tradition, you know?"

"They do like their tradition," I said. "Speaking of, you heard from my father lately?"

Griffen's eyes were amused, his tone light as he said, "Yep, we had a meeting yesterday."

"He still being an asshole?" I asked.

"You know your dad. He doesn't like change, but I think he'll come around."

"I told him to stop wasting his time, that you weren't going to play his game," I said.

"Yeah, I know, and thanks. But we're going to have to work it out between the two of us." Griffen let out a breath, gripping my shoulder in a tight squeeze as we walked into the dining room. "Your dad's not a bad man, West. Frustrating. Stubborn. Buried in the past, but he's not a bad guy, you know what I mean?"

"Yeah, I know what you mean," I said. While my father could be short-sighted, selfish, old-fashioned, and kind of a blowhard, Griffen was right. He wasn't a bad man. He'd been a decent enough father, particularly considering the standards he'd grown up with. He loved my mom, and in his own way, he tried to do right by the town. As far as I was concerned, *his way* was outdated, but my dad was a whole different ball of wax than Griffen's had been. Prentice Sawyer had been a lot of things, and a shit human being was at the top of the list.

My eyes caught Avery's across the room. I couldn't stop the goofy smile I felt spread across my face. Griffen stepped closer. In a low voice, he said, "Avery seems happy."

"I hope so," I said.

"Good." Griffen gave my shoulder another pat and turned for the head of the table and his customary seat by Hope. Paige, the nanny, popped in to take baby Stella.

She had a quick word with Hope and disappeared. The gong sounded again, almost deafening this close. I turned to see it vibrating on the stand, no one within ten feet. I might have wondered, but a youthful giggle sounded to my left, and when I glanced over, I caught sight of the kids—Scarlett and Tenn's boys, August and Thatcher, and Savannah's Nicky. Thatcher, a teenager, had his arms crossed and was rolling his eyes. I'd bet he had not been the one to ring the gong but knew who had. It was hard to guess between August and Nicky. They were both biting their lips, their cheeks pink, eyes guilty. I winked, and they dissolved into another round of giggles.

Savannah turned up beside me. "No shrieking in the dining room," she said, her eyes on the boys. She raised one red eyebrow, and the giggles dissolved into guilty silence. "Go wash your hands."

The boys darted from the room. Sometimes the kids ate dinner with the adults. Sometimes they ate in the kitchen with Finn and Savannah. It looked like tonight would be a grown-up dinner. Thatcher exchanged a look with Tenn, who tilted his head to the doorway with a grin. Thatcher turned and followed his brother and Nicky to the kitchens.

Interesting. I'd had plenty of dinners in Heartstone Manor over the years. Back in the day, children ate in the kitchen or at the breakfast table on the side of the dining room. Since Griffen and Hope had taken over the house, most dinners were informal, despite the grandeur of the dining room. Looked like when Edgar and Harvey stopped by, the house reverted to the formality of Prentice's time.

Avery gestured me over to the seat beside her.

"Thanks. You talked to Edgar and Harvey?" I asked.

Avery shook her head. "They came in with Hope a second ago." I glanced over, watching the two older men getting comfortable on the opposite side of the table. They were talking in low voices. I couldn't catch what they were saying. Harvey had his eyes on the tablecloth in front of him, but Edgar was scanning the room, his eyes pausing as they met mine before moving on.

"They're definitely up to something," I murmured to Avery.

"Agreed," she said.

Savannah and Kitty began serving the salad course and pouring wine. I considered strategies to get Edgar or Harvey to talk. Before I'd settled on a game plan, they went on the offense.

Chapter Eighteen

WEST

"West, glad you're here," Edgar said. "Saves me a trip."

"Yeah?" I said, raising an eyebrow. "Something I can do for you, Edgar?" Considering his offices were a short walk from the police station, I didn't figure he'd been doing much work to track me down. As one of the town's leading citizens, he had all my numbers, but we could play this his way to start.

"I want to know what progress you're making on that break-in at Sawyers Bend Brewing," Edgar said.

"Edgar!" Avery protested. "Don't badger West."

"Hush, girl," Edgar said with a wave of his hand.

She narrowed her eyes. "I'm not a girl. I'm thirty-one years old, and West isn't some kid you can boss around. He's the Chief of Police."

I squeezed her knee under the table. When it mattered, I wouldn't let Edgar push me an inch. But for now, I wanted him to talk.

"You know I can't give you information about an

ongoing investigation," I reminded Edgar. Everyone knew it, and nobody cared. They could ask. Didn't mean I'd tell them anything. I knew how to keep my mouth shut, even if no one else in this town did.

"You don't have any fingerprints. They didn't leave any evidence. How do we know she's safe there?" Edgar asked.

"I have her covered," Hawk growled from the far end of the table. "And when I don't have her, West does," he finished. "She's as safe as we can make her."

"Not safe enough," Harvey said, his eyes going to her arm.

"That wasn't about me," Avery said, lifting a hand to trace the almost healed wound running down her arm. "That was about Ford."

"Was it?" Edgar asked, his eyes shifting to Ford, sitting at the opposite end of the table from Griffen, observing us in silence. This was the Ford who'd come back from prison—watchful, quiet, seemingly content to let his brother run the family as he'd always been meant to. From everything I'd seen, it looked like Ford had learned his lesson. Envy and greed had led him down a path that sent him to prison for a crime he hadn't committed. I would have guessed that if he got out of prison, he'd have been long gone. The strictures of Prentice's will didn't apply to Ford.

Ford had been disinherited. There was nothing for him here. Nothing except home and family. A family that had welcomed him back even as he remained withdrawn from them. The distance with Griffen hadn't been healed, might never be. But Ford was fiercely protective of his younger sisters. He'd been fighting for them even when Prentice had still been alive. I didn't know if he was hanging around to watch over them or because he couldn't move forward while the cloud of murder hung over his head.

Finally, Ford asked, "What makes you think Avery was the target?"

Harvey munched on his salad, his eyes on Edgar, waiting. Edgar's focus on me, he said, "Because whoever broke into the brewery stole Avery's file on Prentice's murder."

"What do you know about that file?" I asked, quashing the surge of irritation at Edgar's interference. He was so like Prentice, stirring the pot, manipulating everyone around him until he got what he wanted. I didn't think he'd killed Prentice, and I didn't think he was the one who'd gone after the rest of the Sawyers, but that didn't mean I trusted him.

"I only know what Harvey told me," Edgar answered smoothly.

"Bullshit," Avery whispered beside me.

I agreed but squeezed her knee again, half to warn her to be quiet and more because I loved the feel of her leg under my hand and the casual intimacy of sitting next to her at a family dinner. How the fuck had I missed this my whole life? We'd practically grown up together. Granted, I'd been just old enough that she'd seemed like a kid for far too long, but she wasn't a child. Far from it. As she'd reminded Edgar, she was a grown woman—one I was realizing I wanted at my side, not just in bed or for a beer. I pushed that thought aside for the moment.

"What are you getting at?" Sterling asked, leaning forward, bracing her elbows on the table. Harvey winced at her lack of manners, but Sterling could not have given less of a shit.

"Do you think Avery had something in that file that pointed to the killer?" Sterling asked. She sat up straighter, sliding her elbows back, her eyes sparkling with intrigue. She flashed a look at Avery. "Damn, I wish we had a copy of your file. I wonder if you saw something and didn't know what it was. You know, like proof. And if we had more pieces to the puzzle, maybe we'd know it was proof."

"Don't get too excited, Sterling," Avery reminded her. "I don't have a copy of the file they stole, and whoever broke into the brewery isn't going to give it back."

Sterling let out a breath, deflating. "Yeah, good point. Too bad you don't have a photographic memory."

"Believe me, it would make a lot of things easier," Avery said, and I knew she was thinking of the recipe. I squeezed her leg again, leaning close to whisper, "The new one will be even better."

The smile that flashed across her face made my chest tight.

"What was that?" Harvey said. I looked up, expecting to have his attention on us, but he was looking at Sterling.

Sterling flipped her hair off her shoulder. "Nothing, just that we have another lead, so you know, it's not a complete dead end."

"What do you mean you have another lead?" Harvey asked. He set down his fork on the edge of his plate with a clang. "You girls need to let this go. Avery and Ford could have been killed, Sterling. For what? Ford's out of prison, and he doesn't want you hurt."

Everyone turned to look at Ford. He set his fork down on the tablecloth with a quiet thunk and swallowed, wiping his mouth before saying, "I've made my feelings clear to everyone. We've been through enough. I appreciate all the help to get me out of prison, but this is dangerous. I don't need you to save me. I'm here, I'm free. Let's just move on."

The table erupted in protests, Avery and Sterling's being the loudest. From beside me, Avery said, "You may have given up, Ford, but that doesn't mean we will. I want to clear your name. You shouldn't have to live like this."

"Live like what?" Ford shot back. "In a castle surrounded by my family? Eating Finn's cooking every day? Believe me, this is heaven compared to where I spent the last year. I'm not complaining. Let it go."

"Listen to your brother, girls," Edgar said.

"No," Avery shouted. "I will not." She leaned past me to spear Ford with a hard glance. "You don't want to clear your name, fine. Maybe I want to know who killed our father. Did you ever think about that? I don't want you living with this for the rest of your life, but you're an adult. You don't want to pursue it. I can't make you. But I want to know who killed Dad."

"Why, so you can thank them?" Royal asked.

"No," Avery shook her head, then paused. "If it hadn't ended up with Ford in prison, then maybe."

"I can't believe you would say such a thing about your

father," Edgar said, his words falling like stones in the center of the table.

"Edgar, get real," Sterling said. "You and Harvey, and West's dad are pretty much the only people who are sorry Prentice is gone."

For a second, I thought I saw real grief flash across Edgar's face before he set his jaw and shook his head. "I'm glad he doesn't have to hear this disrespect," Edgar said. As monstrous as Prentice had been, it was easy to forget he'd been someone's friend.

"Uncle Edgar," Hope's clear, strong voice filled the room. She was one of the kindest people I knew, but when she was pissed, watch out. Edgar had rescued her from a tough childhood and brought her up as his own. For most of her life, she'd been an obedient niece until Edgar had figured out a way to marry her off to Griffen. It could have been a disaster, but those two had been in love before they understood what love was. In the end, they were like our own personal fairy tale. And over the last two years, I'd seen Hope grow a strong spine, especially when it came to her uncle. She loved him, but she was done taking his crap.

"This is Griffen's house now," she continued. "We're done with the worship of Prentice Sawyer. I know he was your friend, and I know you miss him, but no one here wants to hear it."

He pointed a finger at his niece. "Disrespectful," he said again.

"I don't really care. Can it or go home."

They locked eyes for a long moment, then Edgar gave

a short nod and took a bite of salad. Harvey picked up the baton, focusing back on Sterling.

"So, what lead will you be following next? Did you finally track down that jewelry designer?"

To her credit, Sterling didn't give anything away. "Oh, you know, we've been asking questions here and there. Losing the file is a blow for sure, but we'll figure it out."

"It sounded like you had something specific," Harvey said. "If you tell me what it is, maybe I can help."

"Help?" Sterling said, her tone innocent despite the wicked gleam in her eyes. "Like you did when you let the necklace get stolen from your office? No thanks, I don't think we need that kind of help."

Harvey flushed. "I told you I was sorry about that."

"Not sorry enough to report it to the police," Sterling said. "It wasn't yours to lose." Her last words had an edge.

Harvey shifted to face Griffen. "Can't you put a stop to this?" His gaze flicked to me. "You're the police chief. Tell them you'll arrest them if they interfere with your investigation."

"I would if they were," I said, keeping my tone mild, "but they're not."

"Edgar, Harvey," Griffen said, waiting until he had their attention. "Drop it. As Hope said, change the subject, or you can go. Avery and Sterling are fine. They don't need you to step in for Dad."

"Your sister got stabbed," Edgar erupted. "She could have been killed. I don't understand—"

The silverware jumped and clattered as Griffen

smacked his hand on the table. "Drop it, or leave," he said. "Those are your choices. I would hate to rescind your welcome at this table, but we're done talking about this."

Edgar and Harvey exchanged a glance, seeming to conduct a whole conversation in silence. Edgar shook his head and stabbed a lettuce leaf with his fork. "Fine. I'll drop it." And he did, at least for the rest of dinner.

Not that we finished the remainder of the meal in peace—conversation touched on everything and nothing. The food was amazing, as it always was, but when I wasn't puzzling over Edgar and Harvey's behavior, all I could think about was getting Avery alone. I'd rather have taken her back to my place, but staying at Heartstone was a solid second choice. We'd only spent one night together, but I wasn't interested in going to bed without her.

The second we finished dessert, Avery grabbed my hand and pulled me out of my seat. "Come on, I want to show you something," she said.

"Really?" I asked, following her from the dining room, jogging up the stairs beside her. We took a right into the family wing, stopping at her bedroom door.

"Come on," she said, pulling me inside.

"What did you want to show me?" I asked.

Her eyes bright, a smile curving her full mouth, she whipped her t-shirt over her head, taking her tank top with it. A second later, her jeans and underwear hit the floor around her feet.

"This," she said brightly.

"It's the best thing I've seen all year," I said, reaching for her. I had enough presence of mind to flip the lock of the door behind me before scooping her into my arms and heading for her bed.

Chapter Nineteen

AVERY

"Did you put the address in the nav?" I asked.

West shot me a quick grin. I loved the way it made his eyes crinkle in the corners. "I got it," he said. "Should take about forty minutes to get to Wolf Mountain, give or take."

"Cool," I said, settling back into my seat, sipping from the latte I'd grabbed when we'd stopped by Sweetheart Bakery. "I hope this isn't another dead end."

"Could be. We won't know until we get there. I'm just hoping she's home."

"True," I agreed. "Considering she doesn't like answering her phone, who knows where she is? At the least, we can look around outside, see if we can pick up any signs she's been around home recently."

We had tried calling the designer three times over the last two days, but had struck out—voicemail every time.

He reached across the console to squeeze my hand. "Don't stress about it. It'll be what it is."

"How are you so chill?" I asked. We might be forty

minutes from answers about the necklace—about my father and who'd killed him—if the necklace was related. I shifted in my seat, my fingers tapping on the armrest, unable to calm the tension inside me.

He shrugged. "Because this is what investigations are like. One step forward, two steps back. Things you think you know but can't verify. Witnesses who disappear. It's all about building a case piece by piece, and those pieces rarely fit together cleanly or as fast as we want them to. So, you just keep going, digging away until you find enough. Maybe this will be enough. Likely it won't. But one way or another, we'll know more at the end of the day than we do right now."

"That's encouraging," I said. "I think. But kind of unsatisfying. I want to know everything, not bits and pieces."

"I've heard that before." West rolled his eyes. "People think it's going to be fun and dramatic, like stumbling on the secret diary filled with evidence or someone confessing everything. And sometimes—rarely—that does happen. But most of the time it's more like this—little pieces that eventually add up to *enough*."

I sipped my coffee and watched as the last of the town faded behind us. Trees flashed by, a riot of fall color. It wouldn't last much longer. It was getting decidedly chilly in the mountains. Snow seemed to come later and later these days, but we'd get some, eventually.

"What are you doing for Thanksgiving?" I asked, thinking idly about the holidays to come.

"I usually eat at my parents'," West said. "Why? Want to come?"

I looked at him, surprised. I hadn't gotten that far on a lot of levels. He laughed at my expression. I wondered if I looked shocked or nervous—both emotions were fighting for dominance in my gut.

"You don't have to," he said with a smile.

"Maybe you guys should come to Heartstone," I offered before I thought about it. Instead of wishing I'd kept my mouth shut, the idea settled. Did I want to be on the hot seat in West's mother's dining room? No. But could the Garfield family fold into the mayhem of Thanksgiving at Heartstone Manor? Definitely. Edgar would be there. Harvey would probably show up, too, which would give West's dad some company.

"That's an idea," West said. "I don't know if my mom would go for it, but we can figure it out."

"Yeah," I said. "We've got time." A thought popped into my head. "Sterling thinks Harvey and Edgar know something."

"They know a lot of things," West said. "She thinks they know something about what?"

"My dad's murder," I said, taking another sip of coffee.

West's eyebrows raised, his eyes on the road, and he made a sound in his throat I couldn't decipher.

"You don't think so?" I asked.

"I haven't ruled anyone out," he said. "It's possible. Prentice had a lot of secrets, and if anyone knew them, it was Edgar, Harvey, or maybe my father. But I don't know." West shook his head. "My gut says none of them would have let Ford go to jail if they'd had evidence to stop it. Be arrested, maybe. But once he pled guilty for a lighter sentence, once those charges went officially on his record, I don't know. I can't see it, but that doesn't mean it's impossible."

"Sterling didn't like the way Harvey seemed to know we'd found the designer's address. I thought that was weird, too." I waited for his response, curious how that had landed for West. He lifted his chin and glanced my way before fixing his eyes back on the road.

"I hear you. That felt weird to me, too."

"Shit," I said under my breath.

"I don't want to think Harvey's in on anything, but he let the necklace get stolen," West said, "and he didn't report it to me. He was thick with your dad. His hands are not entirely clean. Nothing I can arrest him for, but..."

I nodded. "I know what you mean. And then he's nosing around to see what we know. It's just weird."

"I can't arrest him for being weird, but I'm with you. I didn't like it." He let out a sigh. "I've been considering the possibility that I have a leak."

"I hate not knowing who to trust," I said, not liking the idea that there was anyone at the police station who didn't have West's back. "Any idea who?"

West let out a short laugh. "It could be anyone," he said. "I thought I knew this town when I became police chief. I thought it'd be a cinch. I'd spent a couple of years working in Charlotte, got some big-city police work under my belt. I thought I could roll back into Sawyers Bend, and handle stuff just fine."

"It didn't work that way?" I asked, suddenly curious. I was in high school and college back then and hadn't really clocked West being gone. Then he'd been back and took over as police chief. He'd slid into the role so seamlessly that it seemed like he'd always been police chief.

"Everybody has secrets," he said. "No one is exactly who they seem to be. And when you're the police chief, you learn a lot you'd rather not know."

I didn't bother to ask for details. West understood discretion. "I don't want to know everybody's secrets," I said. "Just this one."

West shook his head. "I have a feeling when we finally get the answer to that one secret, it's going to open up a can of worms."

"Hmm." I had nothing to say to that. He might be right. He might be wrong. It didn't matter. I wanted to know who'd killed my father and tried to put Ford in jail for the rest of his life. Who'd come after my family over and over since my father had been killed. I wanted the answer. I'd deal with the fallout later.

We lapsed into silence, West finally switching on some music. As we left the valley and climbed up to Wolf Mountain, the small town where the jewelry designer lived, the trees grew denser, the roads narrower. We made a wrong turn but finally found the overgrown gravel drive marked only by a single mailbox that clearly led to her house.

West stopped at the head of the drive and checked the rusted mailbox. It was stuffed full of letters and advertising circulars. He shut it and climbed back in the SUV. "There's a good chance she's not home," West said as our tires crunched down the drive.

"Or she might not have gone out in the last few days," I said, hopeful.

"We'll see soon enough."

At the end of the drive, the densely packed trees parted to reveal a small clearing, a bright blue cottage sitting in the center. The trim and front door were a vibrant purple, and orange pumpkins sat on either side of the porch, uncarved. A car was parked under the carport. Nothing looked abandoned or as if the owner hadn't been here recently. My palms tingled, itching to knock on the door. She could be right there with the answers as to who'd ordered that necklace made and for whom. One more piece in the puzzle. We were so close I could taste it.

I unclicked my seatbelt. "Avery," West said, reaching out a hand to stop me.

I hopped out before he could. He met me at the front of the SUV. "Avery, for now, let me take the lead. Understand?"

I wanted to argue. I didn't. West wasn't wrong. He was the police chief. It made more sense to let him take the lead. I was just impatient. We were so close. Ever since we'd found the necklace, we'd been trying to get here.

"All right, let's go," I said.

We climbed the front steps of her tiny porch. The concrete looked recently swept, the mat arranged just so. It did not look like the front porch of someone who had been out of town for a while. The doorbell sounded, a happy chime echoing through the small house. I waited, breath held, for the answering sound of footsteps. There was nothing.

"Her car's here," I said to West.

"I know. It doesn't mean she is. Or she could be in the shower or working. Relax."

His hand rested on my lower back, the heat of his palm spreading through me, anchoring me, but not slowing the frantic beat of my heart. My anticipation was too heady to shut down.

West rang a second time, and again we waited. Still nothing. No sound, just the chime of the bells and silence. After the third time, West gave up on the bell, opening the storm door to pound on the wood of the door. "Ms. Novak? This is West Garfield, the police chief in Sawyers Bend. I need to have a word with you."

Nothing.

"So now what?" I asked.

"Now we peek in some windows. Stay close to me. Don't wander off by yourself."

"I'm not going anywhere," I said, following him down off the porch, staying a pace behind as he circled the house. The side windows were too high to see in from ground level. At the back, there was a small deck and a sliding glass door.

"Bingo," West said. The house was small enough that we'd be able to see most of the first floor from there, assuming there weren't curtains or something. I turned to scan the woods behind the porch. She had plenty of privacy. I guessed that an artist who liked to recreate nature in her work wouldn't have blinds to block out the woods. As we rounded the stairs and went up to the deck, I saw I'd been right.

It was too bright outside to see much until we got

close. When the shadows gathered enough to block the reflection off the window, I wished I'd stayed in the car.

Two smeared red handprints marked the bottom of the sliding door. I wasn't a cop or a doctor, but I knew blood when I saw it.

Fuck.

I took a step closer, peering into the house.

The living room was a disaster. Chairs were overturned, stuffing coming out of the couch, and blood splashed across the golden pine floors. So much blood.

"Avery, stop." West's arm shot out, catching me in the chest. "Off the deck. Now."

"Why? What do you see?" I wasn't sure I wanted to know, but I had to.

"Get off the deck now," he repeated. I turned and jogged down the stairs, the fight draining out of me. There hadn't just been blood splashed across the floors. There had been a puddle of it by what I guessed had been the kitchen table, now broken boards and splinters on the floor.

A puddle that looked big enough that it had to have come out of a body.

I watched, numb, as West pulled his phone out of his pocket, calling for backup. He pulled a glove from inside his jacket, protected his hand, and carefully tugged at the handle of the sliding glass door. It slid open. I didn't know what that meant, except it left me with a hollow feeling in my stomach. Something bad had happened in there. Whoever did it had probably left through that door.

"West," I called out. "Be careful."

His eyes landed on me as he nodded, then looked

behind me at the empty clearing in the woods beyond. "Come back up on the deck," he said. "I want you in sight. I won't be more than a minute."

He opened the door just wide enough to enter and disappeared inside. True to his word, he reappeared less than a minute later, his eyes grim, his phone to his ear. Carefully, he shut the door behind him.

"We've got a body." That was all I heard clearly. The rest was a jumble of cop speak—something about calling the SBI and the ME. I didn't know what the SBI was, but I'd watched enough TV to guess the ME was the Medical Examiner.

I didn't want to see, but I had to know. I inched around West as he paced and barked orders into his phone, moving closer to the sliding glass door. When I saw her, I wished I'd listened to West. She was splayed face down, long strands of blonde hair streaked with red spread around her. I thought she'd been wearing red until I realized her blood had stained everything: her hair, her dress, the floor.

"What happened?" I breathed.

Then West was there, pulling me back. "Hold on a sec," he said into the phone. "Avery, don't. Don't look. You don't need to see this."

I barely heard him. "But how? How long?"

"We don't know yet. We'll wait here," he said into the phone, then hung up, shoving it in his pocket. "I can't take you back to Sawyers Bend yet. I'm sorry. I don't want you to see any of this."

"What happens now?" I asked, my voice shaking.

"Hold on." He tapped a contact on his phone, putting

it back to his ear. A second later, he said, "I have a crime scene here in Wolf Mountain, and I need to get Avery back to Sawyers Bend. Can you send someone to pick her up?" A pause. "Yeah. Yeah. Same address. Thanks." He shoved his phone back in his pocket. "Hawk is sending someone to get you. We have to process the scene."

"I don't want to go back," I protested, not sure if I was telling the truth.

West shook his head, his dark eyes grave. "Listen, honey, this is outside of my jurisdiction, but I'm going to stick around assuming Bill doesn't have a problem with that." I didn't know who Bill was, but I could guess he was law enforcement for Wolf Mountain. It made sense they'd all know each other.

"You're a civilian, and you don't belong here. You've seen enough. You don't need these pictures in your head. Trust me. On top of that, it's going to be a long day. You get me? You don't want to be stuck sitting in my car for hours."

I wanted to protest. I wanted to stay by his side to know what was happening, but I could see the wisdom in getting the hell out of here. I closed my eyes, envisioning a gurney with a black bag on it, the dark red of the puddle of blood. No, I didn't want to stay. I didn't want to see. This wasn't a movie or my imagination. This was a real woman who was dead.

"How long?" I asked. West knew what I meant.

"My guess is she was killed sometime yesterday."

"How do you know?" I asked. I wasn't sure how he could have looked at the violent chaos in that house and known anything about what had happened inside.

"Rigor mortis has passed, but she doesn't smell like she's been there for days. The blood is mostly dry," he said. "We'll know more after the scene is processed. And if we're lucky, whoever did this left something behind that will help us find them." He let out a short burst of air. "She fought, Avery. She fought hard. My guess is not all of that blood is hers. Maybe we'll get lucky."

Lucky didn't seem like the right word for anything about the scene in that house. A horrible thought occurred to me.

"Did we do this?" I asked. "Sterling and me trying to find her? Is this our fault?"

West put his hands on my shoulders and shook me, just a little. "No, Avery, no. This is not your fault. This is the fault of whoever killed her. Not you."

"But if we led them here—"

"No," he said, his voice gruff. "Let go of that idea. You didn't do anything wrong. But for now, I have to get you out of here."

"Okay," I agreed. I let West lead me back to his SUV.

"I know you're going to talk to Sterling when you get back to Sawyers Bend," he said. "You need to tell her to keep her mouth shut. Neither of you should talk to anyone else. I don't want gossip to get in the way of the investigation. You understand?"

I wasn't sure I did entirely, but I got that part of it. I could keep my mouth shut. "Got it," I said.

Five minutes later, the first cop car pulled into the driveway. Not long after that, the place was crawling with people—police in uniform, people not in uniform, I was pretty sure were also cops, people with boxes and kits, somebody in what looked like a hazmat suit, and then the medical examiner's van. I went from wishing I understood what was happening to wondering how long it would take for someone to show up to take me away.

West appeared here and there, always looking serious, talking in low tones, occasionally glancing over to me with concern. Normally, I liked watching him work, but not this. Not with the dead woman inside.

When my ride showed up, I was glad it wasn't someone I knew well enough to chat with on the way back to Sawyers Bend. I didn't feel like talking. I wasn't sure what I felt like. Scared. Sad. And angry. So fucking angry. Whoever killed my father hadn't stopped with him. And this woman, as far as I knew, had been innocent.

You don't know this has to do with Prentice's murder, I reminded myself. *Maybe she had an angry ex, or someone thought a jeweler had diamonds hidden away. It could be anything.* I tried to make myself believe it, but the picture wouldn't gel. This hadn't been the first body we'd come across in the search for my father's killer. It felt like too much to hope it was the last.

Chapter Twenty

I put my SUV in gear and reversed out of the driveway, leaving behind the officers still at the crime scene. Not my town, not my jurisdiction. Wolf Mountain hadn't seen a murder like this in decades, and their chief had been happy to let me stay once I'd explained who I was and why I was there. He'd cleared his throat, given me a hard look, and said, "Best you stick around then, but keep your hands to yourself. Don't want the evidence gettin' spoiled."

I knew what he meant, and he was right. But I watched, and I listened, and I saw so much more than I wanted to. I couldn't get the image of her body out of my head. The jewelry designer, Anna Novak, had been thirty-one, single, and a resident of Wolf Mountain since birth. The house she lived in had been her grandmother's, and she'd made a pretty decent living recreating the nature she'd loved with precious metals and stones. Had she made the necklace Avery and Sterling found? We'd never know. Anna wasn't just dead. She'd been murdered. Brutally.

As far as he could tell before the autopsy, the medical examiner estimated she'd been stabbed over twenty times, possibly as many as forty. That many stab wounds indicated a chilling level of rage. Based on the pool around her, she'd lost most of her blood, which indicated her heart had continued beating. She'd been alive through most of the attack.

I was a cop, but I hadn't always been a cop in a small town. I'd seen bodies. I'd seen murder victims. More gunshot wounds than I cared to think about. But this murder held a level of savagery I'd never seen before. As far as we could tell, whoever killed her had been there for that purpose.

It begged the question of why.

Nothing seemed to be missing. The small house hadn't been ransacked. The only disorder came from the fight Anna had put up to save her life. Chairs overturned. The kitchen table was in pieces on the floor. Broken glassware. The bloody handprints on the sliding glass door. I guessed they'd come from Anna crawling, trying to get away, desperate to live. Smears on the floor said they dragged her back and finished the job.

I tried to stay impartial. I couldn't be a cop if I let my emotions get twisted up with every case. There were too many. I wouldn't be able to function. But this... I swallowed, trying to force the roil of feelings down into my chest, to lock them away. I didn't have time for this, for fear, or pain, or grief. But when I thought of Anna's body on the floor, all I could see was Avery and that knife slice across her shoulder and down her arm. She'd escaped with barely a scar, but seeing Anna's brutal attack, her life stolen, reminded me how close Avery had come to the same fate. They had so much in common. Small-town girls who'd grown up to be independent businesswomen. They were the same age. And they were connected by that necklace.

Was it coincidence that Avery and Sterling had been poking around and Anna ended up dead? It could be. We hadn't found any proof that this murder was related to their search for evidence. But the timing...

It's not that I don't believe in coincidences. I've seen enough to know they happen. But they're a lot less common than people think they are. This didn't feel like a coincidence. Had the attack on Avery and Ford actually been about this damn necklace?

That I couldn't answer, but I intended to.

One thing I did know: Harvey might be up to something. He surely knew more than he was telling, but he hadn't done this.

I didn't have proof, and I'd be getting an alibi. If he didn't have one, his name was going straight to the police chief of Wolf Mountain. But my gut said this wasn't Harvey or Edgar, but was screaming something else. Something Avery wasn't going to like.

My phone rang. I looked down to see Avery's name on the screen. I thought for a second before I picked up.

"Are you still there?" she asked.

"On my way back," I replied.

She was quiet, her breathing the only sound on the line. Finally, she said, "Are you okay?"

"Not really," I answered. "Are you at the brewery?"

"In my office," she said.

"I'll be there in half an hour. We need to talk."

"Okay," she said, her voice hesitant. "I'll see you soon."

"Yep, see you soon," I said, hanging up.

I blinked hard into the bright afternoon sun. The world went on. Leaves on the trees were vibrant, and tourists filled the roads. It was fall in the mountains, a time for family and fun, and Anna Novak was going to miss all of it because someone, maybe the same someone who'd murdered Prentice Sawyer, had decided she was in the way and that stealing her life was the best way to neutralize her. Someone willing to kill to keep their secret wouldn't balk at killing again.

The drive back through town had me gritting my teeth at the sidewalks clogged with tourists wandering into the street. Maybe we should start giving tickets for jaywalking again, I thought, with a cranky sense of satisfaction. See how they'd feel about wandering in front of a car then. I doubted I'd do it. Tourist season kept the lights on through the winter for a lot of businesses. I didn't want to scare them off with petty tickets, as annoying as they were. I crawled through town, tapping the brakes, silently urging the drivers ahead of me to *just go, damn it*, until I got to the other side of town and flicked on my blinker to pull into Avery's brewery.

I went in through the side, not in the mood to play friendly police chief with any locals in the taproom. Avery looked up from her desk when I walked in, her eyes worried.

"Hey," she said. "Can I get you anything?"

I shook my head and closed the door behind me.

"She's dead?" Avery asked.

I could tell she knew the answer. She had eyes, had seen most of what I'd seen. But she needed to hear it.

"Very," I said. I wanted to give her the words, if only to scare her off her pursuit, but I couldn't do it. I couldn't put those pictures in her head. Bad enough they were in mine. I settled for, "She was stabbed at least twenty times. She bled out on her kitchen floor."

"You said she fought." Avery's voice was thin, as if she couldn't force enough air through her throat.

"She did," I agreed. "Based on what we saw in there, she fought like hell. Sometimes it's not enough."

"Fuck," Avery said, sinking into her seat. "Fuck." She jolted and looked up. "This is our fault. Sterling and mine. We did this."

"No. I told you, Avery. You didn't do this. You didn't stab her. You're not responsible."

She wrapped her arms around herself, shaking her head. "Maybe not the way you mean, but if we'd left this alone... If she had the information we were looking for, and someone else knew it..."

"Avery," I said. I wanted to tell her she was wrong, but I couldn't.

Had she or Sterling killed Anna Novak? No, absolutely not. Were they responsible for her death? Also no. The person responsible for her death was the one who'd stabbed her. Had their investigation reminded the killer that Anna Novak was a loose end? That was very possible. I didn't want to tell Avery that. I didn't want to see the weight on her soul, but I had to. Because what I really didn't want was to see her dead.

"Avery," I said, leaning against the closed door and crossing my arms over my chest. "You and Sterling have to walk away from this."

"What?" Avery's head snapped up. "No, obviously we were on the right track."

"Avery," I snapped. "A woman is dead."

"You just said that's not my fault," Avery said, brushing her hair behind her ear with a shaking hand.

"And it's not," I agreed. "It's not your fault."

"But?" she pressed.

I thought about my words, thought about how to make her understand. "It's possible that the person you're looking for, the person who killed your father, is also the person who killed Anna Novak. Especially if she was the jeweler who made that necklace. There was no evidence of a search or a robbery. As far as we can tell, the only reason the killer was there was to take her life."

"To shut her up," Avery said.

"That seems likely. People know you and Sterling are looking for your father's killer. They know you're looking for evidence. Someone stole that file out of your desk. Someone attacked you with a knife," I reminded her.

"That was about Ford," she protested, shaking her head.

"You don't know that," I said, my words rising into a shout.

My hands curled into fists at my side. *Control, asshole*, I reminded myself. Losing my shit was not going to help. I was the police chief, not a spoiled child throwing a fit. I didn't need to yell at her, but I couldn't seem to keep my feelings from ricocheting all over the place. My heart twisted every time I thought about Anna's body, picturing Avery in her place. I couldn't forget the blood on Avery's Halloween costume. She'd been lucky, but luck doesn't last forever.

Eventually, it always runs out.

"Avery, this isn't a game," I said, trying for calm and not succeeding. "This is life or death. You need to leave this alone."

"I'm not giving up," she said, lifting her chin and crossing her arms over her chest.

I couldn't understand why she didn't get it. "Are you even fucking listening to me?" I said, losing my grip on my temper again. "This woman was brutally murdered, Avery. I'll be having nightmares about what I saw in that house for the rest of my life. It could have been you."

"It's not the same," she insisted, not meeting my eyes. "I have security. I'm not going to get killed."

"You don't know that," I shouted, giving up on trying to keep my head straight. "You're just bumbling around, gathering up things you and your sister find like it's a game, or another scavenger hunt. It's not anything like that. I know you want to clear Ford's name, but he asked you to let this go. He's out of prison. There aren't any charges hanging over him. He doesn't need this, and neither do you."

"Don't fucking tell me what I need," Avery said, dropping her hands to her sides and coming to her feet in a surge of anger. "I want to know who killed my father. I have a right to know."

"No, you don't," I said, suddenly exhausted. "You have a desire to know, not a right. Look, I've been a cop a long time, long enough to know sometimes you don't get the answers. Sometimes, all you get are question marks, and you have to live with that. But that means you live. Whoever wanted to keep Anna Novak quiet got what they wanted. Stop trying to make yourself the next target."

"And do what?" she demanded. "Just walk away and hope you find the answer? Are you even looking anymore?"

Helpless rage choked me. I'd been looking, goddammit. I'd been looking for any clue I could find since Prentice had been shot. I lay awake at night wondering what I'd missed. This would never be over for me. Not until we found Prentice's killer. With Anna Novak's murder, the stakes had changed. Avery was in danger.

I waited for her to apologize. She wrapped her arms around her chest and raised her chin.

I tried again. "You need to keep yourself off his radar, Avery. Hawk and I can't protect you all the time. And even if we could, you'd hate living like that. You know you would."

"I'm not giving up," she said through gritted teeth, her brown eyes sparking fire.

"You go anywhere near my open case, and I'll arrest you for obstruction of justice," I said, regretting the words almost as soon as they left my mouth. But I didn't take them back. I didn't know how else to make her listen.

"That's an abuse of power," she said, her hand coming up to point at me, her finger stabbing the air.

"Not if you're actually obstructing my investigation, which you will be if you fucking get yourself murdered," I said, struggling to believe we were having this conversation. Avery was a smart woman. Why did she have to be so stubborn?

"Are you serious?" she asked, her dark brows flying up. "You'd really arrest me?"

"In a heartbeat," I said, meaning it. "I won't let you end up like Anna Novak, even if I have to throw you in jail to keep you safe."

"You've got to be kidding me," she said, shoving her hands in her pockets. "You're fucking nuts. I'm sorry that woman died." Tears sprang to her eyes. She dashed them away with the back of her hand. "I'm sorry," she said again, her voice cracking. "I'm so sorry she died, and I'm so, so sorry if what Sterling and I did brought the killer to her door. But doesn't that make you want to find them more? They killed my father. They killed Vanessa. And now they killed this woman, who of the three was probably the most innocent. Where will they stop?"

Finally, she understood. "That's my goddamn point, Avery. They won't. Especially not if you're in their way."

"I'm not in anybody's way," she shouted. "I don't even have my evidence file anymore. You can't just come in here and shut me down. I don't work for you."

"I'm the fucking Chief of Police," I reminded her, trying frantically to figure out how to drag this fight back into the land of reason. I couldn't. Not if she wouldn't recognize she had to get as far from this investigation as possible.

"I'm not breaking any laws at the moment." Her voice caught, and she forced out the rest. "So, I think you should leave." She swallowed hard, yanking her hands from her pockets and crossing her arms across her chest.

"Are you kidding?" I asked, wondering how this had gone so far off the rails so fast. "I'm trying to keep you alive."

"No, you're trying to control me. You aren't my boss or my father. I don't need this from you."

What was she talking about? I was trying to save her. "You don't need this from me?" I shook my head. "You don't want me to look out for you? To protect you? You just want a good fuck and then I get out of your way?"

She stared back at me, her eyes flat. Finally, she shrugged. "Right now, I just want you to leave my brewery."

I turned and strode from the building without another word, my chest hollow and my lungs fighting each breath. That hadn't gone the way I planned. Not that I'd planned it very well.

She'd come around. She had to. I wasn't going to lose her over a stupid argument. The image of the dead woman flashed into my head again. No, I wasn't going to lose her to a knife or a bullet. And if her hating me was the price of keeping her safe, I'd have to find a way to live with that. Because whatever happened, I wouldn't let Avery's body be the next one we found.

Chapter Twenty-One

AVERY

The taproom was slow—not unusual for early Sunday afternoon, even during leaf season. But was it slower than normal? Or was I just paranoid? Hard to tell. I couldn't gauge how much damage Matthew's gossip had been doing to my relationships with other brewers. Clearly, some damage considering what had happened with the Christmas fundraiser. But to our popularity as a local spot to grab a good beer? That was harder to gauge, especially this time of year, when there were so many outsiders around.

I wanted to pretend my crap mood was because I wasn't selling as much beer as usual. But that was a lie. My crap mood was because I hadn't spoken to West in four days. I wanted to say that this was his fault. That he was an overbearing, domineering asshole who wanted to control me. And who was he to tell me what to do? If he really cared about me, really knew me, he'd understand that asking me to walk away from *my* investigation was ridiculous and unfair.

The problem was, I had a sinking feeling in my gut that all of my justifications were bullshit, and that, in this scenario, West was not the one who was wrong.

I'd looked at his number on my phone probably twenty times since our fight, and stopped myself from calling every time. What was I supposed to say? *I'm sorry, you were right?* Was I willing to go that far? *Was* he right —all the way right?

I didn't know, because I was still fucking pissed off, and underneath that, maybe more than a little terrified.

I'd read the article that a local journalist had written about the murder. West hadn't mentioned all the details. Anna Novak could have been stabbed as many as forty times. I couldn't wrap my head around that kind of brutality. Who would do that? Did I want to be in the crosshairs of someone who could stab an innocent woman forty times?

Why would I be that reckless?

Ford's face flashed in my mind. My older brother, who'd been awful to Griffen, but was also the reason I had Sawyers Bend Brewing. He'd looked out for me, run interference with Prentice, and helped give me time to figure out my life rather than let Prentice mold me into the daughter he'd wanted. I wouldn't be who I was or where I was without Ford. And he'd spent a year in prison for our father's murder. Whoever killed Prentice had set Ford up to take that fall and was probably also Anna Novak's murderer.

I didn't know what prison was like—I hoped I'd never find out—but I knew the brother who had gone in was not the same man who came out. And if I turned my back on this quest for answers, I turned my back on Ford and the possibility of him having a future free and clear of Prentice's murder. Unless we found the killer, for the rest of his life, everyone he met would assume he'd killed our father. Ford wasn't a perfect man, but did he deserve that? My heart said no.

I could decide to leave this in West's hands, I knew. But that felt like giving up. He couldn't possibly care as much about this as I did, care about Ford as much as I did.

So, what the fuck did I do?

What I did was pull some beers for a few tourists who trickled in. I gave them my best version of the cheerful bartender smile and made my way down to the other end of the bar, where it was quiet and I didn't have to talk to people. Dave wasn't coming in for a few hours. Until he got here, I'd have to deal with customers, whether I liked it or not.

My phone chimed with a text. Sterling.

Did you call him yet?

I'd been shocked to discover that my baby sister was firmly on West's side. She'd looked a little green when I told her about Anna Novak. Her face had drained of blood, and she'd shaken her head.

"We're in too deep," she'd said. "I need to think about this. Make some calls." I'd left her in her room, her phone to her ear. The next time I saw her, she'd given me a heavy look. "I talked to some people who looked into what happened, and they said to keep our heads down and stay far away."

"So, it's over?" I'd asked, feeling off balance. "We're just going to let it go?"

Sterling had tossed her hair back over her shoulder and rolled her eyes. "Yeah, duh. I don't want to get stabbed forty times."

"Don't we want to find out who—"

Sterling was shaking her head before I could finish. "Not that much, Avery. Seriously, not that much. I have a lot to live for, you know." Her face shifted, the levity draining away. She'd reached out to pull me into a hug—awkward because I was so much taller—but I wrapped my arms around her and we rocked side to side for a minute, my cheek resting on her soft hair.

"Ave," she'd said into my shoulder, "I know you want to solve this. I know you want this to be over."

I squeezed my eyes shut, tears pricking behind my lids. God, did I want this to be over.

"But now's not the time," she'd continued. "At the least, we need to step back and take a break. As a friend told me, it's too hot right now. Let things cool down, and then we can reassess."

When did my sister start sounding so much like Hawk?

"Yeah," I'd said, giving her a squeeze. Sterling had guts. She and Forrest had embarked on a wild scavenger hunt to solve a riddle left behind by his father. They'd made some questionable decisions, put themselves in real danger, and Sterling had been unapologetic about every bit of it. So, if she was saying things were too hot and we needed to back off, maybe my sense of danger was completely out of whack.

I'd been in a holding pattern—too stubborn and mad to talk to West, heartsick at the divide between us, and angry that this was an issue at all.

The door opened, and I pasted a fake smile across my face, letting it fall as I saw Ford walk in. A shadow of shame swept over me as I realized I was disappointed. Somewhere deep inside, I'd secretly been hoping to see West.

Why? My snotty inner voice asked. *So he can apologize for not being wrong?*

Fuck. I shook off the thought and went to greet Ford as he slid onto a barstool.

"Hey, what brings you in here? Need to get out of the house?"

"This is one of the few places it's recommended I go, given the level of security." His eyes flicked up to a camera discreetly installed above the bar, new since the break-in and courtesy of Hawk's team. You'd have to know it was there to spot it, but it had a wide-angle view of the whole taproom.

"What can I get you?" I asked.

"Bartender's choice," Ford said.

I pulled him our stout. A hint of coffee, a hint of chocolate. Perfect for early on Sunday afternoon. He raised an eyebrow as he watched me build his pint, and I smiled, this one genuine.

"Mocha stout," I said. "It's almost a breakfast beer."

"Sounds perfect." Ford nodded, the faintest hint of a

smile curving the side of his mouth. "Quiet this morning."

"Yeah. It could be leaf season starting to taper off. And it's still early."

"Any more trouble from Matthew?" he asked, following my train of thought.

I shrugged. "Not that I know of." I slid the stout across the bar to him.

"You work things out with West?"

Grabbing a damp rag, I wiped the already clean bar in front of me, not meeting Ford's eyes. I jerked a shoulder up in a shrug. I hated this sticky, dark hole in my chest. Guilt. I didn't want to admit I was wrong because I didn't want to be wrong. But I couldn't change what I couldn't change.

"No," I finally said.

Ford nodded again.

"Nothing to say?" I asked, wishing I could just leave well enough alone.

He raised an eyebrow. "I'm not exactly one to advise on romance."

"True," I agreed. Ford had married Vanessa, Griffen's fiancée, and soon regretted it. They'd stuck it out a few years, but he'd ended up divorcing her, and she'd been as miserable an ex-wife as she'd been a wife. He hadn't dated much that I knew of since then. No serious relationships.

"But," I prompted, "since you brought it up."

Ford let out a sigh. "West is a good man."

"He threw you in jail," I said, my voice rising with a sharp edge. Heads turned at the other end of the bar, and

I wished I'd kept my voice down. I was usually better with this whole customer service thing.

"He was doing his job," Ford said, as if it should be obvious. "I respect him. When I was playing things Dad's way, he annoyed the shit out of me. Everything always had to be black and white, by the book. He believes in what he does, Ave. He cares about this town and the people in it. And yeah, he threw me in jail, but he didn't have a choice. Trust me, if I'd had any evidence to clear my name, I would have given it to him. And he would have used it to get me back out. He's never stopped looking. He doesn't even like me, which is fair enough, given that I royally screwed over his best friend. But I know if he had the slightest shred of evidence to clear my name, he'd use it. Because that's the kind of man he is."

"Yeah," I agreed. What else was I going to say? Ford was right. He was fucking right about everything. "I'm an asshole," I muttered.

Ford tipped his chin up. "You're a Sawyer. We don't like to admit when we're wrong."

I didn't like the way that landed. "I don't want to be Dad," I said.

Ford barked out a laugh, his amusement rusty but there. "Ave, you're nothing like Dad. None of us is like Dad, and thank God for that."

We both looked up as the door opened again. My stupid heart wished for West, and again I was disappointed. Then the face came into focus, and I smiled. Here was a friend. Andy Weber, fellow brewer. He worked for one of the big multi-nationals based out of Asheville, saying he liked the health insurance, and the work environment was top-notch. I hadn't seen him in a while, but we'd taken classes on brewing together at AB Tech ages ago and had always been friends.

"Ave, tell me you have some of that fall brew left." He said, leaning on the bar and shooting me a familiar grin.

There was only a slight prick to my heart as I shook my head. "We sold every drop at the thing on Halloween. I have a harvest lager."

"I heard that was good. I'll take that." Andy settled onto a stool.

Ford got up quietly and wandered away, leaving us alone to talk. I was grateful I didn't have to introduce them. After our father's murder, Ford's name wasn't low profile. Neither of us wanted to talk about it.

"How are things going?" Andy asked.

"You mean in general or since I fired Matthew?" I asked.

"Both."

I saw the look on Andy's face and had a sinking feeling in my gut. "This isn't a random visit with an old friend, is it?" I asked, sliding him his beer. He took a long sip, really tasting the beer, and smiled.

"Fucking A, this is great," he said appreciatively. Then he shook his head. "I wish it were a friendly visit." He let out a long sigh. "There's been some talk. The Holiday Jam food truck thing."

"Yeah?" I asked, already feeling the weight of dread pressing on my chest. "Let me guess. The organizers feel that I'm not reliable enough to handle my usual spot, so they're replacing me."

Andy's face fell. "How'd you know? It's not official. Just talk, but—"

"Because it wouldn't be the first time that's happened since I fired Matthew," I said, resigned to the fact that it also wouldn't be the last.

"He's got a mouth on him, that's for sure," Andy said. "I didn't like him when you hired him, but he had the resume." Andy shrugged. "He talks a good game. And a lot of these assholes want to believe it, Ave. You're female and you're a Sawyer. You know, nepo baby, plus what's a woman doing brewing beer? It all snowballs into a big pile of bullshit."

I laughed bitterly. "Yeah, I know."

And I did. That was the core of it. The problem was, I couldn't change who I was, nor did I want to. My father aside, I was proud of where I came from and what I'd made of myself, despite how it looked on the outside.

And fuck anyone who said that I couldn't do this because I was a woman.

"I put in a word for you," he said, leaning forward. "You've got friends in the Brewers Association." He took another long sip of his lager. "I wanted to give you a heads up and tell you to hang in there—there are a lot of people who have your back, and Matthew's still a newcomer, you know? This is going to work itself out. You just keep brewing awesome beer."

"Beer solves all problems, right?" I said with a wry smile.

"Always." Andy came around the bar to give me a hug.

Andy left after draining the rest of his beer. I

watched the door shut behind him and wondered how long I was going to have to *hang in there* before Matthew's poison lost its strength. How long it was going to take before the universe decided I'd learned my lesson and he stopped being such a fucking pain in my ass.

Ford wandered back over, shoving his hands in his back pockets. "Matthew again?"

"Yeah," I said, rolling back my shoulders and lifting my chin. "I can handle it."

"I know you can, Ave. Maybe you should think about asking for help."

I had no idea what he meant by that. Before I could puzzle it out, he said, "Show me your new beer. The one you're formulating to replace the fall brew."

"There's not much to see," I said. After glancing around to see that no one needed a fresh beer, I led Ford back into the brewery. The door swung shut behind us, and I brought him to the long table in the corner covered in rows of brown bottles, all neatly labeled XP 2: experimental version two.

"If it's in bottles, can we drink it?" he asked, glancing at me with curiosity bright in his eyes.

"Not yet. I was thinking we'd try it on Thanksgiving." I'd been toying with the idea. Maybe it would be awful. And if it was, we'd laugh it off and I'd try again. Doing it as a family felt right.

"So, you're almost there." Ford wrapped an arm around my shoulders and gave me a squeeze. I leaned into his side.

"Maybe. If it sucks, I'll tinker with the recipe some more."

"It's not going to suck," he said.

We stood there for a moment, staring at the rows of brown bottles. My new beginning. Maybe.

Ford spoke quietly into the silence. "He's not worth it, Avery."

"Who? Matthew?" I didn't understand what he meant.

"No. Dad. He's not worth you risking your life. You've got talent and a good business, and a man who cares about you. Don't throw it away over Prentice. You'll get yourself killed trying to find out who shot him. The world is a better place with Dad dead, and we both know it. Don't throw away everything you have trying to get him justice."

I stepped back and glared up at my older brother. "This isn't about Prentice. They threw you in prison for a year."

"And now I'm out," Ford said. "I'm here, and I'm fine."

"You're not fine." How could he say he was fine? He was a shadow of the man he'd been.

"Did it ever occur to you that I deserved what I got?" he asked, his tone so reasonable it knocked me back a step.

"What the fuck are you talking about?"

"Avery, I was complicit in so many of the things Dad did. I was involved in letting our brother get kidnapped and almost killed. I could have stopped it, and I didn't, and he—" Ford's voice cut off, and he looked at the floor. "We almost lost Finn, Avery, and it would have been my fault. And that's not even the worst thing I did. If my penance is spending a year in prison and everyone thinking I'm a murderer, I can live with that. If you get yourself killed trying to clear my name..." His voice cracked, and my breath caught in my chest.

"Ford, I..."

His eyes met mine, raw pain burning in the green depths. "Everything I've already done is bad enough. Don't make me live with losing you, too." He blinked, and the intensity of his emotion dimmed. "Go talk to West," he said seriously. "I get that after Matthew, you're wary of being manipulated or controlled, but that's not what's happening here."

I sighed, seeing it clearly for the first time in four days.

"Yeah, okay," I said, feeling like the biggest jerk on the planet. Did I only think about myself and what I wanted?

"You'll back off and let the investigation go?" Ford pressed.

I nodded. "I'm sorry. I was so focused on finding the answers, I didn't think about getting hurt or how you'd feel about it."

"I know you didn't, Ave," he said, pulling me into a tight hug.

He hung around for another stout, and we played a game of checkers at the bar before his phone chimed and he pushed back his seat. "My ride back to the Manor is here."

I watched him go, wondering how my independent brother could tolerate being driven around, always under guard. He was essentially a prisoner again. It made me wonder how bad actual prison had been, if this was tolerable.

Dave came through the door, and I waved, ready to hand off the bar to him and disappear into my office or go home. I stared at the screen of my phone, thinking. I could text West, ask if he could talk. Or I could go by his place. I could do something other than wallow, feeling like a brat for taking out all my frustration on him when he was just trying to do his job.

As I stared blindly at the screen, a text message popped up. It was Bob James from Wild Haven Brewing.

> Do you have time to talk? I'm in my office until 6.
>
> There are things you should know.

Bob had replaced me with Bear Run Brewing for the kids' Christmas charity event. Did he want me to come back? No, that couldn't be it. He would have said in the text. But maybe not. What did he know that I should know? It had to do with Matthew. I was sure of that. When it came to Matthew, I could use all the ammo I could get.

> Be there in 15.

Seconds later, a thumbs-up emoji popped up on the screen. Maybe Bob could tell me something I could use to shut Matthew up once and for all.

And then afterwards, I could pop by West's. And we'd talk.

Chapter Twenty-Two

AVERY

There are things you should know.

Bob's text ran through my head on repeat as I made the fifteen-minute drive to Wild Haven Brewing. My mind was racing, trying to figure out all the things he could tell me. He'd changed his mind again on the holiday event—Matthew was out, and I was back in. Or Matthew had told him some outrageous lie, and he wanted to know if it was true. Maybe Matthew had been fired from Bear Run Brewing.

Wishful thinking. There wouldn't be a satisfying resolution to the situation with Matthew. I'd made my bed, and I'd used poor judgment in who I'd invited into it. Now I was dealing with the fallout.

It wasn't just that I'd broken up with Matthew. Knowing him, my guess was that being fired was a bigger hit to his ego than the end of our relationship, but the fact that I'd dumped him first couldn't help. I'm sure in his mind that's not how this was supposed to go. I was supposed to fall in line, happily providing him with sex and my business to run, while I did what I was told and brewed amazing beer. There was only one part of that I was interested in, and it was the part about brewing amazing beer. Not Matthew.

One thing I could say about myself—I wasn't perfect, but at least when I made mistakes, I tried not to repeat them. No more workplace romances. Of course, that thought sent my brain ricocheting straight to West.

After I talked to Bob, I was going to hunt down West Garfield, apologize for being a jerk, tell him to stop trying to boss me around, and hope we could put this bullshit behind us. I felt a flush of shame at the way I'd overreacted. I was on a hair trigger these days when it came to being told what to do by men who thought they knew everything. But my issues with my father weren't West's fault, they were mine. It wasn't cool of me to make West pay for my bad judgment with Matthew, or my instinctive pushback when it came to being told what to do.

Anxiety tugged at my gut. West might not give me another chance. I hadn't said anything unforgivable, but I'd been a jerk. But everybody was sometimes, right? Mentally, I crossed my fingers, hoping West was as forgiving as I thought he was.

The parking lot of Wild Haven Brewing was deserted except for a single car, parked on the edge of the lot. I didn't recognize it, but I didn't know what Bob drove. Since Wild Haven didn't have a taproom, do tours, or sell beer on-site, it made sense that no one would be here on a Sunday. And I knew better than anyone how much paperwork I could plow through when no one else was around. Still, there was an abandoned air to the place. If that was Bob's car, why had he parked so far from the door?

I shook my head. I was just looking for trouble, that's all. I pulled in, choosing a spot a few spaces from the door —unlike Bob—and hopped out. The glass door sported a colorful logo with illustrated hops and wheat spilling from a basket. I tugged at the handle. It swung open in silence to reveal the cavernous interior of the brewery. With concrete floors and high ceilings, the building was basically a big warehouse divided into sections. In one corner, tall stainless-steel vats were lined up in neat rows. On the other side, Bob had set up his bottling and labeling equipment. Wild Haven wasn't a rival to one of the big commercial breweries closer to Asheville, but it was a whole lot bigger than Sawyers Bend Brewing. I looked around with envy.

Someday, I told myself, I'd have a big, fancy bottling machine like this one. Someday, I'd brew beer in vats the size of Bob's. I'd have to recover from the current slow-down in business first, but I could get there. I wasn't going to give up, no matter how much trouble Matthew caused.

It was dim inside, and only half of the overhead lights were on. I walked in further, calling out, "Bob? It's Avery."

I'd never been in his office, so I wasn't sure which direction to head. My eyes scanned the big space. On the other side of the bottling machine, I caught sight of a few doors, all closed. Two had windows that looked out into the main space of the brewery, and in one of them, the lights were on. Bingo. With his door closed, he probably hadn't heard me arrive.

I made my way across the brewery, ducking under the rolling track of the bottling machine. "Bob?" I called out again, not wanting to sneak up on him.

No answer. No sound at all. A tickle of nerves went up my spine.

There wasn't anything wrong that I could see, but still—it was too quiet. Why was it so quiet?

Because no one's here, Avery, I told myself.

I reached the door to the office I thought was Bob's and knocked. No answer. Okay, that was weird. I stood there for a second, my hands at my sides, wondering what to do. Knock again?

I did. Still no answer. I tried the knob, and it turned in my hand. I pushed the door open.

"Hey Bob, sorry to barge in, but—"

The office was empty.

Not what I was expecting. Lights on, door unlocked, Bob nowhere in sight. Could he be in the bathroom or something? Maybe. I pulled out my phone and texted him.

> Bob, I'm here. Can't find you.

The message went undelivered.

"Bob?" I called out again. I'd take a walk around. If I didn't spot him, then what? Logic said: go home and try again later. *There are things you should know.* Fuck, I wanted to know the things I should know, and I didn't want to wait. I wanted to know now.

Something on the other side of the room caught my eye—a shadow of movement and a sound. A rustle. Kind of a splash. A splash of what? My heart stopped at the thought that maybe one of the vats was leaking. But no. No. These looked like perfectly maintained, newish stainless-steel vats. No way they had a leak.

The smell hit me, acrid and sharp. That wasn't beer. That was... Gas.

What?

I barely had time to register the scent filling the vast room when flames exploded on the other side of the brewery. Holy shit, that was a lot of fire. I wasn't close enough to be singed, and still the heat was a slap in the face, the smell choking my lungs.

Fuck, fuck, fuck. How the hell had that happened? My mind raced, thinking through what could cause spontaneous combustion. Nothing came to mind.

I bolted for the front door, only to find it locked. It must have locked behind me, but even as I had the thought, I realized, wouldn't it open from the inside? There was no reason for it to lock from the outside on its own.

My brain caught up with my panic in a rush. The fire was moving fast, licking up the walls to touch the metal ceiling, consuming the drywall as if it were ravenous. Thank God most of what was in here was metal and glass, but that wouldn't stop those flames. And I was right in the center of it, thick, black smoke displacing the breathable air faster than I could have imagined.

There had to be another door. *Think*, Avery. The metal receiving door was on the side of the building where the flames had started. If it had been open, I might have been able to get out that way. But not if I had to stop, unlatch it, and wrestle it up. The whole wall was on fire, and I didn't know how long it would be before this whole place collapsed on my head. I knew fire could move fast, but not like this. What had it been—a minute, a minute and a half?

Backing away, I didn't even realize I was retreating from the flames until I slammed into a metal vat. I had to get out. The front door was glass, but... Could I break it by throwing something through it?

I inched past the vat, looking along the wall for another exit. There couldn't be just the two doors. There had to be another way out. I ran, jumping over a crate on the floor, turning to ease past another vat, looking for a window—anything—and finding only white drywall. Fuck. Black smoke was filling the room. I pulled my shirt over my face, coughing, and got down on my hands and knees.

My brain couldn't catch up with my body. My nervous system had tilted straight into abject terror. I had to get out, and I couldn't believe how fast those flames were devouring the walls, already nibbling at the edges of the ceiling above. Was the whole thing going to fall on my head? It could, but I'd probably be dead from smoke inhalation first. Fuck.

My shoulder bumped into a metal stool, and I thought of the glass front door. I was probably shatter-proof, but I'd seen enough movies to know there was some kind of backdraft thing with opening doors and a fire. But my other choice was to stay here, and that would definitely kill me. Metal stool and glass door it was.

Dragging the stool, I crawled as fast as I could to the door, trying to stay under the smoke. I only stood when I was there, struggling to drag in a breath through my shirt and coughing instead. I swung the stool, the hit glancing off. Spiderwebs crackled across the glass. I swung again, my lungs catching on the black, acrid smoke, the cough doubling me over. I didn't have time to cough. The heat was unbearable, sweat pouring down my face and stinging my eyes.

I slammed the metal stool into the door again, the distant shriek of sirens hitting my ears. Thank fucking God. I held my breath until I saw stars, slamming the stool into the door again and again, the spiderweb of cracks spreading, deepening, bits of glass crumbling out. My vision was going grey, I gave one last desperate swing of the stool, and the glass shattered enough for me to dive through.

Sweet, fresh air teased my nose. I tried to drag in a breath and choked on it, rolling to my side, lungs heaving, desperate for oxygen. A shadow fell across my face, and I blinked up at a firefighter in uniform, his face grave. He looked across me at someone else. I turned my head to see Jim, one of West's deputies, staring down at me.

"Thought you were smarter than this, Avery," he said. "You need medical attention?"

I shook my head slowly, my lungs finally relaxed enough to pull in air. I lay flat on my back on the pavement, staring up at the blue sky and the clouds of smoke billowing from Wild Haven Brewing. Firefighters streamed into the building. More sirens wailed in the distance. I forced myself to focus on Jim, still leaning over me, a look of disgust on his face that I couldn't process.

"On your feet," he said.

I wobbled as I stood, not quite understanding what was happening. I was alive and breathing fresh air, while behind me, Wild Haven Brewing burned. It had happened so fast. I'd only been in the building for minutes. How had they gotten here so quickly? I hadn't called, too focused on getting out before the smoke and flames took me.

I straightened, drawing in a breath, and my lungs caught. A second later, I doubled over, hands on my knees, hacking, tears streaming from my eyes. When I thought I could talk, I rasped out, "How did you get here so fast?"

I straightened, and a hand closed over my wrist. Jim. He grabbed my other wrist, slapped on cold, metal cuffs, and said, "Call came in ten minutes ago. A trespasser at Wild Haven Brewing. Someone saw a tall, dark-haired woman unloading gas cans from the back of her vehicle." He looked over to my car and the three red gas cans sitting behind it on the pavement.

"Those aren't mine," I said, blinking stinging tears from my eyes.

"Sure," Jim said. "But considering I got a report of arson and found you here with gas cans by your car, I'm going to arrest you, and we'll let the judge sort it out."

I froze, struggling to understand what was happening as he roughly grabbed my arm and led me to his cruiser. "I didn't—I just got here. Bob texted me." I was babbling, but I couldn't get my head around what the deputy had said.

The call came in ten minutes ago? Had I even been here ten minutes ago? Maybe, but barely. How? There definitely hadn't been a fire ten minutes ago unless—I felt like I was in a puzzle someone had tossed in the air, the pieces falling everywhere, and I couldn't put them together to make a picture that made sense.

"I didn't set a fire," I said. "I just got here."

"Save it." Jim splayed his hand over the top of my head and pushed me into the back seat of his cruiser, closing the door with a thunk.

"Don't I get a phone call?" I asked as soon as he got in the driver's seat.

"Later," was all he said.

I craned my neck to see another fire truck pulling into the parking lot. I hoped they could save Bob's brewery. Whatever was going on here, I was pretty sure he was an innocent victim, just like me.

"This is absurd," I said. "I didn't set that fire, and if I did, I wouldn't have been stupid enough to leave gas cans right behind my car."

"You would if you didn't think you were going to get caught," Jim said. "Bad move, locking yourself inside."

"I didn't lock myself inside," I said, trying to control the temper that wanted to fill the space left behind by adrenaline. I needed a shower. To see a doctor about the raw scrape of every breath I took. Instead, I was cuffed and locked in the back of a police cruiser.

Jim let out a sigh and met my eyes in the rearview mirror. "Avery, I'm not in the habit of helping arsonists.

But since I know our chief has a soft spot for you and your brother's a good guy, I'm going to tell you this: keep your mouth shut. We have you at the scene of a reported arson with three empty cans of gas next to your car, and you were the only person on the property. It doesn't look great. If you're innocent, you're going to have to hope someone can sort it out for you. But right now, every word you say can only make things worse. Do us both a favor and shut up."

I nodded, in shock, but with it enough to listen. He made a good point. I wasn't an arsonist. I also wasn't a lawyer. Or a cop. If I knew the right thing to say to get these cuffs off my wrists, I'd say it. But I didn't. All I could do was wait for my phone call or for someone to tell West I'd been arrested.

And then I remembered what happened when my father died. Someone had seen Ford driving away from Heartstone Manor, in a rush, looking angry. They'd found his shoe prints outside the window and the murder weapon in his closet. That was enough. He'd spent a year in prison because even with that shitty evidence, he hadn't been able to prove that he didn't do it.

Just like I couldn't prove I hadn't set the fire.

Fuck. My gut turned cold, and my heart raced. Ten minutes before, I'd been hoping I didn't die in the fire. Now, I wasn't that much better off. I was alive, and that was something. I'd take it. But someone had set me up for arson. And the last time that happened to my family, the victim had gone to prison. Ford only got back out because whoever set him up wanted him somewhere he was easier to kill. That was our best guess, at least. So, what did that mean for me?

I gritted my teeth and let out a long breath. I hated being helpless. I hated not being able to solve my own problems. And here I was, in the back of a police cruiser, my hands cuffed, and there wasn't a goddamn thing I could do about it. Not yet.

The police station wasn't a long ride. Jim led me into the building, one hand tight on my arm. Did he think I was going to run? Booking went by in a blur—the mug shot, the fingerprints—and then the cuffs came off, and I was shoved into a holding cell. The Sawyers Bend Police Station only had a few cells. Today, they were all empty, except for one on the end that had a big guy snoring on a bench, probably picked up the night before for being drunk and disorderly.

I sat, braced my arms on my knees, and prepared to wait for rescue.

Chapter Twenty-Three

WEST

"**W**hat the fuck are you talking about?" I demanded into my phone. It was the only thing I could think of to say. Jim had arrested Avery for arson? "Back up and tell me again what happened."

Jim went through it a second time. The call to emergency services reporting a trespasser at Wild Haven Brewing, someone claiming they'd seen a tall woman with dark hair carrying gas cans inside. A second call reporting flames at the back of the brewery. Jim had arrived along with the firefighters to see smoke pouring from the building. Then Avery exploded out of the door. He said it looked like she'd used a metal stool to break her way out. They'd already seen gas cans by her car.

There wasn't a world where I could picture Avery doing something like this. But the evidence was damning all around.

Whatever had happened, Avery was in the thick of it.

I drove by the scene. The cans had been taken into

evidence already, and it looked like they had the fire under control. It had been dry the past few weeks, and there were dead leaves everywhere. It was just good luck that the wind had been quiet enough not to spread embers. As it was, the fire crew had been busy beating down the flames that had popped up in the grasses around the brewery.

"I had a word with the fire chief," Jim said. "Definitely arson. You could smell the accelerant."

And Avery was in jail. My jail.

I got back in the car, made the short drive into town, and parked in front of the station, my mind slowly turning over everything I knew. The thing was, when I'd arrested Ford for killing Prentice, I'd been seventy-five percent sure he hadn't done it. After I'd talked to him, I'd been ninety percent sure he hadn't done it.

But with people, you never knew. I'd learned in doing this job that you could think you understood everything about a human, but there were always hidden layers. Everyone had secrets. I hadn't had a choice with Ford. The evidence had been too good. My gut wasn't any help when we had the murder weapon in his closet, witnesses who saw him fleeing the scene, and his footprints outside his father's window.

With Avery, I had a caller describing her at the scene and the gas cans by her car. But if what Jim and the fire crew had told me was true, she'd been trapped in the building. My heart stuttered at the thought of what would have happened if she hadn't found that stool and broken through the door. I couldn't function if I let the picture develop in my mind. Avery, on the floor, passed out as flames raced closer, the air gone.

Stop thinking about it.

Right now, I had to focus on being a cop. I had an arson to deal with—that I knew with one hundred percent certainty. I'd smelled the gas myself through the acrid black smoke. But was Avery my arsonist? My heart and my gut said no fucking way. But there were those gas cans. And the witness who described her at the scene.

I walked through the front doors, nodding at Amanda at the front desk. She called out, "Chief," but I waved her off. I unlocked and pushed through the multiple sets of doors between the reception area and the cells.

Avery sat on the bench in the first cell, her arms braced on her knees, head down. At the sound of the door opening, she looked up. Soot and sweat streaked her face, her eyes bloodshot and swollen.

"West! West, I swear I didn't—"

I held up a hand, but she kept going.

"I know they said they found gas cans, that someone saw me, but I—"

"I know," I said, cutting her off.

She fell silent, staring up at me from across the cell. I didn't say anything else. I knew, down to the core of my soul, that Avery Sawyer had not set that fire. It didn't matter that all the evidence said she did it.

This was where I was supposed to turn around and walk away. Let her have her phone call, probably to Harvey, or Cole Haywood, since this was a criminal offence. My job was to get the wheels of justice turning and leave this to the system I believed in. That was my job. I was West Garfield. I always did my job. No bending the rules. No exceptions.

But looking at Avery—her sweat-stained face and tangled hair, the smell of smoke poisoning the air around her—all I could feel was grateful that she was alive. Fire moved fast, and she'd been trapped. I forced the thought from my mind. If I thought about what could have happened...

I needed a clear head. I had to follow the evidence, but this time the evidence was pointing at the wrong person. And this time, I couldn't let the wheels of justice do their job. Not if it meant keeping Avery locked in a cell.

"Do you need anything?" I asked. "Water, coffee, food?"

Her eyes slid away as she realized I wasn't going to let her out. She shook her head, then said, her voice scratchy and low, "Water. Can I have some water?"

I nodded and turned for the door. I grabbed a few waters and a granola bar from my office, brought them back, and handed them to her through the bars.

"Do I get a phone call?" she asked, hesitant, trying, I guessed, to read my mood.

I couldn't give her anything.

"Not yet," I said. "Drink that water. Eat the granola bar. I'll be back."

I turned to leave. From behind me, I heard her call, "West!" but I didn't stop. I couldn't.

I left the station as abruptly as I'd entered, ignoring Amanda at the front desk yet again. Jim caught up to me as I strode into the parking lot.

"Chief, I'm sorry. I had to. We got that call, and the cans were right by her car. But, Avery? I wouldn't have thought— Maybe I shouldn't have—"

I shook my head. "You did exactly what you're supposed to."

"She had her phone call?" he asked.

I shook my head. "Not yet."

"Should I—"

"She's fine. I gave her some water. I have to check on a few things, then I'll take care of it. You do your job. Process the evidence. Go take another look at the scene. Bring someone else out with you. Find out who called it in. Talk to the fire crew. Get their statements. You know the drill."

"Yes, Chief," he said, ducking his head as he went into the station. He didn't like this much more than I did. Avery wasn't her father. Not even close. No one in town would want to see her in jail for arson. And there wouldn't be a thing I could do about it if I didn't find a reason to let her out.

I went to the only person who could help me. Normally, I'd walk to my parents' house, but I didn't want to run into anyone on the street. I drove the short distance and let myself in, finding my father in his study, watching a football game.

"Can I turn this off for a minute?" I asked.

He looked up in surprise. "West. Didn't expect to see you today." He paused, taking in my expression. "What happened?"

I sat in the leather armchair opposite his. "Avery Sawyer was just arrested for arson. Wild Haven Brewing.

No casualties, but it's looking like a total loss; burned to the ground."

He stared at me, jaw dropped. I didn't think I'd ever seen such an undignified expression on my father's face. He recovered quickly, snapping his mouth closed. He rose from his chair slowly.

"That calls for a bourbon." He raised his eyebrow my way.

Normally, I'd say, "No, I'm working." But it was my day off, and a bourbon sounded like a great fucking idea. I answered with a short nod, and his eyes flared just enough to let me know he'd been expecting me to decline. I would have expected myself to decline. But I was upside down and inside out, and nothing felt normal. Avery was in jail. My jail.

"You arrested her brother when you knew he was innocent," my father said, handing me a cut crystal glass with a finger of bourbon.

I leaned in and took a sniff. He'd gone for the good stuff. That wasn't a great sign. I sipped and then nodded. "I did," I said.

"Even though you knew he didn't do it."

"I didn't know," I said.

"But you were pretty damn sure."

"I was pretty damn sure," I agreed. "But the evidence —we had too much pointing to guilt and none pointing to innocence. I had to do my job."

"You always do your job, West," my father said, sitting back down in his chair and taking a sip of bourbon. "I give you a hard time about it, but I've always admired that about you. You don't take shit from anyone, and you do your job—even when it's hard and uncomfortable and inconvenient. You do your job." He sat back. "What kind of evidence do you have on Avery?"

I told him.

He shook his head. "Seems a little thin."

"Agreed," I said. "The problem is, she was there in the building while it was burning. Jim already checked with Bob—he didn't ask her to come to the brewery. She didn't have a reason to be there, but she was."

"Someone is messing with her," he said, taking a slow sip from his glass. "Sounds like she almost died. Anyone checked her lungs out?"

Both thoughts sent a spike of fear through me. Someone had tried to have her killed; that was obvious to me now. And her lungs? Shit. No. She wasn't coughing, seemed like she was breathing okay. Other than being disheveled and dirty, she hadn't looked injured. The shock of seeing her in jail had knocked all logic out of my head.

"I should have had her checked out," I said under my breath.

"Well, you still can," my father said reasonably.

Sudden urgency to get Avery to the doctor pushed me forward. "I need a favor."

My father's eyebrows flew up, and he took another sip of bourbon. "Well, pigs must be flying if you're asking me for a favor. What can I do for you, son?"

"I need you to call Judge Claremont. I want her released on her own recognizance."

My father drew in a long breath and let it out slowly.

"I've never asked—" I reminded him.

He cut me off with a shake of his head. "I know you've never asked." He studied my face for a long moment. "She didn't do it," he said, and I wasn't sure if it was a question or a statement.

"No," I said, setting the bourbon on the side table. A sip had been enough. I needed to keep my head straight.

"And you're sure?" he pressed. "Even with thin evidence, it doesn't mean she's innocent. Even if someone was trying to set her up, she may be into something you don't know about."

"You don't know her," I said. "You don't know anything about her if you think she would have done this."

My father leaned forward in his chair. "I know enough. I know people are capable of a lot of things we don't want to think they could do." He raised an eyebrow. "I know you two have been seeing each other. Your mother wants to know why she hasn't come to dinner yet."

I scrubbed a hand across my face. "Because it's new. Because we hadn't gotten to that yet." I drew in a breath and let it out. "We talked about Thanksgiving."

My father's eyes brightened. "Really? Well, that's interesting. Your mother would love to have her for Thanksgiving."

I shook my head. How could we be having this conversation right now? Avery needed to see the doctor. And she was safe enough in my jail, for now, but if someone was setting her up, I needed to get her out of there, not talk holiday plans with my father. It was easier to answer than to try to put him off. "She wanted to invite us to Heartstone Manor for Thanksgiving. She thought it'd be fun—a big family holiday. Edgar and Harvey will be there."

"So, it has gotten that far," he said, and the simple confirmation shook me.

I nodded, trying to swallow past the lump in my throat. Despite our argument the other day, and her kicking me out of the brewery, I hadn't doubted we'd figure it out. I could be an overbearing, bossy pain in the ass sometimes. It went with the job.

Who was I kidding? It was who I was. I wanted everyone safe and happy and whole, and sometimes I thought the best way to do that was for everyone to do what I said. Made sense to me. She was wrong about chasing the necklace. But I understood why she didn't want to give up. I got the pull of family and justice better than most people. We would have worked it out.

But now—

"How are you so sure she didn't set that fire?" my father asked, interrupting my thoughts.

"She didn't do it, Dad. Not in a million years. She doesn't have it in her." There was a lot I didn't know, but I was dead certain about that. Avery hadn't set that fire.

My father nodded and stood. "Finish that bourbon. I'll be back." He took his phone with him.

I looked at my abandoned glass and left it where it was. I had work to do. Step one: get Avery out of jail. There was the fast way and the slow way. The slow way was to investigate the crime until we found proof of her innocence, or wait, press charges, and hope the judge granted bail. All of that meant leaving Avery in jail overnight. And that wasn't going to happen. No fucking way.

She hadn't set that fire. But someone had. And unfortunately, the list of prospects was too long. At the top of the list was Matthew, the main person I knew who had a specific grudge against Avery. But since Prentice's death, the Sawyers had faced varying kinds of sabotage and outright attacks. Someone had gone after the Inn at Sawyers Bend, trying to dump cockroaches in the air intake and canceling produce orders. That had escalated to an outright attack that had been meant for Royal Sawyer. Not long after that, Ford's ex-wife had been killed in the gardens of the Inn in such a way that if Tenn's wife, Scarlett, hadn't been at the right place at the right time, the murder most certainly would have been pinned on him.

And now we had another Sawyer who looked guilty of a crime I was absolutely certain she hadn't committed. But someone wanted me to think Avery Sawyer was at fault.

Who? And how the hell was I going to figure it out in time to keep her out of jail for good?

One thing at a time, I reminded myself as my father walked back into the room.

"Paperwork's being faxed over. You'll have it in a few minutes. You can go get your woman out of jail, though I'd recommend you keep it quiet."

I raised an eyebrow, and he explained what I would have put together already if I hadn't been so rattled by the sight of the woman I loved behind bars. The thought rocked me. Was that who she was? The woman

I loved? Wasn't this too fast? Weren't we just having fun?

No. This wasn't just fun. Avery was more than a woman I'd known most of my life, more than my best friend's little sister. She was mine. I'd claimed her with that first kiss, and I wasn't letting go. We could do this slowly, if that's what she needed, but Avery belonged with me.

My father watched with amused patience as my brain caught up with my heart. When he knew he had my attention, he said, "Whoever did this wants you to think she's guilty."

I followed his train of thought. "So, I'll let him think I bought it, though, if that's the plan, I should leave her in jail."

My father shook his head. "But you're not going to do that."

"No, I'm not." I wasn't leaving her sitting in that cell, even if it was the strategic thing to do. She needed a doctor, a hot shower, and rest. And I needed her behind the walls of Heartstone Manor, insulated by Hawk's security team, out of reach of whoever had set that fire and almost killed her.

"I'm proud of you, son," my father said.

"Because I'm breaking the law to get my girlfriend out of jail?" I asked, a tiny smile cracking the side of my mouth.

He smiled and shook his head. "You make it sound so simple, but I know it's not. Not for you who wants everything to be black and white, right or wrong. But life isn't like that, West. You know as well as I do, most of life is grey, and sometimes we have to do the wrong thing to do the right thing. That girl doesn't belong in jail, and we both know it."

"You don't know her well enough to say that," I said.

"But I know you." His eyes warmed as he stood, crossing the room to open a cabinet that hid his home office equipment. He pulled papers off the fax machine and handed them to me. "If you believe she's innocent, that's good enough for me."

"Thanks, Dad." I leaned in to give him a one-armed hug.

"Tell Avery we'll be at Thanksgiving dinner," he called after me.

I drove back to the station in a daze. On the way to my parents' house, I'd imagined begging my father for help while he lorded it over me. We'd fought so often over my refusal to bend the rules, I'd figured he'd make me work for it. I'd forgotten that at the end of the day, he was still my father. He might wish I were more like him, but he loved me. He wanted me to be happy. And, the cynical side of my mind reminded me, he probably didn't hate the idea of me hooking up with a Sawyer.

Putting my vehicle in park, I sat behind the wheel for a minute, trying to put together a game plan. I had the judge's order to get Avery out of jail. That was step one. Now I had to figure out what came next.

Chapter Twenty-Four

AVERY

I was not enjoying jail.

I'd made the mistake of drinking both waters along with the granola bar before I realized that if I wanted to do anything about my full bladder, I'd have to use the exposed toilet in the corner—and that was not happening. I could probably start shouting to get someone's attention, but the indignity of that kept my mouth shut. I could hold it for now.

I paced the cell, waiting for something to happen—anything. Since West left, I'd been alone in here except for the still-sleeping drunk at the other end. The door at the end of the hall was closed, cutting off the rest of the police station from this small block of cells.

I couldn't stop trying to play out what would happen next. I knew West wouldn't abandon me here, even if he was still angry at me over our argument. He would, at the very least, call Griffen and tell him his sister was in jail. He wouldn't trash a lifelong friendship over the small fight we'd had. Unless he was angrier than I'd realized.

I shook my head, striding from one side of the cell to the other. It was possible, but it didn't feel right. West was mad. I'd been mad. Neither of us was pissed off enough to do anything unforgivable.

But I couldn't stop thinking about Ford—about his guilty plea and the year he'd spent in prison. They hadn't had much more on him than they seemed to have on me. At least no one had been hurt at the brewery. That I knew of. Fuck, I didn't know anything, locked back here by myself.

Hold it together, Avery.

And I would. I could. I was not going to fall apart now, but I hated this cell. The cold concrete and metal bars, the flaking paint, and the smell of sweat and the reek of smoke coming from me. I needed a shower and clean clothes. I wanted to go to sleep for a week. I wanted out.

I crossed my arms over my chest and slowed my pacing, my bladder making itself more known. Finally, I gave up and sat, squeezing my knees together. How long had I been here? I didn't wear a watch these days, and they'd taken my phone. It was hard to gauge the passage of time. There was a window opposite the cell, but it was frosted over, with metal lines crisscrossing the glass. The light coming through was the same shade of weak yellow it had been when I'd arrived.

The door at the end of the hall swung open, and West was there. He met my eyes but said nothing. I couldn't read his expression. He looked serious. Was he mad? He was something, but whatever it was, he kept it tucked deep inside, and I couldn't read his face.

He approached the door to the cell and pulled out a set of keys. "Let's go," he said, unlocking the door and swinging it open.

I followed him to the door at the end of the hall. When he stayed silent, I swallowed my humiliation and said, "Bathroom?"

West's step hitched, and he stopped, turning and pointing to a door on the same hall as his office. "Be quick," he said.

I popped in, relieved my painful bladder, and washed my hands longer than usual, as if I could somehow get the smell of smoke off me just by cleaning my hands. West was waiting for me in the hall when I exited the bathroom. He lifted his chin, pointing to a door I hadn't noticed off to the left. I followed and found myself in the rear parking lot of the police station.

"Where are we going?" I asked.

"Clinic first, to get you checked out," he said, leading me to his SUV.

"I think I'm fine," I said, very aware that I was not wearing handcuffs. Why not? I wanted to ask, but I kept my mouth shut, not entirely sure I wanted the answer. "I haven't coughed in a while."

"I want the doc to check out your lungs," West said. I knew by his tone that resisting would be a waste of time.

"Okay," I agreed. I'd had one argument with West over stupid shit this week. I didn't want to another. I'd been caught in a burning building, too frantic to get out to really think about how much smoke I might have inhaled. I knew that could be dangerous. Considering he might bring me straight back to that cell afterward, it made sense to enjoy the fresh air while I had it.

The short drive to the clinic was silent. West appeared occupied by his thoughts, and I was too much of a chicken to start a conversation. It felt like an awkward time to apologize for my part in our fight. And considering I was a suspect in a felony, maybe I should take Jim's advice and keep my mouth shut.

West led me into the clinic, where the receptionist waved us straight back to an exam room. We weren't there more than a minute before Dr. Green stepped in. I didn't know him well; he was new to town, but he'd been in for a beer once or twice.

He slipped a pulse ox monitor on my finger and pulled out his stethoscope. "I don't need you to get into a gown," he said, "but if you could pull up the back of your shirt, I'll have a listen."

The cold stethoscope burned icy circles into my skin as I drew in the deepest breaths I could manage without hacking my lungs out.

"I think you got lucky, Avery," Dr. Green said. "Your lungs sound okay, blood oxygen and pulse rate are normal. It was smart to come in and get checked, but you're good to go."

"Thanks, Doc," I said.

"Anytime."

My gut went cold again as I followed West out of the clinic and back to his SUV. That had been too fast, and I wasn't ready to go back to that concrete box, to breathe in stale sweat and the reek of smoke clinging to my skin. But when we pulled out onto the main road, West didn't turn toward the station.

"Where are we going?" I asked, breaking the heavy silence.

"My place," he said.

I stared at him, eyes wide, mouth hanging open just enough that I probably looked like a stunned fish. "Aren't I supposed to be in prison?"

"Jail," West corrected, "not prison. Prison is something else. And no."

"Did you find who set the fire?" I asked, thoroughly confused. They must have found the arsonist if he was letting me out.

West shook his head. "Not yet. But I will."

"Then how? Jim arrested me." I couldn't make the pieces fit in my head. Nothing I knew of West jived with him letting a prisoner out of jail just because. I'd known West most of my life; he'd always been a by-the-book, black and white kind of guy, even when he was a kid. "Then how?" I asked again.

West pulled into his driveway, put the SUV in park, and turned to look at me, really look at me. I still couldn't read his expression, or maybe I was afraid to.

"I called in a favor. Judge Claremont released you on your own recognizance. You can't leave town, but for now, you don't need to sit in jail either." He rounded the hood and came to open my door.

I sat there feeling poleaxed. West had called in a favor to get me out of jail. I couldn't believe the words that came out of my mouth as I jumped out of the car. "You can't, West. Why would you—"

"Not out here," he said, closing my door and guiding me up the steps to his porch, staying close, as if shielding me from view.

I followed him inside, tension building until I wanted to explode with words. The second the door was shut, I did. "You called in a favor to get me out? West, is that going to get you in trouble? You can't... You never call in favors. You never make exceptions."

"Avery," he shot out, cutting me off. "I wasn't leaving you in there."

"I didn't set the fire," I said.

"I know that," he shouted, throwing his arms out. "For fuck's sake, Avery, of course I know that. In a million years you'd never, ever set another brewer's place on fire—even one who screwed you over."

His words startled a laugh out of me. "I noticed you didn't say *in a million years you'd never set a fire.*"

West raised an eyebrow and crossed his arms over his chest. "I can think of a few scenarios in which you might be inspired to burn something to the ground. I haven't forgotten that bonfire of your father's things. But not like this. I know you didn't do it."

"West," I took a step closer, reaching up to lay a hand on his crossed arms. "Jim found evidence. You didn't let Ford—"

"I'm not in love with Ford," he burst out. "Okay? And I wasn't leaving you sitting in that cell. No fucking way. Understand?"

"What?" I stared up at him, shocked to my core. I hadn't thought about love, but the idea didn't make me want to run. I didn't know what to say about that part.

Not yet. But I knew something else. "West," I said, squeezing his arm, "I don't want you to sacrifice who you are for me."

"You want to go back to that cell?" he asked.

"I really don't." I couldn't lie about that.

"Good, because I'm not taking you back. I need you to lie low. If we were really playing this smart, I'd leave you in there so whoever really set that fire thinks they're in the clear. But that plan involves letting you sit in jail alone, and I'm not doing that. We'll have to go with Plan B."

"What's Plan B?" I asked.

"Plan B is you lie low, and I do everything I can to find whoever set that fire as fast as possible before I have to send you back to jail."

"What if we can't find the person responsible?" I asked, my head spinning.

West loved me? He was putting his integrity on the line to keep me out of jail. He had to love me to do that.

"I'll find them," West said. "And just to be clear, I'm investigating this one, not you. Got it?"

I let out a breath, dropping my hand from his arm. Stepping back, I shoved my hands in my pockets and forced myself to meet his eyes. "Yeah, I get it. And I'm sorry about the thing the other day. I shouldn't have kicked you out of my brewery. It was childish. I was just really fucking mad, and I didn't want to say anything I'd regret, and then I did anyway. I'm sorry. I just—"

"Yeah, I know," he said. "You've had it up to here with people, especially men, telling you what to do and how to do it and acting like you aren't smart enough to figure out your own life."

The tension in my shoulders drained away as his words flowed over me, saying exactly what was in my heart. I was pretty sure it was a good thing West thought he loved me, because I definitely loved him back.

"Yeah, basically, but I overreacted. I know you're not Matthew or my father, or any of these assholes who think I should stay in the kitchen and out of a brewery. I know you just want me to be safe."

"Avery, I'm always going to want you to be safe. I can't turn that off. And yeah, I'm probably going to be more cautious about that than you are. I can't promise that I won't be bossy or overbearing sometimes. That's who I am. But I can promise to listen and not treat you like a child. I would just ask you to keep in mind that I love you, and I can't stand the idea of something happening to you."

I smiled up at him. "Can I borrow your shower? I smell like the fire."

"Go for it," he said with a gentle smile. He dropped his head, brushing his lips across mine.

"I won't be long," I said. The prospect of a shower had me half-jogging down the hall. Turning on the hot water, I let steam fill the room. I'd smell like spice and pine trees, but that was a hell of a lot better than smoke and sweat.

I washed the stink out of my hair and thought about West and his "I love you," and what exactly I was going to do about that. I had a few ideas, but mostly, I was winging it. As clean as I was going to get, I shut off the water and did my best to squeeze my hair dry and finger-comb it into less of a mess. Grabbing West's soft robe off the back of the bathroom door, I went to find my guy.

I had a lot of things I wanted to say, feelings in a swirl inside me I didn't have words for. But there were other ways to communicate than with words.

"Hey, West, can you come here for a sec?" I called from the door of his bedroom. I didn't have to wait long. "I need you to check and make sure I got all the jail smell off me." Tilting my head to the side, I let my hair fall down my back, baring my neck.

West didn't hesitate. He dropped his head, running his lips from my collarbone up to the base of my jaw, nuzzling, sniffing. "You smell pretty fucking good to me," he whispered in my ear.

"So do you," I said, loving the spicy pine scent of the body wash I'd used clinging to his skin. The smell was richer, fuller coming from West, like the natural smell of him added something that made it irresistible, because he was irresistible.

"West," I breathed, reaching up to frame his face in my hands, kissing him, nibbling that full lower lip, losing myself in his mouth. So good. His arms came around me, one hand closing over the curve of my ass, pulling me close. He fit me so perfectly—big enough to make me feel almost delicate, but not so big that I was overwhelmed.

He scooped me up off the floor, startling a laugh out of me before he lay me in the bed. I don't think I've ever seen a man get undressed that fast. Naked, he stretched out beside me, untying the belt of the robe and peeling back the sides. Reaching up, he cupped my cheek in his hand, turning my face to his.

"I love you," he said. "I love your spirit and your fire. I love your heart. I love that we can butt heads and figure it out later." He brushed his lips across mine. "I love everything about you."

I reached for him, my lips seeking his, pulling him into a kiss and then another, pulling him on top of me. He stroked my skin, his fingers memorizing every inch of me, cupping my breasts, closing around my nipples to tug and tease. I couldn't stay still, little moans escaping my mouth, my hips rocking up, so ready for him. One of his big hands slid between my thighs, his fingertip tracing the seam of my pussy, finding me slick and ready.

I needed West, all of him, strong and naked and in my arms. He pushed up off of me for a second, opening his bedside drawer to grab a condom. I heard plastic tear, and he was there, nudging my entrance. The stretch of him was so good it sent shards of bliss straight into my brain. He filled me slowly, pulling my knees back and wide, opening me for him, hitting just the right spot. My eyes squeezed shut from the flood of sensations—his chest hair scraping my nipples, the solid heat of him against me as he moved in long, slow thrusts, pushing me higher and higher until my body closed around him in tight, heavenly pulses.

"I love you, West," I breathed in his ear, holding on to him until I left marks in his skin with my nails. "I love you."

His sigh of contentment reached straight into my core.

And then later, as I lay naked and draped across him, I raised up on my elbows and met his eyes. "It wasn't just the orgasms. I love you."

"Good to know," he said, cupping my cheek and raising his head for a kiss. "We're going to figure the rest of this out."

"I hope so," I said, tucking my head against his neck.

"We will. I promise."

We ate leftovers and went back to bed, where I pinned him down and teased him until his impressive length was hard, then rolled on the condom and rode him until he screamed my name. I loved everything about West Garfield—his integrity, his empathy, his brain—but the sex sure as hell didn't hurt.

I thought I could spend a week naked in bed with him and still not get enough of his body, despite the chaos of the world outside. The murdered jewelry designer. Whoever had tried to set me up. Whatever the fuck was going on with all of this. I could face it all, as long as I was with West.

Chapter Twenty-Five

AVERY

I came awake gradually, in warm, snuggly increments. My legs were twined with West's, the rough hair on his thighs a delicious scratch on my skin. My head pillowed on his chest, his arm tight around me. I don't think I've ever wanted to get out of bed less. He smelled so good—like West, pine, and spice and everything I wanted to burrow into.

A finger traced the shell of my ear, brushing my hair off my face.

"You awake?" His voice was low and husky, stirring me.

I would have thought we'd had enough sex the night before, but I was learning that when it came to West, there was no such thing as enough. I wondered if there ever would be. Maybe someday, after lots and lots of naked time. Maybe.

"No," I said, answering his question. "I'm not awake." I nuzzled my head into his chest, pressing a kiss to his collarbone. "I don't want to get up," I admitted.

"I know," he said. His chest rose and fell as he let out a sigh. "I'm going to clear your name," he said. "Don't worry."

"I know you are, but I can't help worrying." I rolled to my side so I could stay pressed to West's body, not wanting to leave our cocoon of warmth. I liked this—stretched against him, our feet tangling, my hair across his chest. I felt cherished and loved and safe.

It was that last word that snagged in my head—*safe*—but at what cost? What cost to who West was, to the heart of the man I loved?

I propped myself up on an elbow so I could meet West's eyes, loving the sated, warm brown. I'd never seen him so unguarded. I loved that he didn't just make me feel safe; he felt safe enough with me to be this West—relaxed and open. And it was that part that really got to me, forcing me to open my mouth and say, "I'm scared."

"Avery, you don't—" His hand came up to brush my cheek, and I caught it in mine, pulling it down between us, wrapping my fingers around his.

"Wait, West. Just listen to me for a second, okay?"

He pressed his lips together as if it took a force of will not to interrupt me. I loved him even more for trying.

"I'm scared about what happens next," I said. "I don't want to go back to jail. But I don't want you to compromise who you are for me. I love you. That means I love all of you, West. Even when I think you're being bullheaded, and you think everything is black and white. I get annoyed you won't bend the rules, but I love that you won't. I love your honor and your integrity. And I can't stand the idea—"

My voice caught in my throat, my eyes filling with sudden tears. I swallowed hard, knowing I had to get the words out before he interrupted. "I don't want you to do anything you'll regret, anything that feels wrong, for my sake. But," I said as his lips parted, "the other thing is—"

I squeezed my eyes shut, feeling a hot tear streak down my cheek. I hated crying, but I couldn't help it, because the real truth was that as much as I meant everything I'd just said, I was also terrified of following in Ford's footsteps. "I'm scared of what could happen to me if you don't."

I buried my face in his chest. Shame washed through me. I should have kept that last part to myself. If I didn't let him see how scared I was, maybe he wouldn't do anything he'd regret later. And I did not want to be a regret for West. I didn't want to be the thing that pushed him into betraying who he was.

"Avery, no," he said, brushing my hair off my cheek and wiping away a tear with the pad of his thumb. "Oh, baby, no. I won't let anything happen to you. Do you understand me?"

"You can't promise—" I began.

"Avery, look at me."

I lifted my head up and saw the strangest combination of resolve and amusement swirling in his dark eyes. "Baby, I love that you understand who I am, that you know what this job means to me, what my integrity means to me."

"West, I do, and I don't want—"

"Just wait," he said, pressing a fingertip to my lips. "I listened to you. Now you listen to me."

I nodded and pursed my lips against his fingertip in a kiss.

"If you think there's even a question that I'm going to protect you," he said, the amusement draining from his eyes and leaving only resolve, "then you don't understand what's happening here."

I raised an eyebrow. I didn't have a response because he was right. I didn't understand. There was always a choice.

West shook his head, seeing that I didn't get it. "It's important to me to have honor, to follow the rules, to uphold the law. I believe in it. I believe that if we do it right, it makes everyone's lives better. All of that is true. But Avery, you're not everyone. You're mine. I love you. This isn't some fling. I've known you for most of my life. I didn't know we'd end up here, not when we were kids. But now that we are..." He shook his head. "For anyone else, yeah, the rules are the rules. The law is the law. But I'm not letting you go to jail for a crime you did not commit. You're not your brother. Ford was innocent of killing your father—I'm sure of that—but Ford was not innocent. You understand?"

I nodded. As much as I hated it, Ford himself would be the first one to make that argument—and had not that long ago. "Yeah, but I'm not—"

This time, West wasn't just amused; he laughed out loud. "Ave, you're not naïve. You're not a kid. But in the ways that matter, you're as innocent as you could be. I will not let you get set up to do hard time. It's not happening. And if you love me the way you say you do, if you see me the way I know you do, you already know you can't ask me not to protect you."

At that, my eyes narrowed. "West Garfield," I started, "if you think you can—"

He grinned. "I know you're smart and capable. I won't put you in a box, though sometimes it's going to be a struggle, and I'm sure we'll butt heads."

"Probably," I agreed.

"But in this, you need to let me do what I need to do. Because there is no world in which I'd let you go to jail over this. It's not happening. This isn't me bending my ethics for you. This is me protecting the woman I love. It's not a compromise. It's a privilege."

"But how are you going to—" I pressed, his speech giving me the warm fuzzies even as I was trying to figure out how he'd keep me safe without tanking his career. If he couldn't find the real arsonist, what were our options?

West shook his head. "I'm going to find out who set the fire."

"But how?"

His dark eyes narrowed in aggravated amusement. "You do know this is my job, yeah? Before I was police chief, I was a detective."

I'd forgotten. Somewhere in the depths of my memories, I guess I'd known West had gotten promoted to detective before he'd left to come back to Sawyers Bend. But I hadn't really thought about what that meant. Police chief and detective weren't the same thing.

He reached up to smooth my hair back, his eyes so sweet I braced. "I need you to do me a favor."

"What?" I asked, suspicious but too mushy from his romantic speech to give him attitude.

"I'm going to bring you back to Heartstone, and I need you to stay there."

I didn't love that. "For how long?"

"I don't know," he said. "I'm not leaving you in jail, but you're best off hidden. I want whoever set that fire to think you're out of the picture." He propped himself up on an elbow and looked down at me. "I want you to close Sawyers Bend Brewing for a few days. The brewery and the taproom."

"Now?" I asked. "In leaf season?" I squeezed my eyes shut, knowing he was right. Cammie and Dave were good at their jobs—well, Dave was. Cammie was a little flaky, but still, they knew how to do their jobs and mostly did them well, whether it was tending bar or helping me out in the brewery.

But they didn't run the place. If I kept it open, someone would have to make bank deposits, lock up, and get there early to open. What if whoever set me up went after the brewery? Dave and Cammie would be caught in the crossfire. I had a flash of swinging that stool at the door to Wild Haven, smoke filling my lungs. I shivered against West, suddenly cold. I wouldn't wish those moments on anyone, especially my employees.

I let out a sigh. "Okay. Will you put up a sign?"

West kissed the top of my head. "Thanks for not arguing about it. I'll put up a sign and call Cammie and Dave. I don't want you to talk to anyone except your family and me. Not yet."

"So, the idea is to make whoever did this think I'm under arrest?"

"Something like that," West said. "Jim and Amanda at the front desk know you were in that cell, but they don't know when you left or where I took you. I want to keep it that way. If whoever did this thinks I believe you're guilty, maybe they'll get careless. We could use some luck."

"Okay," I agreed.

"Okay." West leaned down and kissed me, lingering, his tongue sliding against mine.

"We have to get moving," I said with some regret as he pulled back, his eyes skating down my bare shoulder, catching on the curve of my breast.

"Shower?" he asked.

"Definitely."

West had a big, square, glassed-in shower with a deep bench on one side. I rolled out of bed, stopping just long enough to dip a hand in his bedside drawer and pull out a condom. Tossing my hair back, I peeked over my shoulder, eyes drinking in the sight of his long body stretched out in bed, his dark hair mussed, his eyes hot as they scanned my naked form.

"Race you," I said, and took off.

West caught me by the time I cleared the bathroom door, turning the water up steamy hot and plucking the condom wrapper from my hands. His mouth went to that spot behind my ear that made me crazy, and for a while, I didn't worry about anything but getting my hands on West.

After, I borrowed a pair of old track pants and a t-shirt, not willing to put my smoky clothes back on. West walked me out, shielding me from his neighbors' view until I was safely in the SUV. As soon as he was buckled in, I ducked down for the trip back through town. Anyone who looked would see West driving by himself. Fortunately, his SUV was jacked up high enough that it would be hard for anyone to see me. They'd have had to climb up on the running boards, and West wasn't slowing down long enough for anyone to do that. I stayed where I was, uncomfortably draped over the center console and out of sight, until we turned into the long drive to Heartstone.

I'd been tempted—so tempted—to tease him with my head practically in his lap. I'd traced a fingertip up the inside of his thigh, and his hand had come down to grab mine.

"Behave," he'd said, with a little regret in his voice. "If I run off the road and smash into one of my citizens' cars, it's going to be awkward. And the whole point of this is to keep you hidden, which will be a little difficult if I have to write up a police report on myself for distracted driving."

We stopped in front of the gates, West waving at the camera. Hawk's team knew West and his SUV. The gate swung open, and we proceeded down the drive.

"I forgot to ask last night," I said. "Did you talk to Griffen after the fire?"

West nodded. "He's been briefed. I'm going to take care of this, Avery. You trust me?"

"You know I do," I said. "I don't think there's anyone I trust more."

"Okay then. I know you're going to be bored and

you're going to go stir-crazy, but I need you to be patient and smart, okay? I'm going to find who set that fire and get your name cleared."

"I believe you," I said, reaching to unsnap my seatbelt and get out of the car.

"I'll walk you in," he said. "I'm going to talk to Griffen again."

Whoever was on the cameras must have called ahead. Sterling and Griffen met us in the hall.

We'd barely made it through the front door when Sterling started in on West. "West Garfield, did you seriously arrest Avery?"

"He didn't arrest me," I started. "That was Jim."

"Same difference! Are you kidding me? You put her in jail? You know she wouldn't set a fire." Sterling's gaze shifted to me, and one blonde eyebrow raised. "Right?" she asked.

I knew if I said I'd set that fire, she'd still be on my side. Because that's the kind of sister Sterling was—ride or die, even if I was committing arson. Fortunately, we didn't have to worry about that.

"Right, because I didn't do it," I said with a firm nod.

She relaxed a little but turned her fury back on West. "You just left her there in jail after she almost died in a fire? I'm so disappointed in you."

West didn't seem bothered. "She's fine, Sterling. Everything's going to be okay."

"Do you have whoever did it?" she demanded, her eyes blue fire.

"Not yet," he said. "First priority was getting Avery

out of jail and home where she's safe. Next on the list is finding whoever set that fire."

"We can help," Sterling said. "Avery and I can—"

"No." West shut her down. "You're not helping. I've got this. I need Avery to stay out of sight. No visitors. No phone calls. Got it?" He looked down at me.

"Crystal clear, Chief. Lie low, stay out of sight, and let you do the detective work."

"That's my girl," he said. He turned to Sterling. "I know you're mad and scared and you want to help, but for now I need you to just—"

"Yeah, I get it. Lie low and let you play the detective." She rolled her eyes. "Fine."

"Why do I not believe her?" West asked, looping his arm around my shoulders.

"Probably because she's full of it," I said.

"And are you full of it?" he asked, a smile curling the side of his mouth.

"Sometimes," I admitted. "But not about this. I'm serious, West. Getting arrested for arson is bad enough. I don't want to end up like Anna Novak."

West tightened his arm, squeezing me into his side. "It's going to be okay, Ave."

"I know it is. You'll be back tonight?" I asked, suddenly wishing he didn't have to go.

"Hopefully in time for dinner," West said. He brushed his lips across mine, keeping things PG, considering my big brother was standing several feet away, not bothering to pretend he wasn't watching.

West's lips moved to my ear, and he whispered, "Don't worry. Enjoy having a day off, maybe find Finn and plan for your new restaurant. But don't worry, okay? I've got this."

"Okay," I promised, knowing it was a lie.

"Okay," he said, dropping another quick kiss on my mouth. "I'll see you at dinner."

"Come on," I said to Sterling. "I'm going to go see if I can get Finn to give me some breakfast."

"Good luck with that," Sterling said. "You know he doesn't like to feed us once the dining room is closed."

"True, but I got arrested yesterday, so maybe he'll be feeling some pity." I headed for the stairs to the lower level, trying to turn off all my worries and think about the plans Finn and I were making for adding a restaurant to the brewery. That was it—focus on the future, don't worry about the present. West had asked me to trust him, and I did.

"I have an idea," Sterling said. "Go see Finn. I'll be there in a minute."

I stopped at the head of the stairs. "What kind of idea?"

Sterling smirked at me. "A secret idea. If it doesn't pan out, it's better if you don't know."

"You can't just leave me with that. It's bad enough I have to sit here while West goes out and finds the bad guy," I protested.

"I'll be down in a few minutes," she promised, "and then I'll tell you."

"All right," I said, knowing I'd have to be satisfied with that. Ever since Sterling had started working with Sinclair Security, she'd gotten mysterious at times, and I'd already learned there was nothing I could do to get her to talk if she didn't want to.

Hoping Finn had enough pity in him to make me a cappuccino, I jogged down the stairs, crossing my fingers that it wouldn't take West long to find what he needed to clear my name. Heartstone Manor was almost a castle, but if I couldn't leave, it wouldn't take long before it would feel like the jail I'd just escaped.

Chapter Twenty-Six

WEST

Griffen watched his sisters stride across the entry hall to the stairs, then turned back to me. "Got a minute?"

I followed him to his office, taking a seat in one of the armchairs opposite his desk.

"You need a coffee?" Griffen asked.

I shook my head. "I'll get one later."

"What's the plan?" Griffen asked.

I propped my ankle on my knee. "The plan is I find out who set that fucking fire."

Griffen nodded. "If you need any help—"

I shook my head. "Hopefully, it won't come to that. I want to do this thing by the book. I don't want there to be any question that Avery is innocent."

"And you're sure—" Griffen began.

I squinted and shook my head. "There's no way she did it. I can't believe you'd even ask," I said.

Griffen shrugged a shoulder. "Avery's got a pretty good moral compass," he said. "Always has. And I absolutely can't see her burning down a fellow brewer's place, but..." Griffen shrugged again, lifting his chin. "If you'd told me the brewmaster's house had burned to the ground—"

I barked out a laugh. "I might have been a little less sure if that were the case," I agreed. "Though Avery has too much class to play games like that with her ex."

"Good point," Griffen agreed. "You'll keep me posted?"

"Of course. I'm not going to let her get railroaded like Ford. It's not happening," I said, knowing Griffen would understand why I'd let Ford go to prison but would do anything to keep Avery from the same fate.

I didn't have to tell my best friend I was in love with his sister. The fact that I'd gotten her out of jail, when by all rights she should still be sitting there, told him everything he needed to know. It also saved us an awkward, mushy conversation neither of us wanted to have. One of the many benefits of a long friendship.

Griffen sat back in his chair, propping his ankle on his knee in a mirror of my position. His eyes level on mine, he asked, "You coming to Thanksgiving?"

"Yep," I said. "Avery invited me and my parents. Already asked my dad—he says they're in."

"Good deal," Griffen said, nodding.

And now Griffen knew I wasn't just in love with his sister, but that this was serious—again saving us a conversation we didn't really want to have. I'd grown up running in and out of this house, never thinking I'd feel like a part of the family. But now, sitting in my best friend's office in perfect accord over my relationship with his sister, one I hadn't seen coming and would fight to the death to keep, a warm glow spread in my chest that offset my worry over Avery.

I had no doubt I was going to find who set that fire. There was no room for failure, and I wasn't alone. Avery would be better off in the long run if I could do this by the book, but if I couldn't, Griffen had access to all sorts of ways to solve this problem that I'd normally never touch. But this was Avery. There was nothing I wouldn't do to keep her safe.

I stood. "I'll be back for dinner. I want her to stay here at Heartstone, out of sight. She's on lockdown. If anyone comes to the house, make sure they don't see her."

"Got it," Griffen agreed, then paused. "Be careful out there. If she hadn't gotten out of that fire—"

I nodded in agreement. "Whoever set that fire wasn't overly worried about killing her." I rubbed the heel of my palm on my chest to chase off the icy hollow of fear.

"Yeah, well, you can't clear her name if they take you out too," Griffen reminded me.

"I'm aware," I agreed. "I'll keep you posted," I said with a short nod and strode out the door.

I had an arsonist to find and Avery's name to clear.

And the clock was ticking.

I left Heartstone Manor behind, knowing time was running short. I couldn't keep Avery caged forever. Her business was closed, losing money every day, and the judge's orders would only keep her out of jail for so long.

Matthew was the obvious suspect. He had a motive. Almost anyone had the means. But arson was a big step from spreading gossip. Going after her business reputation and sabotaging her relationships with other brewers was one thing. But if she hadn't been able to get that door open—

I pushed the thought away. She had. She'd escaped with a few bruises and a sore throat. She'd been extraordinarily lucky, all things considered.

I had a lot of problems. One of them was that I couldn't know if Avery getting trapped in Wild Haven was intentional or an accident. The whole thing had been fairly basic: lure her to the location, set it on fire. Gas wasn't a sophisticated accelerant. Anyone could get it, and everyone knew it would start a fire. I already had my deputies checking the local stations to see if anyone remembered someone filling up gas cans, but the town was busy with leaf season. So far, no one remembered a thing.

Zeroing in on Matthew, while tempting, wasn't the answer. If the evidence pointed his way, great. But I wouldn't run the risk of missing the real culprit by assuming I knew what was going on. Been there, done that. I'd start with the evidence.

Before that, I called Cammie and Dave, explaining only that Avery had a family situation and Sawyers Bend Brewing would be closed for the next few days.

Dave had asked, "Avery okay?"

When I assured him she was, he'd answered, "Cool. I'm going to go see my brother in Chattanooga. Tell her to text when she's ready to reopen, and I'll hop back. Cool?"

"Sounds good," I assured him.

Cammie had seemed more troubled. "But I need my hours. Rent's coming due, you know?"

"It'll only be for a few days," I'd said, not sure if that was true or not.

"Well, can I talk to Avery?" she asked, a faint whine in her voice.

"Not right now. Like I said, she has a family thing."

"You sure I can't just go in and open?" she wheedled.

"Avery will let you know when she's ready to reopen," I said. "For now, Sawyers Bend Brewing is closed. No one should be on the property. Understand?"

"Okay, I guess." She'd hung up, leaving me curious about her reaction.

Cammie had closed the night of the break-in. She swore she'd locked the door, but we only had her word for it. And now she hadn't asked about her boss or what the family emergency was—only worried she wouldn't make her hours for the week. On one hand, I got it. We all need money to live, and Cammie had rent to pay. On the other hand, her lack of concern about Avery felt off. I tucked the mental note in the back of my mind for the future. It could be nothing, or it could be something.

I parked my SUV in the lot of the county fire department and sent Avery a quick text.

> If Cammie calls, don't talk to her. Let it go to voicemail.

The answer came back immediately.

> You already told me not to talk to anyone. Don't worry. I'm bugging Finn and staying out of trouble. I promise.

A tight feeling in my chest relaxed a fraction. She'd

promised she'd keep her head down, but I couldn't discount Sterling's influence. If Finn was keeping her occupied with plans for their joint venture, it would take her longer to get restless.

The County Fire Marshal was expecting me. After getting checked in at the front desk, I headed back to his office, taking the seat he offered.

"What have you found?" I asked. Henry Boone had been the Fire Marshal for a decade, after serving as the Deputy Fire Marshal for almost fifteen years. We weren't buddies, but we'd known each other most of our lives. I trusted his judgement, and as far as I knew, he trusted mine.

I wasn't surprised when he sat back in his desk chair, raising one bushy gray eyebrow, and crossed his arms over his chest. "I hear you're dating the prime suspect, who also happens to be Griffen Sawyer's younger sister. Correct?"

I nodded. "True."

"If it were anyone else, West, I'd say we had a real conflict of interest here. But considering you threw her brother in jail when you had to, I'll give you the benefit of the doubt. I can tell you this is interesting."

"Interesting how?" I asked.

Henry shrugged, dropping his arms to his sides before picking up the papers on his desk. "Report says a call went out about a trespasser matching Avery Sawyer's description carrying gas cans. It's impossible to tell from the 911 call if the caller was a man or a woman. The voice is scratchy—could be modified, could be a bad line. The timing is a little fuzzy. They say they saw her at 4:45 p.m. That could be accurate. But Jim verified that the text telling her to come to Wild Haven came in at 4:38 p.m. It's possible she got the text at 4:38 p.m. and was on site by 4:45 p.m. with those gas cans, but..." He tipped his head from side to side. "It's unlikely."

I nodded. "Possible, but difficult, especially with weekend traffic clogging up town."

"Exactly," he agreed. "We know Avery was in the building. She says she went in to meet with Bob, though Bob was in Hickory for the day with family, and the brewery is usually closed on Sundays, anyway. The fire was started from the inside, against the north wall, using an accelerant—gasoline_based on what we saw inside and with tests of the residue in the cans."

He leaned forward to open a file on his monitor, turning the screen so I could see the pictures of the scene. My heart chilled as I imagined Avery trapped in the center of the destruction.

"It appears that whoever set the fire poured the gas out along the base of the wall." He traced a line along the screen to show what had been the north wall. "If we're going with the story that Avery Sawyer did this—" He raised an eyebrow, waiting for me to object. When I kept my mouth shut, he went on. "She would have had to go in with the cans, empty them along the north wall, then bring them back out, set them by the trunk of her car, and return to the brewery, locking herself inside, all before she set the fire."

I sat back, thinking it through. "Why would anyone take the cans back outside, put them outside their vehicle instead of in the trunk, then return to start the fire, locking the door behind themselves?"

"My question exactly." Henry agreed. "I could make a case for locking the door to keep a random person from interfering or getting caught in the fire. But then why break through the front door when she could have escaped out the back? If she were the arsonist, she'd have to know that would increase her chances of being caught. What happened to the key she used to lock the door? And why park right out front?"

"It doesn't make sense," I said. "Did you get any prints off the gas cans?"

"We got a few partials. They don't match Avery's prints. Otherwise, the cans were clean. Very clean."

"Odd," I said, turning over the details in my head.

Henry nodded. "All of this is odd, West. On the surface, when Jim showed up, I can see why he thought it was a slam dunk. And it could be. People are stupid. It doesn't make much sense to go in, pour out the gas, bring the cans back out, but not bother to put them in the back of her car, leave them out in the parking lot, then set a fire, locking herself inside." He shook his head. "I don't know Avery Sawyer personally, but from what I've heard —" He shrugged a shoulder. "She's never struck me as dumb."

"She's not," I said. "Though smart people do dumb shit every day."

"Don't we know it," Henry agreed. "I don't have anything here that directly pins this on Avery Sawyer. I also don't have anything that lets her off the hook."

I nodded, standing. "I appreciate your time, Henry. I

know you're going to keep investigating." I rapped the surface of his desk with my knuckles. "I'll do the same. One way or another, we'll find out who set that fire."

"But you don't think it was your girlfriend?"

I was smart enough not to answer that one directly. "I follow the evidence, Henry. You know that. We'll find the evidence, and then we'll know the truth."

"Fair enough," he said. "If we turn up anything else, I'll let you know."

I stopped as something occurred to me. "Did you check the surrounding buildings for cameras? I already know Bob didn't have any at Wild Haven."

Henry shook his head. "I haven't gotten to that yet."

"I'll take care of it," I said. "I'll let you know what I find."

"Appreciate that. Good luck, West."

I nodded. I wanted to say I didn't need luck, that old-fashioned detective work would get the job done. But luck never hurt, especially when I was looking for a needle in a haystack.

I drove back out to Wild Haven Brewing. The building wasn't in great shape—the north wall burned away, and the roof was sagging. Whoever had done this deserved to pay, but I knew it hadn't been Avery.

Wild Haven Brewing was surrounded by other warehouse-style buildings, close but not right on top of each other. One of them looked like it had cameras up by the roof that might have been pointed close enough to Wild Haven to catch something. No one was there when I knocked. I'd go back later and track down the owner if they still weren't there.

My next stop was Bear Run Brewing, Matthew Holt's new place of employment. I wasn't getting tunnel vision, but it'd be foolish not to check on the one person I knew had a motive to frame Avery for arson—her former brewmaster and ex. Unless Prentice's killer had set the fire, Matthew was the only person in Sawyers Bend who had reason to go after Avery.

My phone rang as I turned into the parking lot. Sterling. I answered, and she started talking before I got a word out.

"You can't ask how I know, but Matthew was at Wild Haven when the fire started."

"How do you know that?" I demanded, despite her warning.

"I'm not telling you," Sterling said with a huff of exasperation. "That's why I said you can't ask how I know."

"Fine," I said, reframing my question to find out what I really needed to know. "How solid is that information?"

"His phone's location showed he was at Wild Haven Brewing between 4:40 p.m. and 5:15 p.m. on the day of the fire."

"And if that information had been obtained legally," I asked, annoyed and grateful at the same time, "would it stand up in court?"

"Yes," she said.

"Sterling," I admonished.

"Hey, look, I made some calls, okay? I'm not going to let my sister go to jail for something she didn't do."

"Neither am I," I reminded her.

"Yeah, well, now you know it was him. You won't waste your time looking for somebody else."

I wanted to argue, but I wasn't going to waste my time. "I'm at Bear Run Brewing right now," I told her.

"Oh, good," she said cheerfully. "When you arrest him, I want a copy of the mugshot."

"Uh-huh," I said. She could want one. Didn't mean she'd get it. "Are you at home or Sawyer Outdoor Adventures?"

"I'm at work," Sterling said. "Quinn just had a group go out, and I'm working on a project. Top secret."

"All your work is top secret these days," I said, "but thanks."

"Anytime, Chief," Sterling said with a laugh, hanging up on me.

I should be mad she'd gone around me. If we'd really needed it, I could have figured out a way to get a warrant for Matthew's cell phone records—probably bending the rules in ways that would grate on me because I didn't have enough yet to get that warrant. And while I couldn't use that information to arrest him, Sterling was right. Now I had no doubt who was responsible. I just had to prove it.

Chapter Twenty-Seven
WEST

Bear Run Brewing had a shop and a taproom, neither of which was open at this hour of the morning. I went around to the side and tried the door that led into the brewery itself. It was unlocked, so I wandered in, looking for Chris Fields, the owner. I knew him by name and sight, though not well. We'd met a few times, but I wouldn't say we were friends or even really friendly.

An employee spotted me and came over. "Hey, Chief Garfield, what can I do for you?" The young man gave me a friendly smile, and I returned it. I was good at making people feel like there wasn't anything wrong when there was. It was a handy trick when the mere sight of you could strike fear.

"I'm looking for Chris. He around today?"

"Yeah, in his office. Back this way," he said, leading me to an office that reminded me of Avery's. It was bigger —the whole place was bigger—but his desk was stacked with papers, crammed with files and books, boxes of labels, samples of bottles, a few pony kegs, and a random assortment of things a brewer might want to have at hand.

"Hey, Chief Garfield. Problem?" Chris stood, extending his hand. He wore a tie-dyed shirt advertising Bear Run's signature lager, his long sandy hair caught in a low ponytail, a friendly smile on his face.

"Nope, just some routine follow-up on an investigation." I shook his hand.

"Have a seat," he said, leaning forward to pull a box of labels out of the extra chair in his office. "How can I help?"

"I just have a few questions. Were you open on Sunday afternoon?"

Chris nodded, a smile spreading across his face. "All day, actually. We did a fall fun-fest kind of thing—had a few food trucks, bluegrass band, family games and stuff."

"What time did it start?" I asked.

"Noon until 6 p.m.. The staff and I were here a few hours before and after."

"And were all of your employees here?" I asked, not wanting to point specifically to Matthew yet.

He looked at the ceiling as he thought, then shook his head. "Some of the staff who just work in the brewery didn't show, but pretty much everyone else was here."

"Can you give me the names of the staff who weren't here?" I asked.

Chris rattled off a handful of names, none of which were Matthew's.

"What about your new brewmaster?" I asked. "Matthew Holt?"

Chris let out a breath and sat back, watching me with

considering eyes. "He was here. Helped with set-up. Worked the event. He left a little after 7 p.m."

I nodded. "It must have been busy."

"It was a madhouse. You know how things are this time of year."

"I do," I agreed. "Do you have any kind of video security here? Cameras on the parking lot, anything like that?"

"No," Chris said, shaking his head. "We've never needed it. Why? Is this about the fire at Wild Haven?"

I knew the fire wouldn't be a secret. Word travels fast in a small community, and the brewers in the area were tight. I didn't answer his question directly. Instead, I asked what I needed to know the most. "Is it possible that Matthew Holt wasn't here for a period of time on Sunday afternoon?" Before he could answer, I added, "Think carefully."

He snapped his mouth shut for a moment, tipping his head up to scan the ceiling as he thought back. Finally, he said, "I know he was here for the first few hours. He helped with the setup, served beer—I saw him behind the bar pretty much non-stop until about 3 p.m. Then he switched off with somebody else, and he was kind of everywhere." I raised an eyebrow in question, and Chris explained. "Refilling supplies, troubleshooting some power issues at one of the food trucks, setting up music while the band was on a break."

He paused, scanning the ceiling again. "Things got a little iffy later in the afternoon in terms of keeping track of everybody. Like I said, it was a madhouse—lines everywhere, and it was loud with the band playing. Tons of fun, everybody had a great time, but—" He sat back in his chair. "I guess I can't swear I know where he was every second of the afternoon. If anybody left, they weren't gone long. He had a lot of demands on his time. We would have noticed if he'd been missing for an extended period, definitely."

"Good to know," I said. "So, if he was gone, he wasn't gone for very long, but you can't verify his presence or absence during any specific time between around 3 p.m. and when?"

"He was definitely here at 6 p.m. when we started shutting things down," Chris said.

That gave Matthew plenty of time to sneak out and come back. It was a five-minute drive to Wild Haven from here, and I knew Matthew had been there between 4:40 p.m. and 5:15 p.m. The timing checked out, not that I was surprised.

"Okay. That's helpful. Thank you. Anyone else you're aware of who could have left and come back?"

Chris thought again and shook his head. "Not that I can think of. Like I said, it was really busy."

"Well, busy is always good news," I said. "Gotta love those tourists."

Chris answered with a grin. "You know we do."

I stood. "Do you mind if I wander around and ask some questions?"

"Nope," he said, standing with me. "Feel free. Every-body's busy, but not so busy they can't stop and talk to the Chief of Police. Let me know if there's anything else you need."

"Will do. Thanks, Chris."

I wandered back out into the main area of the brewery. Like Avery's place, it was immaculate. The stainless-steel vats, bigger than hers, gleamed just as bright. People worked with quiet efficiency. A jam band played from the speaker in the corner, the music cheerful, looping swirls of sound without a discernible beginning or end.

I hadn't been specific with Chris, but I hadn't wanted permission to talk to all of his employees—just the one. I found Matthew beside a big, circular, copper kettle with windows in it that looked like portholes. He had one open, and he and another man were leaning in, inhaling deeply. The yeasty scent wasn't what I thought of when I thought of beer, but it was close.

Matthew spotted me as I approached, his face going hard. Whether it was out of guilt or because he knew I was with Avery was unclear, but I was betting on the former. He had a curt word with the employee beside him, and the man disappeared. Matthew closed the porthole and latched it shut.

"Chief Garfield. Interesting seeing you here. Problem?"

"I don't think so," I said. "Just wanted to talk to you about yesterday afternoon. Chris said you had an event here."

"We did. It was great. Huge crowd." He crossed his arms over his chest.

"That's what I heard," I said, keeping my tone affable and a little distant. Just a cop doing his job. "And you were here all afternoon?"

"Yep." He raised his chin a fraction. "Ask anyone."

"I'll get to that," I assured him. "And no one saw you

leave? Did you run out to get supplies, anything like that?"

"No." Matthew flicked his hair out of his eyes. "We were packed. All hands on deck. You know how it is." His tone was friendly, but his eyes were hard. "What's this about?"

I had no doubt he knew exactly what this was about—first, because with every word that came out of his mouth, I was more sure he was guilty as hell, and second, because everyone knew what had happened at Wild Haven. Matthew pretending that he didn't wasn't a check in the column of innocence.

"I'm investigating the fire at Wild Haven Brewing. Checking to make sure I have a clear picture of where everyone was."

"I thought you'd made an arrest already," Matthew said, and I wondered if he was going to mention Avery's name specifically.

I nodded. "That doesn't mean we stop investigating."

"Gotta collect that evidence, I guess," Matthew said, dropping his crossed arms and shoving his hands in his pockets as if this was just a relaxed chat. I was almost impressed with his ability to fake it. "Wish I could help you, but I was here all day. I didn't see a thing except happy customers drinking beer and having fun."

I nodded again. "If anything comes to mind—if you remember something from yesterday that seems suspicious—you let me know."

"Sure thing, Chief," he said.

I felt his eyes on my back as I crossed the room for the door. I might not have a smoking gun pointing at

Matthew yet, but there was no doubt in my mind he was guilty. Sterling's info was the first nail in the coffin. But the way he'd handled my questions was the second.

It was almost lunchtime. I had to get back to the station, but I'd make one more stop first. I drove back to Wild Haven and knocked on the door of the nearby warehouse that had cameras on the roof. This time, someone answered—a scruffy guy with a round belly and frizzy hair that looked like it hadn't been washed in a while.

"Chief," he said slowly. "What's up? Here about the fire?" His words were sluggish, as if he'd already hit his morning joint based on the light haze of smoke hanging in the air. Marijuana was illegal in North Carolina, and I knew if I searched him, I'd find enough for a misdemeanor, maybe more. But a little weed wasn't why I was there.

"Notice you have a camera up there on the corner of the building."

He looked faintly surprised and leaned past me to look up. Then nodded. "Yeah, I do. Brother-in-law set it up for me after somebody robbed the place a couple of years ago."

"Is it turned on?" I asked, searching for patience.

"Oh yeah, it records to a tape in my office. Goes back to the beginning when it's full. I don't mess with it much. Never had another break-in." He scratched his elbow, waiting with bleary eyes for me to get to the point.

"Any chance I could look at the tape from yesterday?" I asked.

"For the fire, right? Sure, sure, yeah. Come in." He led me into the building, stopping short as we both encountered the haze of smoke and the pungent scent of weed.

"I just want to see the camera, bud," I said, and he visibly relaxed.

"Yeah, cool, okay." He led me through stacks of what I would call junk—an ancient broken highchair with a Formica tray, a pile of lawn ornaments that looked like windmills, a row of stacked doors in various states of decay.

"You sell a lot of this stuff?" I asked, trying to imagine who would want any of it.

He brightened and shot me a bleary grin. "You'd be surprised. I polish up some of this junk and take it down to the flea market. Most of it moves. Enough to make a living, you know?"

If he said so. I'd seen enough of the local flea markets to know one person's junk was another's treasure. The cramped office in the back corner of the building was dim, the overhead light flickering. The computer monitor on the desk, a sleek flat screen, looked new, as did the black box on the desk with blinking lights.

"Guess it's not a tape." He turned on the monitor and poked at the black box. "Like I said, my brother-in-law set it up for me. Just give me a sec to remember." He poked a few buttons. Nothing happened. "Uh, hold on." He pulled a cell phone out of his pocket, tapped the screen a few times. "Hey Dan, listen, I'm trying to get into the camera on the barn to see what happened yesterday. I can't remember how to pull it up on the screen."

I listened as his brother-in-law walked him through the steps on speakerphone, half afraid he was going to hit the wrong button and delete the footage before I got a chance to check it. That luck I'd been hoping for came through, and he pulled up the footage I was looking for.

"Any way you can zoom in on that corner?" I reached out to trace the section that caught Wild Haven's parking lot and front door.

The voice from the phone answered, "It doesn't really do that. You'd have to download the footage. If you find something you're looking for, I can tell you how."

"All right, good to know," I said, and waited, watching the events of the day before unfold on the screen.

The camera system didn't run nonstop. Instead, it took five-second clips every minute. Clip after clip, the lot remained empty. At 4:37 p.m., a car appeared. Not Matthew's truck. This was a compact two-door I didn't recognize. It parked in the far corner of the lot. A tall male figure appeared beside it. In the next clip, his back was to the camera, but height, frame, and hair color were all a fit for Matthew Holt. The next five-second chunk of footage showed that figure at the front door. In the next, the figure was gone. The car remained.

The next person I saw was Avery. Her car was parked next to the door as she pushed the front door open and disappeared inside. In the next short clip, the gas cans appeared beside her car, and the vehicle in the corner of the lot was gone. Then, a harrowing five-second clip of Avery pounding at the glass door with a metal chair as smoke poured from the north side of the building. At this distance, I couldn't see the fear on her face, but I didn't need to see it to feel her terror.

Clearing my throat, I asked, "How do I download a copy of this? All right with you if I do?"

"Ah, sure, Chief. Whatever you need."

The brother-in-law carefully explained how to export the file and email it to me. I thanked him and the scruffy guy for their help and headed back into town, my teeth grinding at the desire to drive back to Bear Run Brewing and beat the ever-loving shit out of Matthew Holt.

That fucking smug bastard. It wasn't enough that he'd tried to ruin Avery's reputation. The spiteful little shit couldn't leave it at that. No, he'd tried to get her arrested and almost ended up killing her, destroying another brewer's business in the process. I didn't have enough to arrest him, not without a clear view of his face on the security camera, which I didn't have, not if I wanted to make it stick. But I would. Because one thing I knew—Matthew was not getting away with this. When I had what I needed, he was going down, and Avery wouldn't have to worry about him ever again.

The business of being police chief got in the way of my investigation for the rest of the day. We were nearing the end of leaf season, but the town was still overrun with tourists, keeping my people hopping. I made it back to Heartstone just in time for dinner, sliding into my seat beside Avery with a nod for Griffen at the other end of the table.

"You going stir-crazy yet?" I asked.

Her dark eyes sparkled with humor. "Not yet, but I may be making Finn crazy. I invaded his kitchens to talk about our project and ended up bullying him into letting me help cook."

"Did you make this?" I nodded to the meal Savannah and April were serving. It looked like something with pasta.

Avery rolled her eyes. "Cooking might be a stretch. I sliced some things." She leaned forward and snagged a piece of garlic bread from the platter at our end of the table. "You know, I never think about brewing like cooking, but not being able to go into the brewery, not knowing how long this is going to take... I don't know. It left me wanting to make something. Finn let me get in his way to shut me up."

"I don't think it'll be too long until you can get back to your beer," I said, wishing I could give her a guarantee.

"Nothing solid?" she asked, one eyebrow raised.

"Did you talk to Sterling?" I asked, pretty sure Avery had been Sterling's second phone call after she'd gotten her info on Matthew, if not her first. Avery nodded.

"What she gave me was helpful," I said, "but so far, it's not enough. Not yet. Can you wait for the rest until after dinner? I need to talk to Griffen and Hawk."

She smiled up at me, curling her palm over my thigh under the table. "I can wait. Thanks, West."

"For what?" I asked, temporarily distracted by her hand on my leg.

"For being you, I guess. I hate all of this. This whole situation sucks. But it's temporary." She squeezed my leg. "Because we're going to figure it out."

"Absolutely," I promised, a little staggered by her trust. "I'm not going to let you down, Avery."

"Not even a question, West." She leaned into me,

resting her head on my shoulder for a second. "Any crazy tourist stuff happen today?"

I told her about a toddler who'd gotten his hand stuck in a candy jar in the general store because he wouldn't relax his fist-full of gummy bears long enough to pull his arm free. I loved the way she laughed, tipping her head back, the sound full-throated and joyful.

I'm sure there was conversation around us as we ate, but I didn't hear it—happy to end my day sitting next to Avery. After dessert, a wild berry crumble, I nodded to Griffen. He raised his chin in return.

"What was that?" Avery asked, looking between us.

"Meeting in Griffen's office," I explained.

She smiled and shook her head. On the way down the hall, her hand slid into mine, and she tugged. I looked down to see her eyes hesitant, her smile a little tentative.

"Keep an open mind, okay?"

"What do you mean?" I asked, sudden nerves tightening in my stomach.

Avery didn't answer, just nudged me ahead of her into Griffen's office. Hawk was already there.

"What did you find out?" Griffen asked, ignoring his desk, to sit on the sofa closest to the fireplace. Avery and I sat opposite him, while Hawk remained standing. "Did you get anything?"

"Not enough to make a solid arrest, but enough that I know Holt's our guy," I said, and filled them in on the investigation so far.

"You can't arrest him with that?" Avery asked.

Hawk answered before I could. "He could probably get a judge to sign off on it. But West wants more than just enough to make an arrest. He wants something rock solid. Grab Holt too early, and he could spook and hide his trail."

I nodded. "I'm going to arrest this guy, Avery, but I'm going to do it when I know I won't have to let him go, when I know he can't snake free. He could have killed you. The last thing I want is for him to be on guard."

"He thinks I'm under arrest, right?" Avery asked.

"Technically, you are. You're just not sitting in jail."

"But Matthew wouldn't expect me to stay in jail," she said. "There's no judge in this part of the state that wouldn't grant bail to a Sawyer."

"Unless you murdered another Sawyer," I said, thinking of Ford.

"Good point," she agreed. "You were at Wild Haven. How bad is it?"

"It's bad," I said. "The structure is going to need to be rebuilt. Some of the equipment may have made it."

"That sucks," she said, looking down at the rug beneath her feet. "Bob doesn't deserve to be caught in whatever this is with Matthew. How could he do that?"

No one answered her question. Griffen stood, paced to the tall French doors, and looked out into the dark gardens behind the Manor. When he turned, I didn't like the look on his face. He had that same hesitance I'd seen in Avery, and beneath that, a resolve that made me sit straighter.

"What?" I asked.

"We have an idea," he said, "but you aren't going to like it."

Chapter Twenty-Eight

AVERY

I took a deep breath through my nose to calm my racing heart, soothed as I always was by the piney, stringent scent of hops. I wasn't in my own place—the hops room at Bear Run was far bigger than my storage closet. But still, the scent soothed me. I needed it.

A half hour ago, I'd been fired up, ready to put our plan into action. Now that I was here, in this too-quiet, dimly lit room, I was having second thoughts. Too late. I was in it. No escape.

And then it really was too late, as the door swung open, and Matthew walked in.

He stopped short when he saw me. "Avery?" Quickly, he shut the door behind him, turning the lock. "What are you doing here? I thought Chris—" He shook his head. "Did anyone see you come in?"

"No," I said, trying to look scared and desperate, knowing I was better off if Matthew felt like he had the upper hand. I tucked my hair behind my ears and wrapped my arms around my chest.

"I thought you were under arrest," Matt said, his eyes narrowing. "I heard you got caught with gas cans at Wild Haven."

I wound my arms tighter, hugging myself as if for comfort. "West let me out. I guess he found evidence that I didn't do it."

"Faked evidence, you mean," Matt said with a sneer.

"I didn't do it, Matt."

He scoffed. "Sure, you didn't. You're the only person I knew who had a grudge against Bob. Everyone knows you did it."

I stared at him with wide eyes, trying to look hurt. I'm no actress, but I hoped I could fake it well enough to get what I needed. "How could you? You should know I'd never do something like that." I hated the thin, weak tone of my voice. Matthew let a slow smile slide across his face.

"I saw Sawyers Bend Brewing is closed," he said. "Looks like you need someone to run the place. You here to talk me into taking my old job back?"

"I haven't figured that out yet. This whole thing has been terrifying," I said, my voice wavering. "I almost died in that fire."

Matthew lifted his chin, looking away. "It didn't sound like it was that bad."

I dropped my gaze to my feet, my hair sliding into my eyes. My words came out in a whisper that wasn't entirely an act. "The front door was locked. I couldn't get out. The doctor said if I'd been in there much longer, the smoke would have killed me."

His eyes flared wide, and I was suddenly positive that

while Matthew had set that fire, he hadn't planned to kill me. I went with my gut and said what I was thinking.

"You weren't trying to kill me, were you?"

His head shook in a *No* before his brain caught up, and he froze. "I didn't—that's not—"

I dropped my arms to my side, letting tears fill my eyes. "That's a relief. Setting me up for arson was one thing, but trying to kill me? That's a whole new level."

"I wasn't trying to kill you," he ground out, shooting a panicked look at the locked door behind him. "I swear."

"Then why did you lock the door? I couldn't get out, and there was so much smoke."

Matthew shook his head, letting out a huff of air. "I didn't think about it being the only way out of the building. I just wanted to keep anyone from wandering in once the fire started. I didn't know how fast it would go up."

I didn't react to his confession, focused on getting as much from him as I could before he realized what he was saying.

"But how did you get out?" I asked, needing to know. "I didn't see the loading bay door go up."

"There's a regular door beside it," Matthew said. "I let myself out and took off."

"Your car wasn't there. I wouldn't have gone in if I'd seen it," I said.

"Obviously," he said, staring up at the ceiling as if searching for patience. "I borrowed a co-worker's. They never even knew." He shoved his hands in his pockets. "It got a little out of hand. I wasn't planning to lock you in there, for one. Or for the damage to be that bad."

"Why?" I asked, genuinely confused. "What did Bob

ever do to you? I could see you coming after Sawyers Bend Brewing, but why Wild Haven?"

"Because you needed to learn a lesson," he spat out with a sneer. "If I burned your place down, your family would just help you rebuild. This way, you can't fix it. Even if Garfield figures out a way to keep you out of jail, no one will believe you're innocent." He straightened, lifting his chin, a triumphant grin twisting his mouth. "I told you that you'd never run that place without me. Turns out, I was right."

"Bob is going to have to completely rebuild. It could take months. You don't feel the least bit guilty about that, though, do you?" I searched his face, hoping for some hint of empathy. It wasn't there. He truly was the worst.

Proving me right, Matthew shrugged. "Shit happens. Bob was convenient. And you needed to come down a peg or two."

I wondered if that was enough. I forced myself to stay facing Matthew, eyes on him, though every muscle in my body strained to turn to the shelves at the back of the room. But there were things I needed to know, and if Matthew was arrogant enough to talk, I sure as hell wasn't going to stop him.

"What about the break-in at Sawyers Bend Brewing?" I pressed. "How did you pull that off?"

"You're so dumb," he said with a curl of his upper lip. "Cammie. She had a thing for me before you and I hooked up. I kept her on the side." He shrugged. "She didn't have a brewery to go with her, but she was very eager to please. Unlike you."

I rolled my eyes, then reminded myself I'd get more

out of him if I looked meek. Meek was so not my thing. But surely, I could pretend for a little longer. I went back to hugging my arms around my chest, letting my head dip a little. *Think small and scared, Avery*, I reminded myself.

"Cammie let you in?" I asked. "Or she broke into my office?"

"I wasn't even there," he said. "That was all Cammie. She emptied out your drawer and took everything because she didn't know what was important. She stole Bob's phone for me, too. He's as dumb as you are. All about being a family man, but Cammie flashed her tits and lifted his phone without him noticing. I cloned it while she kept him distracted. It's easy if you know where to look on the internet."

He stared me down, taking a step closer to loom over me. I had to fight the urge to move out of reach. "There's nothing to prove I did any of it. Everyone saw me at Bear Run on Sunday, and Cammie did the break-in all by herself. But you, you were there while Wild Haven burned. Your name and your brother's money won't be able to get you out of this. Maybe you should sell me Sawyers Bend Brewing while you can."

I backed up a step, wanting space from the menace in his eyes. I'd wanted him to think he had the upper hand, but his confidence was unnerving.

"I'm not selling you my brewery," I said, and the waver of fear in my voice wasn't entirely an act.

"You sure about that? I know you can't reproduce the beer everyone loved so much on Halloween. Even if you managed to remember the recipe, I added something you don't know about. Only I have the real recipe."

I narrowed my eyes on him, dropping the whole meek act. He was fucking diabolical. Bad enough he'd broken into my office, set Bob's brewery on fire, framed me for arson, and almost killed me. But now he was fucking with my beer?

"Are you kidding me?" I demanded.

"Nope," his grin so smug I struggled not to take a swing at him, even though he could probably knock me out with one good hit. He tilted his head to the side. "I'll tell you what. For the right price, I'll give you the whole recipe. Secret additions and all."

"Fuck you," was all I could say. Did I want to know how to make that magnificent brew we'd sold on Halloween? Yeah, I did, but I was not giving this asshole a dime.

"Are you sure about that, Avery? You won't get it any other way."

I shook my head. He wasn't worth another word out of my mouth.

"You want to think about that?" he asked, closing the distance between us. "Think real hard about what more you have to lose."

He reached for my arm. I stepped back, hitting a tall stack of bags stuffed with hops. Fuck. I'd forgotten how tall Matthew was. My heart kicked in my chest, my throat dry—

And then I heard the sound I'd been waiting for, growing louder as West came out from behind the shelves at the back of the room.

"Matthew Holt. You're under arrest for breaking and entering, arson, and attempted murder."

Matthew's face went slack, his eyes wide with shock. I took advantage of his distraction to slip off to the side, far out of his reach, biting my lip to stop a semi-hysterical laugh of relief. I hadn't been sure I could pull it off, but Griffen had been right—Matthew was just arrogant enough to think he could get away with it. He only needed a little prodding.

West had the cuffs on Matthew and was pushing him out the door when Chris came to my side. He tugged at his sandy ponytail, his eyes heavy.

"Hey, Avery. I'm so sorry. I didn't know. I didn't—"

"It's okay," I said. "Don't worry about it. I hired him in the first place. I had no idea he was this level of crazy."

"He knew his stuff," Chris said, leaning one shoulder against the tall stack of hops.

I nodded. "He did. But poor Bob." I let out a breath, my chest tight at the memory of watching Matthew's fire devour Bob's brewery. If it had been me, I'd be grieving. This was a business, but we were all in it because we loved what we did. Every brewery around here was a little different, reflecting the personalities of the owners and their staff. And Bob's was effectively gone. I turned to Chris.

"I was thinking," I said, "we should all get together, do a fundraising thing for Bob. I'm sure he's got insurance, but you know how that goes. It doesn't cover much."

"Yeah," Chris said, grinning at me. "That's a great idea. I'll make some calls. I know he'd appreciate it. And it's cool of you to think of it, especially after—" He raised his chin at the door Matthew had so recently been pushed through.

I rubbed the heel of my palm against my chest. I didn't want to hold grudges. I just wanted to put Matthew behind me. "Well, I can't blame you guys too much for falling for his bullshit, considering I fell for it first. I'm just glad he was a jackass enough to confess."

Chris flipped his ponytail behind his shoulder, shaking his head. "I didn't believe it till he said it. I just —" His gaze darted my way. "I didn't believe you did it either, Avery. But I wouldn't have thought of Matt."

"I'm just glad this is over," I said. "We can all move on."

Chris sighed. "I guess I'm looking for a new brewmaster."

"You'll find somebody good," I said, patting him on the shoulder. "I'm going to talk to some people about this thing for Bob, see if we can get some music, some food trucks. Will you talk to Bob?"

"I'm on it," Chris said. "We'll put together something awesome."

"Damn straight we will," I agreed, catching sight of Hawk and Griffen just outside the door to Chris's hops room. "I'll be in touch." I left Chris with another pat on his shoulder and followed Hawk and Griffen out of the brewery into the bright sunshine.

The three of us stood together in the parking lot, watching West drive a handcuffed Matthew back to the police station.

Griffen gave me a hug and kissed the top of my head. "You've got balls of steel, kid," he said.

"I thought I was going to throw up for a minute there." My stomach rolled at the memory of facing down Matthew.

"But you didn't," Hawk added. "You got what you needed. Cleared your name. That confession, on top of everything else West has? He might get off on the breaking and entering, depending on what Cammie has to say, but the arson and attempted second-degree murder charges are going to be a lot harder to dodge. Holt isn't getting out of jail for a long time."

"Let's hope not," I agreed. "It's a little early, but you guys want a beer? I want to go open my brewery."

Chapter Twenty-Nine

AVERY

I stood in front of the small table beside the stainless-steel vat, where my flagship IPA was fermenting. Beside that, my attempt at recreating the Fall brew was bottle conditioning, the process that added carbonation to the fermented beer. One more day before I found out how close I'd come to the original. It was hard to resist popping one open early, just to see.

Thanksgiving—I reminded myself. Tomorrow I'd see what I had. Could be nothing. It probably wouldn't be awful, but it could be just *meh*. Or it could be amazing. And if it wasn't, I'd try again. Whatever Matthew had added—and I did believe he'd added something, his smugness had the ring of truth—I'd figure it out.

I looked down at the table in front of me. I'd set up a random-ish collection of flavors that could have been in that beer— dried orange peel, lemon peel, and one of grapefruit. A knuckle of ginger, a stick of cinnamon, and a slice of star anise.

I wasn't sure. The orange and lemon were in the beer

currently bottle conditioning, as was a hint of the cinnamon and ginger. I'd used the star anise before, in a stout, but the flavor was too specific, too dense for this fall brew, and my memory of what Matt and I had bottled didn't have that flavor profile. But the others—they were possible.

I didn't know. Had there been a hint of lemon? I thought so, but I wasn't sure. The original recipe was no longer helpful, since I doubted he'd written down what he'd added. Or maybe he had, and that's why he'd had Cammie steal it. I couldn't be sure, and it didn't matter anyway. I had to figure this out on my own, for my own sake. I wanted this for myself.

I was trying not to obsess, but when I had a break or needed a distraction, I wandered this way and studied the table, thinking, tasting beer in my imagination. I'd get it eventually. I glanced at my watch. It was time to open the taproom. Dave had the day off to visit with family who'd come to town for the holiday, and since West had arrested Cammie, she wouldn't be coming in to work. That whole thing was a bummer. Cammie and I hadn't been BFFs, and she hadn't been a stellar employee, but I thought we'd been friends. I didn't think she'd steal from me or lie to me. But she had, and now I was down a third of my staff. It sucked, but I could live with it.

I didn't feel like manning the bar. I was more in the mood to do beer stuff than people stuff, but I didn't have a choice. Finn was coming in, which would be a good distraction. Thanks to a few storms in the past week, most of the leaves were on the ground instead of in the trees, and fewer tourists crowded Sawyers Bend. The Inn was packed full and would do a gorgeous Thanksgiving dinner the next day, but overall, the town was quieter than it had been. I didn't mind the downturn in business.

My phone rang as I unlocked the front door of the taproom, propping it open to let in the crisp breeze. I pulled it from my pocket. Sterling.

"Hey, what's up?" I asked.

"I got a call from Emmett," she said, her voice vibrating with excitement. "You know Emmett?"

"Emmett, who works with Sinclair Security? Mysterious friend of Hawk's? That Emmett?" I asked to egg her on. Of course, I knew who Emmett was.

"That Emmett," she confirmed. "He's been looking into Dad's murder. Investigating the way..." She paused, as if searching for the right words. "The way he specifically can investigate," she said, which didn't tell me anything, considering the only thing I really knew about Emmett, other than that he was friends with Hawk and worked at Sinclair Security, was that I didn't know anything about Emmett. And I had the feeling there was a lot to not know.

"So?" I prompted.

"He found something weird."

"How weird?" I asked, interested on a whole new level. I wasn't sure if weird was good, but it was a hell of a lot better than nothing, which is what we'd had in our investigation since Anna Novak had been murdered and we'd agreed to stop poking around. It was frustrating, but—

"Well," Sterling said, her words coming slowly, as if she didn't quite understand them yet, "he said that Dad created a trust over two years before he was killed, for someone named Caroline Sawyer."

"Caroline Sawyer?" I repeated, moving behind the bar to check that the fridge was fully stocked with a few beers we didn't have on tap and a selection of soft drinks. "Are we related to someone named Caroline Sawyer? Do we know anyone named Caroline Sawyer?" I racked my brain, but the name wasn't familiar.

"No," Sterling said. "And Emmett searched—did a genealogy kind of thing—and he said there isn't anyone in the family by that name."

"That is weird. What does it mean?" I asked, not sure in this case whether *weird* was useful.

I practically heard Sterling shrug through the phone. "I don't know. I was kind of hoping you would."

"No," I said, shaking my head as if she could see me. "Maybe—I don't know. It seems like the woman he was seeing could have been pregnant, based on the stuff that Savannah found in the attic. So maybe the baby was going to be Caroline?"

"That's what Emmett guessed," Sterling said.

"What do you think?" I asked.

"I don't know," she said. "That could be it. Though if he were setting up trusts for his children, which we know he did, because ours exist—and this was for a potential daughter, why wouldn't Harvey have known about it?"

"Maybe Dad didn't tell him," I said. "Or maybe he did. But from what we can tell, there was never a newborn at Heartstone—none of the baby things were used—so maybe that's why Harvey didn't mention it."

"Good point," Sterling said. "This feels like big news

and also nothing, because we have no idea what it means, or who the mother was."

"I know," I agreed. "Exciting and disappointing."

"I'm going to ask Miss Martha," Sterling said. "She and Aunt Ophelia know the most about our family. Aunt Ophelia is in New York with Nash's mom, but if Miss Martha doesn't know anything, I'll call her."

"Keep me posted." I looked up as a shadow fell across the open door. Finn stepped in, raising one hand in a wave. I wasn't expecting to see Ford right behind him, a foil to Finn. Ford was taller, his hair darker, face somber, whereas Finn's had an easy, open grin. But then, everything was right in Finn's world these days—he had an amazing wife, a cool kid, and a job he loved. I'd never seen Finn smile this much. Not since before his mother died when we were kids. And Ford—well, I couldn't remember the last time I'd seen him really smile. Ford wasn't living these days. He was just existing. Not the same at all.

"Finn just got here," I said to Sterling. "If Miss Martha thinks of anything, call me back."

"Definitely," Sterling said, and hung up.

"What's up?" Finn asked.

"Sterling," I said in answer, but didn't tell him why she'd called. My brothers were not fans of Sterling's and my interest in our father's death. And since I didn't have any useful information, Finn didn't need to know. He knew even less Sawyer family lore than I did, having been away so many years. If Miss Martha and Aunt Ophelia couldn't think of anything, we'd open it up to the rest of the family—but not yet.

"I'm going to poke around." Finn lifted his chin in the direction of the tiny kitchen off the bar.

"Go for it," I said, and turned to Ford. "Hey, did you come to hang out?"

He shook his head. "Had to see Haywood about some old business. He was going to be in Sawyers Bend, so I grabbed a ride with Finn. Figured I'd take care of that and then hang out if Finn wasn't done. Do you need any help behind the bar?"

"No," I laughed. "Why, are you offering?"

"I can pull pints if you need a break later," he said, his eyes lighting briefly with interest.

"I'll let you know," I said, intrigued at the idea of my staid older brother tending bar.

A dark figure stepped in front of the open door, and I stared for a moment, waiting for my eyes to adjust. Ford turned, lifted a hand. "You want a beer?" he called.

Cole Haywood took a step out of the glare, his features coming into focus. I blinked. Even dressed casually, in a sweater and jeans, he looked model-perfect. Cole had always been almost painfully handsome, but oddly, not actually attractive. At least not to me. There was something about him—like he was carved from marble, the cheekbones a little too sharp, his lower lip a little too full, his blue eyes cold.

I don't know, maybe I just resented him for being the genius lawyer, but not genius enough to get Ford out of jail. Whatever. He was a friend of the family, and I could play nicely.

"Beer?" I asked with a smile as Cole approached the bar.

"Whatever Ford's having," he said.

I looked at Ford. "Ford hasn't ordered yet."

"I want that stout I had the other day."

"Ah, the breakfast stout," I said. "It's a little late in the day for a breakfast beer, but a solid choice. That good for you?" I asked Cole.

"Sounds great," he said, and I thought he would have said the exact same thing if Ford had ordered an IPA or a lager.

"I'll bring them over in a minute," I said.

"Thanks, Ave." Ford led Cole across the room to his usual table. Too far away for me to eavesdrop, unfortunately. Both of them looked serious, but not particularly upset.

When I was done building their stouts, I carried them to the table, hoping to eavesdrop just a little, but Ford saw me coming and waited until I was back out of earshot to resume their conversation. He'd always been cagey, my older brother.

My phone buzzed with a text. West.

> Lunch? I can pick you up a sandwich and chips, bring it by.

> Sounds perfect. Thanks.

A sweet fizz of anticipation hit my chest. West and I had spent all of our free time together since he'd arrested Matthew, and it wasn't enough. I suspected it would never be enough. There was no such thing as too much West. And now he was bringing me lunch. Because that was the guy he was. Thoughtful. And hot. Maybe I'd give

Ford his chance at the taps and drag West off to my office. I could lock the door and—

From across the room, I watched as Ford reached into his back pocket and pulled out an envelope, sliding it across the table to Cole, who picked it up and tucked it into his own back pocket. Very interesting—or it would be, if I had any idea what was in that envelope. It made me uneasy trying to imagine what it could be. A check for services rendered?

I'm sure Ford would tell me it was none of my business. And that was true. But I was his little sister, and I was curious. Maybe I'd work up the nerve to ask at some point. Ford wasn't exactly approachable when it came to the details of his personal life, but if the right moment would present itself... Until then, I'd have to live with not knowing. It felt like I did that a lot these days, and oddly, I was getting more okay with it.

Ford pushed his seat back and stood. Cole Haywood followed suit. They clasped hands over the table with a firm shake, saying something I couldn't quite catch.

Ford sat back down, and Cole headed toward me.

"I liked that breakfast stout, Avery," Cole said, with a smile that didn't reach his eyes.

"I'm so glad," I said. "It's one of my favorites."

"What do I owe you?" He reached for his back pocket.

"It's on the house," I said.

"Are you sure?" he asked, giving me another, friendlier smile, the one I always thought of as his campaign smile—the same smile he might use if he were running for office, shaking hands and kissing babies, his perfect wife by his side. I'd always thought Cole looked like he'd be perfect for politics.

And at that thought, a cascade of images crashed over me.

Cole, standing beside his perfect wife, who'd died in childbirth right around the time Prentice had stopped the renovations on Heartstone Manor.

Cole. Whose perfect wife had been named Caro Haywood.

Caro, short for Caroline.

I felt the blood drain from my face, prickles in my fingers spreading up my arms and down my spine. My mouth sagged open. Could it...? But he was Ford's lawyer. He would have—

A wave of icy horror went over me as I stared up into Cole Haywood's cool blue eyes. As Ford's lawyer, he would have been in a perfect position to make sure Ford was convicted of Prentice's murder.

Oh, fuck.

I snapped my mouth shut and blinked, trying to get myself together.

"You okay, Avery?" Cole asked, a chill in his tone that sent a blade of ice up my spine.

We locked gazes, and for a split second, I saw comprehension in his blue eyes. Then it was gone, masked by that genial campaign smile.

"You looked a little dizzy there for a second," he said. "Do you need to sit down?"

"I'm fine," I said. "Just tired, I guess."

"Well," he reached across the bar and patted me on

the shoulder, "get some rest. It's a lot, running a place like this by yourself."

"Don't I know it," I said, my stomach twisting, wishing he would just leave so I could fucking think. I needed to think. I felt crazy standing here having this friendly conversation with the man who might have shot my father and framed my brother for murder. Who'd tried to kill Griffen and then Royal and had likely murdered Ford's ex-wife, Vanessa.

I nodded at Cole, watching as he turned, lifted a hand in farewell to Ford, and headed out the door, the edge of the white envelope Ford had given him sticking out of his back pocket.

"Avery, you all right?" Ford asked.

I was so not ready to voice what I knew in my gut was the truth. Not until I could think it through, talk to West. Sterling. Something.

"I, uh, yeah. I just need to go in the back for a second," I said. "Can you watch the taps if anybody comes in?"

"Sure, I got it," Ford said. "Take your time. I'll give a shout if I can't figure anything out."

"Okay," I said, pushing through the swinging door to the quiet of the brewery.

I paced the open space in the center of the brewery. Was I crazy? I was connecting dots all over the place. Okay, so Cole's wife had died in childbirth, along with their baby, three years ago. Or was it four? What if Caro was Caroline? Had she been planning to leave Cole? Had he known before her death? Was the baby Prentice's or Cole's? So many questions. I couldn't sort it all out in my head.

I wanted to call Griffen, but I should talk to Sterling first, since she was the only other one who knew about Caroline Sawyer/possibly Caro Haywood. Sterling could tell me if I was crazy. Or maybe I'd go flip the lock on the front door and see what my brothers thought, since they happened to be right there in my taproom. If they didn't think I was nuts, we could call Sterling and—

I caught the noise of a scuff of a shoe on the concrete floor of the brewery. Turning, I froze.

Cole Haywood stood in front of me.

"I don't know how you know," he said, "but you do, don't you?"

I opened my mouth with some vague idea of saying "Know what?" like I was clueless, but I didn't get that far.

Cole raised his hand in a fast arc. I heard a buzz and felt a burn on the side of my neck. Pain arced through me as every muscle in my body locked, and everything went dark.

Chapter Thirty

WEST

I tapped on the steering wheel of my SUV, waiting for the group of tourists—identifiable by all the shopping bags in their hands—to cross the road. Things had calmed down since the leaves had begun to fall. The second the road was clear, I pressed the gas, finishing my slow travel through town. Everything was quiet, exactly the way I liked it. I looked at the bag of sandwiches on the seat beside me. So quiet, I could take a lunch break with Avery.

I frowned as my phone rang, blaring through the dashboard. Sterling's name flashed on the screen. I tapped to answer.

"Sterling, what's up?" I asked, a skitter of nerves going down my spine. Sterling and I weren't strangers, but she didn't usually call me.

"West, I called Avery, and she's not answering. I figured it out."

"You figured what out?" I asked, thinking there were any number of reasons Avery wouldn't answer her phone, especially since she was short-staffed. But those nerves dancing up and down my spine didn't like it.

"No, hold on a second. I just need to take a breath. Hold on." The sound of her sucking in a deep, quick breath filled my car's speakers. She let it out in a whoosh. There was a jingle I imagined was her earrings rattling as she shook her head. "Okay, sorry. It's just. Okay. Emmett called. You know—"

"I know who Emmett is," I said.

"He found out my dad made a trust before he died for a Caroline Sawyer."

"Who the hell is Caroline Sawyer?" I asked.

"Exactly what we were wondering. I called Avery and told her. She didn't know either. I talked to Griffen. He didn't know. Nobody knows who Caroline Sawyer is. And then I realized—Caroline Sawyer. Caro Haywood."

That was all she said, but it was enough. Far-fetched? Maybe. But when I started putting the pieces together. Caro Haywood had died in childbirth, and the timeframe fit the age of the baby things they'd found in the attic— and if Caro Haywood was the Caroline Sawyer that trust had been intended for, that meant that Cole Haywood, Ford's attorney—

"Fuck," I said.

"I know, right?" Sterling said, her voice caught between exhilaration and worry. "I didn't see that one coming. And the thing is, Griffen said Ford went with Finn to Sawyers Bend Brewing because he was going to meet Cole Haywood. So, I'm freaking out that Avery's not answering her phone."

Logical. The skitters down my spine turned to ice.

"Did you call Ford and Finn?"

"Yeah, they didn't answer either. But Ford doesn't take his phone with him half the time, and Finn ignores his a lot, so—"

"And Avery could be serving customers," I said, trying to reassure Sterling. My gut wasn't buying it.

"I know, but— Are you closer than I am?" she asked.

"I—"

"Where are you?" I asked, cutting Sterling off.

"I'm at Heartstone. Quinn closed Outdoor Adventures today."

"Is Hawk at Heartstone? Or did he and Quinn go out somewhere?"

"I don't know," she said. "I think he's here."

"Alright. Don't worry. I was headed to Sawyers Bend Brewing anyway. I'm only a few minutes away. I'll keep you posted. And Sterling—don't leave Heartstone Manor until you hear from me. Got it?"

"Okay. Just let me know when everything's okay. Please."

"I will."

I hung up on Sterling and pressed the gas pedal a little harder. I didn't flick on my reds and blues. If Haywood was there, but Avery hadn't put the pieces together, I didn't want to spook him. Sterling could be wrong. Caro Haywood might not be Caroline Sawyer, and even if she were, it didn't mean that Cole had killed Prentice and come after the rest of the Sawyers. And even if he had, it didn't mean Avery was in danger from him. She didn't always have her phone on her when she was working in the taproom, and both Finn and Ford weren't usually glued to theirs either.

But I could feel it. She was in danger.

Despite those reasonable explanations, I pulled up Hawk's number. He answered on the second ring.

"I need you to head to Sawyers Bend Brewing. Did you talk to Sterling?"

"No, I was out on the grounds with Quinn until a few minutes ago."

I filled him in on the pieces Sterling and Emmett had put together.

"It's a stretch," Hawk said, "but also not a stretch."

"Exactly," I agreed. I remembered the flash of Caro's green eyes, her perfectly styled golden hair. "Cole was head over heels for her, but Caro—I could see her angling at being mistress of Heartstone Manor, the wife of Prentice Sawyer. She would have seen it as trading up."

"I'll take your word for it," Hawk said. "I'm on my way."

He didn't reassure me that everything was probably fine. Hawk had seen too much to fall back on comforting platitudes.

The front door to Sawyers Bend Brewing was propped open, perfect for the crisp fall afternoon. I jogged up the front steps, telling my heart to calm down. Seeing Ford behind the bar didn't relax me.

"Where's Avery?" I barked.

He set a pint glass on the counter, taking in my face before his eyes narrowed. "She went in the back a few minutes ago," Ford said. "Why? What happened?"

"How many minutes ago?" I demanded, looking at the closed door between the taproom and the brewery.

"I don't know." Ford frowned. "Maybe ten?"

Finn came out of the tiny kitchen tacked onto the end of the bar, wiping his hands on a cloth. "God, it's filthy in there." He caught sight of me and stopped. His eyes fixed on my face. "What? What's wrong?"

"Where's Avery?" I asked again.

"In the back." He looked at Ford. "Was she going to be gone that long? I know you said you could handle the bar and it's empty in here, but I lost track of time," he said, his gaze flicking back to me. "What is it?"

I didn't answer. I had more questions. "Haywood still here?"

"No, he left," Ford said.

"Before or after Avery went in the back?" I asked, heading for the swinging door, my hand hovering over the sidearm at my hip.

"Before," Ford said. "Just before," he clarified slowly. "What's wrong, West?"

"I'll tell you in a minute," I said, more interested in locating Avery than explaining Sterling's information.

I pushed through the swinging door, resisting the urge to rush, letting it open slowly, scanning the brewery as it was revealed inch by inch. Empty. If Haywood were in here, he would be hiding. Avery was nowhere to be seen.

I headed to the table in the back, saw the crates of bottled beer—the new recipe. Had she opened one? She'd been waiting for Thanksgiving. On a table beside it was her arrangement of mystery ingredients. The orange peels were on the ground beside a slice of star anise. I glanced up, scanning the room. The door closest to the parking lot was ajar. Just a sliver.

Fuck. Fuck. Avery wouldn't have left these ingredients on the ground, and she definitely wouldn't have left the door open.

Fuck.

I raced across the room and yanked the door open to see the parking lot empty except for Avery's car. I texted Hawk.

> Avery's missing. Check her phone?

A second later, he called. "Phone's at Sawyers Bend Brewing, but I have her tagged."

"Of course you do," I murmured, grateful for Hawk's paranoia.

"It's in her watch," he said. "Since she rarely takes it off. One sec."

"Where are you?" I asked while I waited.

"I'm at the gates of the Manor. I'll be there in ten minutes."

"Get me a location on Avery," I said. "You can catch up."

"She's on the move," Hawk said a moment later. "Headed out of town. East. I'll forward the tracking to you so you can follow."

I raced back through the brewery and taproom, shouting to Avery's brothers, "Lock up and go back to Heartstone. Sterling will fill you in."

I didn't have time to explain. All that mattered was getting to Avery.

Chapter Thirty-One

AVERY

My eyes opened to a sea of brown, the details slowly coming into focus as my body bounced. Brown upholstery beneath me. Brown fabric stretched above me. I was in a vehicle. How had I...?

It all came rushing back—Caro Haywood, Cole. The understanding had hit me so suddenly, I hadn't been able to hide it. And he'd seen. He'd followed me into the brewery. He'd had something... A taser?

I tried to feel for an injury, but my hands were tied behind my back, whatever bound them cutting into my wrists. I shifted and realized my feet were tied as well. He'd trussed me up like a pig for roasting, and somehow, he'd gotten me out of Sawyers Bend Brewing without anyone seeing.

I tried to think. Was I better off pretending I was still unconscious, or should I talk to him? I wanted to know why. Everyone knew how devoted Cole Haywood had been to his wife. If Prentice had been having an affair with her, I could understand Cole shooting him. Not the best way to resolve marital differences, but that made sense. Coming after the rest of us, though—

Why? I needed to know.

Forget playing like I was out cold. I had too many questions for that.

"Where are we going?" I asked, twisting and straining, struggling to bring myself to a seated position. I needed to see his face—or what I could catch from the back seat.

"We're going nowhere," he said with a short laugh.

I tried to figure out if he sounded unhinged or if the laugh was him sounding normal. I couldn't. A man I'd known for years had just kidnapped me. He wasn't my friend. He was eight or nine years older than Griffen and my father's business associate. There were a lot of reasons I'd never sought out Cole Haywood's company, but none of them were because I thought he was dangerous. If anything, I'd always thought he was boring, just another buttoned-up business suit. I'd never pictured him with that taser in his hand, much less holding the knife that had killed Anna Novak.

I lurched my way into a seated position. I couldn't see his eyes. They were, fortunately, focused on the road, but I got a good look at Cole Haywood's profile.

It wasn't what I'd expected. I don't know—maybe I thought when he kidnapped me, the mask would come off and the crazy would be out in the open. But he just looked like Cole Haywood: chiseled jawline, blade-sharp cheekbones, perfectly styled dark hair. I'd been kidnapped by a menswear model.

"What do you mean we're going nowhere?" I asked, confused by both his answer and his laugh.

"We're going to the middle of nowhere," he said, amusement coloring his words, "A little piece of property I walked a couple of years ago. I thought about investing in it with your father, actually. Changed my mind. Too remote. But while we were out there, we discovered that long ago, someone dug a well and covered it up. Weeds grew over the cover, but the well was still there. I thought, someday, that might be the perfect place to hide a body. And look, here you are, a body I need to hide. Convenient, isn't it?"

"Not for me," I muttered.

"Well, no," he agreed. "Not for you." Cole's hands tightened on the steering wheel. "You weren't on my list, Avery. I wasn't planning on getting rid of you. But I'm not done with your family yet. And somehow, you figured it out. So, here we are."

"One of Sterling's contacts found a trust Prentice set up for Caroline Sawyer," I said, watching carefully for a reaction.

The wheel of the car jerked to the left, and my shoulder slammed into the door, my skull cracking against the window and sending painful shudders down my spine.

"Interesting," was all Cole Haywood said.

"Why didn't you put Anna Novak in the well?" I asked.

West had spared me seeing the worst of it, but I'd heard enough—seen enough—before he'd pushed me out of the room.

Cole had done that.

Was that how he was going to kill me?

"I lost my temper. She had a mouth on her." He shook his head. "If she hadn't understood what she'd made and for whom, I might have let her live. But she knew exactly who Caro was. Who Prentice was. And what they were to each other. And she made the necklace anyway."

"So, she had to die?" I asked.

Cole raised an eyebrow and met my eyes in the rearview mirror for just a moment—long enough for me to see the full flare of insanity in his vivid blue eyes.

"No, Avery," he said deliberately, each word falling in careful measure. "She had to die because she had a smart mouth, and she pissed me off. And it seemed like something I'd enjoy."

I looked away, unable to hold that gaze. I could tell by the light in his eyes how much he'd enjoyed it. It followed that he would probably enjoy killing me too. Was he going to stab me before he threw me in the well, or just toss me down into the wet dark to die of starvation?

I wasn't wild about either option. I wriggled, shoving my hands down to feel my back pockets where I usually kept my phone. Empty. Fuck. *Okay, think*, Avery. I knew Hawk could track my phone. Was that all? I wouldn't put it past him to have planted trackers on us. But I didn't know. Hawk could be sneaky. *Oh, please, Hawk, please have been sneaky.* Based on the woods outside the window, we were far out of town. And even when they found out I was missing, without my phone, they wouldn't know where to look or who I was with.

Despair rose in a dark wave, threatening to swamp me. I wasn't giving up. I just didn't know how to fight while I was fucking zip-tied in the back seat of his car. I couldn't stop Cole physically—he was bigger than me, and strong enough to have carried me out of the brewery quickly, before anyone noticed. And I was restrained.

Panic welled, my throat tightening.

If Hawk was tracking me, and if they realized I was missing in time, there might be a chance someone was going to rescue me. And if that was the case, and Cole was feeling as talkative as he seemed to be, I should keep asking questions.

"Why?" I asked. "What did Griffen ever do to you, or Royal, or Vanessa, or Ford?"

"Your father stole my wife," he said, "and killed her with that baby he put in her. He took them both from me. She didn't want to have a baby with me. Did you know that?"

I shook my head. It's not like Cole and Caro had run in the same social circles as me. I lived in my jeans and brewed beer, while Caro had been high heels and ladies' lunches—even though she'd also loved the outdoors and hiking. We hadn't been friends or even acquaintances. I'd known her enough to make polite small talk now and then when I got roped into a family function. That was it.

But even I knew how much Cole Haywood had loved his wife. I had no idea she'd denied him the children he'd wanted.

"It must have burned," I said, "when you found out the baby was Prentice's—that she'd had a baby with my father and not you."

"That's one way to put it," Cole agreed.

"I don't know why she thought my father would be a better parent than you, when he was pretty miserable at it," I said.

"Agreed. But your father had a way of clouding the minds of even the best women. Look at Darcy."

I sighed. Cole was right. I'd never understood how sweet, kind, loving Darcy had fallen for my father. She'd been the closest thing any of us had had to a mother, and she'd had a heart as big as the universe. Why the hell had she fallen for Prentice? I didn't know a more evil man, except maybe Cole. As far as I knew, Prentice hadn't murdered anyone. That definitely put him a rung above Cole in the Ethics Olympics.

"When did you find out?" I asked, my heart twinging the tiniest bit at the thought of Cole finding out the wife he'd worshipped had betrayed him.

"When she died," Cole answered through a tight jaw. "I thought the baby was mine."

"I'm sorry," I said—because I was. He was a murderous psychopath, but he'd loved his wife, and it sounded like he'd wanted the child. A discovery like that could make anyone lose their grip on reality.

"What did Ford do to you?" I pressed. "Why pin Dad's murder on him?"

"Ford was the one who set them up."

"Set them up? What do you mean? Like on a date?" I couldn't make that picture work in my head. Ford had his failings, but I couldn't see him helping our father commit adultery with the wife of someone he'd considered a friend. "I don't believe you. Ford was your friend. He still thinks he's your friend."

"I'm not fucking done with Ford," Cole spit out. "But he'll know exactly where we stand before the end."

"So, what do you mean he set them up?"

"The charity event they co-hosted. It was Ford's idea," Cole said, voice flat. "Ford was the reason they spent so much time together. Went hiking, had lunch—"

"Fell in love," I finished quietly.

"Fuck love," Cole snapped. "Your father didn't know what love was. He knew power and manipulation. He didn't understand love—what it is to die for someone or kill for them."

I'm not sure you do either, I thought to myself. But remembering his comment about Anna Novak's smart mouth, I kept mine shut.

"Ford could be flattered into not paying attention," Cole went on. "Your father—well, he'd do anything if it profited him. But Griffen was more complicated. I could already see it, even at twenty-two. Then he was out of the way—"

"Out of the way of what?" I interrupted.

"Of whatever Prentice and Edgar, and I wanted to do."

So, this was all about business? I couldn't get my head around that. Killing because his wife had betrayed him—not really okay, but I understood. Ruining people's lives to make more money. Didn't they already have enough? I was a businesswoman. I understood the need to make a profit, to keep the doors open. I got wanting to have nice things, but I wasn't going to kill anybody for them.

I wouldn't kidnap and murder anyone either. Obviously, Cole Haywood was working with a completely different value system—one that included dumping people down wells to solve problems. I twisted my wrists against the binding, but whatever he'd tied me with held as if it were iron shackles.

Fuck. Fuck. Fuck.

We turned off the gravel road onto a narrower path that wasn't much more than a wide hiking trail. The car bounced and dipped over the rough terrain, and we drove deeper and deeper into the woods. No one was going to find me back here. Even if there was some way they could track me, we were deep enough in the mountains that there might not be any way to pick up a signal. Cell phones worked better close to town. We were nowhere, just as Cole had said.

The silence was creeping me out. I was almost jolted off the seat as Cole drove over a log. His sedan wouldn't be much good to him after this. He didn't seem to care, which was almost as unnerving as the silence. After another hard bounce, I braced my legs to stay in place and tried to figure out what to do with the little time I had left.

I had to keep Cole talking. If I was going to die for Cole Haywood's fucked up revenge fantasy, I needed to know why. And I couldn't take another second of the quiet. Once he shoved me in that well, I'd have all the quiet I could stand. I squeezed my eyes shut, trying to fight the hopelessness. I couldn't give in to fear. I still had more questions.

"Why did you wait so long to kill Prentice?" I asked

as conversationally as I could manage. Caro had died a few years before Prentice was murdered. Why not kill him then? "And why try to kill Griffen?"

Ignoring my question about Prentice, he said, "Griffen was exiled for betraying his father. Why should he get to slide back in and take the reins just because Prentice was gone? He would undo everything we'd worked for and poke his nose into things that were none of his business. It seemed easier to get rid of him." He let out a sigh. "I underestimated how good his training had been. I did my best. Well, maybe not my best, but I gave it a good effort. He refused to go down easily. So, I moved on."

"To Royal?" I pressed. "And the Inn? And Vanessa?"

"Vanessa also had a smart mouth. And sharp eyes. She figured it out before any of you even got close. Tried to blackmail me." He let out a gust of laughter. "What a fucking moron. She could be so smart and so stupid. She thought those tits and long legs would cloud my mind. But I was married to Caro. When you've had the most beautiful woman in the world, a cheap imitation like Vanessa is nothing." He paused, considering.

"Vanessa was useful at first. I aimed her at Royal just to fuck with the Sawyers. Why should you all be one big happy family with Prentice gone and the family legacy sitting in your laps? You all had everything you ever wanted, while I'd lost my wife, my child. I had nothing. Well, fuck that. Prentice was out of the way. Ford was out of the way, and I realized—wouldn't life be so much better if the Sawyer empire crumbled, piece by piece?"

He rolled his neck, the vertebrae cracking. His easy

tone had my nerves on edge. "I'd almost decided to leave the rest of you alone. To go after the business instead of the people. And then Quinn found that necklace, and I learned that you three were looking for the designer, one of the few people who could connect Caro to Prentice. Bad enough I'd lost my wife, and the child that should have been mine. If you'd put those pieces together, everyone would have known. The only good thing Prentice and Caro did was keep their relationship quiet. The humiliation would have been too much to bear."

He slammed his fist into the dashboard hard enough to leave smears of red on the brown leather.

My heart seized in my chest. So much rage just behind that friendly exterior. I didn't want it turned on me.

"I wasn't having it," he said, his words coming out in crisp, clean bites. "I can't thank you enough for tracking her down for me."

"It wasn't me," I said, sick at the idea that I'd led him straight to the innocent designer. If no one stopped him, he'd go after Sterling, too. If he wanted to keep Prentice and Caro's connection quiet, he'd have to.

"Close enough," he said with a shrug.

"How did you know we found her?" I asked.

"Harvey has a big mouth and shit judgment. He and Edgar were worried about you girls putting yourselves in the line of fire," he said, sarcasm dripping from the words. "Little did they know they were loading the gun, chatting about it in front of me."

"Is that what you're going to use?" I asked. "A gun instead of a knife like you did with Anna Novak?"

Cole's eyes met mine in the rearview mirror, and I thought I saw a flare of remorse before he looked back to the narrow, bumpy road. "I lost my temper. We were in her kitchen. She made a smartass comment, and I was very, very angry. The knife was just there."

Just there for forty stab wounds?

He shook his head, this time with genuine remorse. "It was messy. I don't like messy. But no, I meant a metaphorical gun. If I kill you before you go in the well, I'll probably strangle you. There's nothing like it—hands around the neck, watching the light fade from your eyes." The smile that spread across his mouth was revoltingly handsome, filled with pleasurable anticipation.

Ugh. How had we not seen this beneath his cultured surface? All of this evil. I'd never liked Cole Haywood much, but I'd always thought it was because he was friends with my father and had a stick up his butt. But this? This, I had not seen.

"I'd vote for not being killed at all," I said.

"You don't get a vote," Cole answered with a laugh.

"Who did you strangle? You shot Prentice and Vanessa. You stabbed the jewelry designer," I reminded him.

Cole just shook his head and said, "Over the years, people have gotten in my way. Nobody that mattered."

"They mattered enough for you to kill them," I said.

He cocked his head to the side. "And now they don't matter at all."

The sedan came to a rocking halt. "We walk from here. It isn't far." Cole turned off the engine and got out. He wrenched open the door and reached in, leaning down to cut through the ties around my ankles with a long, shiny blade. The knife disappeared, and when he straightened, there was a black gun in his hand.

"I thought you said you weren't going to shoot me," I said, my stomach turning to ice.

"I'm not planning on it. Doesn't mean I won't. We have a hike ahead of us, and I want you to understand that this can go easily, or this can involve a lot of pain for you. It all depends on how bad a mood I'm in when we get where we're going. I suggest you do as you're told, and don't give me any trouble, because I can guarantee you will regret it."

His words shivered across my skin, leaving me frozen. My throat felt too tight to force out sound. I nodded in rough jerks.

He reached in, closed his hand around my upper arm, and hauled me out of the backseat. "Walk," he said, shoving me in front of him.

I could barely see a trail through the trees. I followed it, putting one foot in front of the other, eyes scanning the terrain. I was not going to peacefully walk to my death. I'd rather he shot me. But I needed to wait for the right moment.

Moments slipped away, the invisible clock in my head ticking, ticking, ticking as my feet ate up the distance between me and the well up ahead. We followed the trail, twisting around a cluster of old-growth trees, and to my right, the ground fell away from the trail into a steep ravine. I saw my opening.

It would be dangerous, but I'd take the woods and the steep incline over the psychopath with the gun any day. Wishing my hands were free so I could protect my head, I took a last step forward on the trail and threw myself to the side, expecting to go over the edge, bracing for the bone-jarring impact. Instead, a hand closed over the back of my shirt, yanking me back onto the trail.

"Don't try that again, or I'll shoot you in the kneecap and drag you."

I didn't like the sound of that any more than I liked the idea of dying at the bottom of a well. What now? I didn't know. I put one foot in front of the other, the muzzle of Cole's gun jammed in my back, trying to figure out a way out of this.

I ran out of time. A few more minutes of walking on the narrow deer path, and it opened into a square clearing, smaller than the one where we'd left the car. On one side, a line of stone extended, meeting another in a crumbling corner. Once upon a time, there had been a house here. Which meant...

"Over there." Cole shoved me with the gun, aiming me at the far corner of the clearing, where trees had begun to encroach on what had been the small side yard of the house. I heard the hollow thunk of my foot on wood before I saw the well. Fuck. I really was out of time. I scanned the woods behind Cole, hoping for some sign of rescue. There was only the sun on the pine needles and bare branches, the ground speckled red and yellow with fallen leaves. His hand closed over my wrists. With a sharp jerk, they were free. I caught the flash of the knife blade in the sun as I turned.

"Take off the cover," Cole ordered, sliding the knife

back in it's sheath and giving me a shove in the back. He raised the gun and aimed it at me.

I shook my head. I knew what happened after I took off the cover. A gunshot, if I were lucky. And if not, those elegant, long-fingered hands wrapped around my neck. No, thank you.

"Take off the cover, Avery, or I'll shoot you," he said, his tone chilly with annoyance. He had the upper hand here. I was wasting his time. But it was all the time I had left. I was going to waste as many seconds as I could.

"I'm not—" I began.

A shot rang out, so much louder than I would have thought, slamming into my ears just as fire burned across my upper arm. My opposite hand flew up, fingers coming away red.

"You shot me!" I shouted, too surprised to think about the wisdom of yelling at the man with the gun.

"I told you I would," he said, the chill now holding faint amusement. "Now take off the cover or I'll shoot you in the kneecap. That hurts a lot more. And I'll still make you take the cover off that well."

I was too much of a coward to push him a second time. Shooting my arm was bad enough. The burn of it made me a little dizzy. I did not want to know what a bullet in the knee would feel like. Slowly, I dropped to my knees and reached for the edge of the well cover, my injured arm protesting in deep spikes of agony. It was awkward, working my fingers under the edge, the weight of the cover pinching the tips as I heaved it up, almost overbalancing and tipping forward into the depths. I managed to get it mostly off when I rose to my feet again, glaring at Cole Haywood over the dark circle in the earth between us.

"What now?" I asked, looking from the hole in the ground to Cole.

He flicked the safety on his gun and shoved it in his back pocket, taking a step to the side, closer to me. "Now, we finish this."

He raised his hands and moved.

I couldn't think. If I thought about what I was going to do, I'd lose my nerve. But if this was it, if I was going to die, it wasn't going to be at those hands.

I looked from Cole to the depths of the well, took a step forward, and dropped into the dark.

Chapter Thirty-Two

WEST

"**W**here the fuck is he taking her?" I demanded, my eyes skipping from the road ahead to the map on my phone, Avery, a blinking red dot moving deeper and deeper into the mountains.

"To the middle of fucking nowhere," Hawk answered, his voice distant through the speaker. He trailed behind, speeding to catch up, watching the same map he'd shared with me.

"I'm going to lose you if we keep going in this direction," I said, watching as the signal bars on my phone vanished one by one until all I had left was a stubby, single bar. Hawk's voice faded in and out, and Avery's red dot on the map had stopped blinking.

No signal meant Hawk's tracker was useless. No signal meant I'd lose Avery, too.

My heart was a block of ice in my chest. Finding a missing person in these mountains was worse than looking for a needle in a haystack. I'd been on search and rescue before. I knew how easy it was to walk right past someone in the woods and not see them. And that was when you had an idea where to start looking.

The map refreshed, and I realized I'd missed a turn.

"You got me, Hawk?" I asked, not expecting an answer. The timer on the call clicked upwards. Hawk was there, but not there. From here, I'd be lucky to get another update to the map. I wouldn't hear from Hawk again until he caught up.

I was on my own.

Rolling to a stop, I threw my SUV into reverse, almost hitting the tail end against the side of the mountain as I negotiated a careful five-point turn to reverse direction on the narrow dirt road. I crept back down a quarter mile to swing to the left, up a trail barely wide enough for a vehicle. The fresh tire tracks in front of me told me I wasn't the first to drive this way.

My heart lurched, thudding against my ribs. How far behind them was I? Ten minutes? Fifteen?

My phone beeped as the call with Hawk officially dropped. The map he'd been sharing hung motionless, Avery's red dot frozen. My SUV crawled past her last tracked location. She'd come this way, but if they'd made any turns or left this trail, I'd lose her again.

Whatever Haywood had been driving wasn't equipped for the terrain. He'd scraped rocks, knocked over fallen branches, and rolled fallen logs, leaving clear evidence of his passage. Slowly, with every turn of my wheels, I was penning him in. As long as he kept going, I'd find him. Unless this trail led to an actual road. Then I'd be screwed. It seemed unlikely based on what I could see on the map. There were no roads for miles.

But where was he taking her? Why here?

This land was privately owned and had been on the market for years. Developers had dreams of exclusive gated communities with luxury homes and panoramic views of the Blue Ridge Mountains. None of those dreams had come to fruition. The cost of bringing in basic utilities, paving the road for regular use, and grading to build those mega mansions had been too high to make any kind of development profitable, and the land remained wild and mostly untraveled. As far as I knew, no one had lived up this way in my lifetime. What was here? Unless Haywood was just looking for somewhere remote to kill her and dump her body. That was the most logical explanation.

I had to get to Avery.

I pushed forward, pressing on the gas. My police issued SUV wasn't equipped for this kind of terrain either, but it could handle it better than whatever Haywood was driving. The woods were tight to the trail, the mountain rising on one side, trees dense on the down-hill slope. If Haywood's vehicle had left this path, I'd see it. But so far, the trail stretched in front of me, the ruts of his tires showing me exactly where he'd been. My gut churned. I was moving too slowly. I needed to get to Avery before he did whatever he was planning to do.

The trail curved to the right, no longer hugging the side of the mountain as it opened onto a patch of tall grass, the clear blue sky visible through the break in the trees.

A single vehicle, a luxury sedan, sat alone in the clearing. How had Haywood managed to get that thing all the way up here? No one was inside the car that I could see. There wasn't any movement in the grass surrounding the parked car, nor in the trees at the edge of the clearing.

I threw the SUV into park at the head of the trail, pocketing the keys. He wouldn't be able to get past me to leave. If he went anywhere, it would have to be on foot. And on foot, I was faster. So was Avery, if she were still able to walk.

I debated for a split second. Stay out of sight or check Haywood's vehicle? I wanted to see what was in the car, but the position was too exposed. Not knowing where Haywood was or what kind of weapon he had made waltzing out into the open risky. If he'd already clocked me, and I knew there was no way he hadn't heard me coming, I'd be visible the second I stepped out of my SUV. But there wasn't any way to help that.

A gunshot shattered the silence, echoing off the mountains and answering my question of whether he was watching. Whoever had pulled the trigger wasn't in the clearing, but they were close. *Avery.* Her name rico-cheted around my mind. If that bullet had been aimed at her, we were already out of time. I went for the trees, circling the edge of the clearing, searching for any sign of where they'd gone.

I found what I was looking for two-thirds of the way around the clearing. A deer path marked by fresh tracks belonging to two people. I wasn't a woodsman who could look at footprints and guess height, weight, or shoe size, but I knew enough to see two distinct sets of tracks. The one in front had dragged their feet, overturing mounds of fallen leaves and making their trail impossible to miss. Avery. She was alive. There was no blood, which there would have been had he shot her.

My heart pounding, I moved forward.

The woods around me were silent, except for bird calls and the occasional crackle of a small animal moving through the underbrush. I moved as silently as I could, weapon in one hand, eyes scanning for any sign of movement.

I heard him before I saw him, his feet moving fast, leaves rustling, branches breaking as he moved down the trail toward me. I ducked into a thicket of rhododendrons, hidden from view until he was even with me, his eyes on the trail ahead, his weapon held loosely in his hand.

I left the cover of the rhododendrons as he passed, stepping out to press the barrel of my gun against the back of his head. "Drop your weapon."

He froze, his hand tightening instinctively on the gun. Taking advantage of his surprise, I reached around to wrench the weapon from his hand. Flicking on the safety, I tossed it out of reach.

"Cole Haywood, you're under arrest."

"For what?" he asked, hanging on to that snooty lawyer tone even with my gun pressed to the base of his skull.

"Kidnapping to start. Put your hands up and behind your head," I said.

He lurched as if preparing to run. I'd been ready for him to make a move. My free hand shot up and closed over his throat, squeezing until he let out a pained squeak of sound. "Just give me a reason to pull the trigger, and I will," I promised. "Where is Avery?" I loosened my hand just enough to let him talk.

"Let me go, and I'll tell you," he rasped out.

"The hell I will. Hands behind your head," I ordered. "Do it now, and I won't shoot you where you stand. Don't fucking try me."

"She's already dead," he sneered, his eyes fixed on the trail behind me. Avery was back that way. She had to be.

His words sent icy fear spiking through me even though I knew they were bullshit. "If she were dead," I said, squeezing his throat tighter, "you wouldn't sound so nervous. She's out there somewhere, and since you won't tell me where, I don't need you."

I saw that bit of logic had seeped into his brain as he raised his hands and placed them behind his head.

"Smart move," I said, slapping a cuff onto one wrist. "I'll shoot you if I have to, but I'd rather bring you in. You have the right to remain silent. You have the right to an attorney—"

Maybe unable to believe he'd finally lost, Cole twisted in my grip, kicking out with one foot. I followed him to the ground, landing flat on top of him. Before he could roll, I slammed a knee into his back and rattled off the rest of his rights as I wrenched his free arm behind his back and slapped on the other cuff.

"I have a feeling resisting arrest is going to be the least of the shit we charge you with," I said, "but I'll be adding it on anyway. Now, we'll try this again. Where the fuck is she?"

Brush crackled. Dead leaves rustled behind me.

I shot a glance over my shoulder, heart leaping, hoping it was Avery. Hawk materialized out of the trees, weapon in hand. He spotted Haywood face down, cuffed, and nodded.

"You want me to bring him back to your vehicle, or go find Avery?"

"You take him," I said, getting up. "I'm going after Avery. And Hawk?"

He raised a dark eyebrow, pulling his gaze up from where it had rested on Cole Haywood, filled with satisfaction and scorn. Protecting the Sawyer family was like a religion for Hawk. Griffen was his closest friend, and Quinn Sawyer was the woman he loved. They were far more than clients. They were his family, one Hawk had never expected and would kill to protect. The man on the ground had threatened his people, and Hawk didn't always play by the rules.

"Hey," I said sharply, catching his dark eyes as they hit mine. "Haywood needs to make it to jail in one piece, yeah? I have a lot of questions I need answered."

"If I'd gotten to him first..." Hawk raised an eyebrow, then shrugged with a half-smile. "But I didn't, so we'll do this your way."

For a split second, I wished I were a different man. One more like Hawk, who made up the rules as I went. A man who'd let Hawk take Cole Haywood for a private conversation before I brought him to jail. But this had to be done right. The last thing I wanted was for Cole Haywood to walk on a technicality.

I watched as Hawk hauled Cole to his feet, his grip

tight on Haywood's cuffed hands as he shoved him down the path. I tossed Hawk the keys to my SUV.

"Hold up," Hawk said after he caught and pocketed the keys. "Take this." He tossed me back a compact walkie-talkie. "Not always great in the mountains, but more useful than your cell. If you need help when you find her, call."

I shoved the walkie into my pocket and nodded, hoping it wouldn't come to that. I stood, watching Hawk march Haywood back to where we'd left our vehicles. In the silence of the forest, I set off on the deer path in the direction Haywood had come from. Had he shot her and left her up ahead somewhere?

I'd gone less than a hundred feet when the trail widened into a clearing. "Avery!" I called out. "Avery!"

No answer. The grasses and weeds in the clearing had been trampled, following a path to the far corner where they'd flattened a wide circle with their footsteps.

"Avery!" I shouted again, scanning the ground as I moved closer. My chest tightened as I saw the wooden circle resting on top of the weeds. It had been moved recently based on the overturned leaves and dirt at the edges.

"Avery!" I went to my knees at the edge of the well cover, yanking it off and peering into the dark.

"West?" Avery's voice drifted up from the dark hole in the earth, weak and pained, but alert.

"I'm going to get you out of there. You okay?" I pulled the flashlight from my belt, flicking it on.

"He shot me," she said weakly. The bright white beam of light caught her, and my heart stopped. She was caught in the well, her back braced against the uneven stone wall, her feet jammed into the wall opposite, barely holding herself in place, her legs straining with effort. She looked down her side into the dark below. "I don't know how deep it is," she said. "But I don't think I can hold this much longer."

Her voice trailed off as her foot slipped, the pressure of it dragging a stone from the side of the well. A high scream erupted from her lungs, her feet scraping and body sliding down half a foot. "West!"

"I've got you!" I threw myself on my stomach, reaching as far into the well as I could. My fingers almost grazed the top of her head. Not close enough. I sat back up, yanking the walkie from my pocket.

"Hawk, you got me?" I waited, every second an eternity, before he answered.

"You find her?"

"She's in a well and she's slipping. Grab the rope in the back of my SUV and follow the deer path."

"Got it." Hawk clicked off.

I leaned back over the edge. "Avery, I can't reach you, but Hawk is coming with a rope. We'll get you out."

"Cole?" she asked, her voice strained.

"Under arrest. Hawk's locking him in the cage in my SUV." I thought about my belt. Sitting up, I unfastened it and pulled it free of my pants. Feeding the end back through the buckle, I lowered the loop to Avery. "Wrap that around your arm," I said. "I have the other end. Just in case you slip again before Hawk gets here with the rope."

Moving slowly, using her legs to brace her back

harder into the side of the well, Avery shifted just enough to pull the belt loop over her right arm, wrapping the length around her forearm for better grip. I saw with horror that her left arm was covered in blood.

"He shot you in the arm?" I asked.

"I wouldn't take the cover off the well," she said in answer.

"How much are you bleeding?" I asked, afraid of the answer.

"Not a lot, I think," she said, her voice strained. "I can't really tell."

"Okay, we'll see when we get you out." Leaves crackled close by. A branch snapped, and Hawk was there, leaning over the side of the well, the climbing rope from my SUV slung over his shoulder.

Straightening, he began to tie a slipknot at the end, creating a wide loop. He leaned over the edge of the well. "Avery, see if you can get this over your head."

She let go of my belt, and I pulled it up, watching as she ducked her head to catch it in the loop and worked it over her shoulders. "That's it, Avery," I said, tossing my belt behind me. "Now get an arm through the loop. Both, if you can."

My racing heart calmed a fraction when her bloody arm cleared the loop along with the other, and Hawk tugged the rope tight around her chest. Standing, I grabbed the rope beside Hawk. "Drop your feet from the wall, Ave. We're going to pull you up."

She shifted, her feet slipping, a short scream escaping as she dropped a foot, almost out of sight in the dark below. The rope jerked in our hands, my feet skidding in the dirt. I hauled back, stopping her fall. "We have you," I promised, and pulled with everything I had.

We walked back, step by step, dragging Avery up until she hit the edge. Hawk braced his feet. "Pull her up," he grunted.

I let go of the rope, waiting a second to make sure Hawk had Avery's weight, and moved to the side of the well, hooking my hands under her arms and lifting her clear. I stood there, Avery in my arms, solid ground under our feet, rocking her back and forth, breathing in the scent of her hair, feeling her heart pound against me. "I've got you," I whispered, over and over. "I've got you."

From my left, Hawk said, "That arm's still bleeding. You need to get her to the hospital."

I eased back, turning Avery to look at her arm. The sleeve of her shirt was torn in a jagged line, exposing a bloody gouge in her bicep. "He grazed you," I said to Avery. "Any other injuries?"

She shivered and shook her head. Her eyes shot to the deer path leading back to the vehicles. "Cole?"

"Haywood's secured," Hawk answered. "He's not going anywhere."

"He still breathing?" I asked. There was a pause before Hawk replied.

"Mostly."

"Good enough for me," I said.

Avery might be able to handle the walk back to the SUV, but she was shaky and pale. Blood loss or shock? I didn't know. "Hold still." I lifted her into my arms. We'd move faster this way, and after the last hour, I needed her close, next to my heart. She rested her head on my shoulder, squeezing her eyes shut.

I followed Hawk back down the trail, the distance so much shorter now that we knew where we were going. The clearing appeared, with Haywood's sedan and my SUV exactly where we'd left them. Hawk turned as we reached the SUV, handing me his keys.

"I'm right behind you," he said. "You take Avery to the ER, and I'll deliver Haywood to the station."

"I'll let them know you're on the way," I agreed, taking his keys. If I were doing everything by the book, it should have been the other way around, with me handling the prisoner and Hawk taking Avery to the hospital, but now that I had Avery back, there was no way in hell I was letting her go.

She was alert as I set her on her feet beside the door of Hawk's oversized black SUV, but still squinting, shielding her eyes from the rays of light that penetrated the canopy of leaves above.

"Everything's going to be okay now," I said. "We've got Haywood, and I've got you."

Avery leaned into me. "I knew you'd find me. I just had to buy enough time, and you'd find me."

"I'll always find you," I said, helping her into the passenger seat and buckling her seatbelt. "No matter what. Always."

Epilogue

AVERY

I woke gradually to an odd combination of absolute comfort and sharp, nagging pain. The pain was isolated to my left bicep. The comfort was everything else—West, solid beside me, his long, slow breaths like the waves of the ocean, and his strong arm curled around my back.

"Arm wake you up?" he said into the quiet.

"Maybe." I ran a hand down his side, fingers tracing the muscle under soft skin, the rough texture of hair on his chest and his upper thigh—and decided to take advantage.

Before I could, West rolled, pinning me to the mattress, careful not to jostle my arm. "Exactly where I want you." He paused, cupping my chin as he looked down at me, his dark eyes serious. "How much does it hurt? Do you need another pill?"

I shook my head slowly. "Maybe later. Ibuprofen—not what the doctor gave me. I don't want to be woozy and out of it."

"Okay," he said, dropping his head to press a kiss to my forehead.

"Is it really over?" I asked.

He caught my hand in his and kissed my fingertips. "The bad part. The bad part's all over now. The rest is just beginning." He pressed another kiss into my palm, and I felt the smile spread across my face, like I was radiating light.

"I love you so much, West. How did I not know all this time that it was you?"

He rubbed his lips against mine. "I don't know. I've been trying to figure that out. But I'm not sure it matters. We know now. And now that I know, I'm keeping you."

"Are you going to move into Heartstone?" I propped myself up on one elbow, surveying my room. It was a suite, but not one of the bigger ones. Still, considering it was in the middle of a house the size of a castle, it was probably big enough for the two of us.

"You want me to?" he asked softly.

"Definitely," I said. "I don't want to wake up without you. I want you to be the last thing I see when I close my eyes at night. Do you mind? I know you love your house."

"Not as much as I love you," he said. "And the house isn't going anywhere."

I reached up to stroke the side of his face. "After the will is over, maybe we can move in there?"

He kissed me again, longer this time, slower—the tip of his tongue tracing the seam of my lips, teasing them apart only to lift his head and smile down at me. "It won't be that long. Just a few years. We can find a tenant or do a short-term rental thing."

"Works for me," I said. "As long as I get you, I don't really care where we are."

"Me either," West said. "Home is with you. Heartstone, my house—it's all good, as long as you're with me."

My heart was so full I thought it might explode. I kissed him, laughing as he rolled onto his back.

"Watch your arm," he murmured, easing me on top of him, reaching up to cradle my breasts, stroking his thumbs across my nipples, sending sparks shooting through every nerve in my body.

"I'll be careful," I promised. And I was. Careful enough that I didn't feel a thing from my arm, any pain was lost in the pleasure of being with West.

After, West carried me to the shower, re-bandaging my arm with gentle hands. I'd always known he had kindness in him, but if I'd known when I was a teenager just how much he had hidden under his hot-guy exterior, the crush would have killed me.

Then I thought of how bossy he could be and knew that all things happened at the right time. I wouldn't have been able to handle West when I was younger. The first time he tried to tell me what to do, I would have bashed him over the head with a crate of beer bottles.

"Are you nervous?" he asked, and I knew exactly what he meant. Today was the day. I'd brought home two plastic milk crates of bottles filled with the new fall brew.

"Nervous? Yeah," I said as if it should be obvious. "And terrified. What if it's—"

He shook his head, cutting me off before I could spiral. "It's going to be phenomenal, Ave. But if it's not, you'll try again. You'll get it. He was fucking with you mostly because he was jealous."

That stopped me in my tracks. I brushed my wet hair back off my face and stared at him. "Jealous?"

"Of course," West said.

I was momentarily distracted by the flex of the muscles in his back as he pulled on a dress shirt. We weren't going black tie, but Thanksgiving wasn't casual in Heartstone Manor, especially not with so many of the older generation present.

I still wasn't pulling out my hair dryer—wasn't sure if it actually worked—but I was going to wear a dress and put on mascara. In my world, that counted as formal.

"Why would Matthew be jealous of me? He still knows more about running a brewery than I do. I'm getting there, but—"

"Ave, you can learn how to do what Matthew does—and you are, you have. You just have to put it into practice. That's where all the awkwardness is coming from. You know how. Now, you just need to do it. Once you've run the place by yourself for a while, you'll know how good you are at that. But the other part, the beer itself?" West shook his head. "I don't know that that's something you learn. Like what Finn does in the kitchen—he has a feel for food that's just different. Like you do for beer. Its instinctive. I don't know how to explain it. I'm not like that with anything."

"What about being a cop? You're damn good at that," I reminded him.

"Maybe," he said. "I hadn't really thought of it that way. But you know flavor and ingredients. You know beer in a way that Matthew doesn't and never will. And yeah, I think he was jealous. He knew he could teach you, but you couldn't really teach him. I think some of his wanting to put you in your place was about taking over the brewery, sure, but the rest of it? That was just old-fashioned jealousy. He wants to be what you are, and he never will be."

I blinked up at West, trying on this new view of Matthew. I liked it. "Well, I wish he hadn't tried to set me on fire to get even," I said.

"Yeah, me too," West said, doing up the buttons on his shirt. "So does Bob."

"Poor Bob," I sighed. I'd already made some progress throwing together the benefit. His friends would help him get back on his feet, but he hadn't deserved to be caught in the middle.

I pulled my dress from the hanger, trying to think about anything but those unopened bottles I'd brought home. Part of me wanted to dash down the stairs—wet hair and no shoes—and pop one open. Just one, so I'd know. If it was awful, I could find out by myself without everybody watching.

No. This was my family. They loved me. If it was awful, we'd all laugh about it together. And if Aunt Ophelia, or God forbid Harvey or Edgar, caught me downstairs half-dressed with wet hair all over the place, I'd get a parental-style lecture, despite the fact that I was a full-grown adult.

Not worth it, I decided.

I still wasn't blow-drying my hair, but I took a minute to swipe on mascara and a little bit of gloss, then put on the sapphire earrings that had been my mother's and the diamond necklace Ford had given me when I turned twenty-one. There. That was as dressed up as I was going to get.

I slid on my heels, wondering as they pinched my toes how long I'd have to keep them on, and turned to see West in gray dress pants and a blue button-down shirt, his tie patterned with tiny yellow rubber duckies. His hair was a little wet, slightly rumpled, and for more than a second, all I wanted was to strip his dress clothes off and have my way with him again.

"You clean up nice, Chief."

"So do you." His eyes went hot as he scanned me from the tip of my black heels, past the earrings, to the top of my head. "Now that's a hell of a dress," he said, doing another slow scan back down.

"Parker's," I said. "When she was cleaning out her closet, she and Sterling decided this one was for me."

"I agree with their taste," he said, slowly spinning me around. "I don't know how you manage to take a perfectly acceptable dress and make it look sexy as hell, but you do."

I had to admit West wasn't wrong. I caught sight of myself in the mirror as his compliment rippled through me. Just above the knee, with a flowing skirt and a halter neck that hinted at but showed zero cleavage, the dress couldn't have been more appropriate for a family dinner, and yet—I looked pretty damn good.

My eyes snagged on the bandage on my arm. "Should I put on a cardigan or something?" I asked, the strip of white incongruous against the elegant black dress.

"Not unless you're cold," West said. "You look gorgeous, bandage or no bandage." He handed me two brown pills. "Ibuprofen. You have to stay ahead of the pain. Once you start moving around, it's going to hurt."

I took them with the bottle of water he handed me. My phone beeped with a text. Savannah.

> West's parents are here. You guys coming down?

Knowing Savannah, she was probably everywhere at once today, though officially all of the staff had the day off. Today, she wasn't the housekeeper, she was a Sawyer and Finn's wife, and as determined as Finn to put on a hell of a Thanksgiving. We had a full house. Aunt Ophelia and Nash's mom, Claudia, had come back to Sawyers Bend to celebrate. West's parents were here, along with Harvey and Edgar. Miss Martha, Savannah's mother, would be there, probably trying to help. You could turn the housekeeper into family, but you couldn't stop her from fussing—I'd learned that well enough over the past few years.

We made our way down the front stairs to find the hall empty. The sound of voices came from our left, where Savannah had transformed the family gathering room, usually dominated by a huge sectional and big TV, into its original intended purpose. She'd scattered small tables here and there with trays of snacks and small bites. There a bar set up on one side of the room, and beside it, a galvanized steel tub stood filled with ice and the bottles of beer I'd brought from Sawyers Bend Brewing.

A cheer went up as we entered the room, and I stopped short at all the smiling faces.

"What?" I said. "I mean, Happy Thanksgiving?"

"Avery." My brother, Tenn, stood with his arm around Scarlett. "Royal here has threatened to open your beer about ten times in the last half-hour. We told him he had to wait until you got here." His eyes narrowed on West. "I'm not going to ask what took you so long."

I felt heat hit my cheeks and scowled at my brother. "You can wait for a beer. It's not even lunchtime."

"It's Thanksgiving. Normal drinking rules don't count," Royal said. Daisy leaned into his side, her smile warm, her riot of curls hot pink, perfectly suiting her dusky skin.

"They've threatened to text you about a million times in the last hour. We made them leave you alone. She got shot yesterday, you idiot," Daisy said, smacking her palm against Royal's chest. "She gets to sleep in."

"Whatever," Royal said. "Come on, open the beer."

I looked over to see Ford standing next to the tub, an opener in hand. He held it out to me. "Only you can do the honors," he said. "Come on, don't keep us in suspense any longer."

I glanced up at West. "I'm nervous," I said under my breath.

"It's going to be great," he promised. I wanted to believe him.

I took a deep breath and reached into the tub to pull out a brown bottle dripping with ice water. I took the opener from Ford's hand. I muttered, "Thanks." This was it. Scents, flavors, memories swirled in my mind, lit by hope, bright and sharp and a little desperate. Please, please...

I fit the opener to the cap and flicked my wrist in a practiced move that felt suddenly like I was opening a beer for the first time. With a gasp, the cap lifted, and the scent of it hit me. So far, so good. I lifted the bottle to my nose, breathing in.

It smelled like what I'd been going for. A touch hoppy, a hint of spice, and citrus. I lifted the bottle to my mouth and took a slow, experimental sip, my eyes closing as the beer washed across my taste buds, feeling the promise I'd hoped for.

This wasn't the Fall brew. Not exactly. It was better.

I took another sip, swishing the beer in my mouth, letting the aftertaste settle in. It was brighter somehow. Less heavy on the finish, but it still had substance. Not a light summer brew. It had weight, but not too much. The hints of spice were just enough to bring depth without density. A tinge of apple, the spark of lemon, the sweetness of orange—it was all here, but the beer took the lead. Water. Malt. Yeast. Hops. I let my eyes slide all the way closed and took another long sip. It was perfect.

I swallowed, my eyes flashing open and locking on West's. He plucked the bottle out of my hand and drank. When he was done, he looked a little dazed and let out a whoop.

"You did it again," he said, stepping back from the tub of beer, pulling me with him. "You good?" West asked me.

I answered him with a wide smile. "Never been better. I did it."

"And then some," West agreed. "I may have to bring Holt a bottle in jail, just to watch him cry at how much better it is than anything he's ever made." He leaned down and kissed me. "I knew you could do it."

"You really did," I agreed. "And now I do, too."

He set the empty bottle on the table, snagged another, and held it out for Ford to open. Then we settled in to enjoy the day. And for the most part, we did. I may have had a few too many beers, and my arm hurt when I paid attention, but mostly I just enjoyed seeing my family —and people who might as well have been family—all together, celebrating. The kids ran around, tearing off their ties and losing their jackets before we made it halfway through the hors d'oeuvres Savannah had set out. Finn even came up for a bit, leaving the turkey and ham and whatever else he had going on in the kitchen to congratulate me on the beer and hang out with the family.

West's parents blended in as if they'd always been at our Thanksgiving table. I liked the way his mother stood with Aunt Ophelia and Nash's mom—the youngest of the three, but a similar kind of lady all the same—gossiping and laughing together. West's dad huddled up with Edgar and Harvey, occasionally haranguing our genera-tion, complaining about how willful and modern we all were. When my father had said those things, they'd stung. But from these three, it felt like love, and we gave them hell right back.

There was only one thing that dimmed my joy in the day—one thing I couldn't get off my mind. Cole Haywood. He'd been so talkative in the car, but I'd been scared out of my mind. I wasn't sure I remembered every detail of the answers he'd given me, but I absolutely remembered the one he hadn't. I'd asked him why he waited so long to kill Prentice, and it was the one question he'd completely ignored. Was it because it wasn't important, or because it was?

It nagged at me. I hadn't noticed the day before, more concerned with not dying in that well and the bullet graze on my arm than with really thinking about the details. Cole was in handcuffs. West had saved me. Problem solved, right?

But was it, really? Why had he waited so long to get his revenge? If Cole had killed Prentice because of Caro and their affair, wouldn't he have done it in the madness of grief after her death and the loss of his child? Why wait?

"What?" West said, giving me a little shake. I looked over at him. His salad plate was cleared, silverware neatly lined up at an angle, face down. "You barely touched your salad."

"I ate too many appetizers," I admitted. "I'm saving room for turkey and stuffing."

"But you're stuck in your head—I can see it. What is it?"

"Haywood," I answered.

West gave a slow nod and took my hand under the table. "Yeah. Me too."

"What's bugging you?" I asked.

"When I caught him in the woods, I told him I had him for kidnapping and murder, and he said I'd never make it stick."

"How could you not make it stick?" I asked. "The kidnapping is pretty open-and-shut, right? I mean, I'm here saying he kidnapped me. You pulled me out of that well. He shot me."

"Exactly," West agreed. "But he's a criminal attorney. He has to know we had him on the kidnapping. So, what does he think—"

"—you couldn't make stick?" I finished for him.

West shook his head. "I don't know. But he hasn't asked for a lawyer."

"That's odd," I said. Cole was a criminal attorney. He was known as one of the best around, and he knew the rest of them. He knew how important it was to have representation and that even a renowned attorney shouldn't represent himself. "So, he's in your jail?" I asked, the wheels in my head turning. It was over, but I still wanted answers.

"He is," West agreed. "They haven't moved him yet."

We stopped talking as Savannah placed a bowl of soup in front of each of us. I'd already complained that she shouldn't be serving the family for Thanksgiving, but she'd told me to let her do things her way, and she wouldn't tell me how to brew beer. I'd shut up—I knew better than to argue with Savannah. When she left, West looked at me, and I could see the intention in his eyes.

"Tomorrow," he said. "We're going to talk to Haywood tomorrow."

"Works for me," I agreed.

And that was enough to let me push aside my questions for one more day.

I went to bed, sated, my stomach a little too full. My

body, other than the graze on my arm, relaxed and replete. West stretched out beside me in my bed. I'd already started mentally reorganizing my suite to make space for him. The closet wouldn't be a problem—I wasn't the clothes horse some of my sisters were, and had plenty of room for West. I had a feeling he might want to replace my tiny flat screen in the sitting room with something bigger, maybe trade out the sofa for his. But otherwise, it wouldn't take much to make it work.

We'd have to make time to move some of his things into storage. If he decided he wanted to turn his place into a short-term rental, he'd probably make bank. They were a hot commodity in Sawyers Bend, almost year-round. We'd have to weigh that against the wear and tear on his place, but either way, we'd make it work.

I drifted off with a smile on my face and woke with that itch in the back of my head of questions that needed answers. West was already up.

"Is the brewery closed today?" he asked.

"Kind of," I said. "The brewery is closed, but I'm going to go open the taproom. Ford said he wanted me to teach him how to run the register and everything. He's going to fill in until I replace Cammie."

"Not what I would have expected," West said, considering. "But interesting."

"Yeah, I know. I could use the help. And now that Haywood's locked up, Ford needs to get out of the house, so it works for me."

"Then we better get moving," West said. "Finn is taking the day off from cooking. Let's go talk to Haywood, then swing by Sweetheart Bakery and grab some breakfast."

"I'm in," I agreed.

I threw my hair in a ponytail and put on my regular uniform for a day at the brewery—a Sawyers Bend Brewing polo and jeans. We were quiet on the ride into town.

Jim was sitting at Amanda's desk in the front of the station.

"Everything quiet?" West asked when we walked in.

Jim looked at me with interest, but didn't ask why I was there, instead answering West. "All quiet," he said. "Hasn't made a peep. Ate what we gave him, slept a little."

"He hasn't asked for an attorney?"

"Not yet." They shared a look, and then West shook his head.

"We're going to go back."

Jim nodded. "Good luck."

West pulled out his keys, unlocking the doors that led down the hall to the holding cells. Cole was in the one at the far end, where the drunk had been housed the day of the arson. Somehow, Cole still managed to look like a model, if a little worse for wear. His pants were still creased, his button-down smudged with dirt but still tucked in. His sharp blue eyes tracked us as we came down the hall, appraising us as we stood on the other side of the bars.

West crossed his arms over his chest. "I'm curious why you haven't asked for a lawyer," he said into the silence.

Cole gave a casual shrug. I didn't buy it. There was nothing casual about Cole Haywood.

"I have questions," West said. "But I'm reluctant to ask them at the risk of you calling for a mistrial later, as you aren't represented yet."

"That's assuming I answer them," Cole said.

"Good point."

"I haven't decided on representation yet. I'll let you know when I do," Cole said, his voice and eyes cool. He didn't seem particularly worried about being in jail—because he thought he was getting out, or because he knew he could handle whatever was to come? I didn't know.

"And will you," West asked, "answer my questions?"

Cole's head tilted to the side. For a second, he reminded me of a predator examining its prey. I leaned into West's side. Despite the bars between us, I couldn't forget the threat that was Cole Haywood.

"I might. Turn off the cameras, any recording devices, and ask. Can't promise I'll answer, but I'm curious. What is it you think you haven't figured out?"

West weighed the request and nodded. He pulled out his phone, tapping the screen. "I can deactivate them from here." He pointed to the camera high in the corner of the hall, out of reach of the cells, and to another at the other end. "Between the two of them," he said, "they cover all the holding cells."

Cole watched as the lights on each camera flicked off. West showed him the screen on his phone, then me, clearly indicating that both cameras had been deactivated.

"Why did you wait?" I demanded the second West nodded at me. "I asked you in the car, and you didn't answer. Why did you wait so long between what happened to Caro and shooting Prentice?"

Haywood stood, crossed the small cell to stand just on the other side of the bars. He folded his arms over his chest and looked down at me, his eyes smug. "I didn't."

Not the answer I was expecting. "What does that mean?" I demanded. "Obviously, you did. Caro died two years before Prentice."

"I didn't wait," Haywood said slowly, "because I didn't shoot Prentice."

"Bullshit," West said.

"Yeah?" Cole raised an eyebrow, dropping his hands to his sides, tucking his thumbs in his pockets as if we were standing outside the general store and not separated by the bars of a jail cell.

"You think I killed Prentice?" he asked, blandly.

"You as good as said you did when you kidnapped me," I argued.

Cole nodded, considering. "I admitted to a lot of things. And you can likely pin some of them on me, given that I confessed and you're a somewhat reliable witness. But I never said I shot Prentice."

I racked my brain, dredging up every word of the conversation I could remember, and let out a breath, my shoulders curving forward as I deflated. "No, you didn't, did you?"

"No, I didn't," Cole agreed.

"Bullshit," West said again.

"Is it, though?" Cole asked. "You follow the evidence, remember? That's why you arrested Ford. Because you followed the evidence—the evidence I left for you."

"You planted the evidence?" I asked. We'd known someone must have. If Ford had killed our father, he never would have been stupid enough to leave the murder weapon in his own closet. "If you didn't kill Prentice, how did you get your hands on the gun?"

"Good luck and good timing," Cole said with a curve of his lips.

"You happened to show up at exactly the right moment to grab the gun, to see Prentice dead, but you didn't kill him?" West clarified, his voice dripping with suspicion. "Then who did?"

"No idea," Cole said with a shrug. "He was dead when I got there. But I saw an opportunity, and I took it. For years, I'd been planning the downfall of Prentice Sawyer. After Caro died, Prentice was lost in misery. He was suffering just like he deserved to. Locked away in that house, letting everything fall to pieces around him. The rest of you scattered, abandoning him. I was happy to leave him alive as long as every moment was filled with the pain he deserved."

"But you didn't kill him?" I asked. "After all that?" I shook my head.

"I planned and I waited, and then the moment presented itself. Prentice was dead, and I used his murder to get everything I wanted." Cole paused, his eyes surveying his jail cell. "Almost everything," he clarified. "But I didn't pull the trigger."

"I'm not buying it," West said from beside me.

Cole lifted his chin and said, "You think I shot Prentice? Then prove it."

Never Miss a New Release:

Join Ivy's Reader's Group

@ <u>ivylayne.com/readers</u>
&
Get two books for free!

Forbidden Heart

SNEEK PEAK

CHAPTER ONE
PAIGE

I stared into the cold dregs of my coffee and let out a sigh. I wanted to curl up in a ball and sleep for a million years. Slouching back in my chair, I tried a deep breath, hoping some oxygen in my brain would wake me up. I hadn't slept well in months. At night, I'd lay in my childhood bedroom listening to the rattle of my mother's breaths as she struggled for air, dying a little more every day. Now, the silence was oppressive, every creak of the house as loud as a gunshot.

I was alone. I'd thought it was all I wanted.

I hated this house. The walls were a sick mustard shade, stained by years of cigarette smoke. The linoleum in the kitchen was faded and worn through in spots. My mother had refused to update any of it. Decorations were a waste of money, she'd insisted, and waste is sinful.

I'd escaped this house as soon as I could figure out

how, leaving at eighteen for college, paying my way by working as a nanny, a job I'd found out of pure luck for a lovely family. I'd arrived on campus knowing my scholarships would only go so far, and I needed to find a job fast. Then a professor had a friend who had lost their nanny last minute. They were desperate. I was desperate. I didn't have a ton of experience with kids, but neither of us was in a position to quibble. I took the position, and within six months, I'd moved out of the dorms and into their home, changing my major to early childhood education. Who knew I'd love taking care of someone else's kids?

I didn't want my own—not anytime soon—but for the first time in my life I'd seen what a family was supposed to be like. For so many years it had just been my mother and me, after my father had walked out on us. Nothing about growing up with Harriet McKenna brought to mind the concept of family. Constant criticism and a liberal smack of her palm on my cheek when she was displeased had left me feeling like the only point of family was to escape them.

But at eighteen, a freshman in college warmly enfolded into the Bellingham family crew, I saw what it could be. A husband and wife who loved each other, who made time even though they both had busy careers. Who doted on their children despite their packed schedules. The kids were easy to love. Abby, an infant, fussy at nap time and not a fan of the bottle, but otherwise the cutest thing I'd ever seen. And Joshua—a spirited two-year-old. We did well enough once he learned he couldn't charm me, though deep inside I had to fight not to give in when he flashed those dimples.

I stayed with the Bellinghams through college and two years of grad school, intending to leave and find a teaching job from there. The kids were old enough to go to school, and I needed to make a decision. I had the degrees. I'd acquired some in-class experience. What did I want?

I'd been headed to the classroom when a friend of the Bellinghams had made me an offer I couldn't refuse: follow their family as they traveled, minding two young children. It was a chance to see Europe on someone else's dime. I'd met the Smiths in the course of my years with the Bellinghams—they were kind and fun, their kids boisterous but good-hearted. I said yes, packed my bags, and off we went.

Another four years passed that way until halfway through my twenty-ninth year when I got the call. My mother—who I'd barely spoken to in almost a decade—was sick, dying, and alone. Reluctantly, I went home, though 'home' hardly seemed the word to describe this place. I looked around again, and sighed. What a waste. What a sad house she'd lived in; we'd lived in. Now that I'd seen the world and knew how things could be, the stark contrast was all the more apparent.

I'd gone back and forth, organizing things here for my mother, trying to ease her suffering without becoming her servant—which, I realized, was exactly what she wanted. Me at her beck and call, cut off from the rest of the world. Catering to her every whim. This was the life she'd envisioned for me, and she'd only needed to contract a fatal illness to get it.

I took care of her, but I won't lie and say I liked it. Every moment under her roof was one too many. I always felt like a faker when I flew back to the Smiths and was welcomed into their family again, caring for the kids, laughing with Janice at the end of a long day. They thought I was torn, sacrificing to help them, when what I really wanted was to be with my dying mother. They couldn't have been more wrong.

I never told them how bad things were at home. It was embarrassing to admit that my own mother didn't love me. Duty was the only thing between us. Harriett McKenna had raised me to understand that I owed her for my very existence, and she expected payback.

I understood what the problem was. Intellectually, I got it. It wasn't me, or rather, it wasn't anything I'd done. I had the bad luck to look exactly like my father, right down to the pale blue eyes we shared. I'd never met the man. He'd run off with another woman while my mother had been pregnant with me. And when I'd been born with his eyes, his dark curls, his olive skin, she'd hated me.

I think if I'd been a little replica of Harriet—willowy with cornflower-blue eyes and wispy blonde hair—maybe then she would have loved me. I could have been a little mini-me for her to mold. Instead, as she reminded me over and over, I was a replica of him, sent to remind her of her failure as a wife and a woman. I was the visual representation of everything she'd lost, and she'd never forgiven me for it.

She had a heavy hand and high expectations. Some

of them I'd lived up to. I'd been a good student, kept my room clean, knew how to speak respectfully. The flat of her hand taught me to keep my tongue under control. I don't know if my father ran off because Harriet didn't have love in her, or if he'd taken her heart with him when he disappeared. Either way, there'd been none left for me.

The first few years my mother was sick, I helped without living under her roof for more than a week at a time. I arranged rides to and from chemo and coordinated with helpful ladies from her church who brought over food a few times a week. My mother knew I didn't want any of this. So, of course, my presence was what she demanded. Eventually, she reached a point where I was the only one who could care for her. I left the Smiths, my heart breaking as I packed my bags, my tears matching those of the children.

My nanny families had been the only true family I'd ever known, and going home to take care of Harriet felt like a bank vault door clanging shut, locking me away from warm embraces and steaming cocoa, sealing me into this shadowed house that reeked of stale smoke. I was left wondering if time had stood still in these walls; the clock stopped in the early 80s, the avocado countertops cracked and a phone bolted to the wall in the kitchen, the long curly cord trailing on the floor.

Time didn't exist in that house. For a woman who seemed to hate everything about life, my mother held onto it with a steely grip, fading slowly, day by day, dragging it out. If she'd been another kind of parent, I would have been grateful for every day we had together. But she was Harriet McKenna, and though I'd never say it out loud, in my heart, I wished she'd hurry the fuck up and set me free.

And now she was gone. The house was empty, and I answered to no one. If you'd asked me before she died, I would have told you that freedom was all I wanted. Now that it was here, I didn't feel free—I felt hollowed out and empty. Alone.

She'd left me everything. Not that "everything" was much: this house, her car, a small retirement account. I'd buried her quietly in the plot she'd purchased, foregoing a wake, letting the ladies from her church set up a quiet service. I had stacks of frozen casseroles in the freezer and empty boxes everywhere. All I had to do was pack up the house, put it on the market, and take a step into the future.

I picked up the cold coffee cup and tilted it. Still empty, and it was too late in the day for more coffee. What I wanted was an ice-cold soda. Soda had been forbidden in this house, along with any other sweets.

Sugar lets the devil in. I don't know who told her that, but she'd said it often enough.

When she got too sick to come downstairs, I stocked the fridge with whatever I wanted, including ice-cold cans of ginger ale and my favorite, orange soda. I pushed back from the table, the chair legs scraping the worn linoleum, swung open the door of the ancient refrigerator, and grabbed a can. The sugar went straight to my brain, tasting vaguely of oranges and completely like heaven.

I needed to make a list, a plan. When she first got

sick, I was twenty-nine, still in the figuring-it-all-out phase of life, feeling like I had an eternity stretching before me to settle on what I wanted. A career? My own family? Taking care of other people's children had allowed me to see the world with people I loved, while saving almost all of my salary.

I liked clothes, but I was frugal when it came to everything else. My families paid for room and board and supplied a vehicle when I'd needed one. My expenses were low. I had a nest egg—a good one. I had degrees and just enough classroom experience that I could find a job if I was willing to be flexible on location. I thought I'd be ready to jump into a new life the moment Harriet was gone.

Instead, I was still here, the weight of this house crushing my ambitions. In Harriet's last months, I'd begun to clean out the closets, knowing the inevitable was coming. We both knew. The doctors had been kind but clear. There was no last-minute reprieve on the way—she was sick, and she would die. Their concern was making her comfortable. Not that Harriet McKenna could ever be made comfortable. She was too demanding for that. In my opinion, she thrived in a state of complaint. She didn't want to be comfortable. She wanted to harangue, to order, to criticize—and she did all three in abundance.

I managed to sort through the garage and the guest room closet while she was dying, and it felt like I'd made great progress. But now, looking around, there was so much left. The furniture. Paintings on the walls. Boxes and boxes in the attic, all waiting for me to deal with them. So many decisions.

I hadn't expected to feel so apathetic. I didn't want to sort through the detritus of Harriet's life. I wanted to blink and have it all disappear, to be back in Paris, in my little room next to the children, waiting for them to wake up so I could get them dressed and take them to the park or drop them off at school.

I let out another self-pitying sigh and drained the last of my soda. The truth was, I didn't know if that was what I wanted. The Smiths didn't need me back. As always happened, the kids were old enough now— attending school full-time—that they didn't need a live-in nanny. Janice had emailed a week before: So sorry to hear about your mom, Paige. I wish I could be there to give you a hug. We miss you so much, but the kids are loving school. I don't know what you have planned, but I got word from a friend of a friend who's looking for a live-in. Not quite what you're used to, a small town in the mountains, but the family is lovely and a little desperate—they haven't been able to find anyone. Are you interested? Just let me know and I'll pass your infor-mation along.

Was I interested? I'd spent six years traveling the world, and the last eighteen months in a small town in Ohio. I wasn't enjoying the contrast. Did I want to bury myself in another small town? Did I want another family? Or did I want the classroom? That's what I'd trained for, where I'd always intended to end up. In theory, teaching was the goal. But when I closed my eyes and tried to envision it, the picture wouldn't gel.

I hadn't answered Janice. I knew time was running out, and at this point I was just being rude. She'd called, and I'd let it go to voicemail, stuck in this listless state, hating where I was, unable to move on.

I squeezed the empty can of orange soda and dropped it in the recycling bin. I didn't have to decide today. I did have to pack at least a box or two and load the back of my mother's car with things to take to the donation site. I had to do something, or I'd spend the rest of my life here, in this relic of a house, watching the linoleum curl at the corners, staring at the phone on the wall that never rang.

I let out another sigh, disgusted at my own self-pity. Dragging myself up the stairs, I pulled the cord to drop the ladder to the attic. It was less of a disaster up there than I'd remembered. Half of the boxes were old clothes. I tossed them through the ladder hole and watched them roll down the second-floor hallway, destined for the donation pile.

There was a bin of Christmas decorations that hadn't been hung in my lifetime. Another bin contained my mother's wedding dress. I stopped on that for a moment, unfolding it, trying to envision her as a bride—glowing and filled with joy. I couldn't see it. In my memories her face was twisted into a scowl, her lips always pursed so hard they'd been deeply grooved with wrinkles long before her hair had begun to gray.

I folded the wedding dress back up and dropped it through the hole to land with the other items I was donating. Maybe some bride could give it a new life with new love. But she wouldn't be me.

I'd cleared half of the space, a tinge of relief lightening my heart as I looked around and saw progress. I picked up the pace, carrying down boxes of books to donate. I didn't know whose they'd been; maybe my father's. I didn't think I'd ever seen my mother read anything but the Bible or prayer books.

A few hours later, I was down to the last third of the attic. Most of it was straight-up trash. A broken lamp. A cracked aquarium. And behind everything, an old trunk shoved in the corner, WILLIAMS stenciled on the side.

Williams. I didn't know a Williams. We were McKennas. Why would my mother have a truck belonging to a Williams?

The trunk was secured with a padlock. I didn't have the key. Based on the dust and the pile of crap around it, my guess was that if there had ever been a key, it was long gone.

I grabbed one of the handles on the side and dragged it out of the corner. I couldn't get through the lock—but the hinges on the back—those were a different matter. Curiosity gave me a burst of energy. I grabbed the broken lamp, lowered it in front of me, and then climbed down the ladder to the second floor. Picking my way through the piles of stuff I'd tossed down, I jogged to the garage for a crowbar and a drill. Between the two, I'd force my way into that trunk.

I wanted to know who Williams was, and why their trunk was in our attic.

I couldn't get enough leverage with the crowbar, but the drill did the job. I slapped a bit on, and drilled hole after hole around the hinges. When I thought I'd done enough, I grabbed the crowbar and swung. A few good thwacks later, the hinges fell out of the side of the trunk. I opened the top, flipping it back, where it hung loosely by the padlock that had tried to keep me out.

Here was a treasure trove. A neatly folded U.S. Army uniform, a file on top—discharge papers. Paul Williams. I sat in shock. I knew that face. Paul Williams was my father. The black-and-white snapshot of the young man in dress uniform looked like me—same eyes, same hair. I thought his name was McKenna. She told me we had his name, but clearly she'd lied. Because here he was, Paul Williams, who'd served in the army. Another thing I hadn't known.

Carefully, I set aside the uniform and the file folder. I found their marriage certificate on top of the suit I imagined he might have worn at their wedding. A small collection of fishing lures that looked hand-tied. A baseball with signatures. Here was a life that looked well lived, right up until the moment it stopped because Paul had chosen to continue that life with another woman. Had he created a new family with her? I didn't know. He'd disappeared completely. He'd never reached out. Never checked in. He'd known Harriet was pregnant—at least, I thought he had—but he'd never come back.

It used to make me sad, that he'd abandoned me that way, abandoned us. Now, so many years later, it was down to a dull ache. And always, a question. Why had he cared about me so little? Why hadn't I mattered?

I sighed, pushed the feelings down, and moved further into the trunk.

I found books: Rudyard Kipling, Salinger, Fitzgerald. Was this where I'd gotten my love of reading? It felt like there were answers here, if only I knew how to interpret them.

And then, underneath an old Cincinnati Reds baseball cap, was a manila envelope. No label, address, or postage, the top flap sealed by metal prongs folded flat. I worked them open with my fingernail and reached inside. Letters. Handwritten letters, in a curly, feminine script. I wasn't surprised to see a woman's signature at the bottom. Sarah.

Sarah had written to my father. "Dearest Paul, my heart breaks at our separation. I wish there was a way we could be together. It seems unfair we should both be so unhappy, but so happy together. I can't go on like this. I don't want to."

There was a date at the top, the week before he disappeared. This was the woman. This was the one he'd left us for. If he was still out there, somewhere, could I find him through her? Had he married her? Grown old with her?

It occurred to me, for the thousandth time, that he hadn't ever looked for me. Maybe he didn't want to be found. But Harriet was dead. Who knew if he still lived? If he was well, how much time did I have left to find him?

Maybe he didn't want to see me. But I wanted to see him, to find this man who'd left me before I was born— not to demand an explanation or unleash my anger. I just wanted to look into those eyes so like mine.

And the only clue I had was Sarah.

I flipped through the rest of the letters. A photograph slipped out and landed in my lap. A woman, young and beautiful, with pale eyes, and a precisely curled sandy blonde bob that made me think of the '60s. She was lovely. Her eyes looked kind, with a spark of mischief. I turned over the photograph. At the bottom, in that same curly script, was written: Sarah Elizabeth Fordham.

I didn't recognize the name. Tucking the letters and photograph back in the envelope, I set it in my lap and pulled out my phone, searching the internet. I scrolled through the first few results. A teenage volleyball player who'd scored the winning shot in a game—definitely not her. An obituary for a 98-year-old woman—probably not her.

And then—a link to a marriage certificate from North Carolina. In 1980, Sarah Elizabeth Fordham had married Prentice Braxton Sawyer. Sawyer. The name jolted down my spine. Why did I know that name? It sparked in my brain, and I tapped the screen of my phone, flipping to my email.

The email from Janice. The family in the mountains of North Carolina who were looking for a nanny. Hope and Griffen Sawyer.

My heart pounded. My breath sped up. And a few frantic searches told me it had to be a sign. I'd been waiting for direction, and now I had one.

A goal, a job, and a mystery to solve—all of them in Sawyers Bend.

ARE YOU READY FOR PAIGE & FORD'S STORY?
Visit IvyLayne.com/ForbiddenHeart
to see what happens next!

About Ivy Layne

Ivy Layne has had her nose stuck in a book since she first learned to decipher the English language. Sometime in her early teens, she stumbled across her first Romance, and the die was cast. Though she pretended to pay attention to her creative writing professors, she dreamed of writing steamy romance instead of literary fiction. These days, she's neck deep in alpha heroes and the smart, sexy women who love them.

Married to her very own alpha hero (who rubs her back after a long day of typing, but also leaves his socks on the floor). Ivy lives in the mountains of North Carolina where she and her other half are having a blast raising two energetic boys. Aside from her family, Ivy's greatest loves are coffee and chocolate, preferably together.

For More Information:
www.ivylayne.com
books@ivylayne.com
Facebook.com/AuthorIvyLayne
Instagram.com/authorivylayne/

Also by Ivy Layne

Don't Miss Out on New Releases, Exclusive Giveaways, and More!!

Join Ivy's Readers Group @ ivylayne.com/readers

THE HEARTS OF SAWYERS BEND

Stolen Heart

Sweet Heart

Scheming Heart

Rebel Heart

Wicked Heart

Wild Heart

Broken Heart

Reckless Heart

Forbidden Heart

THE UNTANGLED SERIES

Unraveled

Undone

Uncovered

THE WINTERS SAGA

The Billionaire's Secret Heart (Novella)

The Billionaire's Secret Love (Novella)

The Billionaire's Pet

The Billionaire's Promise

The Rebel Billionaire

The Billionaire's Secret Kiss (Novella)

The Billionaire's Angel

Engaging the Billionaire

Compromising the Billionaire

The Counterfeit Billionaire

THE BILLIONAIRE CLUB

The Wedding Rescue

The Courtship Maneuver

The Temptation Trap